FALCON STRIKE

C. H. COBB

Published by Doorway Press,
Greenville, OH, USA
doorwaypress.com

Signed copies are available by ordering from
chcobb.com.
Print version is also available on Amazon.com.
An E-version is available from Amazon for the Kindle.

ISBN: 0-9848875-4-7
ISBN-13: 978-0-9848875-4-5
Library of Congress Control Number: 2014910989
First Edition, 2014

Cover design by Dani Snell,
www.refractedlightreviews.com.
Cover photo © Kris Klop / Clear Sky Photography,
used by permission.

This novel was written using Open Office 4.
The illustrations were produced with Gimp 2.8.

Acknowledgments

A great deal of research goes into a story such as this. Though I have never met either of them, I am indebted to SEALs Marcus Luttrell (*Service: A Navy SEAL at War; Lone Survivor*) and Chuck Pfarrer (*Warrior Soul: The Memoir of a Navy SEAL*). Their books provided a snapshot into the skills, lives, and thoughts of the men who make up America's elite special operators. After reading their books and learning of the almost superhuman feats of a Navy SEAL, I don't know that anyone other than an actual SEAL could depict their deeds with accuracy. I have done my best.

Inside the Aquarium by Viktor Suvorov became the primary lens through which I understood the rocky relationship between the KGB and the GRU, as well as the machinations of the GRU itself.

A declassified *National Intelligence Estimate* became my source for the huge advantage the Warsaw Pact possessed in armor during the 1970s and 80s.

Google Earth and Google Maps gave me an invaluable bird's-eye view of the various places around the world in which the story is set, as well as a means of measuring distances and evaluating terrain.

Wikipedia provided the lion's share of my research into weapons and aircraft and just about everything else, although the Federation of American Scientists web site (fas.org) and the Global Security site (www.globalsecurity.org) also provided a wealth of information. Tom Clancy's various non-fiction works on the military have been helpful as well.

Special thanks to Kris Klop of clearskyphotography.com for the photos from which all the covers of the *Falcon* Series have been produced. Kris is my favorite aviation photographer.

My brother Lou has been a great fount of encouragement and a valuable source of story critique. He's had a great sense of when my writing has gone over the edge in one direction or another.

My oldest daughter, Danielle Snell, has done her typically outstanding job of producing the covers of each book of the

Falcon Series. Dani also coaches me through the difficult aspects of being an independent author.

Last of all I am thankful to my wife Doris, an artist in her own right, who faithfully supports me and encourages me to keep writing. She cheerfully bears with the downside of being married to a guy who imagines he's a writer. Thanks, babe, I love you!

Any errors of fact or grammar that remain are mine.

Soli Deo Gloria!

Dedication

This project—the *Falcon* Series—would not have been possible without the assistance of my sister, Elizabeth. She has worn two hats. As my editor she's gone over my prose with a fine-tooth comb, correcting my mistakes and teaching me along the way with a delightful combination of humor and expertise. I am jealous of her natural facility with the written word and her insights into the syntactical mysteries of the English language. She patiently corrects chapter after chapter, even though I tend to make the same mistakes again and again.

Elizabeth's other hat is that of an excellent source of information about the Russian people and the customs of the Soviet era. A retired Foreign Service Officer who served during and after the Cold War, she passionately loves the Russian people and their rich culture. Some of that passion has rubbed off on me, and I've tried to separate the "evil empire" from the sturdy souls who suffered under it.

Thanks, sis, for your labor of love!

Cast of Characters

Al Mercer- NSA satellite surveillance technician

Anatoly Geredin- Member of the Soviet Politburo, head of the KGB

Arthur Young- Captain, USN, CO of CVN 70, *Carl Vinson*

Benjamin Klausowitz- Former Director of Central Planning, Moscow, now works for Mossad

Kim Choson- Master of the *Lady of Singapore* freighter

Clifton Edwards (CE)- NSA cryptologist

Ed Bausch- Lieutenant Commander, USN, CO of *Thunderbird* SEAL First Platoon

Ed Devlin- Special Investigator in the Alaska Bureau of Investigators (ABI)

Edvard Stepanovich Golinskiy- Operator of the sawmill north of Magadan

Evelyn Stinson- NSA translator

Galina Toporova- Former co-director of Sidima Timber Co-operative, in love with Jacob Kelly

Hank Swift- Master Sergeant, USAF, assigned to the Intelligence Division, Eielson AFB

Jacob Kelly (aka Jake, Falcon, John Smith, Smitty, John Meeker, Yakov Sokolov)- Major, USAF.

James Franks- General, USAF, Project Director of Project *Hydra* (wife is Shandra)

Jerry Auld- Lieutenant, USN, CO of *Thunderbird* SEAL Third Platoon

Jesse Pierce- Lieutenant Commander, USN, intelligence officer at Adak NAS

Jim Stewart- Special agent in the Seattle Office of the FBI, Foreign Counterintelligence Division

John Bridger- Rear Admiral, USN, CO of Naval Special Warfare Group One

Katerina Klausowitz- works for the Mossad (wife of Ben)

Karl Randolph- NSA satellite surveillance technician

Kerry Davis- Lieutenant, USN, CO of *Thunderbird* SEAL Fourth Platoon

Larry Martin- Brigadier General, USAF, CO of Eielson AFB

Marcus Clausen- Commander, USN, CO SEAL Team 3;

Thunderbird Commanding Officer

Matthew (Matt) Loeb- Technical Sergeant, USAF, assigned to IT Department, Eielson AFB

Nikolai Pavlovich Chernikov- Major General GRU, Commandant Prison 87, director of Project *Krasnyy Voskhod*

Paul Pascoe- Lieutenant, USN, CO of *Thunderbird* SEAL Second Platoon

Roger Bates- Captain, USN (wife is Susan)

Sam Bergman- CIA counterintelligence analyst, Soviet Department

Tom Rainer- Lieutenant Commander, USN, *Thunderbird* Executive Officer

Valeriy Ivanovich Patrikeyev- Lieutenant General, GRU, head of the GRU Ninth Directorate

William (Bill) Jensen- Professor of Political Science at Georgetown University, Special Assistant to the DDO, CIA

William (Bill) Ott- Major, USAF, chief of intelligence, 6985th Electronic Security Squadron, Eielson AFB

Zvi Sharon- Mossad station chief, Israeli Embassy, Washington, DC

Chapter 1

"Empty those jerry cans of gas on the floor, Oz," Jake instructed as he threw some rags in a bucket and poured diesel fuel over them. "When this place goes up in smoke, I want it to get their attention." The two Americans were inside the physical plant building of Prison 87, a top-secret facility deep inside Siberia.

Both men, along with eight others, had been kidnapped and brought to the facility as part of a sophisticated espionage-by-kidnapping program run by the Soviet GRU. Dr. Oswald Simmons, a cutting-edge researcher in microcircuitry miniaturization, had been snatched from the mountains of Colorado. Major Jacob "Jake" Kelly, aka Falcon, was the chief test pilot for Project *Hydra*, a secret weapons development effort that could change the tactical balance of power between the Warsaw Pact and NATO forces in Europe. Jake had been shot down and captured in an exquisitely timed and executed ambush over the Bering Sea. A Soviet helicopter snagged his parachute and delivered him to Prison 87.

They were just minutes from making good on what so far had been a flawless plan of escape. After several weeks of acting the part of a frightened coward, Jake had baited the two cellblock guards into his cell and killed them with his bare hands. Ignorant of his cross-training as an Air Force Combat Control Team (CCT) special forces operator, the guards took him for a harmless wimp. Their ignorance proved fatal.

Major Jacob Kelly had released Simmons from his cell and the two donned the dead soldiers' uniforms. When the guard shift changed they killed the two incoming guards, then exited the cellblock, impersonating the two that should have been coming off duty. The soldiers in the guard towers saw what they expected to see: two guards relieved from duty walking over to the barracks on the administrative side of the compound. Only instead of the barracks, the two had entered the physical plant building, intent on shutting off the power and communications of the remote facility.

"This is the biggest Molotov cocktail I've ever made. I always wanted to let my inner delinquent out," Oz responded with an evil grin as he slopped the gasoline all over the floor.

"Didn't know you hoity-toity academics had an inner delinquent," Jake muttered as he worked, "I thought it was just us knuckle-draggin' military guys." Jake tossed a rope over an overhead steam pipe and hauled the bucket up six feet off the floor, then tied the rope off.

"Well, I'd never admit it in the faculty lounge," Oz said, "but I do love making things go bang. Unless, of course, the thing that's cooking off is a printed circuit board on my lab bench. That's usually not good news."

Falcon grinned. "I imagine not. Let's make sure we're out there, and not in here when this baby cooks off. I'm ready; you ready?"

"*Da*. Let's do it." Both men were speaking fluent Russian, another ability that had aided in their escape to this point, and one that their captors had not caught on to. For Jake it was a double deception: years ago when he'd entered the Air Force he'd not volunteered the fact that he'd learned fluent Russian in his grandparents' house. Kelly wanted to be a fighter pilot and had feared that the language skill would shuttle him into another part of the Air Force. So it wasn't on his dossier, which is why the Russians had also been unaware of it.

Jake surveyed their handiwork one last time. A large diesel-powered emergency generator was in front of them, set in a shallow concrete equipment pit. It was a manual-start generator, which meant if the camp lost power someone would have to come into the physical plant building to start it.

Diesel fuel was puddling in the pit from the fuel line the two men had clipped. Falcon guessed the tank held five hundred gallons. *Plenty for our purposes*, he thought to himself. He grabbed the box of wooden kitchen matches and pulled one out, ready to strike it.

"Cut 'em!"

Using the large diagonal cutters he'd found on the tool bench, Oz neatly snipped the cables leading from the telephone demarc to the lines outside the camp. Then he grasped the handle of the master electrical cutoff, and pulled it down. The entire camp plunged into darkness.

Falcon struck the match, intending to throw it into the bucket he'd hung. They'd counted on a minute or two of delay before the flames in the bucket burned through the rope, and the whole assembly crashed to the floor, igniting the gasoline. It should give them enough time to leave the building and hide themselves in a vehicle in the motor pool outside. The idea was that while the camp was responding to the raging inferno, they would drive the vehicle outside the gate, making good their escape.

That was the plan anyway. But when Jake struck the wooden match it snapped in half, and he watched in horror as the burning tip headed for the gasoline-soaked floor. In that instant life slowed to a crawl. He tried to shout a warning but couldn't get the words formed. Seared into his brain was the sight of the flaming match tumbling end over end. Though it took an eternity to hit the floor, his feet seemed glued to the spot and he was unable to move. With penetrating clarity it registered that he was about to die, and a primordial dread filled his mind with terror. In the final milliseconds he wondered what lay on the other side of the curtain. Annihilation? Hell? Eternal li—

BOOOOM!

The explosion blew him out the door. He was violently smashed, head first, against the unyielding side of the big, six-wheeled URAL-375 truck parked outside the building. He dropped to the ground, body broken, clothes afire, and screamed.

Chapter 2

Bill Jensen sat at his kitchen table and stared into his black, steaming coffee. Bait in a very dangerous trap—that's how he was using the son of his deceased best friend, and it didn't sit well with him. *Using,* he thought distastefully, *using. You don't use friends, Bill! Lord God, what am I doing?*

He popped two Rolaids. It was only 0600 but his stomach was already reacting to the stress of the day and the emotional tension of what felt very much like betrayal. The coffee probably wasn't helping—black, bitter, and strong. He shook his head and tried to come up with a better plan. But there wasn't a better plan.

Dr. William Jensen was a professor of political science at Georgetown University. A trim one hundred eighty pounds, the fifty-two-year-old Jensen appeared to the average onlooker as an athletic academic at the zenith of his career. His steely grey eyes were set over a wide mouth and square chin, and he had a haircut like Yul Brynner's—which is to say he was completely bald. His academic specialty was International Relations, and his knowledge of the history and politics of the Pacific Rim nations was encyclopedic.

Jensen was not merely an academic, however—that was just his non-official cover. Other than the chairman of his department, no one at Georgetown was aware that Jensen was the special assistant to the Deputy Director of Operations (DDO) of the CIA. Formerly a top-drawer field agent in classified locations around the Pacific Rim, and then a case officer, Jensen was tapped in 1980 to work with the Directorate of Intelligence, Office of Asian Pacific, Latin American, and African Analysis and later with the Office of Military Affairs.

In 1984 he became the associate director of the CIA's Center for the Study of Intelligence, but finding the work confining and tame, he turned in his resignation in early '87.

Because the professor was untainted by the Iran-Contra affair and he had a sterling reputation within the Agency, the DDO was loath to lose Bill Jensen. Consequently he waved his wand and created a job out of thin air that would put Jensen's experience and ability to best use. Bill accepted the position, withdrew his resignation, and was now somewhat of an analyst and special projects director reporting directly to the DDO.

His friendship with the Kelly family began in 1969 through a fishing accident. Jensen always thought of the event as providential, a word which found frequent use in the professor's vocabulary. He'd been fly fishing in the Snake River and slipped on a round stone as he was shifting position. He fell and struck his head on a rock, losing consciousness. His waders filled and he would have drowned, if not for Clancy and Jake Kelly. They had just rounded the bend in the river with their own fly rods and saw him go down. The two pulled Jensen to safety, revived him, and drove him to their summer cottage on the Snake.

Bill and Susan Jensen, and Clancy and Galina Kelly had immediately grown close. Through their mutual love of books, history and the out-of-doors, the two couples forged a deep friendship. When Clancy had died in '83 and Galina soon after, Bill and Susan became something of surrogate parents for Jake. Though Jacob was a successful adult in his own right, the Jensens wanted to be there for him just as his own parents would have been. Consequently his achievements and special days and events became something they made a point of celebrating with him. It was clear that the young man valued their wisdom and their care. He had no siblings, no living grandparents, aunts, or uncles, and his parents were dead. The Jensens knew they were a link to Jake's past that he no longer had through anyone else.

When Bill and Susan were notified in July of 1986 that Major Jacob Kelly was missing and presumed dead they grieved for him as though he was their own. His F-16 had disappeared over the Bering Sea while Jake was flying a refresher flight, according to the official record. With little to go on the Accident Investigation Board (AIB) had, in the finest of military traditions, concluded the disappearance must have been the result of pilot error. Bill doubted that. Jake was a highly decorated fighter pilot, and had become such an expert on the aircraft that his peers had dubbed him "Falcon."

But then, little more than a week ago, Kelly had contacted Bill with the wildest of stories. He'd been shot down by the Soviets over the Bering Sea, had escaped custody and managed to flee across the length of Siberia, ultimately departing the country in a kayak. But the flier had been overcome by hypothermia before reaching the Alaskan coastline. The kayak was spotted drifting in the Strait, and an intense confrontation developed between Soviet and American forces attempting to retrieve the kayak and its occupant, a confrontation that nearly resulted in a shooting incident. The Americans reeled him in, and Kelly returned to his homeland unconscious and in an advanced state of hypothermia. He was choppered to the hospital in Kotzebue.

Within several days an assassination attempt sanctioned by the GRU was made on Kelly. Barely recovered from his bout with hypothermia, the major narrowly avoided being murdered in his bed. He fled the hospital, but not before cold-cocking his would-be assassin and shackling him to the hospital bed. He stole an aircraft at the Kotzebue Airport and flew to Anchorage before anyone realized he was no longer in his bed.

The young man had related enough detail of his experience to convince Jensen that the initial shootdown was a Soviet espionage effort to learn about Project *Hydra*, a secret weapons development project for which Kelly was the chief test pilot. But when all the data were assembled, an additional, darker conclusion presented itself: there was a spy somewhere embedded in USAF operations. The circumstances of the shootdown made that crystal clear.

Jake had realized this during the long months of his escape

from Siberia. It meant he'd have to stay underground upon returning to the United States until the spy could be identified. Jake didn't know who he could trust. If he simply showed up at an Air Force base, the spy would learn of it and Kelly would wind up dead within forty-eight hours. But the American authorities knew none of this: they interpreted Jake's disappearance from Kotzebue as evidence of Jake's guilt of either treason or criminality. And yesterday the Alaska State Troopers had arrested Kelly. Jensen's answering machine had recorded a phone call from Kelly just before the arrest, providing all the details and asking for help. And Kelly had hinted darkly that more had happened in the Soviet Union than what he'd left in the message.

Bill Jensen paced about his kitchen, arguing with himself. He too was convinced that there was a spy and that Kelly's life was now in danger. *What should I do?* he pondered. *The best chance of ferreting out this spy is leaving Kelly in place, and hoping the bad guy makes a mistake while going after him. But I am also running the risk that Kelly dies if we can't sort things out quickly enough. On the other hand, if I go riding in with all the resources of the Feds, I can save Kelly but the spy will go to ground and we'll never find him. Hmm. Could this be a leftover from the Walker spy ring? No, not likely. John Walker and his cronies were Navy.*

In the end, it was Kelly's commission as an Air Force officer that decided the matter. Kelly had made the decision to risk his life for his country when he joined up. *Members of the armed forces don't get to pick and choose where their threats come from. I've got to leave Kelly in place, swinging in the breeze, so to speak, until I can nail the sellout. My personal friendship cannot be allowed to decide the matter.* Jacob Kelly, Bill realized, was like a fat earthworm dangled on a hook in a pool of hungry fish—even if you hooked the fish it usually didn't go too well for the worm. Jensen buried his face in his hands, and prayed that God would protect his young friend until he'd located the spy.

****

"Mr. Meeker? Are you okay, sir?"

Kelly groaned. He found himself tangled up in his blankets, lying on the floor. He was in jail in Anchorage in the custody of the Alaska State Troopers after having been nabbed the day before. His head throbbed, and a knot was growing where he'd hit it on the concrete floor. He held his arm up to shield his eyes from the guard's flashlight.

"Yeah, I'm fine. Guess I just fell out of the bed." He wasn't about to tell the guard he'd had a nightmare.

"I heard you scream, sir. Are you sure you're all right?"

"Yeah. Thanks for your concern."

As the guard walked back to his desk Kelly got off the floor and sat on the edge of the bed. He gingerly explored the knot on his head with his fingers. *No real damage done*, he decided, *just hurts like a son of a gun.*

The dream had been recurring regularly since early summer. It always ended the same way: he and Oz were killed by the blast in the physical plant. He grinned ruefully to himself in the darkness, thinking *I'm glad that's not what really happened!*

The guard had used the alias he'd invented when first questioned by the hospital personnel in Kotzebue. That must mean that the powers that be were acquiescing to his request to keep his arrest secret. Jake lay down in his bed, thankful for small things, and tried to get back to sleep. He might have been a little more concerned had he known that two more teams of assassins were en route.

****

On the other side of the continent Dr. William Jensen was folding his six-foot frame into his Porsche 944 Turbo. Although he hoped an early start would help him beat Beltway traffic around DC, he knew he was kidding himself. Interstate 95 was the carotid artery of the nation, and the Beltway was its heart. Rush hour was a twenty-four-hour affair.

He had arranged for teaching assistants to take his classes at Georgetown University for the next several weeks, and gotten clearance from the DDO to pursue an intelligence "research project," which is how he was designating the Kelly affair. This gave him official sanction without requiring him to further specify the nature of the research. It would open all the necessary doors.

Before going to his office at Langley he stopped at the DOD's Defense Prisoner of War / Missing Persons Office (DPMO) at the Pentagon. Each branch of the service maintained its own Service Casualty Office, but the DOD's central office at the Pentagon housed the master database, ensured uniform access and security policies, and handled escalated issues with families and loved ones. Four days earlier, the DPMO had received a phone call from an unidentified individual inquiring after Major Jacob Kelly. While taking the call Sheila Turner also noticed that an unsuccessful attempt had been made to modify Kelly's record just several hours earlier. Provoked by the suspicious nature of the phone call and the failed edit, she had reported the attempt to her supervisor, who instructed her to log her suspicions. Turner's report was snagged by the DIA's *Watcher* program, a rudimentary data analysis tool that scanned the traffic flying around MILNET and other networks, looking for occurrences of specified words and phrases. Jensen had entered Kelly's name as a key word, and *Watcher* had dutifully notified him of the activity on Kelly's DPMO record.

It took Jensen several minutes to penetrate the bureaucracy to the point where he was actually able to speak face to face with Ben Jones, Sheila Turner's supervisor.

"Hello, Mr. Jones. I'm Bill Jensen, special assistant to the Deputy Director of Operations over at the CIA. I understand you have a Sheila Turner working for you. I would like a few moments to speak with her. Could you arrange that for me?" As he spoke Jensen pulled out his identity card and showed it to Ben.

Surprised, Ben wondered what Sheila had done to warrant a visit from one of the spooks at the Agency. "Certainly, Mr. Jensen. I'll send for her. May I ask what this is about?"

"I'm not at liberty to say, other than to assure you that it has nothing to do with Ms. Turner herself. I'd really rather speak to her at her desk, if that's permissible. And you're not to log this visit, or maintain any record of it."

"Of course." Several minutes later the professor was pulling a chair into Sheila's cubicle. "Miss Turner, my name is Bill Jensen. I'm with the CIA, and your supervisor has been kind enough to allow me a few moments of your time. How are you today?" Jensen attempted to put the surprised young woman at ease.

"I'm fine, Mr. Jensen," she said cheerfully, "please call me Sheila. What brings the Agency to my desk this morning?"

"Sheila, on Friday you handled a telephone inquiry about an Air Force major by the name of Jacob Kelly. I'd like to ask you a few questions about that call."

"Sure. Fire away, Mr. Jensen."

"Bill—please call me Bill. First, can you bring the record up on your screen?"

She swiveled around to her computer and quickly brought Kelly's record up on her display. Jensen scooted his chair a little closer. "May I?" he asked, reaching for the mouse.

"Be my guest," she replied. "In fact, let's switch chairs, so you can drive."

After trading places, Jensen silently scrolled through the entire record, reading it carefully. Turning to the young woman, he queried, "I've read your entry, but I want you to tell me what it was that set off your internal alarm bells, causing you to flag this access, no matter how unfounded you feel your concerns may be."

She stared at the monitor for a moment before beginning: "I think . . . I think the biggest reason was the coincidence: on the same day as the phone call, someone else attempted to modify the record. As you can see, down at the bottom of Kelly's record, there was an effort on Friday to color the conclusions of the Accident Investigation Board that handled his case." She reached across him and tapped a few keys and the transaction audit log appeared. She pointed at the first line and said, "There! See? On Friday morning—same day I got the call. Someone tried to change the record. Why would someone want to add a statement about the AIB discussions a full year after the fact, when the investigation has been closed?"

"I don't know," the professor admitted. "But that's directly related to what I'm investigating. If this unknown person had been successful, what would the record have looked like? Would it be obvious that it had been modified?" Jensen asked.

"No, not at all. The text would have been added seamlessly to the comments field, there." She pointed to it on the screen. "You would not know that the record had been edited unless you checked the transaction audit log, and this office is the only one that has access to the audit log. None of the Casualty Service Offices even know the transaction audit log exists. It's a security feature."

The professor looked at the monitor and felt a chill go down his spine. Jake Kelly had been correct in his suspicions about the spy and that the Soviet Union would attack his credibility. On the monitor right in front of him was the evidence. Someone was trying to plant a hint of treason on Jake's record but the attempt had backfired, big time. *Everybody makes mistakes,* Jensen thought. *Everybody gets careless now and then. But this is providential! This guy has just left me his calling card and he doesn't even know it!* Jensen smiled to himself. *I'm gonna nail this guy!*

There was not much additional information that Sheila was able to tell the professor. He thanked her, and then admonished, "Sheila, my inquires about this record are not to be logged, under any circumstances. Here's my card. I want to know of any further activity pertaining to Major Kelly immediately. You are not to speak of this meeting or enter anything into your computer about my visit today. Do you understand?" He raised his eyebrows and did his best to look stern.

"I understand. This sort of thing is unusual, but it does come up from time to time and we've been trained to honor requests such as yours."

His last stop before leaving the DPMO was to the database administrator. After exchanging pleasantries and demonstrating his security clearances, Jensen got down to business. "There was a transaction on Friday—an attempt to modify this record." He showed the attractive black woman a hard copy of Kelly's DPMO record. "I would like a dump of every last byte of raw data in the transaction record from that transaction, including the security audit fields. Is that available?"

"No problem, sir. I can bring it up right now." Her fingers stroked the keyboard and in a matter of seconds the line printer behind her burped out a greenbar page containing the raw information. She tore it off and handed it to him.

"Help me interpret this, will you? I am looking for the workstation address and login credentials used by the person who attempted to change this record." He handed the printout back to the administrator. She opened a binder and turned to the record layout in the database definition. Then she ran down the column of data with her index finger.

"Let's see . . . oh, here it is. The request came from IP address 11.107.6.15."

"Where would that terminal be located?"

"Let me check." She brought up a search utility that accessed the Network Information Center's host table for MIL-NET and scanned for the IP address. "Okay, here it is, Mr. Jensen. That IP belongs to a computer somewhere at Eielson Air Force Base in Alaska. Eielson has a whole block of IPs. Their network technicians could tell you exactly which computer it was."

"Excellent. What are the login credentials that were used to access MILNET and the database?"

"Military standards, sir, specify that the user's first initial and last name shall compose the login name by which they authenticate." She examined the data dump again and pointed to a line near the bottom of the sheet. "There. WOTT@EIEL-SONAFB.MIL. Must be someone with the last name of Ott. Evidently he didn't have sufficient clearance to modify the record. The database rejected the transaction."

"Is this thing time-stamped?"

"Yes, sir, right here, see? 2337 hours. That time, by the way, is GMT—not local. So at Eielson it would have been, um . . . 1537 hours," the database administrator said, doing a quick calculation in her head.

"Excellent," Jensen said again. "You've been most helpful.

Thank you!" After cautioning her to not log his visit or his questions he retrieved the printout and locked it his briefcase.

As he returned to his car, the CIA agent mentally checked off two of the five tasks he had set for himself today: interviewing Sheila Turner and getting the data dump of the failed DPMO transaction. His morning had been very productive already. He pulled out of the parking lot and headed west to Langley.

****

In Washington, DC it was now 0815; at NAS Adak, thousands of miles to the west, it was 0315. Under a clear, cold, black sky two F-14 Tomcats roared off Adak's Runway 18, banked right, and headed north for their rendezvous with a KC-130 Hercules tanker orbiting five hundred miles north-northwest of Adak. Two more pairs of fighters would take off with ten-minute intervals between them. Operation *Screen Pass* was commencing.

The target of *Screen Pass* was the Petropavlovsk-Kamchatskiy military complex on the Kamchatka Peninsula. If the two superpowers ever came to blows, the conventional land action would take place in Europe, but most of the sea battles would occur between the Soviet Red Banner Pacific Fleet, headquartered in Vladivostok, and the US Pacific Fleet, headquartered at Pearl.

Periodically, the two potential belligerents engaged in provocative behavior designed to force the other side to show its hand in terms of defensive capability. *Screen Pass* was just such a provocation. Three pairs of F-14s would approach the Petropavlovsk-Kamchatskiy area, one after another, at different altitudes. The responses of the Soviet military would be recorded, plotted, and later analyzed. The operation was designed by the senior intelligence officer at Adak NAS, Lieutenant Commander Jesse Pierce. Although *Screen Pass* was wholly unrelated to the events surrounding Major Jacob Kelly, the two affairs would intersect at a crucial juncture.

Each fighter would refuel with the KC-130 both going and

coming. The flying gas station was their insurance policy—among other things it allowed the pilots to use their afterburners without worrying about running out of fuel. Other than the Electronic Counter Measures (ECM) pods slung under their fuselages and the super-secret Electronic Surveillance Module (ESM) pods, which were not even in the official Tomcat inventory, all six aircraft were outfitted in a ferry configuration in order to give them maximum range. None of the jets carried any ordnance, a fact which didn't make the pilots happy. And it did not help that they were prohibited from activating the ECM pods unless specifically directed to by the Forward Air Controller (FAC) located in the E-2 Hawkeye orbiting several hundred miles offshore of the target area.

****

Just after 0530 hours Adak time (0330 hours the next day on the Kamchatskiy Peninsula), the USS *Honolulu*, SSN 718, silently ascended from the frigid depths of the black water some twenty-four miles southeast of the Petropavlovsk-Kamchatskiy port area. It surfaced to ESM mast depth, all systems and personnel on full quiet.

The *Honolulu* was a silent black shadow in the water, one of the quietest submarines in the United States naval inventory. A *Los Angeles*-class attack sub, she was capable of wreaking destruction on multiple land- and sea-based targets with her horizontally launched Tomahawk cruise missiles. But land and surface targets were not her real forte. Subs in this class were intended to shadow and, in the event of war, eliminate the large Soviet "boomers" before they could launch their nuclear missiles. Capable of a submerged speed in excess of twenty-five knots, the *Honolulu* was designed to be a huntress.

The keel of the boat had been laid in the Newport News Naval Shipyard in 1981. The mission at Petropavlovsk-Kamchatskiy was her first covert operation. New as she was, submarine technology had advanced so rapidly that just one year after commissioning the SSN 718 was already an old boat. Nevertheless, as the *Honolulu* loitered just off the coast it was a formidable and dangerous opponent. If it was discovered the Soviets' response would be unpredictable, a fact that motivated its crew to remain undetected.

Within fifteen minutes of arriving on station the ambient level of electronic emissions from the nearby Soviet military installations had been established and all active radar emitters had been identified, classified, and plotted. Meanwhile, passive sonar was tracking commercial shipping in the area. It did not appear that the *Honolulu* was being shadowed.

"Skipper, aside from numerous surface contacts identified as local shipping, sonar reports an intermittent contact far to the south. Rusty's not able to get a solid bearing on it, much less a course or distance. But the acoustic signature pegs it as a *Kilo*. Probably on patrol." The executive officer was practically whispering.

"A *Kilo?* How the devil did we hear him first?" The newer Soviet *Kilo*-class of submarine was one of the quietest diesel boats in service. Having a run-in with one of them could be lethal.

"Well, sir, we don't *know* that we heard him first. But Rusty says Ivan is snorkeling and making about as much racket as a *Kilo* will ever make. He's not behaving as though he hears us. If he wasn't snorkeling we probably couldn't have picked him up at all."

"Okay. Spread the word. We need to make like a hole in the water. Anybody drops a wrench on the deck, I'll launch him out of one of the forward tubes myself!"

The *Honolulu* had spent eight hours creeping into position. While getting this close to a major Soviet military port was a real coup, it was also very dangerous. The Russians were to be forgiven if upon detecting the American attack sub less than thirty miles from some of their most sensitive military installations, they interpreted the *Honolulu's* intentions as somewhat less than benevolent. It could get real dicey.

Watching his young crew, the captain decided that if the *Kilo* came closer they would abort. The *Honolulu* would hitch a ride with the noisiest merchant freighter leaving the port. They would simply shadow the freighter out of the area, several meters under its keel, until back in blue water. The noise level of the ship would mask their own acoustical signature. At least, that was the hope.

"How are our guests, Bubba?" The captain looked at his short, lean XO and wondered for the thousandth time how such a scrawny sample of humanity had earned the handle "Bubba."

"Happy as clams, Roscoe. They have their stuff all set up and are just waiting for the show to begin. I think they're listening to early morning Soviet talk radio while they wait."

The "guests" were a small contingent of civilians that had boarded at Pearl ten days ago, whose baggage included a great deal of electronic equipment now connected to the receiving end of the *Honolulu's* ESM antenna circuitry. The J2 at Pearl (the Director of Naval Intelligence) had said they were "civilian contractors" who were to be "afforded every courtesy and given every assistance" in carrying out their "testing." That bit of bureaucratic blah-blah was intended for public consumption. Captain Roscoe Raines truly hoped his crew were not so dull of wit that they couldn't see through the charade. The admiral had gone through the entire mission and its purposes with him. The so-called contractors were on the NSA payroll and were assisting the Navy with Operation *Screen Pass*.

"Good, Bubba. See that they have whatever they need. Let's get this thing over with and get those spooks off my boat."

"Will do, Cap'n."

****

Cup of steaming coffee in hand, Jensen opened the sealed manila envelope. It had just been delivered to his office by a secure courier coming from the NSA's facility, and contained the photographs and analysis of the construction site identified by Al Mercer and Karl Randolph the day before. During a routine shipping census of the port of Magadan, the KH-11 spy satellite passing overhead had picked up a construction site in the remote wilderness above Magadan. The two sharp-eyed NSA technicians had spotted it and managed to read off the fuselage number of a military helicopter on site. When their database had pegged the chopper as being assigned to a senior member of Soviet High Command military intelligence, the GRU, Jensen had been notified.

He pulled out the material, and spread it on the desk. After studying the photographs with a magnifying glass for twenty minutes, he began to read the report. Several pages described the various features seen in the photographs and an analysis wrapped it up:

> *The entire site footprint, plus the individual building foundations—especially those where the roofing has not been installed—support our original conclusions. This appears to be a highly secure prison facility. We estimate that the final construction will include six cellblocks, six guard towers, and seven other buildings. Rolls of what are assumed to be chain-link fencing and razor wire can be seen in the photographs. The fencing will apparently be doubled, with an interior space that might be policed by dogs. Small huts within the double-fenced area support this conclusion.*
>
> *The ground plan appears to have a maximum security area containing the cellblocks plus an additional building of unknown purpose, all surrounded by the fencing and guard towers. A second area, which appears to have the same sort of security arrangements (minus the towers) connects to the main compound gate. We believe this second area to be an administrative section of the compound. It contains six buildings, one of which is probably administrative, three appear to be barracks, and another can be identified as the physical plant containing a standard Soviet centralized steam heating system. The purpose of the remaining building in the administrative compound is unknown.*
>
> *Based on an observed history of Soviet construction speed, we estimate this site to be two months, possibly more, from completion. An absolute minimum time-to-completion we estimate to be forty-five days.*

From what we can determine the maximum census for this facility is thirty-six prisoners if each prisoner is kept in isolation. With four prisoners per cell the maximum census would increase to one hundred forty-four prisoners. In order to adequately staff and secure three shifts, we estimate this facility will require slightly over one hundred personnel. There is sufficient barracks capacity to accommodate a staff of this size.

Although we believe we can identify this site as a prison facility, there are three unusual aspects that may call for a revision of our conclusions. First, on the scale of other known Soviet prison facilities, including criminal/political, KGB, and GRU facilities, this site is very small. This fact is admittedly contrary to all previously identified trends in Soviet construction which tend toward the large or even massive. Second, its location and remoteness could argue for a different or at least unusual use. And third, the presence of General Chernikov seems to be highly irregular: it is unusual to have a man of his rank inspecting a prison this small.

Jensen tossed the report on his desk and leaned back in his chair, thinking. *The writers of this analysis captured the anomalies perfectly: the construction site is unusually small and unusually remote, and Chernikov is too distinguished an officer to be cruising around inspecting prison construction. Unless . . . unless you are running an operation so politically explosive that it needs to be kept way, way below the public radar, to the point of even isolating the staff from the public. An operation that could involve interrogating foreigners whom you have acquired illegally. Such as Jake Kelly. I wonder if Chernikov is wrapped up in what happened to Jake? It would make sense.*

He took a sip of his coffee and extended his thoughts another step. *Okay, let's play with the theory that Chernikov is the man behind Jake's kidnapping. Why would they be building this facility now, after Jake Kelly got away from them? Hmm. Answer? Because they have other detainees. Because the program is still going on. They need to move the location of the operation lest Jake is able to compromise it. In fact, their desire to eliminate or discredit Jacob probably has to do with keeping this program secret. Jake mentioned that he has even more to tell me.*

I bet I know what it is!

Little by little the pieces were falling into place, confirming every statement and suspicion Major Kelly had shared with him. *If I keep getting so many good leads, I'm going to need some help running them all down. This whole affair is unfolding very rapidly*, he reflected.

When Jake Kelly had contacted him by phone a week earlier with an account of his shootdown, capture, and interrogation, Jensen had not known what to think. Added to the fantastic and improbable story was Jake's seemingly paranoid fear that a spy was embedded somewhere in USAF operations. And yet everything Jake had told him was checking out.

As Jensen began to investigate, his research was complicated by the fact that the spy would also have security clearances, possibly enough to know when someone was trying to track him down. Consequently Jensen's every move had to be secret. Not knowing who to trust or how far the corruption extended, Jensen had to carry out his investigation without tipping anyone off. The sole exception was his boss at the CIA, the DDO, who had granted him carte blanche to pursue the matter.

Jensen began with the DIA's *Watcher* program. Because of his elevated security clearance at the CIA, Jensen had black access, a fact which kept others from knowing what he was doing. He submitted Kelly's name and immediately got several hits, besides the DPMO report. USAF General James T. Franks had also listed Kelly under *Watcher*, as had Navy Admiral John Bridger.

Franks had been Kelly's commanding officer in *Hydra* and the overall director of the project. Jensen immediately decided that Franks must be clean. If he had been the traitor, there would have been no need to go through the effort of the kidnapping; Franks could have told the Sovs anything they wanted to know.

Bridger, however was another matter. Rear Admiral John Bridger was the commanding officer of Naval Special Warfare Group One (NSWG-1), based out of Coronado. He had a handful of SEAL teams and support teams under his control.

The admiral was neck-deep in security and intelligence, but Jensen hadn't a clue as to why the man would be interested in an Air Force officer like Kelly. The fact that Bridger was nosing about bothered him. If Bridger had been compromised, it would be a national security disaster. Jensen had placed investigating the admiral on the top of his checklist of leads. He now added two more items:

> *1. Investigate John Bridger. Why is he checking intelligence traffic on Kelly?*
>
> *2. Interview Jim Franks. Why did he submit Jake Kelly's name to Watcher? Does he have information that leads him to doubt the AIB report?*
>
> *3. ~~Get a technician to pull up all the data available on the failed access to the DPMO record.~~*
>
> *4. ~~Interview Sheila Turner, the DPMO employee.~~*
>
> *5. Ask Jake Kelly for his ideas on Sheila Turner's mysterious phone call.*
>
> *6. Contact Eielson AFB network people, and find out whose computer has IP address 11.107.6.15.*
>
> *7. Nose around Eielson, and find out who W. Ott is.*

It was too early to make his phone calls: folks on the West Coast were just getting out of bed. He stared at his list. Everyone he needed to talk to was in California or Alaska. It was time to head west. Jensen began throwing stuff he might need into his briefcase. He picked up his short-notice travel bag, locked his office, and headed for Washington National Airport.

****

The first two Tomcats swept in at 0430 hours at the prescribed altitude of one hundred feet. The leading jet broke left, his wingman broke right, and they both executed a tight 180-degree climbing turn, leveling off at four hundred feet. The Soviet air defense system was caught completely off guard. Because of the low altitude approach the ground-based Soviet radar had been unable to pick the F-14s out of the ground clutter, and the bogeys popped up right under their noses.

The ESM pods carried by the F-14s were recording both the aircraft maneuvers as well as all ELINT emissions. Later analysis showed that there was a full forty-five-second window between the pop-up maneuver and initial acquisition by Soviet targeting radar. The FAC in the E2-C Hawkeye speculated that the officer responsible for the air defenses surrounding Petropavlovsk-Kamchatskiy would be losing his job this afternoon.

What none of the Americans could know is that an enraged Soviet commander had been just seconds from issuing orders to fire on the aircraft. He stood down only because there were but two invaders and they were in full retreat, rocketing out to sea at Mach 1.7.

Phase One of Operation *Screen Pass* was complete with a successful penetration of Soviet air defenses operating on a peacetime mode. But now the situation resembled something closer to a wartime scenario, with all the air search and SAM site radar lit up. The next two Tomcats would be making their approach with the opposition at full alert. Phase Two was about to begin.

Meanwhile, in the black waters just off the coast the technicians in the attack sub were quietly recording and plotting the locations of each newly activated Soviet radar site. Other than the NSA workers recording the data and a few of the *Honolulu's* officers, the crew of the submarine was unaware of the action going on overhead, as all three flights of fighters were flying under EMCON conditions, not emitting any signals that could be detected by the submarine's passive sensors.

At 0505 hours the second pair of F-14s approached at one thousand feet, inbound at supersonic speed. Soviet radar picked them up while they were still one hundred sixty miles out. By the time a flight of four MiG-31 Foxhounds was scrambled the Tomcats had reached the turn-around point.

"Diamond Flight, Diamond Flight, this is Lone Wolf. Four bogeys inbound at niner three zero knots, range four zero miles, bearing two one zero, altitude five angels. Request you drop to the deck and light the burners, zone five."

"Roger, Lone Wolf, inbound bogeys. Dropping to the deck and going to full afterburner. Request we go active."

"Negative, Diamond Flight, maintain lights out."

The Foxhounds gave chase and overtook the American bandits, but were unable to match the low-altitude agility of the F-14s. After about one hundred miles of harassment the MiGs gave up the chase.

Phase two of *Screen Pass* had come off with resounding success for the Americans, although the pilots' flying suits were drenched in sweat as well as other bodily fluids by the time they made it back to the Hercules tanker.

Rather than returning immediately to base the four Foxhounds set up an ad hoc CAP, going active with their powerful Zaslon RP-31 phased-array radars. More data was captured by the sophisticated instruments in the Hawkeye and the snoops in the submarine.

The final pair of inbound Tomcats was detected at the maximum range of Petropavlovsk-Kamchatskiy's ground-based radar systems, two hundred thirty miles out, and the Soviet fighters were vectored to intercept the inbound sortie. They closed to within one hundred miles of the F-14s before reaching the margin of safety on their fuel reserves. Forced to return to base, they left the inbound fighters uncontested.

Twelve minutes later the sensitive receivers on the submarine and in the Hawkeye picked up the signature emission of a TIN SHIELD, the NATO designation for a Russian 36D6 surveillance radar belonging to a mobile SA-10 surface-to-air missile defense system. Seconds later a second signature appeared: a 30N6 command guidance radar, known to NATO pilots as FLAP-LID. The firing system radar probed the airspace indicated by the surveillance radar and soon achieved target lock on the inbound US fighters. By this time the Tomcats had closed to within fifty miles.

"Gold Flight, Gold Flight, this is Lone Wolf. You are being painted by a SAM site. Break off, and exit on vector xray alpha. Maintain EMCON." The FAC on the E2-C was taking no chances. Within seconds four new contacts appeared on the Hawkeye's threat display.

"Missiles launched! Missiles launched! Four Grumbles incoming, repeat, four Grumbles incoming, locking on you, Gold Flight! Break off, break off, break off. You are go for ECM!" The FAC was beginning to sweat; he could feel perspiration trickling down between his shoulder blades.

Gold Flight pulled a tight turn, lighting their afterburners and climbing while they accelerated on their new vector. They were now just forty miles from the port. The SAM site was using the improved 5V55R Grumble surface-to-air missile with a powered flight range of about fifty-six miles. The Grumble's guidance system was the semi-active radar homing (SARH) type. With SARH, the FLAP-LID fire-control radar would simply bounce a signal off the target and the Grumble would fly the reflection right to the target. It was remarkably accurate with a disheartening kill-ratio.

The top speed of the missile was thirty-eight hundred miles per hour. The Tomcats of Gold Flight were accelerating past thirteen hundred miles per hour, a mere one third the speed of the missiles. Holding his breath, the FAC on the Hawkeye watched his screen as the blips drew close. The missiles closed to within one thousand feet of the aircraft before they fell, fuel spent, into the sea.

"Gold Flight, you are in the clear." The controller hesitated for a second, and then added, "Mission accomplished. Good job." His voice was clear but his hands were shaking. It had been a close thing.

An hour later, the *Honolulu* retracted its ESM mast and silently returned to the depths. Gliding under a departing merchant ship she crept away, shielded from the listening ears of the *Kilo* by the loud machinery noises of a tramp freighter.

****

The aftershocks of *Screen Pass* would continue for days. After all the local finger-pointing was complete, the old men of the Politburo were convinced by KGB head Anatoly Geredin that it had something to do with the escape of Major Jacob

Kelly from Chernikov's interrogation facility. They assumed that the probe was a prelude to an in-kind covert response from the United States. Chernikov's boss, General Valeriy Patrikeyev, was a member of the Politburo. The commanding officer of the GRU's Ninth Directorate, he had repeatedly assured them that the major had not yet given the US intelligence community any important information. But the council was nonetheless suspicious. Unknown to the GRU or even many in the Politburo itself, Geredin began to forge plans to shut Chernikov down and eliminate the embarrassment he had caused to Mother Russia. Geredin had never been in favor of Project *Krasnyy Voskhod*, Chernikov's kidnapping program. If the GRU did not soon abandon their dangerous program, Geredin's KGB would shut it down for them. The old bear of the KGB had many useful contacts with people who knew how to *do things*—the Russian way.

Chapter 3

Tuesday, October 6, 1987: 1030 hours, local time
Anchorage, AK

It was hard to characterize where Kelly was being held as a jail cell. Certainly there were bars—and the construction was concrete and there were guards and locks. But there was also some furniture and a bed, not a cot. More than likely the small facility was intended for the protective custody of non-violent criminals being granted immunity in return for testimony.

As far as he could tell, at least part of what he'd asked of the arresting officer had been provided: he was isolated and under guard. As to the rest of his requests he had no idea. He hadn't heard a word from Jensen. He guessed that a sequence of events would be launched today leading to some sort of resolution—one way or another—of the fifteen-month odyssey that began with his shootdown over the Bering Sea.

For a brief moment a wave of frustration broke over Jake, and he yielded to it. He'd had his fill of running and hiding. He was home, but he wasn't home. He was tired of the asterisks and footnotes that seemed to plague his life story. He sat back on the bed and dreamed of payback. *One of these days Nikolai Chernikov will regret he ever heard my name. I will make him suffer. I will make him curse the day of his birth!*

The rattle of keys warned him that someone was about to enter. Jacob Kelly looked up as a young lieutenant commander entered, bearing a breakfast tray. Kelly smiled wryly and said, "Not very often that my breakfast is served to me by a naval officer. Makes me feel like an admiral. Good morning."

"Don't get used to it. Good morning yourself." The man gave him a friendly smile. "So how is Major Jacob Kelly feeling this morning?"

Jake grinned and said, "No more Mr. Meeker, eh?"

"Afraid not. You happen to be wearing Mr. Kelly's finger-prints, so I reckon we'll call you Jacob Kelly." Then he noticed the bruise on Kelly's forehead. "Whoa! Where'd you get that knot? You want that looked at?"

"Nah. Accidentally rolled out of the rack last night and landed on my noggin—I'm okay. Actually, I haven't slept so well in over a year," he replied honestly. "It's the first time in the last fifteen months that I've been able to sleep without worrying about somebody coming after me. My hands and feet still ache a bit, but otherwise I feel fine. You have me at a disadvantage, by the way. You know my name but I don't know yours."

Jesse Pierce marveled at the calm, controlled poise his pris-oner displayed. The man appeared to be utterly confident and completely comfortable. "I'm Lieutenant Commander Jesse Pierce, the J2 at Adak NAS. I organized the rescue effort that pulled you out of the drink. We got there just before the Sovs. It was a close thing."

"Thank you, Commander Pierce. I don't believe I was con-scious at the time. It would have been a real disappointment to wake up on Soviet soil again."

"You're quite welcome, Major. Unfortunately, as it turns out, your rescue is the beginning and not the end of this af-fair. My colleagues and I are very interested to learn who you are and why the Soviet Union was so intent on reeling you in that they darn near caused a war to do it."

"Well, Commander, you are in luck because there's nothing I'd rather do than spill the beans, but as I told Agent Devlin yesterday, I will only talk to the CIA or the FBI. I'm sorry, but that's the way it has to be."

Pierce shrugged his shoulders and said, "You'll get your wish. This morning you'll be interrogated by Jim Stewart, who is with the Seattle office of the FBI, and you'll also be talking to Sam Bergman of the CIA. I wonder, though, if you could answer just one question for me: was there a substantial man-hunt in Siberia for you?"

"In all likelihood, Commander, you'll have your answer be-fore the week is out."

"Going to make me wait, are you?"

"Sorry."

Pierce set the tray down in front of Jake and, turning to leave, said over his shoulder, "Bergman and Stewart will be talking to you in the next few hours."

****

"Thanks, gentlemen, for making the effort to be here for this meeting. And thank you, Ed, for playing host again." Devlin nodded and Jesse Pierce continued, "As you know, a great deal has happened since we last met. Let me take just a few minutes to lay out a plan of attack for today before we get started. First, we will review our progress to date. Then Sam and Jim are going to spend several hours interrogating Major Jacob Kelly. We will wrap up the day with a debrief from Sam and Jim, and then a discussion as to whether we need to go any farther with these joint meetings or whether we can simply turn Project *Snowbird* over to one of our respective organizations."

When Jacob Kelly had been retrieved unconscious from the kayak it was not known who he was or why the Soviets wanted him so badly. Pierce and his boss at Adak NAS, Captain Danny Daniels, hadn't a clue as to whether the affair involved national security, or whether the man in the kayak was a defector, a criminal, or someone simply trying to escape the massive police state. Consequently they put together a joint team, designated Project *Snowbird*, composed of both Naval and Air Force Intelligence, the CIA, the FBI, and the Alaska State Troopers. Each member of the team was a veteran of cases involving either counterintelligence or counterespionage. Their objective was to discover who the boater was and what sort of potential intelligence value he had as someone fleeing the Soviet Union.

"Jesse, with all due respect, this is an Air Force matter. Kelly is one of ours, for better or worse. If any organization follows up on this incident, it ought to be the Air Force." The speaker was a weary-looking Major William Ott. Ott commanded the 6985th Intelligence Squadron at Eielson AFB. The squadron was part of the Air Force's Security Service and was referred to by their compatriots as the "Secret Squirrels." Ott carried his two hundred pounds on a well-conditioned, big-boned frame. At the moment his blue eyes were somewhat bleary from lack of sleep, and his weariness was bringing out the imperious side of his nature.

Pierce sensed Ott's frustration and took a conciliatory approach to avoid stirring the pot. "Bill, I have no dispute with you on that point. The only question is whether there are going to be additional organizations besides the Air Force, who will be interested in interrogating Major Kelly. I expect my own leadership in this incident will run its course this week, possibly even today. Of everyone gathered here today the Navy probably has the least claim to *Snowbird*, other than the fact that we were the ones to bag Kelly." Ott conceded, so Pierce continued with the meeting.

"Alright, let's begin. Ed, why don't you start by giving us the details of Kelly's capture?"

Ed Devlin was a special investigator with the Alaska Bureau of Investigations (ABI). A former marine, Devlin possessed a graduate degree in Business Management from Penn State. His work often involved combating efforts by foreign powers to penetrate Alaskan high tech ventures, be it in the boardroom or the laboratory. Somewhat heavy-set, Devlin was a weight lifter with a powerful upper body. He tended to be very focused and businesslike, sometimes to the point of being dour.

"Sure, Jesse." Ed looked down at his notes, and began. "On Monday morning, we got a call from a patron in a diner here in Anchorage, claiming that someone matching the artist's depiction of John Meeker—the name Kelly had given to the hospital staff in Kotzebue—was in the restaurant. Both Alaska State Troopers and the Anchorage PD responded immediately, but Kelly, Meeker, what have you, had already fled the restaurant. Thankfully he was soon spotted by an unmarked car.

"We finally cornered the suspect in an alley behind an office supply store, but he got the drop on one of our agents and held him briefly at gunpoint. By a ruse, he got an employee at the office supply store to let them into the manager's office. Once in the office, Kelly made a phone call to someone named 'Bill.' In that call, Kelly instructed Bill to contact me, and to encourage me to keep his arrest secret. It was obvious —from the conversation—that the major had had other recent conversations with Bill.

"Depending on how this plays out, we may have the additional issue of this Bill assisting a felon. Kelly asked Bill to pull some strings and help him deal with the crimes of pulling a gun on an officer and stealing an airplane. On the basis of this phone call it appears possible that Kelly may be associated with corrupt elements of the judicial or executive branch."

"Has Bill contacted you?" Major Ott asked.

"No, not yet. Anyway, after his phone call Kelly managed to handcuff himself and turn his weapon over to the officer."

"He cuffed himself?" Ott looked dubious.

"Uh-huh. He had the officer turn around and put his hands on the wall. After a moment Kelly told the officer to turn around again. The officer observed that Kelly had slid the gun over to him and was standing across the room in handcuffs."

"That *is* odd!" exclaimed Ott.

"That's what we thought," Devlin agreed, "and then it got a few degrees odder, if that's a word."

"How so?" This was from CIA analyst Sam Bergman, who so far had been listening to the conversation without comment.

"Well, after the officer had secured control of the situation Kelly asked him for four things. First, to check the gun, which the officer did. Both the magazine and the chamber were empty. Kelly asked him to remember that he'd not really been in danger at any time. Second, he asked that the FBI or CIA be involved in the case as quickly as possible. Third, he asked to be placed in isolation and under armed guard at all times. And fourth, he asked that his arrest be kept secret. Although we are not allowing the prisoner to run our investigation, we felt it was in the interest of Project *Snowbird* to follow through on all four requests, and so we have."

"Why all the secrecy? Why does Kelly want to be under guard, or to have his arrest kept under wraps?" queried Ott, eyes narrowing.

"That's just it. We don't know and he's not saying. But he is adamant about it," replied the trooper. "Oh! One more thing. I went to see the prisoner yesterday and he let it slip that he was thankful that the Soviets did not *recapture* him. That's the term he used: 'recapture.' Apparently he had been in their custody at some point and then escaped. Or at least that's what he wants us to think." Devlin turned the floor back over to Jesse, and poured himself a fresh cup of coffee.

"That lines up with something he said to me this morning," the naval officer related. "When he thanked me for his rescue, Kelly said that it would have been a disappointment to wake up on Soviet soil *again*. So his point of departure in that kayak was indeed from the Soviet side of the Strait." Everyone was silent for a few minutes, absorbing these latest details, then Pierce called on the FBI agent, "Jim, it's your turn."

"Oh! Wait, Jesse, I almost forgot," Devlin interrupted, "we cross-referenced the dates on which the IDC assassins, Fred Banks and Jason Devoe, were missing from Banks' repair shop with our files of unsolved crimes and have come up with some pretty interesting possibilities. Four unsolved murders over the last two years align nicely with the dates provided by their assistant in the shop. Additionally, two more deaths that were ruled accidental match up. In all six cases the victims were highly placed in either corporate or political positions in Alaska or other northwestern states. Sorry, Jim, didn't mean to butt in."

The FBI agent made a few new notes on his pad, then looked up. "No problem. Okay, well, we ran the prints on Meeker on the NCIC database over the weekend and came up empty. Then Sam here gave me a buzz on Sunday night and recommended that I run the prints against the database of US law enforcement, intelligence employees, and military personnel. Bingo. The military database matched Meeker's prints to a Major Jacob Kelly, USAF. I asked Major Ott to bring Kelly's Air Force service records, so we will get to hear from him in a moment. The information I'm sharing is the result of some quick work yesterday by agents in the Harrisburg, Pennsylvania office, as well as one of our offices in Idaho." He opened a manila folder, pulled out some faxes, and perused them briefly before continuing.

At fifty-three, Jim Stewart was a highly decorated special agent working out of the FBI's Seattle office, in their Foreign Counterintelligence Division. Tall, slender, and silver-haired, Stewart was built like a runner—which he was. He'd collaborated with Ed Devlin in the ABI for years and the two had developed a fast friendship. Other agents referred to them as "the Odd Couple" because Stewart was as well known for his sense of humor as Devlin was for his lack of one.

"Kelly is the son of Clancy and Galina Kelly, both deceased. He has no siblings or other living family members. He was raised in the Harrisburg area on the Susquehanna River. A top high school athlete, Kelly attended the USAF Academy after graduating. His home above Harrisburg is all closed up, but we got an agent into it yesterday. It's like a big library inside with a couple of bedrooms and a kitchen—books everywhere. Neighbors say that the entire Kelly family were voracious readers. The family had a generally good reputation in the neighborhood and no one had anything negative or suspicious to say about them. There's more information on a briefing sheet included in your folder, but it does not seem relevant to the case so I won't go over it.

"There is one interesting fact we discovered, however. Kelly's maternal grandparents, Yakov and Oksana Remizov, fled Stalin's Russia in 1947 and came to the US. They settled in a community of Russian immigrants in Idaho. We located an old woman who knew them well. According to her, neither Yakov nor Oksana ever learned to speak English. And yet as a boy Jacob Kelly spent most of each summer with his grandparents."

"What are you saying, Jim?" Ed Devlin asked.

"Well, I think we can surmise that Kelly picked up some Russian language ability from his summer vacations with the grandparents."

"No. Not according to our files," Ott said. "Kelly did not list any language abilities on his Academy application, and none of our background checks or vetting for security clearances revealed anything about an ability in the Russian language. Unless . . ." Ott trailed off, his brow furrowed.

"Unless what?" Jesse demanded.

"Unless he lied," Ott replied, shrugging his shoulders.

"I suppose that's always possible. Anyway, that's all I've got. But I think the whole group ought to hear Bergman's thinking that led him to ask me to try the other fingerprint databases. It made a great deal of sense and as it turned out, he was right." Stewart sat back down.

"Go ahead, Sam," said Jesse.

A top-drawer analyst in the CIA's Soviet Department, Sam Bergman had been tracking communications intercepts over the past fourteen months revealing a massive manhunt proceeding eastward through Siberia, and then northeast through the Chukchi Peninsula. He suspected, as did Jesse Pierce, that the manhunt was somehow connected with their prisoner. An exercise fanatic who both lifted and ran, Bergman weighed in at 190, a little on the heavy side for a male who was five-ten. He was addicted to red licorice, and the joke at the Agency was that he maintained an emergency stash in the secure safe in his office.

"When Jim told me the NCIC database contained no matches with the suspect's fingerprints," Bergman began, "it got me thinking. Other than the theft of the airplane, nothing in our data identifies the suspect as a common criminal. I re-examined the note Kelly left in his hospital room and it hit me. Kelly considers himself on our side, the side of law enforcement. He left complete details, even down to the money he lifted from Fred Banks. He seemed to be handling himself as a professional. Once I recognized that, asking Jim to check the military and law enforcement databases was just a short leap.

"Also, yesterday morning at the Agency I received clearance to work with a group of NSA analysts for the purpose of going over all the latest communications intercepts to and from the Caymans. And sure enough, there were calls from the Cayman offices of the International Development Corporation to Anchorage last Friday. One went to Fred Bank's shop, and another went to the offices of Alaskan Corporate Transport. We now have tight links between Banks and IDC, which means we also have a presumptive link to the Soviet Union.

"By the way, I should hasten to add that we don't believe ACT has any illegal or suspicious role in this, nor do we consider that they are anything other than an airline company. They are not suspects in this investigation. As the saying goes, one man's money is as good as another's, and ACT had no reason to view Banks and Devoe as anything other than what their cover story claimed.

"There is one additional development which may be related to this case. Yesterday afternoon I was called back to the NSA to help one of their translators with a very strange intercept from a highly-placed reliable source inside the Soviet Union. Their translator needed some assistance with the Russian context of the intercept in order to make a good translation. The message stated that there was an American military officer returning to the United States as a covert Soviet agent. Gentlemen, I think we need to take seriously the possibility, however remote, that Major Jacob Kelly is the one referred to in this communication intercept."

"I agree with Sam on this," Ott concurred. "At Eielson we, too, have been picking up hints and rumors of a pending agent insertion. We have several intelligence assets not known to the wider intelligence community, and they've been picking up this buzz since Sunday."

"Ditto here," affirmed Jesse Pierce. "I guess most of us have sources we don't normally share, but we at Adak have also been getting this sort of intel since Sunday. What's wrong, Sam?" Jesse noticed Sam was scowling.

"This is almost too simple," the CIA analyst complained.

"What do you mean?" queried Devlin.

"I've been analyzing Soviet intelligence for years. This is way too much data all pointing the same way. Makes me suspicious," Sam muttered.

"That's true. It is an unusual amount of intelligence for what should be a closely held secret by the Soviets," admitted Jesse, "but think about it, Sam. How often do you get to compare notes this closely with intelligence officers in other organizations that have their own independent assets? I mean, usually, we aren't even talking to each other much less sharing our best stuff!"

"He's right, Sam. How many times in the last five years can you remember the FBI and CIA cooperating on a case like this? As soon as there's even a whiff of an international flavor, the FBI is iced out. And you guys are not allowed into domestic matters. So maybe all this confirming data is no more mysterious than the fact that we're all talking to each other. And look, if our respective intelligence organizations are worth anything, the intel we are working actually *should* be pointing in the same direction. I mean, isn't this what we should expect?" Jim Stewart observed.

"Yeah, I guess you guys are right. But it still fits together too neatly. And let's not jump to conclusions because it will color the way we look at the data. Once you buy in to a certain theory, you start trying to make the evidence fit it, rather than the other way around." Bergman's face was still fixed in a frown.

Jesse let the tension subside for a moment before he continued the discussion. "Alright, now for the moment we've all been waiting for . . . Major Bill Ott, tell us about United States Air Force officer Major Jacob Kelly." With a grand flourish Pierce gestured to Ott, giving him the floor.

Ott grinned at the naval officer as he stood. "Wow. Makes me feel like a celebrity." He passed around folders to each of the men and explained, "This is the relevant, declassified portion of Kelly's service record. I say 'declassified' because parts of his record remain classified due to the projects and operations that he was involved with over the years. On this short notice I was not able to get permission to release those parts to you. What I have passed out you men can read at your leisure. But the short story is this: Major Kelly has an impeccable service record. If he were Catholic, I would nominate him as the next pope."

Devlin piped up, "Perhaps he built that 'impeccable service record' in order to get moved into jobs where he would have access to classified information?"

"See! That's exactly what I'm talking about!" Bergman interjected. "That's a great example of trying to make the data fit the theory. Ed, a better explanation might be that he is just a fine officer!"

"Okay, guilty as charged. Sorry, guys!" A chastened Ed Devlin sat back in his chair.

"Yes, well, let me go on," Ott continued. "Major Jacob Kelly, also known as 'Falcon' to his friends, is a top-rated fighter pilot. His expertise in the F-16 as a combat pilot and as a precision test pilot led to his assignment with a special group at Edwards Air Force Base. The group is involved in a top-secret development project under the command of General James Franks, a man who in Air Force circles is considered nothing short of a genius. The details of the project are entirely classified. Not only am I not permitted to discuss them with you, but I don't know anything about it myself. Even the project name is classified.

"An odd feature of his record are the gaps. Notice, for instance, his service record in '83 and '84. It says that he was with the 34th Fighter Squadron during that time, but he logged no hours, he took no training, and was not involved with any operations. For an officer of this caliber that's not only odd, as I have noted, it's highly improbable."

"So, what does it mean?" asked Stewart.

"It might mean that he was involved in some sort of special ops training," said Devlin. "When I was in the Marine Corps, I tried to get into Delta Force. Unfortunately, I washed out at the six-month mark during training, developed a kidney stone. That's how my service record showed those six months. It listed me as with my regular unit during that time, but showed no activity."

"Well, I don't have any information on that supposition, gentlemen. It's probably as bad to speculate on that as it is on other matters surrounding Kelly," Ott rejoined. "Here's what the record does show. Fifteen months ago, on 10 July, 1986, Kelly was flying an F-16 over the Bering Sea. The aircraft and the major disappeared without a trace. An Accident Investigation Board concluded that he had crashed due to pilot error. A small amount of floating debris appeared to corroborate their findings. Since that time Major Jacob Kelly has been listed with the DPMO Office in the Pentagon as *missing and presumed dead.*"

Ott stopped and looked down at his hands before continuing quietly. "Gentlemen, there was one unusual aspect to the AIB investigation. The accident board did, in their discussions, spend a good deal of time on the possibility that Major Kelly had actually defected with his aircraft. They ultimately decided that the theory was too far-fetched, but it is worth noting that they did initially consider it. In light of some of the latest intelligence we've received, I wonder if perhaps we need to consider that possibility again?"

Ott finished his report, "The more mundane elements of the major's service record are in your briefing folders and I'll not waste time going over those details. Jesse, that's all I have."

The room was silent as the men weighed what they had heard. The details surrounding Kelly were so unusual in themselves that an unusual explanation might be warranted, even reasonable.

Jesse Pierce stood up and stretched. "Gentlemen, unless there is further discussion, I recommend that we adjourn until after Sam and Jim have had an opportunity to interrogate the prisoner."

Ed Devlin motioned to Major Ott. "Bill, we have some clean bunks downstairs, set up for guys who are pulling long shifts during emergencies. Let me show you where they are— maybe you can get a few winks until we meet again this afternoon." The sleepy major nodded and followed him out of the room.

****

Captain Roger Bates, USN, loved his duty station at Alameda NAS. He loved the neighborhoods, he loved the fog, he loved the Bay Area. When he had left home this morning the fog was so thick that the twenty-minute drive had stretched to forty-five. It was like driving in a dream-land.

Bates was a liaison to the Australian Navy and worked on developing joint military exercises with the cousins down under. The premier exercise that Bates was involved with was RIMPAC, the largest international maritime military exercise in the world.

Bates' best friend, USAF General James T. Franks, had asked him to check the data tapes from 10 July of last year for any hint of a Soviet jamming signal north of the exercise. Captain Bates had assigned the task to the electronic warfare technicians in the OW Division of the USS *Carl Vinson*, CVN-70.

There was an envelope on his desk from his friends in the OW division when he arrived. As soon as he had waded through the morning's message traffic and dispatches, Bates opened the envelope and read the report. With growing excitement, he picked up the phone and dialed Jim Franks' number.

"Good morning, General Franks! I trust your beauty rest was, well, effective."

"And who is this who thinks he can be so disrespectful to me this time of the morning?" Franks demanded in an imperious tone, already knowing the response.

"What, are you both deaf *and* ugly?" Bates chuckled.

"Oh," Franks said, voice heavily laden with disappointment, "It's just you. I thought perhaps it would be someone important. And what, my little Navy peon, can I do for you?" Franks asked dismissively.

"Well, let's see if I can find a way to justify my unconscionable use of your valuable time, General. Hmm . . . No, I guess not. I doubt you would be interested in a little news about ELINT signals in the Bering Sea on 10 July a year ago.

Nah! My lordship is *too important* to bother with trivia like that. Listen, I'll call back when you aren't so busy polishing your medals." And with that, Bates hung up with a devilish grin and then watched the second hand on his wallclock sweep across its arc.

James Franks had never accepted the AIB conclusions about Jacob Kelly's disappearance. Then, a week ago he was contacted by Admiral John Bridger, CO of NSWG-1, who claimed to have knowledge of Kelly's disappearance. Through various channels, Bridger had learned from one of his former SEAL platoon commanders that a Soviet fighter pilot was claiming to have shot down an F-16 the summer before. A little research into F-16 losses pointed Bridger to General Franks. But in order to avoid endangering his sources, Bridger had sworn not to compromise them. If the lead was to be followed up the two officers would have to find other evidence with which to reopen the investigation, evidence that would not lead back to their sources. Just days later Franks fell upon the idea of checking the RIMPAC tapes.

Bates continued to watch his clock, laughing to himself. Within fifteen seconds, his phone rang, and he answered with, "This is Captain Roger S. Bates, United States Navy, Naval Liaison to the Royal Australian Navy. How may I help you?" He never used his full title, he just wanted to stir the pot a little more. Jim Franks' volatile temper made it easy—and a lot of fun—to push the general's buttons.

"Forget all that hogwash," the voice roared through the receiver, "just tell me what you found out!"

"Oh!" Bate's voice was dripping with innocence, "You mean I can be of assistance to your lordship?"

"Listen, Rog, tell me what I want to know *right now* or I am going to fly up there and cram that telephone where the sun never shines!"

"It's good news, Jim. You were right! Our Hawkeye picked up a Soviet jamming signal at precisely 0147 hours, bearing two-zero degrees true. The signal was about twenty seconds in duration, and then it disappeared. Twelve minutes before the signal there was some chatter on Soviet Air Force comm frequencies on the same bearing, and then about ten minutes after the jamming signal there was a little more chatter. Unfortunately, the range was too great and the comm signals were too weak to distinguish any words. But we have a one hundred percent verification of the jamming. It was a very strong, very clear Soviet military jamming signal."

"Roger, I cannot thank you enough! This provides me with exactly what I need. One of these days I will be able to explain what this is all about and why it's so important. If the Air Force can award naval officers a medal, you might be in line to get one! Then after lo these many years, maybe you'll have something you can polish, too."

****

After getting off the phone with Roger Bates, Franks dialed Admiral John Bridger.

"John, we're in business. Captain Bates has had the data tapes of last summer's RIMPAC exercises analyzed and there *was* a Soviet military jamming signal! I've checked out the timing and the bearing: it originated from precisely where Jacob Kelly would have been. I'm having Captain Bates send us both a classified copy of the analysis."

"Outstanding! Now that we have this verification, we need to determine our next step." Bridger thought for a moment and added, "Between the data that Bates has provided plus the information from my sources, we finally have a smoking gun. The Soviets have committed an act of war."

****

As soon as Jensen landed at LAX he made his way to the freight terminal. A CIA helicopter was waiting for him, rotors spinning. He climbed aboard with his carry-on, and the chopper took off. Their destination was Imperial Beach, just south of San Diego and immediately south of the SEAL base at Coronado where Admiral John Bridger's headquarters was located.

Over the thunder of the blades he shouted to the two men riding with him, "Is everything ready?"

A young, dapper CIA spook shouted back, "Yes, sir. Exactly as you asked. The intelligence guys at Coronado were not real helpful until the Deputy Director got on the phone. He cleared a path for us and the operation is ready. It's just waiting on you, sir."

Jensen looked at the man and nodded, smiling. The fellow looked like a character from Mad Magazine's *Spy versus Spy* cartoon. He was wearing a black suit and dark glasses. *All he is missing is the fedora*, Jensen chuckled to himself. The other agent looked slightly sloppy and quite unremarkable. His face was plain, dull-witted, and sleepy-looking. Jensen knew from the background checks when he had picked his team that morning before leaving Langley that Spy Guy was relatively new; Sleepy was the experienced professional, as sharp as they come.

Earlier that morning, after he had finished interviewing the people at the DPMO office, Jensen decided that he had a window of, at most, two days to investigate Admiral John Bridger. Although Jensen could not imagine that the admiral was a turncoat, he had to be sure.

Jensen was facing the same difficulty as Jacob Kelly: *whom could he trust?* He could not simply stroll in and ask Bridger why he had placed Kelly on the *Watcher* list. If the admiral was in the Soviets' employ the inquiry would alert him that someone was on his back trail, and he would either go to ground and flee, or cut off contact with his handler until suspicion had blown over. Somehow Jensen needed to verify whether Bridger was trustworthy, and he had to do it within forty-eight hours. Any longer than that and Jensen figured that events surrounding Jacob Kelly might then be on a course that he himself would no longer be able to alter.

Prior to leaving Langley Jensen had met with the DDO and laid out the entire problem. He needed the backing of the DDO in order to investigate people of Bridger's rank. Relationship trumped caution and Jensen had decided to trust the DDO with the details. He'd known the man for most of his career and would have trusted him with his own life. Now he was entrusting the man with Jacob Kelly's life.

The hardest part had been keeping the DDO from riding in with the cavalry and bailing the pilot out of the clink. If they were going to catch the spy, whoever it was, they were going to need to let events surrounding Jacob Kelly develop unimpeded. Jensen's actions would have to remain under the radar. The Deputy Director gave him five days to clear the matter up. After that Jensen would have to defer to the official *Snowbird* investigation. The two men decided to compartmentalize Jensen's activity and not inform Sam Bergman of it.

Even with the DDO's support, there was still a certain amount of unavoidable calculated risk. The CIA could not simply march onto a SEAL base and perform surveillance on one of its highest ranking officers without getting some cooperation from base security. The SEALs themselves were half military and half intelligence. Their operations frequently involved working with the highest classifications used by any of the US intelligence services. All of which meant that their own base security and counterintelligence was finely honed. A surveillance operation on their own turf without clearance from their own people would be spotted and compromised within hours.

Consequently, there were a few individuals on the base in Coronado that had to be brought in to the loop. What those individuals had been told was not true. They would later be debriefed and straightened out by the CIA. But for now there were some guys in the SEALs' security apparatus at Coronado who were more than a little nervous about their boss and whom he was really working for.

Chapter 4

Tuesday, October 6, 1987: 1030 hours, local time
Anchorage, AK

The cell door opened and two guards stepped in. They handcuffed Falcon and then escorted him down the hall to an interrogation room. After seating him in a chair, they left him alone.

The walls were bare except for a mirror opposite him. Jacob Kelly guessed there were people on the other side of it, watching. A video camera was mounted on the ceiling in the corner to his right front, another to his left. He folded his hands on the table in front of him, and waited. He knew from experience the interrogation had already begun, and that the interrogators were hoping he would become nervous from the delay. Instead, he relaxed and began to think about Galya.

He'd met Galina Toporova in a rather unconventional way. While fleeing from his pursuers at the train station in Khabarovsk, he'd carjacked an orange ZAZ-968, a little two-door tin box on wheels, equipped with something the Russians claimed was a motor. In the driver seat was a beautiful young woman whose name, he later learned, was Galina Toporova. He forced her to drive him several kilometers from the train station, in the opposite direction from the manhunt. Learning that he was an American and had no intention of harming her, Galina's curiosity was piqued. She talked him back into the car, one thing led to another, and he wound up wintering in the timber cooperative led by Galina and her brother Boris. As the snowy months dragged by, the American pilot and the Siberian woman fell in love. When he resumed his trek to the northeast coast of the Chukchi Peninsula in the spring, he promised to come back for her.

Kelly was head over heels in love with the woman. Not

only did she have the same name as his mother, but she had his mother's dignity and courage. And she was bold, a leader of men in a rough man's industry, but she was neither rough nor crude herself—she wasn't "one of the guys." Galina had feminine compassion and a lively sense of humor. She didn't complain. She enjoyed the out-of-doors. And the woman had enough of a temper to keep things interesting and fun. She was altogether lovely in his eyes. One day she would be his wife. Thinking of her made him smile at the cameras. *Take your time, boys, I can do this all day.*

The difficulties in keeping his promise to her bothered him not at all. Jake knew what he could do. As soon as he got past the current snafu, he had two items on his life agenda. Kill Chernikov, the man running the GRU espionage program; and bring Galina back to America—in that order.

****

Sam Bergman and Jim Stewart watched the subject through the one-way mirror. The only reason Sam was present for the interrogation was because of Kelly's strange request, which Ed Devlin and Jesse Pierce had decided to honor.

"Jim, this is your baby. I've never done an interrogation, and I've no idea how to go about it. I'm an analyst, not a field operative." Bergman was, in fact, a little nervous.

"Relax, Sam. Let me take the lead. All you have to do is to observe Kelly—read his body language. Try to pick up on fear, deception, that sort of thing. Think of it as asking your teenager why he came home late on Friday night. His words will give you one answer; his body language might send a different message.

"Now, it's going to be slightly warm in there. That's intentional. We raise the temperature of an interrogation room to induce a level of nervousness or anxiety into the prisoner. But don't *you* make a comment about it being warm, for crying out loud! We need to pretend it feels normal.

"You are welcome to ask questions but, as I said, I'll take the lead. This is the sort of thing I do all the time. Just remember: do not promise him anything. Right now we have no authority to make promises of any sort. If he presses us for some point or concession, you let me answer.

"Judging from the behavior we're observing at the moment, this guy is a pretty cool customer. Most subjects would be fidgety by now, but he doesn't look the slightest bit rattled. Okay, let's go meet the infamous John Meeker."

Sam and Jim stepped into the room. Jake looked up with an expression that revealed nothing and spoke first: "Good morning, gentlemen. It's good of you to be here."

Stewart picked up the hint of irony in Kelly's voice and responded in kind: "Hello, Major. It's good of you to be here, too. Did you have to rearrange your schedule to make this meeting?"

Jacob Kelly immediately decided that he liked the speaker, and grinned. "Mister, you would not believe the trouble I've gone through to be at this meeting today. It has rearranged not just my schedule, but my whole life for the last sixteen months. My name is Jacob Kelly and I am a major in the United States Air Force, lately returned from the dead. If you gentlemen would care to introduce yourselves, we can get started."

Jesse Pierce had warned Stewart that Kelly would attempt to take command of the interview, and within sixty seconds of their entering the room that's exactly what he did. The only way to avoid the man's request for introductions would be to stonewall, but Jim knew that the major had already refused to speak to anyone except the CIA or FBI, so there was little to be gained from stonewalling. On the other hand, introducing themselves left the initiative in the hands of the prisoner. *Well, I can always grab control later, if need be*, he thought. He decided to ride this horse and see where it was going.

"Very good, Major. My companion here is Sam Bergman, one of the CIA's top analysts in the counterintel division of the Soviet Department. I'm FBI Special Agent Jim Stewart, also working in counterintel. How can we help you?"

Stewart saw Bergman's eyebrow rise at his open invitation for the prisoner to take control of the interview. Bergman began to open his mouth but Stewart kicked him under the table and Sam shut his mouth like a trap.

Jacob Kelly noticed the interaction but ignored it. "Some identification, gentlemen? I would share mine with you, but I seem to have lost it. I'm sure you understand."

"Of course. We have identified your fingerprints, so I am confident of your bona fides." Stewart wondered how long this odd gentility would last. Both he and Sam passed their badges over for Kelly's inspection. The prisoner examined them closely, nodded to himself, and passed them back.

"Thanks. I'm prepared to tell you two anything you ask. Naturally I cannot control who *you* share it with, nor do I even know who is on the other side of that mirror, nor who is watching by camera. I do know I am fortunate that my requests for a guard and isolation have been honored, and it's not often that prisoners can dictate who they want to interrogate them. I am very grateful for the cooperation Officer Devlin has extended thus far, and I desire to reciprocate.

"But I would like to make one final plea. Please allow me five minutes for my opening statement by clearing the observation room and turning off the cameras and any audio devices wired to this room. You are free to tape my statement if you have a personal recorder, but I want you to hear what I have to say before anyone else does. After you have heard me, if you don't think it matters who is listening in, well, there's nothing I can do about that."

Stewart sat for a moment, thinking. His immediate impulse was to ignore the prisoner's request. But something about the man's demeanor nagged him. He remembered Bergman's insight: *this prisoner sitting in front of us thinks he's on our side. If indeed that's the case, he must have a good reason for making this request. Well, it can't hurt*, Stewart finally decided. He looked over at Bergman and raised one eyebrow quizzically; the analyst responded by shrugging his shoulders with a "why not?" expression on his face.

Excusing himself, Stewart stepped out and directed that the observation room be emptied and the cameras and audio turned off. He went to his briefcase and pulled out a tape recorder, and then returned to the interrogation room.

"Major, I swear I don't know how you do it, but right now we are all eating out of your hand. That's liable to change in the next five or ten minutes. For now, I have complied with your wishes. But I *am* going to tape this statement. Now without any further ado I would really like to know what the devil is going on. I want to hear how you have managed to go from being one of the country's premier fighter pilots to being in handcuffs on the wrong side of the microphone in this interrogation room."

****

Admiral Bridger's intercom buzzed insistently. "Yes, Mabel, what is it?"

"Admiral, the custodians are here. Apparently tonight is when the floors get stripped and waxed, so they want to get in early to clean the offices. I guess they can't get the floors waxed and do the regular cleaning all in one night. Is that alright?"

Bridger frowned. He had a lot to do. *But,* he thought philosophically, *so does the cleaning crew. Just have to work around it.* "Okay, Mabel. I'll just get an early lunch today. While I'm out, would you contact General Franks at Edwards and set up a lunch meeting for Friday? I'll come to his place. He'll know what it's about." Bridger liked to go to Edwards. He could get flight time in his F-14, plus the food at the Officers' Club at Edwards was better.

"Sure, Admiral. I'll take care of it."

After Admiral Bridger left his office the cleaning crew arrived, only it was a CIA "cleaning crew." While several agents straightened and dusted the office, two men worked quickly to bug his phone and his computer terminal keyboard. The bug in his phone would pick up both sides of a telephone conversation as well as the ambient sounds in his office, even when the handset was not in use. The keyboard bug would pick up all keystrokes entered to his computer. The signals from both bugs were multiplexed into a single signal by a tiny chip in the telephone bug.

The problem was how to get the signals out of Bridger's office undetected. The entire SPECWAR Group One headquarters building had been hardened against surveillance and the offices were electronically swept once a day at random times in an effort to ferret out any transmitters.

The solution turned out to be elegantly simple. The telephone cables with which the office had been wired were four-pair, meaning that there were four twisted pairs of conductors in each cable. But the phone only used two of the pairs. The CIA cleaning crew attached the bug to an unused pair, sending the signals from Bridger's office to the telephone closet in the basement using the building's own wiring. Even the daily sweep would not detect the bugs.

When Bridger returned from lunch, two CIA technicians were recording every sound in his office from within a beat-up van marked *Miguel's Drywall Services*, parked just off the base. By 1600 hours, Bridger's car and home would be bugged as well.

✴✴✴✴✴◻◻◻◻◻✴✴✴

Kelly placed his hands on the table and began his story. "Several years back I was recruited by General James Franks at Edwards to be part of Project *Hydra*. *Hydra* is a top-secret development project for some new strike capabilities for the F-16. I am—or *was* anyway—the chief test pilot.

"On the night of 10 July, 1986, I was flying over the Bering Sea on a test flight and was shot down, probably by a heat-seeking missile since there were no warnings from my threat detection avionics. A jamming signal appeared as soon as the missile hit, preventing a distress call. I bailed out but did not even get wet. A Soviet helicopter snagged my chute and reeled me in. They took me to a detention center in Siberia, where I was interrogated about *Hydra*. Lucky for me, within several weeks I managed to escape."

"You *escaped* from a Soviet prison?" Sam asked incredulously.

"That's right."

"How?"

Falcon hesitated, thinking. He decided to leave Oswald Simmons out of the story until he had a better sense of where this was headed.

"I managed to set part of the camp on fire. It took out their power and communications. During the confusion, I escaped. I've spent the last fifteen months or so staying one step ahead of the Soviet army, making my way across Siberia to the Chukchi Peninsula, where I obtained a kayak. My plans were to paddle across the Strait to Alaska. I made it most of the way before hypothermia took over. You gentlemen know more about my rescue than I do, as I was unconscious at the time. I woke up in the hospital in Kotzebue. Next thing I know, somebody is trying to kill me. I assume he was working for the Russians. In any case, he was unsuccessful and I expect you have him in custody. I left him handcuffed to a bed in Kotzebue.

"The short story is this, then: I was kidnapped by the USSR so that they might interrogate me about a top-secret US weapons development program. I escaped and returned to America. And they have been trying to eliminate me ever since I returned."

"That's a pretty amazing story," responded Stewart, after a brief silence.

"Indeed," agreed Jacob Kelly.

"And so, why the secrecy?" demanded Stewart. "Why the alias given to the hospital? Why didn't you contact the Air Force as soon as you became conscious in Kotzebue?"

"The answer to all three questions is one and the same, and I should think that it would be obvious." There was an expression of mild surprise on the prisoner's face.

"Humor me; enlighten us," Stewart said dryly.

"I was betrayed, gentlemen. The Soviet aircraft that jumped me and the chopper that picked me up knew exactly where I would be and when I would be there. And they knew that it would be me in the cockpit. The only way they could have known all this was if someone told them, someone on our side. This wasn't a random shootdown, it was a hi-tech kidnapping. They wanted me for my knowledge of *Hydra*.

"So when I woke up in Kotzebue, I didn't know whom to trust. I knew the Soviets want me dead. If I talked to the wrong guy or the wrong guy found out I'm back, I would be a dead man. So I tried to hide my identity."

Bergman nodded, "They want to bump you off, because you can finger them in an act of war against the United States."

"Exactly. And they must realize it's just a matter of time till we figure out there's someone wearing an Air Force uniform who really works for the other side. The easiest way to prevent that is to kill me before I can convince you of my story. That's why I asked for isolation and protection, and why I asked you to clear the observation room and turn off the cameras. I don't know who is watching. I expect the spy will maneuver himself into a position where he can report what I say and ar-range a hit.

"Since the bad guy is in the Air Force, I figured I could trust someone from the civilian intelligence agencies—which is why I'm talking to you and not the military. But unless I can convince you two, I will remain the only one who knows for sure there is a spy in Air Force operations."

Jim Stewart considered Kelly's explanations. The entire tale was pretty far-fetched. On the other hand, the facts of the case backed up his improbable story. Kelly *had* been pulled out of a kayak in the Strait, mostly dead from hypothermia; the Soviets *had* contested the rescue almost to the point of trig-gering an international incident; there *had* been that attempt in the hospital at Kotzebue. Nonetheless, he decided to rattle Kelly's cage and see what happened.

"This is all a nice little story, Major, a story which conve-niently casts you as the hero. But here's what I think—I think you defected with your fighter and landed at a Soviet airbase, received a pile of money in some Swiss bank account, and then decided you missed the land of flush toilets, so you came back. Or maybe you even decided to spy for Ivan, I don't know. Money talks, right? So why don't you tell me why I should believe your tale of woe instead of trusting my gut, which tells me you're just another money-grubbin' traitor?"

Kelly's face grew hard and his eyes flashed, "Well, Agent Stewart, I guess you'll just have to sort it out, won't you? Let me give you a piece of advice, though. Don't ever enter the same room with me unless I am shackled hand and foot. I'll take you apart. I'm not going to listen to you accuse me of betraying my country, not after what I've been through."

"You're not shackled now, Major. Want to try your luck?"

"Now wait a minute, gentleme—" Sam interjected before Jim cut him off with a dismissive wave of his hand.

"What about *Hydra*, Kelly?" Stewart flung the question at the pilot.

"What about it?" Jake asked coolly.

"What did you tell 'em?"

"Nothing. I escaped before they had the chance to break me. They knew the name, they knew it's a weapons system, and they knew I'm the chief test pilot. But they knew all that before they grabbed me."

"Okay. Did they ask about anything else?"

"No, just *Hydra*."

"The hospital report from Kotzebue says that you've got some interesting scars on your shoulders. Are they souvenirs of your fun time with Uncle Ivan, or leftovers from interrogation?"

The pilot glared at him without answering. Stewart was pushing hard, trying to get the man to make a mistake. He wasn't sure whether he believed Kelly and was trying not to form an opinion yet. It was too soon for that. He needed to explore multiple possible explanations before he allowed himself to come to conclusions.

"Let's see 'em," the FBI agent directed.

Jake removed his shirt and showed them his shoulders. On one, a heart symbol with the word "Stalin" had been burned into his flesh, producing an ugly raised scar. On the other, the same symbol with the word "Lenin." He also showed them the burn scars on his hands.

"General Chernikov was questioning me. He didn't like my

answers."

Sam Bergman guarded his reaction carefully, but his heart was racing. *Chernikov? Could it be?* He'd been amassing his own private folder on Chernikov for a long time, but the man had dropped out of sight several years earlier and the trail had gone cold.

"What can you tell me about this Chernikov?" Sam asked carefully.

"Major General Nikolai Chernikov. Tall. Grey eyes, black hair. He's probably upper thirties to lower forties. Speaks English fluently. He wears the uniform of the 106th Guards Airborne, but he's actually GRU."

"How do you know that?"

"He told me. Said that he wanted me to know that I was going to die."

"I don't get it. How does telling you whom he works for guarantee your death?" Stewart asked.

"The GRU is the most secretive of all the Soviet intelligence services," Sam explained. "For years very few even knew of its existence. For Chernikov to tell someone he's a GRU officer makes him liable to death. The only way he would risk telling Kelly is if Kelly was himself marked for death. But," he said, rubbing his chin, "what about the guards overhearing him? I wouldn't think he'd take the chance."

"The guards are all *Spetsnaz*," Kelly replied, "so he has nothing to worry about. They are rotating special forces units into the facility as guards, and using it as a rest and refit time for the operators. They stay for several months and then a new unit rotates in."

"How could you possibly know this?" Sam asked.

"I speak fluent Russian—they didn't know. So I overheard them talking among themselves."

Sam considered this carefully. It was the same Chernikov, of that he was sure. But last Sam knew, Chernikov was a colonel and he didn't know that the man had been tapped for the GRU. What he'd just learned was worth all the trouble of being involved with *Snowbird*. He'd have to update Chernikov's dossier when he returned to Langley and nose around for additional information on the general.

Stewart flipped through a manila folder, examining the documents. "Wait a minute, Kelly. Neither your service record nor the security vetting uncovered that. Explain to me, Major, how the fact of your fluency in the Russian language could be missing from your record. It is, I'd say, relevant information."

For the next twenty minutes Kelly explained that he'd learned Russian while spending summer vacation with his maternal grandparents who'd emigrated from the Soviet Union. He'd hidden the fact that he spoke Russian from Air Force investigators because he wanted to fly fighter jets and not get shuttled into intelligence. It was, Stewart thought, a weakness in the major's story and left open the possibility that he was, in fact, working for the Russians all along.

As the interview began to wrap up, the two agents looked over their notes and revisited several points, asking follow-up questions. At last Bergman put down his pen and rubbed his forehead with both hands. "I still am amazed that Chernikov told you he's GRU. That's a pretty gutsy way of making it clear that he would go as far as necessary to break you. Apparently, he wanted to remove all hope of prisoner swaps or transfers. One of you was going to die, and it wasn't going to be him."

"And now it is," Kelly replied.

"No, probably not. The Spets will keep his secret, if they even heard him tell you in the first place."

"It's not the *Spetsnaz* Chernikov has to worry about."

"So—who's going to take him out? *We're* not going to do it. Uncle Sam does not usually do that sort of thing."

"No. But I am."

"Really? How? What will you do?" Stewart asked.

"First, once I'm released from this jail, if I can find the Air Force officer who betrayed me I'll turn him over to the government. But Chernikov, well, he has something else coming."

"And what would that be?" asked Stewart in a slightly mocking tone.

"Let's just say that General Chernikov will want to stay out of Moscow's dark alleys for the rest of his life."

"You're confessing to a felony in advance?"

Kelly just smiled, but it was a grim expression.

Long after this meeting two impressions remained in Sam Bergman's mind. One was the sight of the ugly scars on Kelly's shoulders, a disfigurement only plastic surgery could remove. The other was the memory of the dark smile on the pilot's face when he spoke of revenge on Chernikov. Bergman was glad he was not the one in Kelly's crosshairs. Somehow he knew if the man was ever able to make good his threat against Chernikov, it would not be pretty.

****

"Do either of you believe him?" Jesse Pierce studied Stewart and Bergman, trying to evaluate the fantastic tale. If true, the story had huge implications and could lead to an international incident.

Sam and Jim looked at each other, and shrugged. "I thought the scars were mighty convincing. Jim, you're the man with experience in interrogations. I'm just an analyst. What say you?" Bergman asked.

Jim nodded, and started slowly, "Look, men: even when you take the major's tale of woe out of this event, it's still a highly improbable story. Two Tomcats, four Falcons, a pair of Floggers and two Soviet missile boats duking it out over some half-dead guy floating in a kayak in the Bering Strait? Come *on*, guys! *Really*? But—and this is the kicker—we *know* all that is true, incontrovertibly true."

"And your meaning is . . . what?" asked Major Ott skeptically.

"Simply this: if the facts we know to be true are so incredibly unusual, then it isn't surprising that the story of the man at the center of the storm is also somewhat fantastic. Given the context, yes, I'm inclined to believe him. In all my experience of interrogating people who very much wanted to deceive me, Kelly comes off as quite credible."

"Or," Ott countered, "perhaps he truly is a spy and a very good one at that. Look, for instance, at the fact that he is a fluent speaker of Russian but intentionally hid that fact throughout his entire Air Force career. That's mighty suspicious if you ask me; it's likely he's violated the military code of conduct simply by lying about the matter. This guy has 'traitor' stamped all over him."

"When he first mentioned it I had the same response, Bill. But I've thought about it more and decided it actually exonerates him," replied Jim. "Look at it this way. If he was a Soviet agent it would have been much more valuable for Sovs to have Kelly shuttled into Intelligence, not Flight Ops. And yet the reason he hid his Russian proficiency was to stay *out* of Intelligence.

"And how about the attempt on his life?" the FBI agent added. "They wouldn't be trying to bump off one of their own. That's a pretty powerful fact in his favor."

"Actually, it's not," disagreed Bergman.

"What? Why not?" asked Devlin. "To me that's proof-positive that his story is believable. If they're trying to plant a spy they wouldn't be trying to kill him."

"The Soviets are the best people on the planet when it comes to running disinformation campaigns and camouflaging their intentions," replied Sam Bergman. "Nobody does it better. Just like the military activity in the Strait could have been stage-managed to draw our attention to Kelly and add strength to his story, this assassination attempt also could have been an elaborate ploy."

"But we've got their people! They wouldn't sacrifice their operatives for this," Stewart objected.

"If the guys we bagged in Kotzebue turn out to be IDC men, they aren't 'their people,' they're just contractors, mercenaries for hire. Ivan would sacrifice them with a snap of the fingers if it meant they could embed someone in the officer corps of the Air Force. To IDC it looks like a job gone bad, nothing more. So the assassination attempts don't prove Kelly's story. They might, they might not.

"However, there is something else in his favor," Sam added. "He told us that Chernikov is in the GRU. That's not a fact that would be up for grabs as part of a disinformation campaign; it's simply too valuable."

Sam turned to Bill. "I know you're not happy with the accusation Kelly made regarding a turncoat in the Air Force, but his version of events does make a lot of sense. And if he's right about the spy, he has handled himself properly. Not knowing whom to trust, he trusted no one. All things considered, I'm inclined to believe him."

"Did he identify the person he called from the office supply store?" Pierce flipped through several pages in a file folder. "Um, let's see . . . Oh, here it is. Bill. Did he identify this Bill?"

"Nope. Refused to," answered Stewart. "Said if we wind up not believing his story he needs someone on the outside working on it. Bill is apparently his ace in the hole."

"Ed, where are we with the court order to get the telephone records for the store? Should be a simple matter to get the number he dialed. We know exactly what time it was," Pierce said.

"It got bogged down. The judge started asking questions we weren't ready to answer. We should have it in another day," replied the trooper.

Jesse Pierce shut his briefing folder. "Well, I guess that's all we can do for now. Let's keep running down these leads. Jim, can you schedule a couple more interrogation sessions this week?" When the FBI agent nodded, Pierce continued, "Let's meet again on Monday. For the time being I think Kelly should remain in the Alaska State Troopers' custody."

"Commander, I really don't think that's necessary." Major Bill Ott's tone matched his angry expression. "We were supposed to transfer him to Eielson tomorrow! I've been hoping to send him up there today. He's an Air Force officer suspected of treasonous behavior. Let us handle this, for crying out loud!"

Devlin turned on Ott. "Get real, Bill! If there's even a slight chance that Kelly's story is true, the very *last* place we would want to put him would be in an Air Force brig on the very base that might contain the spy!"

"You know Ed's right, Bill," Sam soothed. "That would be like throwing him in the lion's den. You can't press for the transfer, not now."

Jim Stewart spoke up, "I'm with Jesse on this one, Bill. Even if he's guilty as sin, this jail is the best place to interrogate a guy who, right now, seems to be the target of Soviet assassination squads. This facility was specifically designed to protect government witnesses from people who don't want them to testify. A military brig isn't used for much more than the occasional case of insubordination or a GI who's had too much to drink. You guys are not set up to protect someone who has a contract on their head."

Ott pressed his lips together, but slowly nodded. "Okay. You're right; it does make sense to keep him here." Turning to Jesse, he apologized, "Sorry, Jesse. Been running on a short fuse lately. But please, let's do try to get this cleared up so I can take him on Monday."

****

Once he verified that the surveillance of Admiral Bridger was functioning properly, Jensen baited the trap. From the CIA office in Los Angeles he logged into the secure side of MILNET using an untraceable cover account. He accessed Kelly's Air Force service records, and using the DIA's general personnel database requested a search on Major Jacob Kelly. Both accesses were dutifully logged by the DIA's *Watcher* program and would be included on the *Watcher* report sent late that evening to Admiral Bridger.

The professor was gambling on the probability that the report would spur Bridger to make a contact, the nature of which might either incriminate or exonerate him. If that contact was made from his office, his home, or his car, the CIA would be listening in.

Jensen's team in LA would handle the details of the surveillance. There was no need for him to stick around. By late evening he was on a flight to Fairbanks to investigate the mysterious *WOtt* at Eielson Air Force Base. He wanted to know who this person was who had attempted to change Jacob Kelly's DPMO records. And he wanted to know why.

Chapter 5

Sam Bergman caught an early morning flight out of Anchorage, headed back to Washington, DC. He opened a little bag of red licorice bits that he purchased in the airport and began to chew on one of the candies as he made a list of things to check on back at Langley. He wanted to call Evelyn Stinson, the lovely NSA translator with whom he'd analyzed the strange intercept from source *Leaning Tower.* The communication had alluded to an imminent Soviet agent insertion, and there were several aspects of that intercept which bothered both of them. The encoding language was subtly different from previous intercepts dealing with a similar topic. It was close enough that they were able to decode it, but strange enough to make them wonder if something unusual was going on.

The other oddity was that the message was sent in triplicate, with minor differences between the three copies. Sam knew that someone trying to find a security leak would sometimes transmit subtly different texts of the same message to each addressee. The text that was leaked would pinpoint the source of the leak. But in the case of *Leaning Tower*'s intercept it appeared that all three versions were bundled together, as though all recipients would receive each version. *There must be a different explanation*, Sam thought. Evelyn had received permission to speak with the local NSA propeller head, a brilliant but socially challenged individual. After spewing several paragraphs of incomprehensible technobabble, the man had muttered something about needing several days to examine the packet headers of the message. *Whatever. What was his name? Clifton somebody.*

Bergman also wanted to track down the "Bill" character that Kelly had called. He didn't need a court order to get into the phone company records, he just needed a good hacker. The CIA had plenty of those.

He also wanted to keep tabs on the latest IDC communications. He wondered if there would be any message traffic pertaining to the Kelly case. Unfortunately, there was often as much as a week's delay in getting IDC data from the NSA.

But his main intention when he returned to the Firm was to chase down all the latest information on the Russian, Nikolai Chernikov. Perhaps there was new data that Bergman had missed. Chernikov's recruitment by the GRU was a valuable piece of intelligence. If Major Kelly was being truthful, that would explain why Chernikov had dropped out of sight.

Putting his notepad back in his briefcase, he made himself as comfortable as possible in the economy-class seat. The thoughts that had kept him awake last night began to tease at his mind again. Not normally a philosophical man, Bergman was troubled. He had always wanted to "make a difference" with his life. Ever since hearing his grandfather talk about narrowly surviving the Nazi concentration camps, Sam Bergman's goal had been to ensure that such a horror could never again be perpetrated on the Jewish race, or any other race for that matter.

Sam was a patriot who deeply loved the country that had rescued his beloved grandfather from the hands of Nazi sadists. In his opinion, the one nation best equipped to prevent a repeat of *Kristallnacht* was the United States. America would never tolerate another Holocaust and was largely capable of preventing it. This simple calculus explained why Bergman was serving his country in the CIA. He was not a blind "my country right or wrong" jingoist. Along the way he had seen stuff in the CIA that profoundly disturbed him about America, and he'd known and heard more about the political doings of both major parties than he ever wanted to know. But he was an eyes-wide-open realist and knew that all countries, all ideologies, all parties had both their good and dark sides. All things considered, in his book America was the best of the lot, and by a large margin.

The problem that gnawed at him was making the leap from his evolutionary atheism to any sort of meaningful ethics. Bergman was not a philosopher, but he *was* a deep-thinking analyst, and he did not care for cognitive dissonance. He didn't like contradictions, especially not when they popped up in his own thinking. But the simple judgment that nazism was bad and freedom was good involved him in a contradiction.

According to a strict interpretation of his own worldview, evil did not exist. "Good" was nothing more than a functional statement. In Bergman's world there was no God. So far as Sam was concerned, only matter, energy, and the relation between them were eternal. But such a belief was unable to account for why he knew intuitively that freedom was good and fascism was not. Other atheists he had read tried to answer the dilemma with high-sounding ideas about the happiness and welfare of man being a natural good, but Bergman was not so sure. The naturalist John Muir once said that if it came down to a war between man and the bears, he would side with the bears. *Well, why not?* he thought. *What exactly is it about man that makes his welfare primary? Why is that good? What if it's actually evil? What if Muir was right? Who's to say?*

Bergman groaned. *I really don't want to think about this again. Should have gotten a paperback instead of these licorice bits.* Much as he hated "navel-gazing," he was slowly realizing his atheism left him without any legitimate means of evaluating his own life, or the morality of anything else for that matter. And working in an organization like the CIA without a firm moral compass was a dangerous endeavor. He'd built his life and ambitions upon . . . what? Air? *Was* he making a difference? Was it the *right* difference? How could he know? When it was all over would he be satisfied with what he had done? *Got to stop thinking these stupid questions!*

****

"Good morning, Major Kelly. I trust you slept well."

"Like a baby, Agent Stewart. What is our topic of conversation this morning?"

"Well, you realize you've given us a pretty fantastic tale. We need to verify as much of it as possible."

"Of course."

"What I would like to do this morning is to get a blow-by-blow account of the escape and your trek across Siberia. Names, places, dates, names of rivers, etc. Everything you provide will be checked against our databases, satellite imagery, etc. I think our little committee is tending to side with your version of events and we are trying to gather corroborating evidence."

"I am afraid I don't understand the problem, Agent Stewart. What other version of events is there?"

"The other possible version of events, Major, is that you are a traitor trying to return to the US military so that you can continue selling us out. You defected with your aircraft, you were not shot down. According to this version of events, you are coming back to siphon off the advances of *Hydra*, and provide them to the Soviet Union."

Jacob Kelly nodded his head. "I see," he said. "We had best get started then. I can give you a lot of information, but there is some information I am not going to provide."

"And what would that be?"

"Agent Stewart, one does not survive a Siberian winter at those latitudes without help. There are Soviet citizens who might suffer greatly if I gave up their names. That I will not do."

"You realize those names are our primary way of proving your story, and if you do not give them to me all I will be left with is a travelogue of places." Stewart rubbed his eyes. This was going to be harder than he thought.

"Yes. But I'm not going to compromise people who risked their lives and freedom to help me."

Over the next three hours, Stewart and Kelly worked together to plot as much of his trek as possible. By the end of that time the FBI agent had a complete itinerary, including the names of numerous Soviet soldiers, but no civilians. For Jake, it was the first time that he'd studied a large map closely since returning to the US. He was finally able to see the path that he had taken, and he was impressed in spite of himself. It had been a heroic—even epic—undertaking and best of all, he had succeeded.

****

It took some doing, but Bill Jensen managed to identify the airman on the Eielson Air Force Base Information Technology (IT) team with the highest security clearance. An examination of the man's service record revealed that he had the technical experience Jensen required for the surveillance he'd planned. The next step was getting the base commander to give him access and support, without which Jensen would get nowhere.

Jensen guessed that the base commander could be trusted with at least part of the story. The Soviet mole had to be below flag rank, otherwise they could have obtained information on *Hydra* through much simpler means.

After deplaning in Fairbanks, the CIA operative placed a brief call to the DDO. Jensen then drove to the base, went to the headquarters building and asked to see the base commander, identifying himself as a citizen concerned about the noise of flight operations at the base.

"General Martin, there's a resident out here who insists on seeing you. He wants to register a complaint about noise. I tried to explain that we've already done what the county and city asked of us in noise-abatement procedures, but he simply refuses to believe me."

"That's okay, Cathy, I'll see him. Send him in."

"If you say so, sir. You know that your schedule this morning is jam-packed."

"We need good relations with the neighbors. I'll talk to him."

The bemused secretary ushered Jensen into Brigadier General Larry Martin's office and exited, shutting the door behind her.

"General Martin, Bill Jensen, CIA. Thanks for seeing me on short notice." He handed his identification across the desk to the general, who studied it closely before passing it back.

"Your boss called me ten minutes ago, Jensen, told me to expect you. Said you would explain everything. Now, mister, why the cloak and dagger stuff? What's this all about? I have a lot on my plate this morning!" Martin was miffed to have received a phone call directing him to let Jensen in the door, especially when the call came from a civilian agency like the CIA. But the general was wise enough to know that requests from the CIA Deputy Director of Operations usually had a great deal of political clout behind them.

"May I sit down, sir?"

"Of course, please be seated." Martin was gratified that his visitor was sensitive to military protocol. His temper began subsiding.

"General, there is a situation developing so rapidly we are just barely able to stay ahead of it. With your security clearance and experience, you'll understand if I cannot get into details. But I can say there is a mid-level officer or an upper-level enlisted man on this base who is working for the Soviets."

"What?"

"Sir, an attempt at unauthorized access to a secure military database was traced back to this base. That, plus some other intelligence I am not at liberty to discuss, is indicating there is an actual security breach on this base. Not a potential breach, mind you, but an actual one. One—possibly two—of your people is working for the other guys."

Martin was appalled, but he knew there was no point in disputing the allegation. One does not get phone calls from the DDO arising out of baseless speculation. The impact of what his visitor said began to sink in, turning his emotions to anger. That one of his people could be selling out their country was a heinous offense in his eyes. If a name could be attached to the traitor with certainty he was tempted to exercise summary judgment with the nearest available sidearm. A rope would do nicely. The general responded with a tightly controlled voice. "I see. You must be here to identify the traitor.

How can I help you? What can I do? I'll get you anything you need."

Jensen breathed a sigh of relief. "Thank you, sir. I appreciate your help, and that is precisely why I came to see you. I'll make it brief because I know you are extremely busy. I promise that you will be provided all the information possible under the circumstances, as soon as details become clear.

"First, General, please understand that this investigation is so sensitive that it is an ears-only operation. Nothing is to be written down or committed to a computer because we are not sure what the traitor has access to and we don't want to show our hand. If you are uncomfortable with that condition, sir, the DDO can arrange clearance for this request at any level you require, but it will all be verbal."

"No, Jensen, there is no need. The phone call I have already received is sufficient."

"Thank you, sir. Second, I cannot involve anyone in your intelligence group on the base, as it might be the compromised department. We do have very specific data but it needs to be interpreted by a member of your IT staff in order to attach a name to it. With your permission, sir, I would like to run the investigation on base, and I would like the assistance of Technical Sergeant Matthew Loeb, from your IT department."

"Done. Since you seem to know all about my people, I assume you have already ascertained his security clearances, skills, and training."

"Yes, sir. He will do nicely."

"Okay, what else do you need?"

"Later today I am going to set up video and audio surveillance equipment around the suspect. I will need enough clearance here at Eielson so that Loeb and I can get in any building on the base and install surveillance devices without causing suspicion."

"Hmm. That will be tougher. Tell me, how much experience have you had around the military?"

"Sir, I was heavily involved as a Case Officer for agents in multiple southeast Asian countries during the conflict in Vietnam. I was with military personnel in the Air Force, Army, and Navy constantly for several years. I know the ropes pretty well."

"Well, congratulations. You are now an E-4, a Senior Airman, and Sergeant Loeb is your boss. I'll see that you get outfitted with the uniform. That will give you the cover you need to assist Sergeant Loeb as he installs network gear. I'll see that you two have uninterrupted access and I'll have the base security detail notified that you two will be nosing around in secure areas and are not to be disturbed."

"Actually, sir, I don't think that will work. How many active-duty fifty-year old airmen have you seen?"

"Right. Good point, Jensen." General Martin mulled over that. "Okay, let's make you a civilian contractor with a sufficient security clearance to get you into any building on the base."

"Thank you, sir, that will be perfect. I expect to be back and forth between here, California, and DC over the next seven days. We believe that the surveillance will provide a smoking gun to back up the data we already have. Could I have Sergeant Loeb attached to me during that entire time? I'll need him running the gear and watching the suspect."

"Now you're getting expensive, Jensen. This better not be some cock and bull hunch, or I'll feed your carcass to the intake of a Falcon running on afterburners. Alright, you've got Loeb for a week—one week. I'll give him access to some empty offices where you two can set up shop. Now is there anything else? If you've got half a brain, you'll say 'No'!"

"No, sir, there is nothing else."

"Wise man. Now, I've got work to do."

"Thank you, General Martin."

"Dismissed."

"Yessir."

As Jensen left the office, Martin's secretary shot him a sour look. *I think it would be more dangerous to run afoul of her than of him*, he thought as he shut the door behind him.

****

"Admiral, there's a call for you on line two. It's General Franks."

"Thanks, Mabel. Tell him I'll be with him in a minute."

Admiral John Bridger was wrapping up his weekly intelligence summary briefing with his SEAL team commanders. The SEAL teams received daily intelligence situation reports on developing events in the world regions they were responsible for. As hot spots flared around the globe they were constantly evaluating their teams' personnel, equipment, and training should they be called upon. Once a week Bridger met with his commanders to sort out the larger happenings and to evaluate their readiness to respond within the short windows demanded by crises. After dismissing the men he punched line two and picked up the phone.

"Hi Jim. What's going on?"

"I got another hit last night on the DIA's *Watcher* listing. Somebody is studying our man. It was a basic search through his personnel records."

"Yeah, I saw that too. Funny that there is this activity on Kelly's records all of a sudden. For a year or so, nothing, and then all this. It's like somebody else is fishing around for information."

"Uh-huh. That was my thought," Franks agreed. "Listen, John, when Roger discovered the jamming signal on the RIM-PAC tapes in the vicinity of Kelly's shootdown, he gave us what we needed to reopen the accident investigation without compromising your sources. Maybe simply stirring the pot will cause the Soviets to react. In any case, I don't think we can sit on this thing any longer. If Kelly was shot down I don't plan on letting Ivan simply walk away from it."

Bridger mulled this over and came to a decision. "You're right, Jim. We have what we need to follow up without endangering my source. Okay, why don't I meet you at Edwards on Friday at 0800, and we can plan our next steps over breakfast."

"What'sa matter, Navy?" Franks taunted, "Tired of the grub down there at Coronado? I've noticed, you know, that you never invite me to come your way. How come you aren't asking me over to the O Club down there?" Franks enjoyed prodding Bridger, and the service rivalry was always a good source of ammunition.

"It's not that, Jim. It's just that I know *you* can't fly. And I don't want you putting your life in the hands of some Air Force chopper pilot who thinks he *can*. So, really, I'm just protecting a national treasure by coming to Edwards."

"What national treasure?"

"Why, you, of course! Far as I know, you're the only USAF officer who is actually capable of tying his own shoes each morning!"

Franks roared a loud and colorful response. The CIA technician clandestinely recording the conversation ripped the headset off with Franks' outrage ringing in his ears. The spook looked at his headphones in amazement and wondered if all generals and admirals spoke to each other in these terms. Though he didn't hear it as he rubbed his ears, the tape captured the two officers' agreement to meet on Friday at Edwards.

****

Bill Jensen was sitting in an office at the Eielson AFB headquarters. On a lanyard around his neck was his newly minted base ID, identifying him as a civilian contractor. The office was empty other than several tables and chairs, a standard government-issue metal desk, and a telephone. The door opened and a slender young man walked in. He had intelligent eyes set in an angular, confident face. *He looks like a runner,* Jensen thought, *there's probably not an ounce of fat on him.*

"Good afternoon, sir. I am Sergeant Matt Loeb, and I was told to report to this room."

"Have you been told why you're here, Sergeant?"

"No, sir, but I have been told that I am attached to Bill Jensen for one week."

"That's me. Pull up a chair, son, and let me tell you what you're going to be doing for the next five or six days."

Jensen pulled out his CIA identification and passed it over

to the sergeant. "This is who I really work for. The only people on this base who know that I'm with the CIA are you and General Martin. It needs to stay that way. Understand?"

"Yes, sir."

"Call me Bill. Do you mind if I call you Matt?"

"Not at all, sir. Why does the CIA need me?"

"Matt, I chose you in part because of your security clearances. Understand that what I am going to tell you is secret. The work we will be doing is secret. You can't talk about it with anybody. Is that clear? Not with your wife, not with your coworkers, not with your supervisor. Other than God Himself, the only two people on the planet you can discuss our activities with are General Martin and me, and if you talk to God, make sure you are doing it silently. Do you understand?"

Loeb's eyes were wide as he nodded his assent, "Yes, sir, I understand."

"*Bill!*"

"What?"

"I told you to call me Bill!"

"Oh! Yes, sir. I mean, yes, Bill."

"Okay. Matt, the security of this base has been compromised. Someone on this base works for the bad guys and you are going to help me find him. If he even gets the slightest whiff that we're searching for him, we'll never catch him. So we have to do this very, very carefully."

"How come you aren't asking the guys in intel to do this? I've never been trained for surveillance or intelligence work." Matt looked slightly confused.

"The problem is, I don't know whom I can trust. It may be that the bad guy is in the intelligence section, I just don't know. But I have a good clue, and this is where you come in. I have the IP address of a computer that made an unauthorized access, and I have the login name. The login name is *WOtt,* and the IP address is 11.107.6.15."

Loeb wrote the information down and said, "I'll be right back. This won't take long."

Ten minutes later he returned. "*WOtt* is the account name for Major William Ott, who does in fact head up the intelli-

gence section on base. And the IP address is for his computer."

"Oh, that's bad news. Really bad news. If Major Ott is truly working for the bad guys, then I hope for our sake this
command's intelligence section does not work with sensitive
stuff. That's probably a vain hope, though."

"I wouldn't know, Bill. Not my area."

"Right. Tell me, how tightly are the IT security policies followed on the base? Is it common that people could login with
other people's accounts? Are account passwords properly secured?"

"Absolutely," the technician affirmed, "General Martin is
unbending on security issues. He has directed the IT department to inform him if people are telling one another their
passwords, or hiding them under their keyboards, or putting
them on sticky notes on their monitors. He actually issued a
reprimand this summer to an officer who got careless. I'd say
there's not much chance at all that someone else could be logging in with Major Ott's account."

"How about the IP address. Are you certain it's his?"

"Yep. Our IP addresses are given to the client computers
by what's called a DHCP server. We use address reservations
that are keyed to the unique MAC address of the network
card in the client computer. Bottom line is that the same MAC
address always gets assigned the same IP address. Always. The
IP you gave me has been assigned to Major Ott's computer."

Jensen rubbed his face. This was not going to be easy. On
most bases, the intelligence section ran twenty-four hours a
day. Somehow they were going to have to be able to install
surveillance equipment without being seen.

Sergeant Loeb spoke again, "The good news, Bill, is that
the intel section is in this building on the floor right below us.
If we have to set up some sort of surveillance equipment, at
least we won't have far to to pull the wires. It might be that we
could snake them through the HVAC ducts. I could check at
the base maintenance area. They have up-to-date blueprints
on all the base facilities. We've used the prints frequently in
the IT department for pulling network cables."

"Good idea. Matt, you check with base maintenance and figure out how we can get wires up here. A pallet of surveillance gear arrived from the Firm this morning at the airport, I'm going to drive over and pick it up. And we've also got to figure how to get the intel guys out of their department for the couple of hours it will take to place the surveillance."

"I don't think that will be difficult, Bill. I'll just start pulling coax, and if I can use the ducting I will. It's against the local building codes, but I doubt that the Agency worries about building codes anyway. I'll spin a good story and the boys down in intel won't even wonder what's going on. They're used to seeing the IT guys around, even in secure areas. Once I get the cables pulled, it won't take thirty minutes to connect them to cameras."

****

By late afternoon Jensen and Loeb had most of the spaces in the intel section covered by video and audio surveillance. The cameras were positioned behind the HVAC grillwork; the view was somewhat obstructed but for a quick and dirty job it would suffice. The inside of Major Ott's office was viewed from several different angles, and all of the desk areas of the other men in the intel section were also visible.

The pallet of surveillance equipment was damaged, Jensen learned to his frustration. Everything was intact except the high-speed video viewer that would allow Loeb to skim the recorded surveillance videos at high speed, without which eight hours of video would require eight hours of observation. Jensen arranged to have another airfreighted from the Agency's technical department. It was slated to arrive on Thursday night.

The sergeant had pulled and positioned all the cabling in full view of the department, telling them that the IT department was "upgrading the backbone of the network." The intelligence boys knew their own trade, but as far as they were concerned network topology was but one step beyond black magic, best administered by copious quantities of pixie dust.

It never even occurred to them to be suspicious.

The final trick was to get the guys out of the department long enough to connect the cameras to the cabling. With the permission of General Martin, who then communicated with the base fire department, Loeb tossed a smoke grenade into an empty trashcan in the men's restroom. The ensuing alarm emptied the entire building. The fire chief kept his crew away from the intel section, and prolonged his discovery and inspection process as long as possible. By the time the building's occupants were allowed back in, Loeb and Jensen had placed and tested their equipment.

A phone call to the CIA's San Francisco office obtained a small surveillance team that would fly up and bug Ott's home and car. Two more agents were detailed to look into his banking records and financial situation. By Friday morning, Major William Ott and his activities would be under the CIA's microscope.

Although domestic incidents were normally under the FBI's purview, when foreign intelligence or counterintelligence activities were involved, Executive Order 12333 issued in 1981 permitted the CIA to investigate and collect intelligence. Jensen knew he was on solid ground running this investigation. The FBI might grouse about it, but pursuing this case under the auspices of the CIA was within its official mandate, though a defense attorney might try to raise the issue of jurisdiction. Two mitigating factors were involved: first, the case would be made that Ott was working for a foreign intelligence service, the surveillance of which is clearly under the CIA's purview. The other mitigating factor was that since Ott would be charged under the Military Uniform Code of Justice, he would not be tried in a civilian court. Consequently, he would not go free, CIA involvement notwithstanding.

By late Wednesday night, Professor Bill Jensen, Special Assistant to the Deputy Director of Operations for the CIA, was on a flight back to DC. He was absolutely exhausted and slept until the stewardess woke him up as the aircraft was taxiing up to the terminal at National Airport, on the Virginia side of the Potomac River.

Chapter 6

Thursday, October 8, 1987: 0815 hours, local time
Langley, VA

Sam Bergman sat at his desk and began working through the small mound of telephone messages, reports, and briefs which had accumulated while he was in Anchorage. The quality of the coffee in his mug brightened his mood considerably. Someone in the office had tired of the brackish-looking hot water produced in the canteen down the hall, and had brought a coffee maker into their area. Now the java was robust and strong, just the way he liked it.

Two messages caught his attention. One was from Evelyn Stinson at the NSA. She had left an urgent request yesterday afternoon, asking him to return her call. The other was from the NSA group he had been working with regarding the IDC communications going to and from the Cayman Islands.

Most of the other items in his stack were articles, news reports, and intelligence estimates regarding various sectors of the Soviet economy. One rather interesting report he scanned seemed to indicate that the USSR was not capable of maintaining their current level of defense spending for more than another three years.

The larger part of the pile he stuffed into his briefcase to be read and evaluated while on the road. For an analyst Bergman did a great deal of traveling. As the CIA's premier Soviet expert he was in constant demand. Between trips to the West Coast, London, Berlin, and Tel Aviv, he actually spent more time sitting on an aircraft than he did sitting behind his desk at Langley. *Now that the coffee has improved, I'll have to stick around here a little more,* he thought to himself.

****

Not far from where Sam Bergman sat, Bill Jensen was staring morosely into his cup of brackish-looking hot water from the canteen down the hall. *I wonder if this means we've had another budget cut?* Jensen had just finished updating the DDO on the progress of the Kelly investigation. He hadn't even gone home after landing at National. *I'm getting too old for this*, he reflected wearily.

Though Bergman and Jensen worked in different sections at the Agency they were acquainted and knew of one another's work. However, Bergman was not aware of Jensen's pursuit of the Kelly affair, nor of the close friendship between the Kelly and Jensen families. For the moment it served Jensen's purpose that the left hand not know what the right hand was doing. It would all come out eventually, but he hoped that the revelation would be attached to a news report detailing the arrest of the spy at Eielson.

****

"Hi, Evelyn. This is Sam Bergman over at Langley, returning your call. I was out of the office yesterday. What's up?"

"Hello, Sam. I received a new intercept from *Leaning Tower.* I really think you need to see it."

"Okay. Let's see . . . would ten o'clock work for you?"

"Sure, that will work great."

"See you then."

Twenty minutes later Bergman was headed for the NSA facility in Maryland. He decided that after his visit to Evelyn Stinson he would stop in and see the team monitoring IDC message traffic.

****

The technician backed up the tape and pushed *Play* again, for the fifth time.

> *[intercom buzzes, followed by sound of a woman's voice] Admiral, there's a call for you on line two. It's General Franks.*
> *[Bridger] Thanks, Mabel. Tell him I'll be with him in a minute.*
> *[noise of Bridger dismissing men from a briefing. Sounds fade, a door shuts.] Hi Jim. What's going on?*
> *[Other party] I got another hit last night on the DIA's Watcher listing. Somebody is studying our man. It was a basic search through his personnel records.*
> *[Bridger] Yeah, I saw that too. Funny that there is this activity on Kelly's records all of a sudden. For a year or so, nothing, and then all this. It's like somebody else is fishing around for information.*
> *[Other party] Uh-huh. That was my thought. Listen, John, when Roger discovered the jamming signal on the RIMPAC tapes in the vicinity of Kelly's shootdown, he gave us what we needed to reopen the accident investigation without compromising your sources. Maybe simply stirring the pot will cause the Soviets to react. In any case, I don't think we can sit on this thing any longer. If Kelly was shot down I don't plan on letting Ivan simply walk away from it.*
> *[Bridger] You're right, Jim. We have what we need to follow up without endangering my source. Okay, why don't I meet you at Edwards on Friday at 0800, and we can plan our next steps over breakfast?"*

The conversation had been recorded yesterday. This was the technician's first opportunity to listen to it carefully, and it was exactly what they were looking for. The surveillance on Bridger, the CIA technician knew, was being conducted in the hopes of either incriminating or exonerating Admiral Bridger with respect to his interest in the Jacob Kelly affair. This brief recording cleared the admiral by demonstrating he was working with General Jim Franks to uncover additional information about Kelly's disappearance.

The tech dialed Jensen's number at Langley, and replayed

the segment. Ten minutes later the CIA surveillance group at Coronado was packing up their gear with orders to discontinue the surveillance on Admiral Bridger immediately and destroy all tapes. Later on Thursday the Naval Intelligence section at Coronado would remove the bugs.

****

There's no place in the world quite as beautiful as Virginia and Maryland in the fall. The hardwoods that populate the forested lands of these lovely states blaze into multiple hues of breathtaking beauty. Often the colors are so brilliant the trees seem to be illuminated from within. Bergman took his time on the drive to the NSA's Maryland facility, enjoying each new vista as the road wound toward his destination. The day was a rare one for the East: low humidity and crisp temperatures made the horizon as deep a blue as the zenith. It was invigorating.

Precisely at 1000 hours he strolled into Evelyn Stinson's cubicle after enduring the biometric hurdles at each door. "Hello, Miss Stinson. How is my favorite Russian grammar teacher today?" The drive had put him in an ebullient mood.

She looked up, surprised and slightly confused. "I'm fine, Sam, fine. And how are you?"

He was suddenly embarrassed by his boyish enthusiasm and backpeddled, "I wasn't making a pass at you, Evelyn, I'm sorry. It's just such a beautiful day outside, not even this concrete cave can quench it. The leaves out there are just gorgeous."

She smiled warmly, "I know. I seriously considered not showing up today. This would be a great day to get out on the Skyline Drive, or visit Gettysburg."

"Gettysburg? Do you enjoy history?"

"Yes, I do. Civil War history in particular is a hobby of mine, and Gettysburg is one of my favorite places. Whenever I go, I feel such a mix of admiration and sadness for the people who fought and fell there."

"Me too," Sam agreed. "On one hand it seems like such a

tragic waste. On the other, I'm glad Lincoln found the Union worth preserving, even at the cost of thousands. Well, I won't take up your time with small talk. You said that the latest intercept from *Leaning Tower* was really important. What's up?" Sam parked himself in a chair next to her desk.

She pulled a folder out of the small stack on her desk, and opened it up. "Sam, there's more news on the agent that is allegedly infiltrating the country. Supposedly he's an Air Force pilot. The intercept we received contains the cover story he'll be using, which is intended to explain the extended time he was absent from the US. The story goes like this: he was shot down and recovered by the Soviets. During his time in captivity he was interrogated for anything of intelligence value he might know. After a brief incarceration he escaped, trekked across Siberia, and managed to get across the Bering Strait.

"Frankly, Sam, this is so fantastic I can hardly believe what I myself translated and decoded. It would make a fascinating novel or movie, but it certainly does not sound like a plausible cover story. The message is addressed to the Soviet embassies in Germany, France, and the United States. It appears to be sort of an 'FYI' so that the ambassadors are not blind-sided if the US should register a complaint."

Bergman was dumbfounded. The cover story in the *Leaning Tower* intercept was precisely what he had heard from Major Kelly two days ago. He himself had accepted Kelly's explanation along with most of the *Snowbird* project group. Major Ott was the lone exception. The tale did strain his credulity but the fantastic context of the *known* facts—Kelly's recovery from the Bering Strait, the assassination attempt at Kotzebue, and his subsequent flight to Anchorage—made the pilot's whole story believable. Bergman supposed it was roughly analogous to Lewis Carroll's *Alice in Wonderland*. Once you're in *Wonderland*, talking to the Mad Hatter probably seems quite normal.

"When was this transmitted, Evelyn?"

"Late in the day on Monday, Moscow time. Oh, there's something else, too: the message names a Soviet officer who's going to be identified as mixed up in the scheme. It's a general by the name of Nikolai Chernikov."

"I see. In the last message you spotted several anomalies. How's this one?"

"It has the same characteristics as the previous message: three copies of the message with identical wording, containing one spelling error in each copy, though the error is in a different place in each message. And just like the previous message, the exact same word appears in the wrong verbal aspect—*begat'* rather than *bezhat'*. You might remember that's the code word for an agent insertion, but they're using the wrong aspect. These oddities make me think something's going on with this communique, something we've not yet identified."

"I'm curious: do you ever see spelling errors in other messages?"

"Oh, sure. They appear with roughly the same frequency that you would find them in English documents. The difference is this is the same exact message appearing three times, and the errors are in different places. The word they misspell in copy A is spelled correctly in copy B, and so on."

"There is a technique in counterespionage work, Evelyn, that would normally explain the misspellings. When you suspect your communications are compromised, one way to ferret out the leak is to give a slightly different version of the same confidential message to different individuals. If the message shows up in the enemy's hands, all that is necessary to identify the leaker is find out which version was leaked. But I don't think that explains what we're seeing here. Since these three copies are bundled together, the leaker will detect the differences and know someone's on to him.

"Evelyn, have you heard back from the guy who is examining the 'packet headers,' or whatever they are called?"

"Who? Oh, CE? No, not yet. He told me yesterday that he was having a hard time making the operative at the embassy understand what he wants."

"I'm not surprised. Didn't sound to me as if he was speaking English when he was trying to explain it to us."

"Really," she agreed, laughing. "But he did call late yesterday afternoon to tell me that they finally understood what he wanted, and he should have the data this morning. I'll let you know when he has it figured out."

"Thanks, Evelyn. Gotta run." Sam stood up to leave, and then paused at the door. He cleared his throat and then said, somewhat nervously, "By the way, if some guy from the CIA ever called and asked you out for an afternoon together wandering around Gettysburg, followed by dinner at a classy restaurant, would you be inclined to humor him?"

"Hmm. I'd have to check my busy schedule. But I don't think I would discourage him from at least asking."

Sam's smile was just a little wider as he turned to head for his other appointment at the NSA.

Bergman's meeting with the NSA technicians monitoring message traffic to and from International Development Corporation's office in the Cayman Islands was productive. The technicians provided him a printout of all the phone calls to or from IDC's Cayman office. He decided to complete his research at Langley. Stuffing the paper into his briefcase, Sam enjoyed the prospect of the drive back to his office. It really was a beautiful day.

****

Bill Jensen was several steps ahead of Sam Bergman on the IDC connection. He was wrapping up the analysis of the IDC message traffic in his office at about the same time Sam Bergman was leaving the NSA facility. The chief of the team analyzing the calls was sitting in his office.

"Barry, this is crucial! If you have any doubts about what you are telling me, say so before I commit the resources to set up a team to track and capture these guys. How sure are you that IDC has dispatched several hit squads to Alaska?"

"I am one hundred percent positive, so you'd better set up your team. If I was the target I would either be leaving the country or putting my affairs in order. These guys are good, and you know as well as I do that they're hard to spot and even more so since we don't know who the target is."

"I *do* know who the target is."

"Then you'd better warn him."

"That's just it—I can't. We'll just have to find these guys before they find their mark," Jensen rubbed his eyes, and then continued, "Okay, you said one team is heading for Anchorage and another is headed for Fairbanks, right?"

"That's right."

"Why Fairbanks?" Jensen asked himself, aloud. Kelly was in Anchorage. *Ah! Of course! Eielson Air Force Base is in Fairbanks. They must be expecting Jake to be transferred there.*

Barry thought the question was directed to him. "How the devil should I know? Why Anchorage? Why Fairbanks? Why not Disney World?"

"Sorry, Barry, just thinking out loud. Look, man, you've done a terrific job, thanks. I need your guys to keep this a top priority just a little longer."

"You got it, Bill."

Jensen gnawed on the problem for a few minutes and came to a decision. He compiled a mental to-do list, and then wrote up a mission profile to counter the IDC hit squads. Bill knew just the man to lead the operation in the field. Roger Carson was a former Delta Force operator the CIA had recruited. Jensen had worked with him in the past and had a high regard for the man's abilities. Carson had a sharp mind, was a decisive leader, and most importantly was not squeamish about violent action if it was officially sanctioned. Jensen picked up the phone and asked the department secretary to locate Carson. Ten minutes later the man strolled casually into his office and draped his lanky six-foot-two frame over a chair. Carson was built like a marathoner—wiry, skinny, and tough as shoe leather—and was one of the CIA's go-to guys for covert direct action.

"What's up, Bill?"

"Got a tough little job available, RC, wondered if maybe you were getting bored and needed a bit of action?" Jensen didn't miss the happy grin that spread across Roger's narrow face.

"For you, Billy boy? Always! Don't know how you do it, but you always seem to draw the best projects. Everybody on the Ops side of the Firm knows you have the most interesting assignments."

Jensen shook his head and grinned. "Keep those cards and letters coming, Rog, flattery will get you everywhere. Listen, Rog, this is a black op even inside the Firm. Other than the DDO, no one else is aware of this project. Don't tell anybody but your team, and only after you've got the whole group assembled. Nothing gets written down, nothing goes into the computer, understand? Make sure your guys toe the line on that requirement. Go see the DDO to satisfy yourself that the job has official sanction, but that's it—no other contact with anyone within the Firm. When you draw your equipment, your story is that you're doing some live-fire direct action team training in Alaska. And that, by the way, is the only good news about this project: it's all within CONUS so you have no worries regarding capture."

"Why the extreme secrecy? How come I can't even talk about it inside the Agency?"

"Because we think some of the good guys are working for the bad guys, and we haven't sorted out who is who yet. We don't want the bad guys to find out the cavalry is on the way."

Carson chewed on that for a moment and then asked, "Okay. What else do I need to know?"

"You have two primary objectives and one secondary. The primary objectives are to protect the target and neutralize the hostiles who are trying to off him. The secondary objective is to capture them."

"Who's the target?"

"Major Jacob Kelly. He's an Air Force officer being held in custody in Anchorage by the Alaska State Troopers. At some point he's probably going to be transferred under guard to Eielson in Fairbanks. Two IDC goon squads have been dispatched, one to Anchorage, one to Fairbanks. If IDC follows their normal pattern, these will be three-man squads. You probably won't have to worry about a direct attempt on the target, such as a sniper attack. If they follow their usual MO, they will arrange a fatal accident."

"Oh, great. One of those!" Carson groaned. "So we have

to protect this guy from tripping over his shoelaces or slipping on a conveniently placed banana peel?"

"It's more likely you are going to have to protect him from getting into a vehicle or aircraft that has been sabotaged. Now, there are a few minor complexities."

"Uh-oh. Why do I get the feeling these aren't so minor? What are these 'minor complexities'?" the field agent asked.

"Well, first of all, you cannot make contact with the target."

"That's not so bad. What else?"

"You cannot make contact with the State Troopers, either. They can't know you are there."

"Oh, that's bad. Real bad. So we can't coordinate with them? Hmm. Is he under protective custody, or is he under arrest?"

"Well, they're trying to figure that out now." Jensen held up his hand to cut off the man's protests, "Hey! It's not relevant, Roger. For the time being, assume arrest."

"Any other 'complexities'?"

"Uh-huh. Just one. We don't have a make on either hit squad. We don't know who they are, what they look like, or even if they've arrived on site yet. We don't have names, not even aliases. You're going to have to spot them by surveillance alone. I'll have a small team here trying to work up their names from hotel ledgers, flight rosters, and other transactions, but I can't guarantee that we'll get anywhere."

Carson fixed his eyes on Jensen and slowly shook his head. "Bill, you're going to have to start living right. I can't believe that anyone would give you such an impossible task. We don't know who the bad guys are. We don't have access to the mark. We can't coordinate with local law enforcement. If we get caught sweeping their vehicles and aircraft for bugs and bombs, they're liable to throw *us* in the pokey. And the worst of all is, you're sending us to *Alaska*, for crying out loud, and it is practically wintertime! How come this couldn't be unfolding in Orlando, or Hawaii?"

With a twinkle in his eye, Jensen replied, "No, RC, *you* are the one who needs to start living right. After all—I'm giving the task to *you*."

Carson stood up and rejoined dryly, "You are a kind and thoughtful man. I'd better get my team formed up. What are the rules of engagement?"

"First priority is the safety of Major Kelly. The second priority is remaining undetected. You may use deadly force only if attacked, or if you believe that Kelly is in imminent danger. Do not put civilians at risk, however."

****

The first thing Sam Bergman did upon arriving back at his office was contact one of the hackers on the CIA payroll. He asked the man to locate and identify the number that the major had dialed when he was arrested in the furniture store. The second thing he did was call Jesse Pierce.

"Jesse, something's come up that's going to make us rethink the *Snowbird* case. I've received some additional intelligence on that defector story I mentioned on Tuesday. A highly placed source outlined the cover story to be used by the spy who is attempting to infiltrate the military. Get this: it's the one we heard from Major Kelly—it matches exactly."

Pierce groaned. "Oh, boy. Bill Ott just called me a few minutes ago and said the same thing. According to his sources, Kelly's account is part of an elaborate ruse. You realize, Sam, that between the intelligence intercepts and the interrogations we are being presented with two radically different possibilities. According to one story, with the help of a spy in US Air Force Operations, the USSR has committed an officially sanctioned criminal act—an act of war, really—by shooting down and kidnapping one of our pilots. According to the competing story, however, neither of those things actually happened. Instead, our guy has been turned and he defected with his F-16, and now the Soviets are intentionally implicating themselves by these fanciful tales with the hopes of re-implanting the guy in the Air Force.

"If we believe Kelly's story, we may be abetting the Soviets in their efforts to penetrate the Air Force by clearing Kelly and returning him to duty. If we believe the story we're picking up in our intelligence intercepts, and consequently charge Kelly with treason, we may be accusing an innocent man while we are—again—aiding and abetting the Soviets by leaving a spy—of whose presence we have been informed—in place in USAF Operations. Either way, we could be complicit in the penetration of a Soviet spy into the Air Force. There is no safe option here."

Sam did not answer. What could he say? The commander was right, after all—it was an unpleasant dilemma. Whatever decision they made would be fraught with danger.

"Sam, are you still there?"

"Yeah, Jesse, I'm here. Just don't know how to respond. You've hit the nail on the head. We really have to get this right. As of the moment, I am inclined to believe that Kelly is the spy. I left Anchorage thinking he was clean. One of the biggest reasons was that he identified Chernikov as GRU. I really didn't think the Sovs would give up that piece of information willingly—it's too valuable. But this latest intel and the reliability of the source has caused me to change my mind, and now I wonder if he really is a spy. Perhaps it would be best to turn him over to Bill Ott. I imagine that the major should be interrogated to see how far the damage goes. If Kelly's working for the Sovs, *Hydra* has been totally compromised, along with who knows what else."

"Do you think Kelly was telling the truth about Chernikov, Sam?"

"Yes, I do. That piece of data about Chernikov explains all the other intel I've been collecting on the general. It's kind of like finding the missing jigsaw puzzle piece: it really fits the picture. I don't know why I didn't see it sooner—I've been studying Nikolai Chernikov for years.

"Contrary to my initial conclusion, Jesse, the information about Chernikov doesn't help us make a decision about Kelly because there are two equally plausible explanations. On the one hand, Kelly's innocent and he's just passing along a valuable piece of data that he picked up while in their custody. Or, on the other hand, Kelly's guilty and the Sovs were willing to let him give away that little gem about Chernikov to make us *think* he's innocent. Remember, they wrote the book on disinformation."

Jesse sighed. "Good grief—the plot thickens! Well, let's wait until Monday before we decide about the transfer. Maybe something new will crop up in the meantime. Other than Ott's impatience, I don't think it can hurt anything."

****

The Politburo was engaged in a heated debate about Afghanistan. Things were not going well, and the nineteen members were badly divided. Some wanted to pull out, others wanted to insert more troops, and some recommended turning the region into a glass-encrusted parking lot through an extended, high-altitude bombing campaign. Andrei Gromyko, the Chairman of the Presidium of the Supreme Soviet, was in favor of the latter option. In his mind, Afghanistan had turned into a test of Soviet military might before the eyes of the world, and more importantly, in the eyes of the increasingly restless Soviet satellite states. Gromyko feared that if the army did not win decisively in Afghanistan, the USSR would begin to unravel from within. Standing against him was General Secretary Mikhail Gorbachev, who had begun speaking in favor of a withdrawal. Gorbachev had his eye on the faltering Soviet economy and knew that the war had become very unpopular.

Patrikeyev himself preferred to raise the troop levels significantly and give the Soviet military one more year to subdue the opposition. It was during a break in the debate that his aide came and touched his elbow. He followed the man back into an anteroom. As he left, he felt the eyes of Comrade Anatoly Geredin boring a hole in his back. The old spook had spies everywhere monitoring his success—or lack of it—in silencing Kelly.

"What is it, Igor?"

"Sir, we received word an hour ago that our man in Fairbanks was unable to accelerate the transfer of Major Kelly. In fact, word is that the move will probably not take place until Monday, their time. Our operatives need to know whether this changes their operational instructions."

General Patrikeyev mulled the question over before coming to a decision. "No, the instructions are unchanged. Kelly is to be eliminated if at all possible. It is vital, Igor, that you stress this one point: his death must, I repeat, *must* appear to be accidental. Otherwise things for us will go from bad to worse. Do you understand me, Igor?" He gripped the aide by his upper arm and squeezed hard until the man winced.

"Yes, General. I understand. I will make it quite clear. The communication also indicated that the group interrogating the American pilot are now convinced that he is a traitor."

"Excellent. Is there anything else?"

"No, sir. That was it."

"Good. You were right to interrupt me, Igor. This was very important. Now, I must get back."

Igor was unimaginative, but he was more than competent as an aide. Patrikeyev knew his message would be transmitted in very clear terms. He re-entered the conference room and flashed a sardonic smile to Comrade Geredin as he returned to his seat.

****

Bill Jensen could not suppress a groan as he boarded an overnight flight to LA at Washington National Airport. He was dog-tired, but he had to be at Edwards on Friday morning in time to crash the breakfast meeting between Admiral Bridger and General Franks. Things were unfolding rapidly, but he felt himself able to manage the pace as long as it did not go for more than another week.

As he settled back into his seat, Jensen found himself thinking about Clancy Kelly, Jake's father. He was the most highly educated self-taught man Bill had ever met. The son of an Irishman, Clancy had inherited a large library of classics from his father and had added to it extensively. Clancy had read every book in his library cover to cover at least once and some of them many times over. When cancer cut his life short, he was teaching himself Greek and working his way through a Greek copy of Xenophon's *Anabasis*. The man literally lived to learn. He could discourse intelligently on military history from virtually any era.

Shared interests drew Bill, Clancy, and Clancy's son, Jake together: the enjoyment of the outdoors, fly fishing, reading, learning, and military history. It was a bond that persisted even through the deaths of both of Jake's parents. Bill and Susan Jensen had made a point of being there for all the major landmarks in Jacob Kelly's life.

Jensen squirmed in his seat. One thing he had noticed about airliner seats especially when traveling coach: they always seem to be designed for someone shaped differently from oneself. Perhaps for a munchkin. "Comfort" and "air travel" were becoming mutually exclusive notions. As he sought to find a position in the Boeing 767's seat in which he could catch a few winks, Bill told himself once again that there was no way he was going to allow the son of Clancy Kelly to be hung out to dry for an act of treason he did not commit. Not on his watch.

Chapter 7

Friday, October 9, 1987: 0630 hours, local time
Georgetown, DC

As Evelyn Stinson left her Georgetown apartment and walked to her car, she enjoyed the snap in the chill air and the promise of another day of brilliant color. The beauty of the morning reminded her of yesterday's conversation with Sam Bergman, the analyst from the CIA. She idly wondered if he would call her for a date at Gettysburg, as he had hinted. She was torn between hoping he would and hoping he wouldn't. As to the latter, her experience with men had been pretty unpleasant. She knew she possessed a face and a figure that turned heads. And she also knew that many men who asked her out weren't interested in her as a person, they wanted to use her to gratify their desires. She wasn't interested in spending any time with a guy who was looking for the shortest distance between a date and the bed.

On the other hand, Sam had seemed genuinely embarrassed when he thought she mistook his exuberance for flirting. She was pleased to meet a man who possessed the capacity to be embarrassed. His hint about a date had been genuinely shy, and that intrigued her, too.

She was attracted to Sam because he was obviously a thinker who loved his work. As an individual he appeared to be emotionally complete, not needy. And, she got the impression he was something of a gentleman in the old-school sense of the word. She liked that. Evelyn didn't want to be one of the guys—she didn't need to be one of the guys. She enjoyed a genteel deference from men. On the other hand, if a guy was condescending to her, well, she was ready for that, too. If it was an older fellow, she just thought of him as a doddering old grandfather who meant well but was living in the wrong century. If the offender was a younger man, she had ways of putting arrogant males in their place.

She decided that she hoped Sam would call. It really was a beautiful morning!

****

As Evelyn Stinson hummed her way to the super-secret NSA facility in Maryland, a bleary-eyed CIA counterespionage team was dropping their gear in a rented room in Fairbanks. Roger Carson pulled out a sat phone, adjusted the scrambler, and called home.

"Carson here, with Team Baker in Fairbanks. Has Team Alpha checked in yet?"

There was a brief delay as the signal was transmitted to a satellite in stationary orbit twenty-two thousand miles above San Francisco, relayed to an identical bird floating above West Virginia, then bounced down to a receiving station in northern Virginia, from whence it was directed by a packet-switching network to the Operations Center at Langley.

"Negative, no contact yet."

"What do you have for us?"

"Nothing so far. We're still running matches and searches on the passenger manifests for all the incoming flights to Fairbanks. It's going to be another three hours, anyway."

"Roger that. I'll call again at 1100 your time."

Carson put the sat phone away and turned to his four-man team. "There's nothing we can do yet. Get some sack time. We are getting up at 0700."

****

Lieutenant Commander Jesse Pierce reviewed the after-action intelligence analysis of the foray against Petropavlovsk, Operation *Screen Pass*. They had clearly caught the Russians with their pants down. The Navy was beginning to tinker with the idea of outfitting the Tomcats with the AGM-88 High-

Speed Anti-Radiation (HARM) missile. If *Screen Pass* had been a wartime sortie, the first flight of F-14s had gotten close enough to launch a volley of the advanced HARM missiles which would have degraded the port's anti-aircraft capability significantly, opening the door for additional strike aircraft to take down the remaining SAM coverage. He inspected the maps detailing where the *Honolulu*'s sensitive ESM equipment had detected gaps and seams in the radar coverage. There were enough approach vectors available that a significant strike force could be sent against the Petropavlovsk-Kamchatskiy military complex with an anticipated high degree of success. Also of interest were the details on the *Kilo* coverage of the undersea lanes into the port. Several potential areas of approach had been mapped. All in all, *Screen Pass* had been an entirely successful operation. But Jesse knew that within a month those open doors would be shut, nailed down forever by the Soviets' own analysis of the same operation, with the exception of the undersea weaknesses. Ivan probably did not know about those, even now.

He buzzed his communications officer. "Joey, send this pronto to USPACOM at Pearl, and then send a copy to Major Ott at Eielson AFB, and ask him to distribute it to the appropriate Air Force installations."

"By courier, sir?"

"Nope, use MILNET. This thing isn't going to have a long shelf life. Might as well get it to 'em while it's still fresh."

What Jesse Pierce could not have known is that the thirty-two-page report of the incursion into Soviet airspace was going to turn the Kelly case on its head. It was yet another intrusion of providence into the affairs of men.

****

"This time we've got something for you, Roger. Three men took a United Airlines flight from Chicago to the Seattle-Tacoma airport, and then boarded Alaska Airlines flight AS103, landing in Fairbanks at 1830 local. We caught them because their baggage was transferred in Chicago from a United flight originating in Dallas, but none of the three names appeared on the Dallas manifest, meaning they were traveling under different names for that leg. Once they arrived in Fairbanks, we lost 'em again. No one has booked any hotels using the names they were traveling under."

"They are probably running on cash at this point," Carson surmised.

"Yeah, that's what Jensen guessed, too," responded the CIA man.

Carson took the information down. There had been a chance photograph of the three taken by an airport security camera in Chicago. Though it was grainy it was better than nothing. The agent arranged to have the image faxed to the hotel office.

"What about Team Alpha, have they checked in yet?"

"Yes, they called in. Unfortunately, we had less for them than we do for you. Our best lead so far is that a block of three tickets to SeaTac was purchased with cash at the TWA counter in San Francisco on Tuesday. The trail goes cold from there."

"What about the cameras?"

"Surprise, surprise, none of the TWA cameras were working in that wing of the terminal. The cables are routed through a public stairwell, and guess what? The coax carrying all the security cameras was clipped."

"Well, I'd say that's a pretty good sign it was our boys."

"I agree. But other than that, it gives us exactly nothing. We are chasing down a theory that they might have taken ground transportation from SeaTac to Portland, and caught a flight to Anchorage from there."

Roger Carson hung up the sat phone and turned to his team. "Jimmy, you check out Highway 3, as far as Denali. Alpha Team is responsible for everything south of Denali; we've got everything north. Locate the most likely points for planning an automobile accident. Mike, you get on base at Eielson and check out the airfield, and likely spots for an accident to occur. Mr. Jensen has arranged access with base security. Skip and Randy have the hotel circuit once that fax arrives. You two need to locate the bad guys so we can keep an eye on 'em. Skip, you're in charge."

"What are you going to do, Rog?" Randy was always suspicious that he was going to have to work harder than everybody else.

"Park on the couch, eat chocolates, and watch reruns of *Green Acres*. What did you think I was going to do, knothead?" Roger snapped at the youngest man on the team. Relenting, he said, "I'm flying down to Anchorage to check on Alpha Team. There's no make on their target yet, and they may need an extra man. At least you guys know who you're looking for. Skip, check in every six hours on the sat phone; I want to stay in contact. Randy, if you'll run me out to the airport, I'll share some of my chocolates with you." This last was said with an apologetic smile.

The young man knew it was a peace offering and responded with a grin, "Sure boss. Just installed the TV in the limo last week. You'll be able to watch your show on the way to the airport."

****

Howard Mumford drove the Chevy Suburban east on Tudor Road. His companion in the front seat had a map of Anchorage spread over his knees. "Got it," he muttered. "It should be three blocks farther on the right side of the road, Howard."

"Yep, here it is, Clayton," the big man affirmed. His heavily muscled six-foot-four frame was one reason they had rented the large vehicle. The man in the passenger seat had a similar build, though he was somewhat shorter. While their wiry companion in the back seat didn't look particularly intimidating, it would be a fatal mistake to underestimate his abilities. The three were a finely honed, professional assassination squad and were very, very good at what they did. They were also paid very well to do it.

Snow was falling as they passed the Alaska Troopers Anchorage headquarters. "I don't like the snow," said the man in the back seat. "Too easy to follow tracks."

Howard glanced in the rearview mirror, looking at his sour companion. "You just don't like getting your butt wet and cold, Pat, be honest. Okay, Clayton, which building is the mark in?"

The man in the back seat muttered resentfully, "It *does* leave tracks, all the same."

Clayton consulted a sketch. "It's that one, just to the left of the big building. It's a low security detention area."

Pat studied the scene. "Bad place for sniping. There's too much in the way, especially if they bring him out the front. Every angle that gives me a clear field of fire leaves me exposed, without a good exit."

"I told you before, Pat, we're not making a direct hit on the target! It's gotta look like an accident. I don't even know why you brought the sniper rifle. It's just that much more to lug around." Howard's exasperation was evident and was greeted with resentful silence from the back seat.

"Would you two stop bickering! I feel like I have my kids with me! This hit is going to be hard enough without you guys making it worse, for crying out loud!" Clayton exclaimed.

The team was silent as Howard drove about two miles past the headquarters, then negotiated an unplowed turnout as he turned the Suburban around to drive back.

Pat asked in a conciliatory tone, "Do we know yet whether the transfer will be by air, or are they going to drive him up to Eielson?"

"As of the moment it's going to be by air. If this snow keeps up, the highway will close for the rest of the winter and they won't have a choice," Howard replied. "Our source says they are planning to move him on Monday."

"That means we have to pop him somewhere between here and the airport, or we'll have to sabotage the plane. What kind of aircraft will they be using for transport?"

"The troopers have a Beechcraft King Air for prisoner transport, according to what I was told. A model C90." Howard looked in the rearview mirror at his wiry companion and asked, "What about it, Pat? Can you do a Beech?"

Pat smirked. "I can do a Beech, and it will look just like an accident. Piece of cake."

****

Franks met Bridger's Tomcat on the tarmac. They stopped briefly at Flight Ops and the admiral removed his flight suit, which he'd worn over his uniform.

"It's a good thing the American taxpayer isn't keeping an eye on your budget, Admiral. That F-14's a pretty fancy taxi, even for a naval aircraft. It's a mighty expensive way to get from Coronado to Edwards," Franks groused.

"Actually, Jim, the way I see it I'm saving the taxpayer big shekels. I get my flight hours in, and not by flat-hatting the good citizens' homes, either, like those Air Force plumbers you call pilots. I'm on official Navy business, and if you think about my extraordinarily valuable time that would otherwise be wasted sitting in southern California traffic, why, I'm saving so much money I'm probably a profit center!"

"Oh, heaven help us! That's the sort of tortured logic that justifies those floating bull's-eyes you call 'aircraft carriers.' One well-aimed torpedo would send two percent of our national GDP to the bottom of the Pacific in five minutes."

The two friends kept up their verbal jabs all the way to the Officers' Club, causing the driver to wonder if the men actually liked one another at all. As they walked up the sidewalk leading into the Club, a stranger approached them.

"General Franks, Admiral Bridger, good morning, sirs. My name is Bill Jensen, I'm a special assistant to the Deputy Director of Operations, CIA. I apologize for the intrusion, gentlemen, but I wonder if you might allow me to join you for breakfast. I have some information that will be of interest to you both." He passed his CIA identification badge over to Franks, who inspected it and then handed it back.

"I'm sorry, Mr. Jensen, I'm afraid not. The admiral and I have matters to discuss that can't be shared with anyone else. Here's my card—you can contact my secretary and set up an appointment and I'd be glad to talk to you. But not now."

"Please, sir, it's vital—"

"The answer is no, Mr. Jensen. Excuse us." Franks said firmly, cutting the CIA agent off.

The two officers stepped around Jensen and were entering the door when he called out, "I have information on Kelly!"

Franks stopped, and slowly turned around. "What did you say?"

Jensen looked around to make sure no one was within earshot before repeating quietly, "I have information on Major Jacob Kelly."

Franks glared at Jensen, saying nothing, and then looked at Bridger. The admiral shrugged his shoulders in a "why not" gesture. Franks looked back at the agent and asked, "How can you know anything about Kelly?"

"With all due respect, sir, I'd really rather discuss this with you two where we can do it in confidence."

Franks nodded. "Come in, Jensen."

"Thank you, sir."

Franks had asked the staff to move his personal table to a private room in the Officer's Club, and had his security staff scan the area for listening devices. When the three seated themselves he was sure they could speak of classified matters in confidence. The waiter took their orders, and then disappeared.

"Okay, Mr. Jensen, this better be good," Franks warned.

"Oh, it is, sir. First, thank you for letting me join your meeting this morning. It's going to save all kinds of time. The clock is winding down and we have a long way to move the ball in order to score, if you'll forgive the football metaphor."

"We?" Bridger asked coldly.

"Yes, Admiral, we need to work together. I know this whole situation must seem quite strange, but for some very important security reasons I couldn't go through normal channels to contact either of you. Since I knew you were meeting today I thought I'd invite myself to the party."

"Okay, Jensen, the first thing I want to know is how on God's green earth did you know that we would be meeting today? My schedule is not published in the newspaper, and I don't expect Jim's is, either!"

"Please, call me Bill. Admiral, you've been under surveillance for the last forty eight hours. I've been investigating the major's disappearance, and because of the odd circumstances surrounding Kelly your interest in him came to my attention. I am also aware of the general's curiosity, but I knew I could trust General Franks. I apologize, Admiral Bridger, but I did not know if I could trust you. By the directive of the DDO and with the full—but reluctant, I might add—cooperation of base security at Coronado, we have surveilled your communications. That surveillance has cleared you from all suspicion, and it's also how I learned of this meeting, which is really quite providential. It's going to save some time and trouble."

Bridger was furious. "You had *me* placed under surveillance? Do you have any idea what you have done? Have you lost your mind? Don't you know that as the commanding officer of SPECWAR Group One, I'm dealing with highly classified information practically every time I pick up the phone? How many technicians and operatives were listening in? How many people now know about the operations we are running? How many lives and missions have you put in danger?"

"Slow down, John," Franks soothed, "don't forget that every operation you and your SEALs run is vetted or augmented by CIA intelligence and cooperation. And if I'm hearing Jensen correctly, his aim is the same as ours. It sounds like he wants to get to the bottom of the Kelly disappearance."

"Quite right," affirmed Jensen. He turned back to the agitated admiral. "Everyone who was involved in your surveillance, Admiral Bridger, had the appropriate security classifications and, I might add, the moral and legal right to do what they were doing. Sometimes, sir, we can't tell the difference between the good guys and the bad guys just by looking at the uniform. In order to protect Kelly and our larger mission, I *had* to check you out. Your very interest in Kelly made you a suspect, and I'll explain why in a moment. It's understandable that you're angry because as it turns out, our goals *are* the same. But I didn't know that two days ago. To answer your questions, none of your operations or your people have been compromised, the tapes have been destroyed, and the listening devices removed."

"Was my secretary involved?" Bridger was slowly calming down and his face returning to its normal sun-browned color.

"She knew nothing about it and still doesn't. And no one on your base was even willing to talk to me without some direct arm-twisting from the DDO himself. They are all loyal to you, Admiral."

"Okay. Okay. But I am curious. Why was it you knew you could trust Jim, but did not know that about me?"

"Rather than answer that question yet, let me explain the entire affair to you: what happened on 10 July, 1986, and why, what has happened since, and what is happening now."

"Hold on," Franks interrupted, "you could have no idea of any of that unless the CIA was involved in his disappearance. Was this some kind of crazy CIA operation run amuck?"

"Not at all. The CIA had nothing to do with Kelly's disappearance."

"Then how can you possibly know what happened?"

"Because Jacob Kelly told me what happened," Jensen patiently explained.

"He told you?" Bridger and Franks exclaimed in unison.

"Yes, of course. He told me everything."

With the slightest tremor in his voice Franks, asked, "Then he is alive?"

"He is, and none the worse for the wear. I can see that this news has affected you, General." The last statement was more of a question.

A single tear rolled down the side of his face and Franks cleared his throat, taking a sip of water before responding. "Sorry. I was not expecting this news and it caught me off guard. No officer ever wants to lose the men in his command. But Major Kelly was—is, thank God—close to my family, especially my children. He's, well, very special to us. We have been grieving the loss ever since he disappeared."

"If we can extricate him from this trouble, General, he'll be just fine. I knew Jake and his family when he was still in high school. His dad and I were close friends. He's like a son to my wife and me. I know how you feel."

"When did he contact you," asked Bridger.

"On the telephone, last week. He called me because he didn't know whom he could trust. Wait," he said to Franks who was about to interrupt again, "hold your questions. Let me tell you the story first, then I'll take questions."

Both officers nodded so the CIA agent continued. "On 10 July last year Jacob Kelly was flying an F-16 over the Bering Sea on a test flight for *Hydra*, which is your super-secret project, General Franks, to upgrade the battle control and co-ordination of Paveway-guided munitions."

Franks nodded his affirmation. "It's very irritating that everyone seems to know about my super-secret project, but what you say is correct. Go on, please."

"On this particular night the Sovs had stationed one of their fighters along Kelly's flight path. They shot him down, retrieved him after he ejected, and took him to a secret detention facility in Siberia to interrogate him about *Hydra*." Franks grimaced, and his shoulders slumped. Jensen went on, "Yes, general, they know about your project, a little bit anyway. But not from Jake. He told them nothing.

"This is where the tale goes from merely amazing to totally unbelievable. One of these days we're going to see this story as a blockbuster book or a major motion picture if the details ever become public. But I digress.

"Major Kelly managed to escape from the detention facility. He survived a Siberian winter, eluded a major manhunt for some thirteen months, and made his way up to the northern edge of the Chukchi Peninsula, traveling over forty-five hundred miles through some of the most difficult terrain on the planet. Then he kayaked back to the United States.

"The next part of the story became public several weeks ago. Did either of you gentlemen read in the newspapers about a fellow named John Meeker who was found unconscious in a kayak out in the Bering Strait, and was taken to the hospital in Kotzebue, Alaska?"

"Yeah, I saw that story. It was an odd one, too, because Meeker disappeared from the hospital. There were allegations that someone attempted to kill him," Bridger affirmed.

The CIA agent paused, unfolding his napkin, and then said quietly, "John Meeker, my friends, is Major Jacob Kelly. He has returned to the United States. The men who attempted to assassinate him were under contract to the GRU, Soviet military intelligence."

The waiter appeared and began serving their food. Bridger and Franks sat in silence, processing the unexpected news. When the waiter left Jensen asked, "May I return thanks?" Franks responded quickly, cutting off the smart remark he knew was forming on Bridger's lips, "Please."

After a brief prayer giving thanks for the food and for Kelly's safe return to the States, Jensen continued, "Here's where the tale gets complicated. This is where I can answer your question about trust, Admiral. Jacob Kelly believes—as do I—that someone in Air Force operations compromised him. A spy, in other words, and probably at Eielson Air Force Base. The Soviets were all set up and waiting to grab him. And when they did get him, it was *Hydra* they interrogated him about. The only way they could have known his precise flight path was if someone wearing an Air Force uniform was feeding them the information. And I didn't know how far the corruption might go—remember the John Walker case.

"I knew that you, General Franks, were clean since you're the director of *Hydra*. If you had been the turncoat there would have been no need to kidnap Kelly. You could have passed along whatever they wanted. Simple logic eliminated you as a suspect.

"But I did not know why you were interested in Jacob Kelly, Admiral, especially as a Navy man. That's why I couldn't trust you initially. I feared you could be part of a wider network of Soviet spies, trying to locate Jake to finish the job the assassins botched. So I had little choice but to spy on you until your own actions clarified your intentions. They did, and now I know you're working on our side."

"But how did you know that I was interested in Kelly to begin with?" the Admiral asked.

"That's a state secret, sir, and it's a question I'm not permitted to answer. I can assure you there was no breach in your security."

"So where is he and what do we do now?" asked Franks.

"He's being held under arrest by the Alaska State Troopers in Anchorage. He and I had been communicating by phone before they picked him up. I haven't talked to him since he was arrested."

"Why is he under arrest?" queried Bridger.

"Two reasons. One is that his escape from Kotzebue involved the theft of an aircraft. Along the way he drugged a Navy MP and held a state trooper at gunpoint. So he's technically broken several laws and committed an assortment of felonies. The second reason is that they are not quite sure what to do with him. There is a group of five men, a mix of military intelligence, FBI, CIA, and Alaska State Troopers who are interrogating him to ascertain whether he is telling them the truth about his escape from the Soviet Union. There is some concern among them that Jacob Kelly is a traitor and that his disappearance was a defection and not a shootdown. They worry that he is being *planted* back in the Air Force to resume spying. They are working with several communications intercepts buttressing the idea that he is a spy working for the bad guys. I believe the Sovs are playing mind games with them, running a disinformation campaign designed to discredit anything Kelly might say—especially about his own kidnapping." Bill Jensen paused at this point, and began working on his omelet.

Bridger spoke up, "That's where we can help. Between Jim and me, we have two independent means of corroborating Kelly's claims. I have testimony given to me by sources I trust, involving the admission of a Soviet fighter pilot to the effect that he was vectored to a specific location and directed to shoot down an approaching F-16 on the night of 10 July, 1986. Secondly, we have hard ELINT evidence, on RIMPAC data tapes, of a Soviet jamming signal in the vicinity of the shootdown, on the exact date and time the F-16 was splashed."

Jensen nodded. "That's conclusive. It's improbable under

any scenario that the Soviet Union would stage the shoot-down. Getting their hands on the jet while it was loaded out with *Hydra* avionics would be too tempting a prize if the pilot actually was working for them."

Franks asked, "Bill, are you in communication with the group interrogating Jacob?"

"No, not yet. Don't want to tip off the spy. It's possible that one of these five men is actually the traitor."

"But that means you have to leave Kelly in jail," Franks objected.

"It means more than that. It means I leave him in jail, it means that I cannot contact him, it means that I have to allow him to be arraigned if necessary. And it involves some risk that the Sovs will get to Jake and kill him before I can bag the spy. But as I said, we can't afford to tip him off or show our hand. Any investigating I do has to be done quietly. That's why I don't want you two to reopen the accident investigation into his disappearance." Jensen finished his breakfast and pushed away from the table, preparing to leave.

"Listen," he added, "you men are among the very best at what you do. But counterespionage is not your stock-in-trade; spying is not your thing. It *is* my thing and I'm very good at it. All I am asking you to do is keep your ears open, but please, don't take any action. You can talk to each other, you can talk to me, or you can talk to the DDO. But, please, no one else.

"By the way, Admiral Bridger, before this is all over we might need your very special talent."

"How's that?"

"Jacob Kelly hinted in one phone call that he has an ace in the hole if it begins to look like the investigation is going sour and charges are going to be brought against him. He would not tell me but I think I know what his ace is. I believe Jake knows of others who have been kidnapped for their specialized knowledge. They are probably being held at that same Siberian detention facility. At the appropriate time he'll tell us what he knows. And when that happens we may need several SEAL teams to rescue those people and destroy the camp. I believe that when all the data is in, the President would approve such an action."

Franks' eyes narrowed, "Surely not! *We* would be committing an act of war. The President would never approve that action. The USSR would trumpet it abroad and we would look like international pariahs."

John Bridger's eyes glittered a steely grey as he replied, "No, Jim, you're wrong. You stick with your avionics and let Jensen and me save the world. He's right. We could take that camp out and plant an American flag in the middle of the smoking rubble and Ivan would never say a word. One peep out of them and we would parade their captives across the stages of the world. The eyewitness testimony of the victims would be irrefutable. The USSR would never live it down. It would be a foreign policy disaster if the world learned of their kidnapping plot.

"Bill," Bridger said, standing up and extending his hand, "if you call on my SEALs, we'll be ready."

****

The teletype in the secure-room of the intelligence office at Eielson AFB clattered to life and began clacking out the thirty-two-page summation of the Navy's recent penetration of Soviet airspace surrounding Petropavlovsk-Kamchatskiy.

After all the racket had ceased the spy got up from his desk and pecked the secure-room's entry code into the digital lock, and retrieved the report. One of his responsibilities in Eielson's intelligence section was to read and digest the report, distribute it to interested parties with sufficient clearance, and write a précis which would be part of Monday's regular intelligence briefing for the base commander and the operations officer.

Walking slowly back to his desk, he skimmed the report with growing interest. This would be pure gold in the hands of his Soviet spymasters. They would pay a premium for it! Not only did it detail US intentions and techniques in a high-stakes surveillance operation against the most important port of the Soviet Pacific Fleet, it also revealed multiple weaknesses in the port's air defenses. The report disclosed a daring incursion by an attack submarine into waters near the heavily guarded port. As an American the spy felt pride that US forces were able to pull off such an operation undetected by the USSR. But as a very *greedy* American he could not wait to sell the news to the Russians. Thirty-two pages! This was going to be a challenge.

He sat down and pulled out a cigarette. Taking his cigarette lighter in his hand, he leaned his elbows on his desk and lit up. Through a pinhole in the bottom of the Zippo, a miniature set of precision-ground lenses directed the image of the cover page of the classified document onto a frame of six millimeter film inside the lighter. A spring mechanism silently advanced the film to the next frame. The camera was a descendant of the KGB-produced Svouk Camera, tailored to fit in a specially modified Zippo lighter. The only downside was that using it had turned him into a chain smoker. He was going to be smoking a lot of cigarettes today.

He photographed the report as he read it. Fiddling with the Zippo as though it had a problem, he quickly photographed the first three pages. By the fourth page he lost his nerve and pulled out a Marlboro. Lighting up, he snapped a shot of page four. Over the space of several hours and several packs of cigarettes, he photographed the entire document.

While the spy believed the report to be vital, the next regular drop for his Soviet handler wouldn't be until Monday evening. Alternatively, he could risk setting up an emergency transfer. After weighing the pros and cons he decided to wait for his regular drop on Monday. It was, as it turned out, another providential decision.

****

The CIA's Alpha Team was getting frustrated. Searching for the IDC hit squad in Anchorage was like hunting blindfolded. No one had been able to provide them with either descriptions or location of their quarry. They didn't even possess any evidence the IDC team had arrived in Anchorage.

They were hunting for a team of professional assassins whose purposes included remaining undetected. The only way to spot them was to look for a team of three men conducting clandestine surveillance. The only bright spot was they knew the target was Major Jacob Kelly.

Carson's satellite phone chirped. He answered wearily, "Carson here."

"Roger, we've found them!" It was Skip, reporting on Baker Team's progress in Fairbanks. "They're staying at the Holiday Inn close to Eielson. I've got them under surveillance now. If they move, we'll know it."

"Good job, Skip! Do you need any additional assets?"

"Negative, Rog. Jimmy finished checking the highway to Denali, and returned late this afternoon. Mike is done at Eielson. So all four of us are watching them now, by shifts. We should be in good shape. Jimmy rented a helicopter at Fairbanks International, so we can get around quickly when we need to, as long as the weather doesn't get bad. I've set up a watch schedule for tonight. If they try to slip out, we'll see 'em."

"Nice work. Keep your distance. We don't want to spook them. Try to figure out what their plans are, but don't move in. Not yet, anyway."

"Got it. How is it going with Alpha Team?"

"Terrible. Alpha has nothing to go on. We have no idea who the bad guys are, where they are, or what they are up to. We don't have pictures, nothing. Alpha is pretty frustrated right now. I am going to stay down here with these guys to help out. Sounds like you boys can manage by yourselves."

"We can, RC. I'll keep you informed. Good luck."

****

Bill Jensen buckled his seatbelt and asked the stewardess for a pillow. If he was lucky he'd sleep for most of the flight. He was on a TWA non-stop from LA to Washington and he was exhausted. Just before drifting off, he wondered how his wife Susan was getting along in Texas. Her sister's birthday had been today, and he had forgotten to call and wish her well. He'd do it tomorrow.

Meanwhile, it was late in the evening at Langley when Sam Bergman finally tossed the thick intelligence briefing on the state of the Soviet Union's economy onto his "finished reading" stack. It did not take a genius to see that the USSR was headed for turbulent waters economically. They were trying to match the Reagan build up, ship for ship. While the United States was spending itself into a larger budget deficit, the effect on its capitalist, market-based economy was electric. Everything, including tax revenue, was increasing. Not so in the Soviet Union. In the centrally planned socialist economy, the increased demand did not result in increased profit, but was an added—and resented—burden on already unproductive manufacturing and industrial sectors. It was like asking a patient on a ventilator to do jumping jacks. Bergman wondered how long it would take before something gave way.

As he locked away confidential materials, preparing to call it a night, he noticed a sealed envelope on his desk that he had overlooked. It was from Wally, the friend he had enlisted to hack the Anchorage telephone company's records in order to learn whom Major Kelly had called from the office supply store in Anchorage just before giving himself up.

Tearing open the envelope, he sat down and pulled out the handwritten note. Wally had found the number, all right. Sam was surprised to see that it had a northern Virginia area code. He was also miffed that his friend had not taken the obvious next step to find out who the number belonged to but instead had written a little note, *Call me about this.*

That's odd. Oh well—one more task for tomorrow, he thought as he stuck the note in his pocket, picked up his briefcase and headed for the door.

Chapter 8

Saturday, October 10, 1987: 0800 hours, local time
Langley, VA

Saturday morning dawned grey and sullen over the Eastern Seaboard. The high pressure system responsible for the sparkling, clear, cold mornings of the past week was now over the northern Atlantic, and a low pressure system was skating up the coast pushing moisture and rain ahead of it. Sam Bergman clambered out of his car realizing that the number of Saturdays available to visit Gettysburg before winter was diminishing, which to his somewhat backward way of thinking meant the lovely Evelyn Stinson wouldn't have any reason to go out with him. It hadn't occurred to him that she might like to accompany him pretty much anywhere. As he entered the CIA headquarters he decided, somewhat lamely, maybe Gettysburg wasn't all that bad in the winter.

His thoughts turned to business and he pushed the Stinson girl out of his thoughts as he unlocked his office. He needed to call Wally about that phone number. *Why the mystery? The man could have simply written the information on the paper and saved me another phone call!*

After grabbing a cup of coffee Sam picked up the phone. No one answered at Wally's desk, so he pulled out the CIA directory and dialed the man at home.

"Hey, Wally! Sam Bergman. I got your note about the phone number you tracked down for me. What's all the mystery about?"

"Sam, it's Saturday. You aren't in the office, are you?"

"Of course I am. Why not? I was wondering why you weren't!" Bergman knew what was coming and he gritted his teeth and closed his eyes. He didn't want to talk about it.

"I'm not in the office today because I have a life. Something you need, by the way." The voice on the other end of the phone was patient and caring, Sam grudgingly admitted to himself.

"I have a life," Sam insisted.

"Yes, I know, and it's called the 'CIA,'" Wally chided. "You need a *real* life, Sam. How many Saturdays have you worked since we went to the Baltimore Orioles game together in July?"

How can this guy have such an incredible capacity to make me feel guilty, Sam wondered to himself, *I'm glad he doesn't know how many Sundays I've worked since then*. Sam responded, "Well . . . all of them, I guess."

"Thank you for making my point. You need a life."

"Thanks for your opinion, but I like my life. We can take this up next week, Wally, but I have a question. You scribbled on the bottom of your note that I was to call you about this number. Thanks, by the way, for getting it for me."

"No problem. The phone company's computer system in Anchorage has a security hole I could drive a truck through. Piece of cake. But I didn't think it wise to write down the name of the person who owns that phone number."

"Why is that?" asked Bergman, beginning to feel a little uncomfortable.

"Because it belongs to someone you know, and I don't want to say their name over this line. It's a professor at a local university."

Bergman thought for a moment, remembering that the arresting officer had testified that Kelly called a man named Bill. He sat up straight at his desk. *Oh, no.* "Um, not that professor, surely!"

"The very same."

"You are kidding, right?"

"No, I am not, and your response tells me that we are thinking about the same professor."

Sam thought the conversation was getting just a bit ridiculous, but he knew CIA policies prevented Wally from naming the the individual in question on an unsecured line. "Well, right. He's the only prof I know, which narrows it down.

Wow! Okay, thanks, man!"

"Anytime, pal. Listen, next time you want to spend a Saturday living, give me a buzz. There are all sorts of interesting things normal people do on Saturdays. I realize you wouldn't know, but I'd be glad to show you the ropes."

"Thanks, Wally! Next time I want to be, uh, normal, I'll give you a call. Bye!" Sam hung up the phone before his friend could come back with another silly response. *I'm not spending my next Saturday out with you, Wally*, he thought. *There's this drop-dead gorgeous NSA employee I'm going to spend it with. She's a lot better looking than you, my friend!*

****

Randy, of the CIA Baker Team in Fairbanks, was in trouble and he didn't even know it. The youngest member of the team, he was not two months out of CIA training and this was his first real surveillance assignment. He hadn't been in the spy business long enough to understand his own body and its responses to the long hours, strange temperatures, and other challenges surrounding clandestine operations. This fact was about to become clear to him.

It was a minor mistake, really. He had a thermos of coffee with him and was working on his second cup while he kept an eye on Room 107 of the rather old and shabby Holiday Inn. It was 0427 hours and very cold. Randy was sitting in a rented Jeep Cherokee XJ about one hundred fifty feet down the street from the hotel. In ninety minutes he would be relieved by Skip. Mike was on a similar four-hour shift monitoring the radio back at their hotel, which served as their base of operations. If their targets emerged from the Holiday Inn, a radio call from Randy would have the rest of Baker Team up and ready to move within a few minutes.

He couldn't run the engine to keep warm—that would make his surveillance obvious. He couldn't keep the windows rolled up either, because his body heat and the moisture from his breath would cause them to fog up, not only giving away the fact that he was in the car but also obscuring his vision. So the two windows facing away from the hotel were rolled down about one third of the way with the consequence that he was shivering with the deep Alaska cold. The coffee warmed up his insides, but it also made him sleepy. In another twenty minutes or so the caffeine would kick in, but at the moment he could hardly keep his eyes open. He told himself that, though sleepy, he was alert. But he wasn't—in fact, all his attention was consumed with merely *staying* awake; he had precious little left for actual surveillance or situational awareness.

For instance, he didn't notice the shadow flitting from tree to tree behind his vehicle, drawing ever closer. If he'd been watching closely, he might have seen the momentary glint of the gun as the street light hit it. Since two of the car's windows were open, he might have heard the dull metallic clink as the shadow quietly mated a sound suppressor to the custom-made barrel of an old but well-maintained M1911A1 Colt pistol. But Randy was aware of none of these things. He was focused on just keeping his eyes open.

"Son, what are you doing out here in the cold? Looks to me like you're spying on somebody." The voice was barely audible, but it registered like a thunderclap in Randy's ears. He snapped his head around and found himself looking straight into the .45 caliber opening on the business end of a pistol. In the dim light he recognized his assailant's face as one of the assassins on the IDC team he was supposed to be surveilling. Suddenly he was wide awake.

Randy was inexperienced, but not dumb. He didn't move a muscle, though he was dying inside. He stared into that awful little black hole. He'd never before considered it in these terms, but that little hole could deliver a pretty significant dose of eternity in just one bloom of flame. The thought made him shiver even more.

"Mister," he said with just the slightest tremor in his voice, "I'd be mighty obliged if you would relax that trigger finger just a smidgen."

"Put both hands on the steering wheel, son," the older man commanded. When Randy complied, he continued, "Very good. Now, reach over here and unlock this door. And do it very slowly." After Randy unlocked the door, the man climbed into the passenger side of the jeep. In all the maneuvering not once did his eyes or pistol move from Randy's face.

"I've been watching you for an hour or so. You're obviously conducting surveillance, even if you are doing a pretty lousy job of it. I want to know who you are spying on, and why. If you can satisfy me, I might send you on your way with everything intact but your pride. If not, well, too bad for you. So we're going to play a little game. I'll ask a question and you'll answer me immediately. If not, I'll pull the trigger. Understand?"

Randy nodded, mind racing, trying to remember the guest register he'd looked over yesterday. Unless he could construct a convincing lie he figured he was a dead man. But he also knew from his briefing that IDC hit squads preferred to stay under the radar and not draw attention to themselves by committing crimes unrelated to their contract. *If I can weave a plausible lie*, Randy thought, *I just might survive.*

"Who are you and who do you work for?" the man asked.

"I'm a private investigator and I work for the wife of the man in Room 109," Randy answered, regaining his nerve.

"You're a private eye?" the assassin asked, surprised.

"That's me. Mrs. Edison is afraid that her husband is cheating on her. So I follow him on his business trips. This is the fourth one I have taken. The jerk sells cold weather lubricants. I think he is going to all the airports on the Arctic Circle. So lucky me, I get stuck out in the cold keeping an eye on him. Why in the world couldn't he sell something they need in Hawaii, or the Bahamas?" Randy complained bitterly.

"Amazing." The hit man seemed to be turning things over in his mind. He was silent for a moment and then smiled, "Well, is he clean?"

"So far he's been a real boy scout. I actually think the missus is cheating on him. You know how it is: she wants out of the marriage and she wants to soak him on the way out. Gets his money, and gets her boyfriend, too. It's a miserable, fallen world out there, buddy." Randy shook his head sadly.

"Tell me about it," the stranger said ironically.

"You with the government?" Randy asked, playing dumb and giving the man a means of graceful exit.

The fellow paused, thinking, and then responded, "Yeah. FBI. We've got a job—I mean—an operation going here." The man studied Randy and seemed to be satisfied.

"Well, am I messing you up? I mean, if I am in the way or something I can move a little farther down the street." Randy tried to sound impressed and eager to please.

"No, no, you're fine. I had just been watching you out here and thought you might somehow be connected with the operation we are working on. Had no idea you were a PI." This last brought a sardonic chuckle out of the man's lips. He shook his head and turned to get out of the car.

As the man shut the door, Randy leaned over and said, "Hey, I got another buddy with me on this gig. He relieves me at 0600. Just wanted to let you know."

"Okay, son. It's no problem. If you see me around tomorrow, you've never seen me before. Don't walk up or acknowledge me in any way. I'm working on an important case here. Do you understand? Stay out of my hair."

"Got it, Mister. I'll stay clear."

The man disappeared into the shadows. Randy wondered how he had gotten out of his hotel room without being seen. *Must have climbed out the back window.* He'd have to report that. The good thing about the confrontation was that they could conduct the hotel surveillance openly, now that they had a cover for it. The bad thing about it was that Randy could not take part in any other surveillance operation on the IDC team. They knew him now, and his alibi would only work once.

Randy had no trouble staying awake the rest of his shift.

****

Sam Bergman sat at his desk, uncertain what to do. The revelation that Major Kelly had placed a call to Dr. Bill Jensen was startling. Sam knew that Jensen was a highly sought-after professor of political science at Georgetown University. He also knew that position was a cover intended to obscure the fact that Jensen was a CIA employee. Among CIA operatives, Jensen's name was near legend. What connection did the man have to Kelly?

Sam wondered if Jensen had been turned. After a moment's reflection he discarded that possibility. If Kelly was working for the bad guys he would never expose another spy operating under such deep cover in such a careless way. No, Jensen was probably just a friend whose phone number happened to be in Kelly's thinking at the time he was arrested. Perhaps Kelly thought Jensen had some political connections that might be helpful in getting him off his felony charges.

Bergman picked up the phone and dialed Jensen's office in the CIA. No answer. *Where are all these people today? Just because it's Saturday does not mean the world of intelligence grinds to a halt!* He tried Jensen's home number and got no answer there either.

He puttered around his office for another hour or so and then booked tomorrow's flight back to Anchorage. He needed to be there early Monday morning for another joint interrogation of Kelly with Jim Stewart. After filling his briefcase with reading for the long flight out and back, he locked up and headed for home.

****

Clayton sketched the airport layout on a legal pad and talked as he drew. "These are the commercial passenger facilities for the big airlines. Over here are the general aviation hangars and facilities. The Beech is parked right here, at the end of this row of hangars. You can enter from the highway here and get to the passenger side of the general aviation parking lots without going through any security. However, if you are going to get a vehicle into the hangar area you have to go through either one of these two gates. The main gate, here, is manned from 0600 until 2200 by a security guard. After hours it is locked and well lit, and has a security camera on it.

"There is another gate, a manually operated aircraft owner's gate, right here, that has an Ingersoll-Rand digital lock on it. It is available twenty-four hours a day, and there are no security cameras on it. I watched for an hour this morning and both gates were in use. There is a parking area on the outside of the gate, so with a little work we could read off the access code by sitting in the parking lot with a pair of binoculars.

"I posed as a prospective owner considering renting tie-down and hangar space. I lounged around the general aviation facilities and struck up a couple conversations with other owners. The airport security is pretty lax. They are relying on locks and gates and limited access. For instance, there is only one scheduled security patrol of the general aviation hangar and tie-down areas. It takes place between midnight and one in the morning.

"Bottom line: it will be easy to get in as long as we get the access code for the owner's gate."

"Great, Clayton. Okay, Pat, what do you propose?" Although Howard was the leader of the three, Pat was the best thinker and planner of the team.

"It's pretty simple, really. I will calculate the amount of fuel needed to get them to the roughest country between here and Eielson. We'll pump the tanks dry and refill them with just that much fuel. And finally, I'll monkey with the fuel gauges and the wing tanks, so that the gauges and the dipstick will both show a full load of fuel on board. So, it *will* be an accident—a 'pilot error' accident. They'll run out of fuel over the mountains and crash. There won't be any survivors." Pat smirked. It was a good plan and he knew it.

In Pat's world, people were just an annoyance. He was contemptuous of most, including his present companions. He considered himself to be unusually intelligent and took great pleasure in demonstrating it. Companions were but a means to an end: they were the foils against which he could display his superior mind. Other than that, people were a nuisance. He tolerated them only because he needed an audience; brilliance such as his deserved appreciation and the role of those around him was to appreciate him.

Clayton frowned, "What if they fill the tanks after we do the plane?"

"They won't. Trooper policy is to refuel aircraft immediately upon landing, on the idea that they never know when they will need to go back up in a hurry. So the Beech is sitting there right now with full tanks. The pilot will do his pre-flight walk around before he takes off, and he'll check his fuel level with the dipstick, but he already knows he won't have to fill up. So we don't have to worry about somebody messing with the plane after I'm done with it." Pat sat back with a smile.

Howard nodded. "It's a good plan. What will you need?"

"Well, we need to rent a pickup truck with a large capacity transfer tank, plus an electric pump, meter, and hoses. We'll need the key code for the gate, and I have to pick up some miscellaneous hardware to jimmy the fuel gauges and wing tanks. That's about it."

"Okay. Clayton, you do the rental. If the folks see you again at the airport they might get suspicious, so I'll get the key code. Pat, you buy your widgets. How much time will the job require once we get through the gate?"

Pat scratched his chin and thought for a moment. "If you guys can handle the fuel transfer, I'd say we're looking at a maximum of two hours."

"Perfect. The forecast is calling for fog and snow tonight. That will cloak our activities, but also make it harder to spot a security patrol. Can't be helped. Let's plan on going through the gate at 0200."

****

Technical Sergeant Matt Loeb was weary. In addition to his regular duties, he was working on the special surveillance project for which CIA agent Bill Jensen had recruited him. After a long Saturday spent reviewing the videotaped record of activities in the Eielson Intelligence Section, Loeb had arrived at two conclusions. First, that it takes eight hours of watching to view eight hours' worth of surveillance tapes. It was a one-to-one correspondence, something that had not occurred to him when he had taken on the assignment. He'd spent a boring day reviewing Thursday's and half of Friday's tapes.

The second conclusion was that there wasn't any hanky-panky going on in the Intelligence Section. After watching twelve hours of dull videotape, Loeb concluded that the six men in the office were all dedicated to doing their job. Nothing on the tapes raised the slightest bit of suspicion.

Matthew Loeb was trained for the wizardry of computer networking and system maintenance. He wasn't trained for surveillance. He wearily decided that he'd had enough for one day, and he had not even begun the after-hours sets of tapes, reviewing what should be an empty office. *If today's movie was boring, that one's going to be stultifying!* As he was preparing to unload the current tape, which was halfway through the Friday duty hours, he accidentally hit the HI-SPEED button. He had assumed it was simply a fast forward and so had never tried it, but now he watched in fascination as the tape began playing with a very good picture at sixteen times normal speed. There was no audio, but the picture was clear—if somewhat jerky— as the subjects were displayed at high speed moving around the office. Loeb hit the STOP button, suddenly furious with himself.

"I can't believe I have just *wasted* TWELVE HOURS today watching this stupid tape at normal speed. WHAT A WASTE!" he growled to his empty office. For a moment he had to restrain himself from jumping up and throwing things. Time was precious and he hated to squander it. And he had just wasted a *full* day. He cursed himself for his pride. Jensen had offered to show him how to use the specialized video player that had been air-freighted from Langley to replace the one that had arrived damaged, but Loeb had condescendingly assured the CIA officer that he had no trouble using technical electronic equipment. Now, he angrily reminded himself, because of his youthful arrogance he had just wasted a day doing the equivalent of watching paint dry.

Calming down, he calculated that watching the final four hours of Friday's tape would take only fifteen minutes at high speed. He sat back down at his desk and decided to redeem at least part of the day by finishing up the tape that had been recorded during business hours on Friday.

Hitting the HI-SPEED button once again, he settled down

to watch. Fifteen minutes scrolled by rapidly, especially compared with the hours of tedious viewing he had done before discovering the high-speed function. When the tape was done, he sat back thinking, vaguely dissatisfied. There was something odd about what he had just watched, but he could not identify exactly what. It was kind of like trying to remember a dream: the image vanishes in the mist of your memory as soon as you attempt to concentrate on it.

Intrigued, Loeb rewound the Friday tape to about midday and watched it again in high speed. This time he was positive that he had seen something, but once again was unable to put his finger on it. He looked at his watch. *One more time couldn't hurt,* he decided. Rewind. Hi-speed.

This time he was closer to realizing what he had seen. There was a man in the tapes, a chain smoker. Something about his behavior was oddly repetitive. Sergeant Loeb decided to watch one more time, and focus on that man. Rewind. Hi-speed.

"*GOTCHA!*" Matt shouted as he punched the STOP button. It was as clear as a bell in high speed. He had missed it completely at regular speed.

The man in the video was chain-smoking. Every time the subject reached for a fresh cigarette, he would pull a page off a stack of papers on the right side of his desk, lean on his elbows over the document as he used his lighter to light his cigarette, and then move the page to the bottom of the stack.

Matt rewound the tape to the beginning of the business day, and watched again in high speed. When the subject arrived in the office, his desk was clear. Matt watched him move about for the first hour, reading and filing documents and doing some writing. Then the subject got up and entered the secure-room, retrieving a batch of papers from the teletype. He carefully stacked it on the right side of his desk and then for the remainder of the day worked through the entire stack, changing pages each time he lit up a smoke.

Matt hit STOP, and sat back with a smile on his face. All weariness was gone. He had done it! He had found the spy! He had just watched the subject photograph an entire classified report, one page at a time, and no one else in the office had noticed a thing.

He looked at his watch, suddenly motivated. Making a decision, Loeb called his wife.

"Hey, babe, it's me."

"Matt, where in the world are you? I have been waiting supper, and it's getting dried out!"

"Listen, sweetie, I am really sorry. I am working late on a special project. You guys go ahead and eat without me. I won't be home for several more hours."

"Well, you should have called an hour ago," complained his wife.

"You're right. I should have. I just got lost in what I was doing."

"All right," she grudgingly offered. "But please do call the next time this happens. The kids and I had no idea where you were, and I couldn't get you at your desk."

"I'm not at my desk, I'm in the main administration building. Got a pencil? I'll give you the number where you can reach me."

After he hung up, Loeb watched all the after-hours tapes at high speed. None had anything of interest on them. Having finished all the tapes, he called Jensen at his home number but no one answered. Not wanting to leave a message, Loeb hung up, mounted fresh tapes for the night's surveillance, and headed home.

Chapter 9

Light snow was falling as predicted, and there was a thick low-lying fog when the three IDC assassins drove to the general aviation owner's gate at the Anchorage Airport. Clayton jumped out of the truck, entered the stolen access code, and then slid the gate open. Five minutes later they had located the Alaska State Troopers' aircraft. The fog was so thick they could not see the hangars though they were close by. The parking area lights appeared as ghostly halos, floating in the mist.

The three men knew their tasks and got to work as soon as they exited the truck. Within minutes Clayton and Howard were transferring JP-4 fuel from the C90's tanks to the transfer tank in the truck while Pat was removing the access panels to the fuel level sender for the nacelle tanks, the main tanks, and each wing tank. After carefully removing the capacitance-type fuel probes, the saboteur fitted them with new spacers to place the electrodes in closer proximity. The result was an increase in capacitance that made an empty tank register as full on the pilot's gauges. He was counting on the violence of the crash to conceal his work. After checking the probes with a capacitance meter he reinstalled them.

By the time Pat had jimmied the senders the other two men had pumped the tanks dry. He metered just enough fuel back into the tanks to get the aircraft to the roughest part of the Alaska Range, a rugged semicircle of mountains halfway between Fairbanks and Anchorage. Mount McKinley is the highest peak in this range, rising to over 20,300 feet above sea level. Running out of fuel over the Alaska Range was a recipe for certain death, and the crash site would be very difficult to locate and access.

The final act of sabotage was to insert a thin-walled plastic cylinder into each fuel tank filler neck. Each cylinder was sealed on the bottom and cut to precisely the correct length, fitting into the filler neck like a sleeve. Pat carefully poured enough JP-4 into each cylinder so that the pilot's dipstick would show the tank's fuel level as full. When the pilot climbed into the cockpit and powered on the aircraft's electrical system, the tank gauges—like the dipstick—would falsely read as full. If there was a fire following the crash, as Pat hoped, it would consume the plastic cylinders. The trace elements remaining would be misidentified as coming from other plastic parts in the aircraft. Pat buttoned up his work and the aircraft was ready to go.

It was a perfect job. They encountered no one. Having worn surgical gloves for the entire procedure, they left no fingerprints. The morning snow plow would eliminate all tire tracks. There was not a shred of evidence placing them at the site.

The hit squad climbed wearily into the truck and returned to their hotel. In a few hours they would fly out of Anchorage, their job complete.

****

The Piper Cub skimmed the Laotian jungle at treetop level. Jensen adjusted his headphones to better hear what the pilot was saying. Amused with himself, he realized the pilot wasn't saying anything; instead the sound coming through his headset was that of a phone ringing. *How incongruous*, he thought.

The pilot descended rapidly into a clearing and executed a perfect short-field landing. US Army Rangers ran from the brush and surrounded the plane, establishing a secure perimeter. Jensen yanked off his headset and grabbed his backpack, preparing to exit the plane. He turned to thank the pilot, who said "The call is for you, sir, on line one."

With a start Bill Jensen woke up in his bed, the dedicated

secure phone ringing angrily on his nightstand. As he picked it up he looked at his alarm clock: 0630 hours.

"Jensen," he mumbled into the phone.

"Dr. Jensen, this is Sam Bergman, CIA. Sorry to wake you, sir, but I'm about to board a flight for Anchorage and don't know when I can next reach you."

"Hello, Mr. Bergman. Oh, wait. Yes! I remember you, Sam. You produced that excellent analysis of the impact of the faltering Soviet economy on their military. I was there at the War College when you gave the lecture last fall. Terrific job, and I agree with your analysis. Now, what can I do for you? It is a little early, and it is Sunday morning, but you've got my attention."

"Sir, I am wo—"

"*Bill*, Sam—call me Bill. You young bucks at the Agency make me feel like an old-timer with all this 'sir' business. Please call me Bill."

"Fine, thank you, er, Bill. Anyway, I'm working on an unusual investigation in Anchorage, and one of the subjects of the investigation called you last Monday. Do you know a Major Jacob Kelly?"

"Sam, I didn't know you were in Operations. I thought you were an Analysis guy." Jensen deflected the question as he considered how to answer Bergman.

"I *am* an analyst. I was thrown into this case because it involves the Soviet Union. Unfortunately I can't really get into that."

"Yes, of course. I understand. Now, what can I do for you?"

Bergman repeated his question, "Jacob Kelly called you last Monday. Do you know him?"

"Yes, Sam, I do. His late father was one of my best friends. Why do you ask?"

"He's the subject of our investigation, as I said. Why did he call?"

"Well, I wasn't here to take the call so he left it on my answering machine. It was something about some trouble he was in, pulling a gun on somebody, and some other stuff. Apparently the son isn't made of the same stuff the father was. I'm not interested in getting involved with him. I really don't know why he called me. I've no intention of returning his call." The lie made him uncomfortable. It was a necessary aspect of his job, but he hated it. But Bill Jensen was not ready to tip his hand to the Project *Snowbird* group. By Jensen's reckoning it was likely that Bill Ott—a member of *Snowbird*—was the spy who had delivered Kelly's flight plan to the Russians.

"That's probably wise, Bill, probably wise."

"Is there anything else?"

"Nope. I'm terribly sorry I woke you up. Enjoy your Sunday."

Jensen hung up the phone and sat on the side of the bed, thinking. After years of working in Operations, including a long stint in the early seventies doing things in Southeast Asia that would never be public knowledge, he had developed reliable intuition concerning when a case was about to break wide open. He was experiencing that feeling now. *If I was a bettin' man, I'd say this thing will be resolved inside of a week.*

Rubbing the back of his neck, he looked at the clock again —0650 hours. He groaned and fought the urge to crawl back in bed. He'd been burning both ends of the candle and he was whipped. *No matter. I'll grab a nap later this afternoon. If I hustle I can make the early service at church.* Jensen got up and padded toward the shower. He didn't enjoy being a bachelor and couldn't wait until his wife returned from Texas.

****

After hanging up the call to Jensen, Sam dialed Evelyn Stinson's office at the NSA on his Agency satellite phone. He knew she wouldn't be there, but he didn't want to risk waking her up at home. Plus, it was easier to ask her on a date through her answering machine.

"This is Stinson. Please leave a message."

The curt recording nearly caused Sam to lose his nerve. He took a deep breath and plunged ahead, "Hi Evelyn, this is Sam Bergman. With the CIA." He added that last bit convinced it was presumptuous to assume she would remember him by name. Sam took another deep breath and continued, "Just wondering if you might be available Saturday for a stroll around Gettysburg, and then dinner. I'll be out of the office Monday and Tuesday, I'm headed for Anchorage on a project with the Agency. I'll contact you when I get back in town. Bye."

He was trembling a bit when he put the phone on the hook. He shook his head, angry with himself. He had no problems working with women at the Agency or elsewhere. It was just when he got to the point of asking one on a date that he became so rattled. If she turned him down he hoped she'd make it easy on him and leave the rejection on *his* answering machine. Always easier to talk to a machine than a real person.

Looking down the concourse he saw that they had begun boarding his plane. He picked up his carry-on and hurried to the gate.

****

Jensen was about to watch the Redskins game on TV when his home phone rang. He was expecting to hear from his wife and picked up the receiver eagerly. "Hello?"

"Bill, this is Matt Loeb, in Fairbanks."

"Hey, Matthew. What's up?" He was disappointed it wasn't Susan, but he could sense the young man was excited about something.

"I've got great news. I've found—"

"WAIT, Matt!" Jensen exclaimed. "This is not a secure line, son! Just speak in vague generalities. No names! Understand? Someone else might be listening in."

"Oh! Huh. Never thought of that. Okay. Well, sir, I found what you were looking for," he said, "and it's not the one we were expecting."

"But we have solid, um, reasons for thinking as we did. I can't imagine that the data was wrong!" Jensen was perplexed.

"Well, sir, it may not be *either-or.* I suppose it could be *both-and.*"

"Yes, I suppose that's possible. In fact, the original theory had two rather than one."

"But sir, there's something else. The, um, papers that exposed the deed, sir, well, we don't want them to get away from us. They're pretty important. We can't just sit on this is what I am trying to say, sir."

"Okay, I'll get a team on it right away, Matt. Meanwhile, you sit tight and continue doing what you're doing. Oh, and Matt, is there any chance you could review our original, um, data? That seemed pretty conclusive."

"I'll get right on it. But when you see what I have seen, sir, you'll understand why I am certain about the other. It's pretty obvious."

Jensen hung up the phone and wondered what his assistant at Eielson had seen that was so obvious. The young man was clearly excited.

A roar from the television set brought Jensen's attention back to the game. Kickoff. The Redskins had run the ball back to the opponent's forty-five yard line. The professor sighed. It looked as though it had the fixings to be a great game—but a game he wouldn't get to see after all.

He turned the set off, went into his study, and dialed Roger Carson's number using his dedicated secure line.

"Carson here."

"Hey, Rog, it's me. What's the latest?"

"Hi, Bill. I'm still with Alpha Team in Anchorage. We've had zero success locating the IDC boys. The research team at the Firm hasn't given us anything. It's pretty frustrating."

"Keep looking, Roger. We can't expect you to do any more than what you are doing. I knew we didn't stand much of a chance, but it was worth a shot. Still is."

"Yes, sir. We'll keep at it. Baker Team is watching their suspects but Randy and Skip have both been compromised."

"What happened to them?" Jensen asked.

"One of the IDC goons spotted Randy on surveillance. He managed to get up to the car last night without being seen and put a gun in Randy's face. Randy convinced him that he was a PI keeping an eye on a traveling salesman for the man's wife. It was a pretty close thing. What probably saved Randy's life in the end was that his surveillance work was too amateurish to peg him as a government agent. Sounds like Randy did a pretty good acting job. Anyway, ninety minutes later Skip relieved Randy. We have to assume the hit squad saw him too. So we can't risk using Randy and Skip where they might be seen by the bad guys, or we'll spook 'em."

"Well, Rog, that actually might be providential."

"There you go again, Sunday school boy. Everything is providential to you."

"Believe it or not, Roger, you are correct. Everything *is* providentially controlled by the hand of God. But I don't have time to give you a Sunday school lesson on it right now. My man at Eielson has managed to uncover a spy, and I need somebody to keep an eye on him. Skip and Randy could handle that."

"Huh. Maybe that *is* providential."

"You'll need to contact Sergeant Matthew Loeb at Eielson. I'll give you his phone number. He has been detached by the base commander to me. Nobody else there knows what he is doing, so don't blow his cover. You're to keep the spy under surveillance whenever he leaves his building. Your mission is to watch for any drops he might be making and retrieve the material before his handler can get to it, and secondly to keep him from fleeing. That second should not be a problem, since he has no idea we're on to him. If you need more men you can call up several more from the Seattle office."

"If we cop his drop, his handler will know he's been made. Then he *will* be a flight risk," Roger objected.

"I know, Rog. But I think this thing will be wrapping up within seventy-two hours or so, and we'll be able to arrest him. But the stuff he's had access to is quite sensitive and we need to stop the flow now."

"So why not reel him in now? Why wait?"

"We think he might be a part of a small network of bad guys there at Eielson, and we want to have a little more time to ID the others. Plus, his spying is related to the Jacob Kelly affair. If we yank him too early it complicates that case. So we have to leave him in place as long as possible."

Carson sighed. "Okay, boss. I'll send Skip and Randy to keep an eye on him, and I'll call up two more agents from the Seattle office. By the way, Bill, when this is over and we get back to Langley, I think Randy needs a little more training and mentoring in field work before he's ready to play against the big boys. His inexperience nearly cost him his life and put the mission at risk."

"I'll trust your judgment, Roger."

Forty-five minutes later, Bill Jensen was boarding a flight to Sea-Tac, where he would transfer to a flight bound for Fairbanks. His intuition that the case was beginning to wrap up was stronger than ever.

****

Immortal, invisible, God only wise,
In light inaccessible hid from our eyes,
Most blessed, most glorious, the Ancient of Days,
Almighty, victorious, Thy great name we praise.

Unresting, unhasting, and silent as light,
Nor wanting, nor wasting, Thou rulest in might;
Thy justice like mountains high soaring above
Thy clouds, which are fountains of goodness and love.

To all life Thou givest, to both great and small;
In all life Thou livest, the true life of all;
We blossom and flourish as leaves on the tree,
And wither and perish, but naught changeth Thee.

Great Father of glory, pure Father of light,
Thine angels adore Thee, all veiling their sight;
All laud we would render: O help us to see
'Tis only the splendor of light hideth Thee!

As the singing ended Galina sat down with the hymnbook open on her lap. The hymn, *Immortal, Invisible*, by W. Chalmers Smith, was a challenge to translate with its esoteric vocabulary. And yet she had an intuitive sense for the grandeur and majesty of what she had just sung, even if she could not completely comprehend it.

The church of Galina's hosts, composed mainly of Chinese-American believers, was meeting on this particular Sunday evening for joint worship and fellowship with its sister church from across the bay. That church was composed of a wild mix of Caucasian, African, Japanese, and Korean believers, many of whom were military families connected with area naval installations. The two churches met together for worship four or five times a year. Leveraging on their rich diversity, they conducted a worship service and fellowship meal with the theme of "every tongue, tribe, and nation," drawn from the book of Revelation. It was a favorite high point in the life of both churches.

Galina was not a believer in Christ, nor a religious person in general. She was an intentional atheist who took her metaphysical beliefs very seriously. Galina did not wind up at atheism by default. She had carefully examined almost all the major world religions and found reasons to reject each one. There were but two that remained—Christianity and Judaism —and she had been studying both for about a year. She had read through the entire Bible and was currently working her way through several books by C. S. Lewis about Christianity. Galina remained unconvinced, but she was not yet ready to pronounce her exploration complete. She found herself strangely drawn to these people, their music, their worship, and their ancient book, the Bible. If pressed, she would be unable to account for why. Nevertheless, the attraction was there.

Both her benefactors in China and her hosts in America were Presbyterian believers. While the customs of worship of the two churches were different, she felt a vibrant continuity in the spirit and belief of both bodies of believers. So far her impressions remained intuitive: she could not categorize or classify what she was experiencing. But the sense of welcome and even homecoming was undeniable.

When the worship service was over the colorful group of people moved into a large hall set up for a meal. Each participant had been encouraged to come in their national dress—which for the Americans meant jeans—and to bring a dish of food representative of their homeland. The sights and smells were wonderful and the babble of multiple languages filled the air. Galina found herself sitting across from a friendly, middle-aged couple.

"Hi! I don't recall seeing you before. My name is Roger, and this is my wife Susan."

"My name is Galina Toporova. I've only been in the country for a week or so."

"Oh, really? Welcome to America! Where are you from?" Susan's warm, motherly tone put Galina at ease.

"I have come from Siberia by way of China. I have applied for asylum in America."

As the trio chatted, Galina learned that Roger was a captain in the US Navy and serving as a liaison to the Royal Australian Navy. Susan was a stay-at-home mom who had a side business as a caterer. Over dinner Galina's own tale came out. The Bates' sympathy and genuine interest caused the young woman to abandon her reserve, and she shared her story freely.

"I am so sorry to hear that your brother died," Susan said. "It must have been terrible for you."

"Boris was all that anyone could ask for in a brother. He was a wonderful person, and I miss him terribly."

"Why did you leave the Soviet Union?" asked Roger.

"My brother and I managed a timber cooperative. Last winter I met an American pilot who had escaped from a detention center in western Siberia. He was injured when fleeing from the military and the KGB, and we took him in and hid him during the winter, while he healed. In the spring the KGB discovered we were hiding him. He barely escaped, but I was caught and deported to China."

Roger's eyes narrowed, "You say an *American* pilot?"

"Yes, an Air Force major."

"And he was being held in a deten— OUCH!"

Susan gave Roger a swift kick, as she said sweetly, "Rog, dear, this is not an interrogation. Let Galina finish her story."

An awkward silence followed until Susan asked the young woman, "What became of your friend, the American?"

At that, Galya dropped her head. When she spoke again, it was barely above a whisper. "I don't know. He was trying to return to America. He told me he would come back for me. And now he won't know where I am." She struggled to hold back the tears.

"You must love him very much."

She nodded, unable to speak. Susan squeezed her hands, comforting her.

Later that evening Roger Bates reflected upon the conversation. If the story the Toporova girl had told him was true, there was a stranded Air Force pilot wandering around Siberia trying to get back to the US. He decided to give his Air Force buddy, General Jim Franks, a call in the morning. Franks would know what to do with the information.

****

Jacob Kelly was feeling increasingly like a caged animal. His worst fears were coming true. Several times during the week Agent Jim Stewart had come to interrogate him. Always the same questions, always asked in different ways and different sequences. Kelly knew the FBI agent was trying to catch him in an inconsistency or contradiction. About mid-week the agent's attitude had changed, and Jake realized it was because his assessment had changed. Stewart no longer believed him and the interrogations became more aggressive. Now he was being treated as a traitor, a Soviet plant. If nothing changed, he could expect to be tried on charges of treason.

Twice he had been questioned by an Air Force officer, Major William Ott. The man had been positively hostile and made no attempt to hide his feelings. Ott told him he would be transferred on Monday or Tuesday to an Air Force brig at Eielson. That, Jake knew, would be the beginning of the end.

When he'd been incarcerated by the Soviets it had not been as bad. They were the enemy and he could rely upon his hate, his thoughts of revenge. He could present a defiant posture. But not now: these were his countrymen, this was his country. He could neither hate them nor dream of vengeance against them. His interrogators were simply doing their job, pursuing allegiance to the same oath he'd taken to protect the country and the Constitution from all enemies.

He had heard nothing from his friend Bill Jensen. *What has happened? Jensen believed me, promised to help me. Where is he?* Jake knew anything could have happened. His friend could have gotten into an auto accident and be lying in a hospital somewhere, unconscious. The man could have keeled over from a heart attack. *Or maybe Bill really doesn't believe me?*

As hope diminished his depression grew. Jake began to think about escape. *Perhaps during the transfer.* He would effectively be a man without a country: no legal standing in any other land and sought by the police in his own. As he weighed this, his thoughts turned to the rugged Snake River country near the Kelly family's summer cottage. He could go there, find an uninhabited corner of the National Forest and simply disappear from humanity, living off the land.

But what of Galina? He'd promised to go back for her. How would that be possible if he was on the run from everybody? For only the second or third time in his life Jake was overcome with despair.

****

"Comrade Geredin, I would like a minute of your time." Another meeting of the committee was breaking up, and General Patrikeyev had followed Geredin out.

"Well, Comrade General, I am here and you are here and I am no longer able to move quickly enough to get away. Thus, you may have as many minutes of my time as it takes me to hobble to my car."

Though blunt it was not said in a spiteful way. *Geredin's problem is, after all, really with Chernikov and not with me*, Patrikeyev thought philosophically. He watched the old man shuffle painfully before responding. "*Spasibo*, Comrade. I thought you might appreciate an update on the situation with the Air Force major. One that was not filtered through your people."

"Indeed, General. I might as well have it filtered by you and *your* people. What have you to say? What of Major Kelly, a man sufficiently skilled to avoid not only our army and our navy, but your assassins as well?"

The old man's sources were better than he had thought, Patrikeyev realized with a shock. Geredin must have spies everywhere. He reminded himself not to underestimate this dangerous, doddering relic of Soviet strong-arm rule.

"The major will be dead within forty-eight hours, Comrade Geredin. I have two teams seeing to it. He's going to be transferred to a different prison facility and will encounter an unfortunate accident during the transfer. And beyond that, we have what the Americans would call an 'insurance policy.' Thanks to a disinformation campaign promulgated by the GRU, the American intelligence community now believes Kelly to be a Soviet spy. If we don't kill him first, the Americans will execute him for treason."

They had reached the old man's car and Geredin, leaning for support on his cane, looked directly at Patrikeyev and said with undisguised disdain, "And I suppose you wish to be congratulated for this, Comrade Patrikeyev? You, whose over-reaching GRU has placed the *Rodina* in such tremendous danger to begin with? You wish me to pat you on the back for your accomplishment?"

General Patrikeyev felt his face go red with anger. He snarled at the decrepit figure before him, "How dare you insult me, Geredin! You voted—the whole committee voted—to pursue Project *Krasnyy Voskhod*. And it has produced good information in several areas of technology. Do not overreach yourself, Comrade! You are not the only one with spies. Yours is not the only voice on the committee, old man!"

Geredin dismissed him with a wave of his hand and said in a conversational tone as he painfully entered into his black Chaika sedan, "It is not my bark, Comrade Patrikeyev, that you should be worrying about." Geredin shut the door and rolled down his window for a parting shot, "It is my bite." Rolling the window up he motioned to his driver, "Take me home, Vasili. I have had enough for one day."

All the way back to his office the commanding officer of the GRU's Ninth Directorate was shaking with rage. The die had been cast. Geredin had never been friendly but now was to be considered an implacable enemy on the committee. Opposition would show up in every direction, ranging from denied GRU missions and projects to slashes in the GRU budget.

In his office he poured a finger of vodka, knocked it back, and poured another, savoring its kick as he nursed his wounded pride. *I'd better put together a contingency plan to deal with Geredin. Perhaps I can arrange an early 'retirement' for the old bear. I'd better double my own security guard at my dacha with men I can trust.*

One more piece of business remained before he left for the day. Picking up the phone, he dialed Chernikov's office at the old detention compound, knowing that the general would still be there.

"Chernikov."

"General Chernikov, it's me, General Patrikeyev. Go secure."

Both men set their encryption devices with the code of the day. After a brief whistling sound, the conversation continued.

"How are things progressing?" Patrikeyev asked.

"Excellent, Comrade General. Thank you for asking. The German chemist broke today! Now he's singing like a Vienna choir boy. I have transmitted information to our scientists in Vladivostok for increasing the specific impulse of our larger launch vehicles by means of a small change in our propellant formulation. It could add as much as five percent to the range of our missiles, I am told."

"Very good, General, very good indeed. I need as much good news as I can get from you."

"Is it Comrade Geredin?" Chernikov sensed the tension in his patron and wondered if Geredin had sufficient clout to make trouble for General Patrikeyev.

"*Da.* He is becoming a problem—a problem I may have to do something about."

"Well, I expect to have more good news for you, sir, in several days. I think that our German scientist can make some 'contributions' to our knowledge in several different areas."

"Excellent. In the meantime I have something for you, General."

"Regarding Jacob Kelly?" Chernikov held his breath. If the American major had been dealt with the problems with Geredin would probably go away on their own.

"*Da.* He should be dead within forty-eight hours. I'll call you as soon as it happens."

Chernikov felt inexpressible relief. If Kelly was terminated the blot on his own record would disappear and all would be right with the world again. "*Spasibo*, Comrade General. I look forward to your call more than I can say."

Chapter 10

The message light was flashing on Evelyn Stinson's telephone when she arrived at her office on Monday morning. She sighed. *I've only just arrived and already people are making demands.* It had been a disappointing weekend. She had hoped to hear from Sam Bergman, had left Saturday and Sunday free in case he called for a date. But he didn't. And so she arrived at her office feeling like she was twenty-eight going on forty.

She powered on her computer and petulantly decided to snub her answering machine. Grabbing her cup she walked down to the canteen. Perhaps she could drown her sorrows in a cup of tea. *Hmm,* she thought ruefully, *as long as I'm binging, might as well do it right.* She looked over the donuts, and bought four of the sweetest, most fattening pastries in the bunch. *You'll pay for this, girl. Gonna have to run an extra two miles tonight.* A few moments later she returned to her desk with her donuts and tea, ready to munch her way through the morning work.

Most of the message traffic waiting for translation came from pretty routine sources. She was disappointed that there were no new messages from source *Leaning Tower.* That would have given her an excuse to contact Sam. *Oh, good grief, girl! Grow up! You went from mild interest last week to infatuation this week! What happened to the disciplined, straight-laced Evelyn?* The self-rebuke snapped her out of her funk, and she buckled down to work. And to the donuts.

It was about 0930 and she'd plowed through the most boring and mundane of the waiting intercepts and was advancing to the more interesting work, when Clifton Edwards knocked on the door of her cubicle. "Hi, CE. Come in. What can I do for you?" She looked at the young man with some amusement. She pointed at a chair and offered him a donut which he gratefully devoured in two bites.

This morning he was wearing a red bandana around his frizzy head, a Grateful Dead T-shirt, and his official uniform of ragged jeans with requisite sandals. It was not quite NSA dress code, but then CE had his own dress code. The man had been one of MIT's most promising products, earning multiple degrees in Mathematics, Computer Science, and Physics. The NSA had pursued him vigorously during the last eight months of his academic work, to no avail. But the frizzy-headed genius finally relented and decided that if the NSA wanted him, well, he was available so long as he could wear whatever he wanted and set his own hours. The result was that CE put in about seventy hours a week because he loved his work, much to the delight of his NSA handlers (one could best describe those with supervisory authority over CE as handlers, not as managers or supervisors—CE simply could not be managed). He'd quickly been recognized as the best cryptologist at the NSA and was gaining a reputation bordering on legendary. Evelyn wondered if they would allow the young genius to report to work nude if the urge struck him. Probably so.

One week ago Evelyn had asked CE to examine an intercept from source *Leaning Tower.* The message contained in the intercept had arrived in triplicate, each copy containing a single spelling error but found in different words. Sam Bergman had been called in to help her assess the intercept. He'd briefly considered whether it was a Soviet attempt to ferret a leak in their own communications, but rejected the idea since the three messages appeared to be bundled together such that each recipient would see all three copies. Evelyn had obtained permission to ask CE to examine the intercept and give them a better understanding of its triplicate nature.

Edwards wiped the donut crumbs from his mouth with the back of his hand (which he then wiped on his jeans), and said, "It took the Moscow people a long time to get me what I wanted. It finally arrived on Friday, but I was working on another project which I wrapped up last night. Anyway, I looked at it this morning and here's the scoop. Those were three separate messages with three separate destinations. They had been packetized by a store-and-forward router and placed in a single digital envelope, probably for a burst transmission. Apparently your source is on the wire somewhere between the store-and-forward router and the next router in the network, which would have separated the messages and sent them on their way to their individual destinations."

Evelyn's head was spinning with the technobabble, but she thought she got the gist of what CE was saying. "You mean, Clifton, that no one person was supposed to see all three messages together?"

"Right. No one was intended to see them bundled. And that's not a security thing, it's just a consequence of the physical transport layer of that part of their network. In other words, the grouping of those three messages into a single packet had nothing to do with intelligence, counterintelligence, or anything else. It was just an artifact of how the routers do their job on that trunk of their network. Those were three separate messages bundled together. It's kind of like the way the mailman does his route. He does not make separate trips from the post office to the mailbox and back again, for every separate mailbox. Instead, he takes a whole bag of mail, the pieces of which are addressed to the various locations on his delivery route. Then he goes from box to box, delivering the mail.

"Now, the fact that we intercepted them as three bundled messages is kind of like Jesse James knocking off the mailman when he is headed from the post office to the first mailbox. Jesse will get all of the mail for everyone on the route, but that does not mean letter A is related to letter B, other than that it's all in the same bag of mail."

"Gotcha. I understand. That last bit about Jesse James helped. Thanks so much, CE. I'll call Sam at the Agency, and give him the news." *Aha!* she thought, *now I have a reason to call him!*

"Anytime, Evelyn. Just keep the donuts coming and I'll do anything you want."

After CE left, Evelyn picked up the phone and dialed the number Sam left for her. She got his answering machine, *"Hello, this is Sam Bergman and I am not in or have stepped away from my desk. If it's an emergency, contact the Division Watch Officer, otherwise please leave a message."*

"Sam, this is Evelyn Stinson at the NSA. I have a critically important message for you. Please call right away."

An hour later Evelyn was growing concerned. Sam had not returned her call and she knew the information CE had given her would affect Sam's conclusions about a critical matter he was working on. She wondered if he was avoiding her for some reason. Frustrated, she debated what to do and concluded that personal issues couldn't interfere. This information had to get to him.

As she reached for the phone to call him again, she noticed her blinking message light. *Oops, forgot all about that. What if someone left an important message for me?* Feeling guilty, she picked up the phone and reviewed the messages. There was only one, and it put a big smile on her face.

"Hi Evelyn, this is Sam Bergman. With the CIA. Just wondering if you might be available Saturday for a stroll around Gettysburg, and then dinner. I'll be out of the office probably Monday and Tuesday, I am headed for Anchorage on a project with the Agency. I'll contact you when I get back in town. Bye."

She reveled for a moment in a happy glow and then remembered her task. Sam was out of town until Wednesday, but this information had to get to him immediately! She pulled out a confidential interagency phone list of the various government intelligence services and located the number of the Analysis Division Duty Watch Officer at the CIA. It was vital that she talk to Sam.

****

Jim Stewart was increasingly discomfited by the *Snowbird* case. The evidence was conflicting—something was not adding up and he knew it. It was irritating.

On the one hand, the major's cover story was coherent.

Try as he might, Stewart had been unable to crack the man's tale or trick him into an inconsistency. And important elements of the case supported the major's version of events. The incident in the Bering Strait did not appear to be staged. Back channels confirmed that several Soviet naval personnel had died in the incident. Interviews with the Tomcat, Falcon, and Orion pilots indicated that the Soviets appeared to be serious about recovering Kelly. Hospital personnel were convinced that the major would have died of hypothermia within ninety minutes had he not been recovered. The FBI labs verified the presence of a deadly toxin on the pin in the lighter recovered from the suspect in Kotzebue. The alleged assassin and his partner, both captured in Kotzebue, had been linked to IDC, a mysterious corporation headquartered in the Cayman Islands and known to the CIA as a front for Soviet assassination teams. None of these facts aligned with the accusation that Jacob Kelly was a Soviet plant.

On the other hand, the intelligence that the *Snowbird* project group was receiving was airtight. It came from the most highly placed sources of the DIA, the CIA, and the naval and Air Force intelligence sections, sources which in the past had proven their reliability. According to all these sources Jacob Kelly was a traitor. The evidence supporting Kelly's story could—with a few adjustments—conceivably fit into a narrative pointing to his guilt.

Although he initially leaned toward the pilot's innocence, the weight of the intelligence intercepts had finally reversed Stewart's opinion. Now he found himself angered that even under intense interrogation Kelly exhibited not a shred of remorse or culpability. *Doesn't he have a conscience?* But in his heart of hearts Stewart wondered if his emotional reaction against the major was his own attempt to convince himself of Kelly's guilt. He shook his head. *What a messy case!*

He stood with Bergman and watched the pilot through a one-way mirror, as Kelly sat alone in the interrogation room, waiting for the next round of questioning.

"This is our last opportunity to break him before we turn him over to Bill Ott. What do you think, Sam?"

"I think he is dirty, Jim. I know the facts don't line up perfectly, but the evidence against him seems strong."

Stewart rubbed the back of his neck. "Yeah. I suppose you're right."

"Look, Jim, I know you have some doubts about it, and you're the expert when it comes to interrogations. But I'm an expert on the Soviet regime. This sort of subterfuge is what they excel in. They're not above wasting five or even ten lives in order to insert a valuable agent. The only nation that shows more cunning in their intelligence services are the Chinese, and it's a bit of a toss-up. I admit that we are not one hundred percent sure of our conclusions. But this might be a case where sixty-five or seventy percent will have to do."

Stewart continued to study the man on the other side of the glass. "Yeah. But what if we *are* wrong? There are some pretty big national security implications there, too. And they are a lot more consequential than just ruining one man's life and reputation, though that is bad enough."

Bergman made no response so Stewart sighed, "Well, let's get this over with," and entered the interrogation room.

An hour later they had made no new progress. Kelly surmised that the men had already decided he was a traitor. When Stewart and Bergman got up to leave he played his final card.

"Agent Stewart, do you remember asking me last week why you should believe my story?"

Stewart's back was turned to him, hand on the door, ready to leave the room. Bergman was right behind him. Jim paused and turned around. "Yes, I do. Why?"

"Well, there's one additional reason I didn't share with you."

"I'm sorry, Major Kelly, but it's too late now. You will be transferred today to Eielson Air Force Base. Whatever you share now will be investigated while you are in their custody."

"I won't be safe in their custody."

"I know you have said that, but we are out of options and out of time. It seems clear to us that you have not been telling the truth. You haven't provided us with any means of independently verifying your story. We have no real reason to believe that your life will be in danger in an Air Force brig, other than your own word, and obviously we're unwilling to take that at face value."

"You will be able to verify what I have to tell you now, and there's no way Ivan can cover it with disinformation." Jacob Kelly remained calm and composed, though Stewart sensed he was discouraged.

Bergman and Stewart returned to their seats.

"Do I need to turn off the video recorders and empty the observation room?" Stewart asked snidely.

Jacob Kelly locked eyes with him and waited a long moment before he responded, "If everything is indeed set in motion as you say, and if in your judgment I am a liar and a traitor, then my answer to that cynical question really does not matter, does it?"

"No, it really doesn't. Now, don't waste our time any longer. What do you have to say?" Stewart was transmitting a message of impatience and dismissal with his posture and body language. It was partly to make the prisoner anxious, and partly because he *felt* impatient and dismissive.

"I am not the only one they kidnapped. I know the names of others that the Russians have in custody, or did when I escaped. You will be able to verify that each of these people have mysteriously disappeared."

"Others?" Stewart sat up and leaned forward, interested. "You are telling me that they have kidnapped others?"

"I have nine names to give you, including two American scientists, three British scientists, an Israeli military officer, a German biologist, a German chemist, and a mathematician from India."

"For the love of Pete! Why did you withhold this until now?" Stewart jumped up and shouted, his pent-up anger and frustration spilling over. "This would have been simple to verify! Why are you playing these games with us?"

"Simple, Agent Stewart. There is a traitor in the Air Force and you can bet he is tracking this case. I expect he knows in some detail what I've told you and what I haven't. As long as I keep these names to myself—as long as no one else knows where these nine are—they're still potentially useful to Chernikov's program. But once I give their names up and their governments start hammering the Soviet government with questions, these men become a liability. Chernikov will put a bullet in their heads, lose the bodies in the vast waste of Siberia, and erase all signs that they were ever in custody.

"So if I provided these names earlier I would have been signing their death warrants. The only reason I am telling you now is because it is my last option. I am the last slim hope these people have of getting out of there alive. I know where the camp is, how it is laid out, how many guards there are, and what the routines are."

Jim Stewart sat down and stared at the man across the table, considering what he should do. After a moment he shrugged his shoulders in frustration and pushed a pad and pencil across the table. "Write 'em down."

He turned to Sam and said tersely, "Stay here. Don't talk."

Stewart left the room, shutting the door behind him, and entered the observation room. No one was there except Ed Devlin; the others had not yet arrived.

"What do you think, Ed?"

"I think we should chop off the tapes when you two got up to go out the door. That's a natural place for the tapes to stop, and they won't appear to be edited. I don't think we should share this part with anyone else, including the *Snowbird* group—not until you have a chance to run those leads down."

"Not even with Jesse?"

"Not even Jesse."

"You believe him, then?"

"No more than you do. But I don't want to gamble nine lives on the chance we could be wrong. These names should be simple to check without raising any suspicions. With the FBI's resources you ought to be able to come up with something in twenty-four hours. And if they prove out, we have to entertain the possibility that Kelly is telling us the truth about everything."

"True. But if we're going to play this hand we've got to

turn him over to Ott today as planned. Otherwise we'll have some explaining to do."

"Better to gamble on one life than nine."

Stewart nodded. He asked, "Will you take care of the tapes?"

"Yep. I'll edit them myself. No one will know."

"Go ahead and shut everything off now. I'll finish this up."

The FBI agent re-entered the interrogation room and observed that nine names, with nationalities, had been written neatly on the pad. He sat down. "Okay. All the observation stuff is off. I will check out these names but it's going to take a day or so. Only Ed Devlin, Sam, and I will know anything about this. Ed is wiping it off the recordings.

"But we still have to turn you over to the Air Force today, otherwise we'd be showing our hand. You should have given us these names several days ago. And besides, I'm not convinced that you aren't just playing mind games with us."

Jacob Kelly nodded, "I understand."

Chapter 11

"Good morning, gentlemen. Our goal today is to wrap up Project *Snowbird*. We'll go around the table for any updates, then make a final decision. Ed, let's start with you." Jesse Pierce sat down at the head of the table.

"G'morning, all. Most of the leads my guys have been pursuing are not germane to the remaining questions in Project *Snowbird*. We've been firming up the case against the IDC goons and preparing the evidence against Major Kelly regarding the felony theft of an aircraft, assaulting an officer with a deadly weapon, and miscellaneous other charges. We'll have enough to convene a grand jury by the end of the week, leading, I believe, to multiple indictments against the major. The case against the IDC people is a little tougher, but we are linking them to other murders and disappearances. We'll have 'em cold in the end. That's it for me, Jesse."

Jim Stewart stood up. "Hi, guys. I will give you a quick summary of our interrogations, but I think it would be most helpful if I restate Major Kelly's claims first. It is Major Kelly's contention that he was shot down while on a test flight over the Bering Sea and recovered by the Soviets. He was then allegedly taken to a GRU detention facility in Siberia, where he was interrogated about a secret Air Force project known as *Hydra*. Escaping from the facility, he made his way across Siberia and the Chukchi Peninsula, all the while eluding a Soviet manhunt and surviving a Siberian winter. He then attempted to kayak back to the US but ran into trouble with the weather and hypothermia, and that's when we picked him up —near death—in the Strait.

"He claims that a spy in the Air Force, probably at Eielson, collaborated in his kidnapping or capture or shootdown, however you want to look at it."

"Do you believe him? Is he credible?" Jesse Pierce asked.

"No, we do not. My original inclination was to grant him credibility based on his record as well as the extreme measures the Soviets took to reel him in. But the weight of recent intelligence causes us to conclude that this is an elegantly conceived plan of the Russians to implant a spy in the Air Force. We believe that he defected with the aircraft—which was loaded with avionics from Project *Hydra*—and turned it over to the bad guys, and now is being reinserted back into the same top-secret Air Force project.

"However, after a week of interrogating him, I have to confess that we have learned nothing to incriminate *or* exonerate him. The transcripts of the interrogations are in your briefing packets and make for some pretty interesting reading.

"I also have to admit that we are lacking *motive*, gentlemen, motive. Nothing in the evidence nor the interrogations provides us with that crucial piece of data explaining why or when he was turned. Everything contained in Major Kelly's record indicates he loves the Air Force and his country. We have combed his financial transactions, bank accounts, telephone records, and tax returns, and I had a team of FBI agents scour his home as well as his quarters at Edwards. There is literally nothing, nothing at all, we have found that would even hint of impropriety. Assuming he is guilty, we find ourselves unable to account for his behavior on the basis of the evidence.

"Nevertheless, on the strength of the combined intelligence intercepts we have been receiving, Sam and I recommend he be handed over to Bill as soon as we are done with this meeting. I suspect there are a lot of questions the Air Force would like to ask him. As far as the other matters, including the FBI's own investigation of the IDC connection, that information appears in this morning's briefing packet and I will not go over it now as it does not impact our recommendation." Stewart nodded to Jesse Pierce and sat back down.

"Sam," Pierce said, "it's your turn."

"Thanks, Jesse. Late last week we received an intelligence intercept from one of our most highly placed sources, which Jim alluded to just now. The information, which we do find credible, stated that an attempt would be made to penetrate the Air Force with an American officer who had turned to the Soviet side. The intercept contained the cover story to be used by this officer. The cover story, gentlemen, matches exactly what the major has said to us almost word for word. Other intelligence traffic coming from less highly placed sources is providing a similar, albeit far less detailed, claim. I concur with Jim; I think Kelly is guilty as sin.

"I also managed to trace the phone number Kelly called from the office supply store. It turned out to be the phone number of a high-ranking CIA officer by the name of Bill Jensen. Jensen has a non-official cover and is not widely known to be in the CIA, so I am giving you this information verbally but it is not in your briefing packet. I asked Jensen about the call and he readily admitted to knowing Kelly. He claims to be a friend of Kelly's father from years ago. The father has since died and Jensen is refusing to get involved in the son's troubles. He has not returned the phone call and has no intention to. He's rather perturbed that the son of his friend has gotten mixed up in illegal activity."

"That would be correct," Ed Devlin spoke up, "Kelly has not received any phone calls while in custody nor has anyone attempted to contact him."

Bergman nodded and continued, "I ran some checks in the background and Jensen's story checks out solid. I believe Jensen was a coincidental contact and is not implicated by the major's phone call."

Bergman finished his summary, "For my part, gentlemen, I don't believe there is any remaining purpose to continue Project *Snowbird*. I think we have gotten to the bottom of it, or at least as far as we can, and I'm convinced Kelly is a spy. I recommend we turn the case over to Bill Ott and disband the *Snowbird* group. I, for one, won't miss the long flights out from DC and back." Bergman reached for his cup and walked over to the coffee pot. "That's it for me, Jesse."

Bill Ott stood up and began his summary, "I find that we are in agreement, gentlemen, though it disappoints me to say so. As an Air Force officer you never want to think that a brother officer would betray his friends, his service, and his country in such a flagrant, vile fashion. I would much rather have found that we had a hero on our hands, a man who courageously escaped an illegal Soviet detention and completed an epic trek across Siberia, all the while making fools of the GRU and the Soviet army. That to me would have been a preferable ending to this story."

Bergman looked on curiously and wondered if Ott was warming up to make a speech. It was beginning to sound like a prosecutor's opening statement in a jury trial.

Ott continued, "Instead, I think we have here a man, a traitor, who has been attempting to make fools of us with a cock-and-bull story about a hi-tech kidnapping." As he paused to take a breath Ott glanced around the table and seemed to remember where he was. He cleared his throat and continued, albeit somewhat sheepishly, "Yes. Well. In this past week we too have continued to receive intelligence of various quality which verifies all that has been said this morning.

"I've had three investigators combing over Kelly's service record and past postings, but he is apparently a very smooth operator, for my men have found nothing suspicious. Jesse," he said, looking the commander in the eye, "I think we can shut this thing down. I'll continue the investigation through Air Force channels." Ott sat down, looking pleased with himself.

Jesse remained silent, nodding his head. "Men," he finally said, "my investigation hasn't picked up anything, any tidbit, any piece of information that's not already been stated here this morning. Naval intelligence assets continue to pick up chatter confirming what you have shared."

"Then you agree?" asked Stewart.

"No," the lieutenant commander said, "I do not. I think he's innocent. But I have no basis for saying so other than a gut feeling."

"And other than the fact that all our investigations around

the periphery of his life turn up no suspicious activity," Stewart said softly, looking down at the table. Sam looked at him sharply.

"Right," Pierce concurred. "He's too clean. There's no motive. And there was nearly a war started in the Strait when we picked him up. Do you remember, Sam, why you had Jim check out the law enforcement and military fingerprint databases when we still knew him as John Meeker and were trying to get an ID on him?"

"Yes, Jesse, I do. It was because the note he left in the hospital at Kotzebue was written from the perspective of someone on our side."

"Exactly. In fact, guys," Jesse persisted, "do you realize that the *only* evidence we have against Kelly are those intelligence intercepts, and we have a fifty-fifty chance that Ivan is messing with our minds?"

"You mean with disinformation?"

"Yep. In other words, *all* the evidence except for those intelligence intercepts points to his innocence. I admit that his story has an 'Alice in Wonderland' feel to it, but I believe there are two reasons for it. First, none of us can imagine that the USSR would be so bold as to do what Kelly claims they did, and second, none of us can imagine that someone could escape from a GRU detention facility thousands of miles inside the Soviet Union, elude the ensuing manhunt, and then *kayak*, for crying out loud, back to the United States. No, gentlemen, I do not think the major is guilty."

"Now wait just a minute, Jesse," Major Ott objected, "that intelligence is *not* inconsequential. It's from several different highly placed sources which have always proven reliable in the past. We have never received anything but solid intel from these particular sources. And so far as we know Ivan has no clue we are getting information through these channels—which means that they would not likely use them for disinformation, since they don't know we are listening."

"Relax, Bill. I am not about to start an interagency or interservice war over this. Of all the people in this room I readily admit to having the least experience in the intelligence trade. I concur with the decision to turn Kelly over to you today; I just don't agree with the idea that he is a spy. I am confident your Air Force investigators will clear him. All I ask is that you place him in protective custody on the chance that his story is true and that someone in the Air Force really is trying to off him."

"I have no problem with that. I will see that he is isolated and protected. And if our investigators are able to clear him then he really *is* a hero and we will treat him that way."

"Bill," Bergman asked, "have you contacted any of the people connected with *Hydra* to let them know their test pilot has shown up?"

"No, not yet. As Kelly asked when the State Troopers bagged him, I've kept his capture a secret from everyone except a small team of investigators in my office. And we will probably keep it a secret for a couple more weeks until my men run down all possible leads."

Jesse nodded, satisfied. "Well, that's it then. Other than working out the details of the transport and hand-over, I think we are done."

Ed Devlin spoke up, "Jesse, Bill and I have already worked that out. The State Troopers have prisoner transport procedures down pat. We'll fly Kelly to Fairbanks in one of our aircraft and the Air Force will reimburse the expense."

"You're flying into Fairbanks International, rather than Eielson itself?" Jesse asked.

"Yes," Ed responded, "it's too difficult for a civilian craft to get landing clearance—they ask too many questions—and we're trying to keep this under wraps a little longer. So we'll have Ott's men pick him up from the General Aviation section at FIA." He turned to Major Ott and added, "Major, there's plenty of room on that Beechcraft. Do you want to fly back with the prisoner?"

"I appreciate the offer, Ed, but no. I'm flying commercial later this afternoon—I have some errands to do here in Anchorage before I return. My team will meet the aircraft on the tarmac in Fairbanks to take custody of the prisoner."

"Suit yourself, but the offer is open."

****

His cell door opened and three guards walked in, one carrying a set of shackles.

"What's going on?" Falcon asked.

One of the guards responded, "Sir, we are transporting you to another location. I am sorry, but we will have to shackle you."

"Where are you taking me?" he asked, as he sat down on his bed and offered his hands and feet to make their job easier. They chained his hands and feet together.

"Sorry, sir, but we're not allowed to communicate with you other than seeing that your basic needs are cared for."

Jacob Kelly's movements were now restricted to not much more than a shuffle. The fatalistic gloom he had been fighting now settled over him like a smothering blanket. He guessed that he was being taken to Eielson as his interrogators this morning had said. *Where is Bill Jensen? Why has he not called?*

There was snow on the ground and a high overcast as he emerged from the building. The cold murkiness of the weather matched that of his soul. Jake wondered if he had finally stepped into a situation from which he could not escape. Was this the end of the road? The guards helped him into the back of a black Suburban and set out for the Anchorage airport.

Chapter 12

Eugene Martin was a blessed man. After thirty years of flying heavy bombers and tankers for the Air Force he was now retired and living the life of his dreams. Martin was the senior pilot for the Alaska State Troopers, which meant he got to fly high-performance aircraft into some very interesting places. He loved his job. Eugene Martin was a completely contented man.

Today he was flying a prisoner transport from Anchorage to Fairbanks. His copilot was a young friend, Beau Ashton. Beau had come up through a civilian path, learning to fly as a teenager. His family had had enough money to pay for training beyond a simple license to fly. After earning his Airman's Certificate he had taken instrument training, then earned a multiengine rating, and finally obtained his commercial license. Ashton's current job was flying organs and tissue from donors to recipients for a medical company that handled the logistics of organ transplants. When Beau was not on call he worked for the Alaska State Troopers on a per-diem basis. Gene had taken Beau under his wing, so to speak, and found the young man to be very teachable. Beau's skills and judgment as a pilot had grown under Gene's influence and the two looked forward to flying together whenever possible.

Gene walked around the Beech King Air C90, doing his pre-flight visual checks. The aircraft was virtually new, having been manufactured in 1982. The Troopers purchased it straight from the factory. It was a dream to fly, the twin Pratt and Whitney PT6A-21 engines providing plenty of thrust for speed, climbing, and maneuvering. He rolled a step stool into place and checked the wing tanks with a dipstick. All was well, the bird was fueled and ready to go. Disconnecting the tie-downs, he threw the wheel chocks into the baggage compartment and climbed into the cockpit, where Beau was already running through the checklist.

"We are green and clean on the pre-start," his copilot affirmed. As pilot-in-charge Gene rescanned the pre-flight checklist, silently teaching Beau what it meant to sit in the left seat when passengers were your cargo. He nodded and affirmed, "Good job, Beau, thanks."

"Propeller and engine area visual check," Gene said after strapping himself in.

"Clear prop right," Beau called out.

"Clear right," Gene acknowledged. Setting the throttle to idle, he reached over and turned the right side fuel pump to the ON position, and after announcing, "Starting right," he turned the ignition switch to the start position until the starboard engine coughed into life. It took a moment for the warning lights and annunciators to extinguish, as the engine warmed up. When the gas generator for the turbine had stabilized at over fifty percent of the engine rpms, he set the right engine start switch to the OFF position, and turned the right generator switch to the ON position.

"Clear prop left." He looked to his left and acknowledged his own check, "Clear left. Starting left." After the sequence had been repeated for the left side engine he scanned the instruments. Everything appeared to be in normal ranges. Gene set the cabin heat on high to cut the chill for his passengers.

"Beau, greet our passengers, would you?"

Ashton unstrapped himself and went back through the cabin to the steps. He motioned to the guards waiting in the hangar. They walked to the aircraft, trudging through the snow, escorting a tall, well-built prisoner who was shackled hand and foot. Beau studied the man as the party approached. Even shuffling in chains the man moved with a certain grace. As the prisoner drew near Beau noticed he ran his eyes over the Beechcraft, evaluating it the way a pilot would. He wondered who the man was and what he had done.

A few minutes later everyone was settled and strapped in

and Beau returned to the cockpit, slapping Gene on the shoulder, "Ready to rock-n-roll, captain!"

After Beau strapped himself in Gene keyed the microphone and announced, "ANCHORAGE GROUND, BEECHCRAFT *NOVEMBER ONE TWO SEVEN DELTA CHARLIE*, PARKING AREA TWO, READY TO TAXI FOR DEPARTURE."

Seconds later came the response, "BEECHCRAFT *NOVEMBER ONE TWO SEVEN DELTA CHARLIE*, ANCHORAGE GROUND, CLEAR TO TAXI TO RUNWAY THREE TWO. CONTACT ANCHORAGE TOWER ON ONE ONE EIGHT POINT THREE."

Gene slowly throttled up to maneuver the aircraft onto the taxiway. In five minutes he was in position as the next aircraft for takeoff. "Beau, tune COM1 to Anchorage Tower on 118.3, and let's get this show on the road."

"You got it, Gene, one one eight point three."

"ANCHORAGE TOWER, BEECHCRAFT *NOVEMBER ONE TWO SEVEN DELTA CHARLIE*, READY FOR TAKEOFF RUNWAY THREE TWO."

"BEECHCRAFT *NOVEMBER ONE TWO SEVEN DELTA CHARLIE*, ANCHORAGE TOWER, HOLD SHORT RUNWAY THREE TWO FOR INCOMING TRAFFIC."

Four minutes later, after holding to allow a United Airlines heavy to land, the Beechcraft King Air took off and climbed to cruise altitude for the trip over the mountains to Fairbanks.

****

Bill Jensen sat with Technical Sergeant Matthew Loeb watching the surveillance videos as the young man pointed out what had drawn his attention. "Watch, Dr. Jensen, er, I mean, Bill. When you play the tape at regular speed the office activity looks quite normal." Matt played about five minutes of the tape at normal speed. During the replay, Jensen could see the office workers going about the unremarkable activities and duties of reading, filing, typing, and so on.

"Now watch this. I'm rewinding the tape, and we'll watch two hours of their day at sixteen times normal speed. It will take a little less than eight minutes." Loeb rewound the tape, then punched the high-speed button. The black and white figures scurried through their activities with comical rapid movements. Jensen tried to suppress a chuckle but was unsuccessful.

Loeb smiled but kept his eyes on the monitor. "I know, sir. I laughed, too, when I first used the high-speed function. It really looks funny watching them in high speed, doesn't it?"

The patterns in the office initially appeared random. But slowly Bill's attention was drawn to a man in the foreground who was evidently a chain smoker. He seemed to be lighting cigarettes every minute or so. As Jensen watched it dawned on him that the smoker's actions were not random, but repetitive. Whenever he lit a cigarette he did it in precisely the same way. He focused on the man and ignored the others. The smoker pulled a paper off his stack, leaned on his forearms over the paper, and lit the cigarette with a lighter. He then put the paper on his desk at the bottom of the stack. Jensen realized that the man was photographing the documents.

"Stop the tape, Matt. Son, you've done an outstanding job. I think you nailed our spy! Now, cue it to one of these cigarette-lighting events. I want to watch it at normal speed."

Loeb positioned the tape and played it at normal speed. Jensen watched, fascinated. *Apparently*, he thought, *there is a camera in that Zippo. I'll bet it's a Svouk.* "Okay, Matt. That's enough. You nailed him. He's got a camera in the lighter and is photographing documents. Who is he?"

"It's Senior Master Sergeant Hank Swift, sir. You sent two men to do off-base surveillance on him late yesterday. I gave them his home address, car make and model, and everything else I could think of. They have been watching him ever since. Sir, although I don't know exactly what that document is, I was able to see from an earlier tape that it came from the printer in the secure room. That printer is reserved for the most confidential information. Whatever the document is, we don't want it to get away from us. We were really lucky that it's such a long report, because the repetitiveness of photographing all those pages is what caught my attention."

"No such thing as luck, Matt. It's providence—God at work."

"Huh?"

"Never mind." The CIA agent leaned back in his chair, thinking. Matt knew better than to interrupt so he rewound the tape and removed it from the machine. After a moment, Jensen spoke. "Okay, we know that Hank Swift is a bad guy. And we have pretty conclusive evidence that Major Ott is a bad guy, too. Isn't that interesting? Jacob Kelly was right! There *were* two of them."

"Who is Jacob Kelly?"

"Forget it, Matt. Doesn't concern you. Just a friend of mine. Do me a favor, Matt, I've got to make some confidential phone calls so I need you to vamoose for a bit. Why don't you see if you can verify from base records that Major Ott was here at his desk when that attempt to modify the DPMO record took place?"

After the sergeant had left the room, Jensen pulled the sat phone out of his briefcase and called Roger Carson.

"Carson here."

"Hi, RC. By the way, thanks for sending Skip and Randy to Sergeant Loeb. We're about to bag a very bad man. I might need your team in Anchorage to pick up a second bad guy today."

"No problem, Bill, but I have some strange news for you."

"What's that?"

"Just five minutes ago I got a call from our support team at Langley. The IDC hit squad here in Anchorage has flown the coop."

"What?"

"We were never able to locate them ourselves. But three tickets were purchased at Sea-Tac last night, at around 2100 hours, using an IDC credit card. The card had been flagged as belonging to IDC several months ago, and our support team at the Firm was notified within the hour. They finally got a look at them with security cameras from the UAL ticketing counter. On a hunch, they checked the cameras at Anchorage International and it paid off. From that point they were able to get the aliases, and even located the hotel they'd stayed in. You know what this means, Bill. Either someone called off the dogs, or they finished what they'd come to do and got out of Dodge before the stuff hits the fan."

"Oh, boy—this is really, really not good. Rog, call Baker Team here in Fairbanks right now and find out what their targets are doing. If someone has called off the dogs, then both teams will have left. If Baker's targets are still in Fairbanks that can only mean that Major Kelly is in great danger. Call me right back."

"You got it, boss. I'll be right back to you."

****

Falcon resisted the temptation to drift off. The drone of the engines and the warmth of the cabin drew him to sleep like the mythological song of the Siren. He shook his head to clear it and looked around the cabin. Two of the Troopers were unarmed and had been detailed as jailers. From conversation among the men he knew they each had a key to his shackles. Four more Troopers comprised an armed escort, each with a sidearm and Mace. Evidently *someone* believed his tales about Siberia or he would not have merited such a large escort. The guards had locked the chain of his ankle shackles through an eyebolt set in the floor. It left him able to sit in the seat comfortably strapped in but he couldn't stretch his legs.

He sensed the plane level out and heard a slight change in pitch as the pilot adjusted the fuel mixture, prop pitch, and engine speed. Kelly figured they must have reached cruising altitude. He looked out the windows. They had climbed above the ceiling, and the sky was bright blue. They had not yet crossed into the Alaska Range, but he could see the tops of the mountains ahead and to his left. Mount McKinley was rising majestically out of a wreath of clouds. *The pilot must be flying up the Susitna Watershed*, he thought. The George Parks Highway, Highway 3, extending from just north of Anchorage to Fairbanks would be right below them. Jake imagined that the ground conditions, underneath the clouds, were bleak and cold.

****

The satellite phone chirped and Mike Young of CIA Team Baker picked it up. "Young here."

"Mike, this is Roger. Listen, give me a quick status update on your targets."

"We've been bouncing a laser off their hotel room window, and managed to eavesdrop on their plans last night. They're going to cause an accident during the landing. They have worked out all the details, but the gist of it is they're going to knock one of the snowplow operators out cold and force some vodka down his throat, then leave him in the cab. When the aircraft is landing, they'll run the plow onto the runway so that the two collide. The IDC goon will bail out just before the collision. They expect the violence of the crash will cover their tracks, and the 'accident' will be blamed on a drunk plow operator.

"We know they are monitoring the aviation frequencies, including the Fairbanks tower, because we heard the monitor in the background last night. They've got everything, including the timing, planned perfectly. Roger, these guys are good."

"What is your counter, Mike?"

"Jimmy and I will be set up with sniper rifles, each on a different angle. As soon as the hostile approaches the plow, one or both of us will take him out. Evidently the time is getting close, because they are packing up their hotel room, about to head for the airport."

"Yeah, the State Troopers took Kelly to the airport earlier today. Plane took off about thirty minutes ago. It's a Beechcraft King Air C90, call-sign *NOVEMBER ONE TWO SEVEN DELTA CHARLIE*. We shadowed the Alaska Troopers all the way to the airport as force protection. I don't think they knew we were there. One last question for you: when you take the hostile out, what are you going to do about the others?"

"The reinforcements you sent arrived early this morning. I put them on the guy at Eielson and pulled Randy and Skip back, so we've got enough guys to grab 'em. Security at the airport will provide backup. If the other members of the IDC team try to run, we should be able to bag them."

"Excellent. Listen, I have to run, but stuff is beginning to cut loose, so be ready. Don't you guys pack up until you hear from me. I might need you to assist with several arrests.

"By the way, Team Alpha's targets have pulled out of Anchorage. That must mean that their dirty work has been accomplished. And that means that the aircraft may not reach Fairbanks. Your targets were evidently designated to provide insurance in case the other hit squad failed. I think the squad that Team Alpha was looking for was always the primary threat. You got any questions for me, Mike?"

"Nah, Rog, we're good. You can count on us. If that aircraft makes it to final approach, it's going to land safely. We'll see to it."

****

"Bill, I just talked with Mike on Team Baker. The IDC squad they're covering is still hard at work fomenting madness and mayhem. So whoever is pulling the strings hasn't reeled 'em in. The good news is they know exactly how the hit is going down if Kelly reaches Fairbanks. They're on it."

"Hmm. Well, that at least is good. Have you got any idea when the prisoner transfer is going to take place, Roger?"

"It's happening now."

"You're kidding? Now? Has the plane taken off yet?"

"Bill, they took off thirty or forty minutes ago."

"Oh, Lord, have mercy! We've got to get that plane back on the ground *now*! Roger, I have to call the Troopers at once. Listen, once Ott arrives in Fairbanks, retask Team Alpha to shadow him. Don't let him know he is being followed, but don't let him leave town, either. Photograph anyone he makes contact with and be prepared to pick him up on my word. If he starts acting like he's going to flee, grab him but avoid the use of deadly force—even if you are about to lose him. I think he is dirty, but I am not yet completely certain."

"Got it. We'll keep an eye on him. I know he was at the State Trooper's headquarters when I last checked. What about the IDC guys?"

"Tell Baker to bag them at the first good opportunity, before Ott arrrives."

****

"Alaska State Troopers main headquarters, how may I direct your call?"

"I need Special Agent Ed Devlin immediately. This is an emergency. My name is Bill Jensen, and I am with the CIA."

"I'll connect you with his office, Mr. Jensen."

The CIA agent fumed as the phone rang and rang.

"Alaska Bureau of Investigations, how may I direct your call?" a young female voice finally said.

"I must talk with Ed Devlin immediately."

"He does not seem to be at his desk. May I take a message?"

"*No, you may not take a message, I need Ed Devlin now*! This is an emergency! Turn the building upside down if you have to, but get Devlin on the phone RIGHT NOW!" The long hours, lack of sleep, and bureaucratically polite inertia of a government agency had finally gotten to Bill, and he knew he had overstepped propriety.

There was a brief shocked silence and then the young woman responded, her voice quavering, "And whom may I say is calling?"

Jensen shut his eyes and tried to contain his panic. "This is Dr. William Jensen. I am a special assistant to the Deputy Director for Operations of the CIA. I am calling on official business that happens to be top secret. There are people's lives at stake, Miss, including a number of State Troopers. I need to talk to Ed Devlin *right now*, please."

Fortunately for all involved, Devlin poked his head in the

office at that moment. The department secretary frantically waved him over. She was so flustered she put the receiver in Devlin's hands without saying a word.

"Hello?"

"Is this Ed Devlin?"

"Yes, it is. And who is this?" His secretary had still not quite recovered and he had no idea to whom he was talking.

"This is Bill Jensen, with the CIA. Listen, Agent Devlin. I know all about Project *Snowbird* and Major Jacob Kelly. I've been tracking your progress for the past week—I'll explain later. But right now it is critical that you get that Beechcraft on the ground *immediately*!"

Devlin was surprised, but he did recognize Jensen's name from the morning briefing. He replied, "I am sorry, Mr. Jensen, but it is too late to recall the aircraft. And we wouldn't anyway. We have decided to turn the major over to the Air For—"

"I did NOT say *recall* the aircraft, Devlin! I SAID GET IT ON THE GROUND, NOW! That Beech is not going to make it to Fairbanks. It has been sabotaged! Everyone aboard that aircraft is going to die, including your guards and your pilot, unless you warn them. Hand Kelly over to the Air Force if you want to, but get that plane down now."

"There are no airports open this time of yea—"

"Doesn't matter," insisted Jensen, cutting him off, "Have him set it down on a straight stretch of any road. Just don't let him fly into the Alaska Range. We'll never find the wreckage. Listen, Agent Devlin: there have been two different assassination squads in Alaska for the last three or four days, one in Anchorage, one in Fairbanks. Their orders are to take Kelly out. These squads were sent out by IDC, a front operation for—"

"Yes, yes, I know about all IDC. They do the dirty work for the KGB and the GRU."

"Precisely. The Anchorage team pulled out last night—which means they sabotaged the plane and aren't sticking around to watch it fall out of the sky."

"Are you confident of this?" Devlin asked, his concern

rapidly mounting.

"Very. If you have any Troopers on that plane and you don't want to be calling their families with bad news, you'd better contact that pilot. It might be too late even now."

"I'll call the dispatcher immediately and have them order the plane down."

"Thank you. Listen, I know this is all very confusing. I will call you back in about fifteen minutes and bring you up to date. Try to keep the Project *Snowbird* group from leaving, but don't tell them what is going on. Trust me on this. You are all going to want to hear what I have to say."

"Okay, Jensen, I'll do it. I don't understand why, but I'll do it."

After hanging up the phone, Devlin called down to the State Troopers dispatch center. "Billy, I need you to contact our Beechcraft right now, priority one. Whatever else you are doing, drop it. This is a life and death emergency! Tell them to put the plane on the ground immediately and then patch me through from my office."

Chapter 13

Beau turned to the communications panel on the Beech and said to Eugene, "Gene, we have a priority one coming from State Troopers Dispatch. I am putting it on your headset . . . Okay, go ahead, Dispatch, we're listening."

"Gene, can you hear me? This is Ed Devlin."

"Of course, Mr. Devlin, what can I do for you?"

"Gene, this is an emergency. You have got to find a place to land that Beech and you have to do it now. Do not, repeat, do not fly into the mountains. Your aircraft has been sabotaged."

As a former Air Force pilot Eugene was accustomed to taking orders without arguing and so even as he continued the conversation he began a turn back to the south.

"Mr. Devlin, there's not an airstrip within miles that isn't thoroughly snowed in. There isn't anywhere to land this thing, sir."

"You'll just have to put it down on Highway 3, Eugene. But it is critical that you get it out of the air as soon as possible."

"Sir, even as we speak I am settling on a course to the southwest. We started over the Alaska Range about five minutes ago. Now, can you tell me what has been done to my airplane?"

"That's the problem, Gene—we don't know. If it is a bomb, it could be triggered by altitude. It might go off as you descend for a landing. We just don't know."

"Sir, if that's the case, we're in luck. Highway 3 in these parts is high enough that maybe we wouldn't set off an altitude-triggered bomb."

"Let's hope so. Gene, we will monitor your situation. Meanwhile, I am lining up some choppers to pick you and your passengers up. As soon as I know more, I'll call you back."

"Roger, sir. We'll be here, I hope."

Beau returned the headsets to intercom mode and looked at his mentor. "Well, Gene, this might get a little interesting. Wonder what has been done to our Beech?"

"Beats me, Beau, but I hope we can put her down before we find out."

"Really."

For a moment they were silent, scanning their instruments and the terrain ahead of them. They were just passing over Cantwell.

"Beau, once we get about twelve miles or so below Cantwell, there are several long, straight sections on Highway 3 between there and Denali that we could probably land on. Go aft and let everybody know what is happening, and then come back and let Anchorage Center know that we have an emergency."

****

Jake felt the aircraft turning sharply to the left and then settling on a new course. He could tell from the angle of the sunlight they were now heading southwest. The guards also noted the change and looked at one another, shrugging their shoulders.

A moment later the copilot came back and shouted over the roar of the engines. "Gentlemen, I have good news and bad news. The good news is that we are still in the air and our aircraft is working fine at the moment." Everyone in the cabin caught the emphasis and leaned forward to hear the punch line. "The bad news is that we really, really want to be on the ground. We've just received word from the Troopers' dispatcher that there is a very strong possibility this aircraft has been sabotaged. We have been told to land immediately, even if we have to land on a highway.

"Please secure everything in the cabin. We don't want stuff flying around loose if things get rough. Once you have done that strap yourselves in and don't leave your seats."

"What about the prisoner?" asked one of the guards. "We don't want to leave him shackled if we are going to have a rough landing."

"For now, leave him locked up. I am sure they will give us instructions." The young man then returned to the cockpit.

Jacob Kelly knew exactly what had happened. It was just as he feared. Chernikov or someone higher up in that chain of command had arranged for his death. Unfortunately, it was also going to kill everyone else on the aircraft. *Collateral damage. I guess Chernikov finds that acceptable.*

There was nothing to be done. He resigned himself to whatever would come and smiled grimly at the irony. He had escaped the entire Soviet Army, Navy, and Air Force. But he was unable to save himself from the various United States intelligence services. He shook his head. His own country! As he had frequently in the last seven days, he wondered what had become of Bill Jensen. *Did he not get my message? Doesn't he care?*

As any pilot would in similar circumstances, the major wished it was his own hands on the control yoke. He hoped the pilot of this Beech was good.

****

Beau strapped himself in and reported to Gene via the headset intercom, "Right now our passengers are not too worried because we still have a working airplane. I instructed them on emergency landing procedures and told them to stay strapped in."

Beau switched his headset to COM2 and contacted Air Traffic Control. "Anchorage Center, this is Beechcraft *NOVEMBER ONE TWO SEVEN DELTA CHARLIE.* We are declaring an in-flight emergency and deviating from our flight plan. Our flight plan is no longer in effect."

"*NOVEMBER ONE TWO SEVEN DELTA CHAR-*

LIE, this is Anchorage Center, we noticed your course change. Please state the nature of your emergency."

"Anchorage Center, we have been informed that our aircraft has been sabotaged and have been instructed by Alaska State Troopers Dispatch Center to land immediately. The sabotage is not yet apparent but we are taking no chances."

"*NOVEMBER ONE TWO SEVEN DELTA CHARLIE,* your nearest option is Palmer Municipal Airport, CTAF on one two three point six."

"Negative, Anchorage Center, negative. We have been advised to land immediately, repeat, we have been advised to land immediately. We are going to put down on Highway 3."

"Copy that, *SEVEN DELTA CHARLIE.* Good luck."

For a while neither pilot spoke, as they were both busy mentally reviewing emergency procedures. Then Ashton spoke up quietly. "I know what the problem is, Gene," he said. "Look at the fuel gauges. We've been in the air for forty minutes and haven't used a pound of fuel. The gauges have been rigged. We're going to run out of gas."

A quick check of the instrument panel confirmed the young man's observations. They radioed the information back to Dispatch and then prayed that the fuel would hold out long enough to allow them to make a powered landing. But it was not to be.

Within two minutes the right engine coughed and died, followed thirty seconds later by the left engine. The Beechcraft King Air C90 is powerful for its small size with its two Pratt and Whitney turboprops. But when the engines are providing no thrust they are about as useful to the aircraft as a pair of boat anchors. Over the snowy, rugged landscape of the southern Alaska Range, the Beech had been transformed into little more than a brick with wings.

Without power the descent of the Beechcraft was simply a matter of mathematics. The C90 was about sixty-five hundred feet above ground level (AGL). Given the aircraft's glide ratio, Gene had about nine minutes to get the airplane on the ground before they ran out of altitude and crashed. With no headwind that would give them a range of roughly fourteen statute miles from their present position.

Gene feathered the props and said, "Beau, I want you to tune the Automatic Direction Finder to the Non-Directional Beacon at Summit. Then get information on the conditions in Cantwell. I need to know how far down this cloud layer goes. We're gonna be dropping through this soup blind, but if the ceiling is high enough and we keep our heading pegged to the NDB at Summit, we shouldn't run into anything before we regain some visibility."

****

The Dispatch Center immediately contacted the State Trooper Post in Cantwell with instructions to clear Highway 3 from Cantwell to thirty miles south of the Chulitna River Bridge. Troopers were instructed to stop any new traffic from entering the area, and the traffic already there was to be gathered at the curves if they were unable to exit the highway. All the straight sections of the road were to be cleared of traffic.

Radio transmissions and patrol cars raced up and down the valley, as the State Troopers sought to clear the road in time. The Trooper Post called the few businesses up and down the route, and secured their assistance as well.

****

Jim Stewart sat in the empty conference room at the Troopers Headquarters. He wanted to make some phone calls. Jesse Pierce's doubts about Kelly's guilt were eating away at him. Even though the young naval commander was fairly new at the intelligence business, he had displayed excellent instincts and judgment. Pricked by his own doubts, Stewart wanted to start running down leads on the names Kelly had provided in the final interrogation session earlier that morning.

Ed Devlin popped his head in the door and queried, "Jim, are you sticking around for a while or are you headed back to the airport immediately?" Devlin did not mention the rapidly developing emergency, as Jensen had requested.

"My flight does not leave until tonight. I was going to hang around till then. Do you mind if I use the phone in here? I need to make several calls."

"Be my guest. Or should I say, be the guest of the State of Alaska?" he said with a grin. "Listen, please don't leave without seeing me first. I just wanted to wrap some stuff up, okay?"

"Sure thing, Ed."

After Devlin had shut the door Stewart dialed his office in Seattle and asked for Sally Wolden, the department data analyst.

"This is Sally Wolden," said the voice on the other end of the phone.

"Sal, this is Jim. I've got some stuff I need researched, and I need it now—yesterday if possible. Are you available?"

"Oh, big boy, it depends on what you mean by . . . *available*," she replied in her most sultry voice, drawing out the last word in a suggestive fashion.

"Stop it, Sal. This is important."

"Can't blame a girl for trying, James. Okay, I'm available. What do you need?"

"First of all, Sally, the information I'm giving you is very sensitive. If we had time for others to review it, it would probably be rated somewhere above Top Secret. So be very discreet. I have the names of eight scientists and one military guy that I need you to locate. The list includes a couple of scientists from the US, three from Britain, two Germans, and one from India. The military guy is an Israeli with the IDF."

"That should not be too hard. Give me the names and I'll get right on it." Sally was secretly pleased to be given a task of some importance. She was tired of tracking down mere drug dealers and bank robbers. Stewart read her the names and then dropped the other shoe.

"Sally, this is not going to be as easy as you think."

"Why is that, Jim?"

"Well, I have a feeling that you're going to get a run-around. If that happens, tell your contact that we know where this person is and then give them my name and phone number here at the Alaska State Troopers Headquarters. Let's see, this phone is extension . . . 5721. Be sure you also give them my office number there in Seattle but tell them to call me here, first, if they want to know where their man is."

"Hold on, big boy. Let me get this straight. You want me to locate these people, but you already know where they are? Let me make this really easy for you. Why don't you just tell *me* where they are and then I'll repeat that back to you and the job is finished, right?"

Stewart smiled in spite of himself. *Count on Sally to have a practical solution.* Aloud, he agreed, "Well, I guess that would make the task a bit quicker, wouldn't it?"

"Uh-huh. In fact, since you already know where they are just tell yourself and I can get back to my donut and whatever else I was doing before you called."

"Listen, Sal, here's the deal. I have been given some information pertaining to these names that I have to verify. If the information is false, when you try to contact these people you are actually going to be successful. You will, in fact, be able to locate them.

"But if my information is true, the people you contact are going to give you some stupid story like, '*I'm sorry, John Doe is out of the country on sabbatical. Can I take a message?*'" Jim mimicked this in his best British accent. "When you tell them that you know where 'John' is and ask them if they would like to know, I'm predicting that all you-know-what is going to break loose, and my phone will be ringing off the hook."

In her most condescending mother-knows-best voice, Sally patiently tried one more time, "Jim! Listen to me. If you know where these people are supposed to be, just look there. Then you'll know if your information is true."

Stewart rolled his eyes, shaking his head. "I can't, Sal. *There* happens to be deep within a country to which we do not have access. And these nine men are *there* against their will."

"Ah. I see. I believe the FBI would call that *kidnapping*. And I am guessing you do not want that piece of information to be given out?"

"Correct. I just need you to get the ball rolling, Sal. If you call back in thirty minutes with a list of nine phone numbers where I can reach these folks, then I'll know my source was lying to me. If, on the other hand, I start getting calls from people in the intelligence services of these various countries, then I'll know we hit the jackpot."

"This should be interesting. I'll get right on it."

****

"Ed, I'm headed for the airport. My flight leaves in a little over an hour. Just wanted to say that it's been great working with you. Perhaps we will get to collaborate on a project again some day." Sam Bergman had his coat and briefcase in hand, and his mind was already beginning to shift to new tasks that awaited him back at Langley.

Devlin stood and motioned the CIA analyst into his office. "Sam, sit down for a minute and shut the door behind you, if you don't mind."

When they were both seated Ed asked, "Is there any way I can get you to stick around for another couple of hours? There are several things to wrap up yet."

Sam shook his head, "No, I really can't. My flight leaves in an hour, and if I miss my connection at Seattle-Tacoma, there's nothing else going to DC today. Can't you guys wrap it up without me?"

As Devlin opened his mouth to respond the phone on his desk rang. He picked it up. "Devlin," he said tersely. As Sam watched, Ed looked up at him and said into the phone, "No, he hasn't left yet. He is sitting right here. Why? . . . Okay, wait a minute." Devlin handed the phone across and said, "It's for you. Apparently your office has tracked you down."

"This is Sam Bergman. Hello?"

"Mr. Bergman, this is the watch officer in the Analysis Division at Langley. I have a call from a translator over at the NSA facility at Fort Meade, an Evelyn Stinson. She insists that she must talk to you immediately. Can you take the call?"

"Sure. Connect me to her."

A few seconds later, he heard Evelyn's voice, "Sam?"

"Yes, Evelyn, it's me. What's up?"

"Listen, do you remember the techie here who was going to take a look at the headers of those odd intercepts we received? I can't be too explicit because I'm assuming your line is not secure."

"Correct, I am not on a secure line. Yes, I remember him. Did he come up with anything?"

"Yes, he did. And it is not at all what we expected. Those different memos were never intended to be seen together. They were addressed to different recipients, none of whom would have seen what the others received."

Sam was silent for a moment, and then asked, "And he is positive of this?"

"Absolutely positive. He was able to explain it to me. There is no question about this whatsoever. Other than our intercept, those memos would not have been seen together, not by anyone."

As Devlin looked on, hearing only one side of the conversation and not understanding any of it, he saw the color drain out of the CIA analyst's face. He wondered what new revelation had just surfaced.

"Evelyn, thanks for calling and thanks for tracking me down. What you just told me is vital to a case I'm working on right now. I'll call you when I get back to Washington." As he spoke, he looked squarely at Devlin and slumped his shoulders, shaking his head. In that moment, Devlin knew that the *Snowbird* group had made a critical error, an error that now threatened the life of everyone on that Beech King Air.

Chapter 14

When the engines died all sound ceased except the flow of frigid air over the wings and fuselage of the C90. The conversation stopped, and the men in the cabin looked at each other.

"Well, at least we don't have to shout at each other anymore," said one guard, trying to lighten up the situation. No one responded.

The jailer sitting nearest to Jake asked dryly, "If I unlock you, promise you won't run for it?"

The major made a show of looking around the cabin and at the exit door, and then smiled, "I promise. That first step would be a little long."

"Quite. What about *after* we land?"

"Hmm. I can see, Officer, that you are an optimist. Okay, how's this? If I am in any shape to run after we land and if you are in any shape to chase me, I promise I'll count to ten before I take off."

The officer smiled back at him, "Works for me." He reached over and unshackled Kelly. "Don't want to crash and have you all locked up. You'd probably wind up sitting on me."

****

Sam Bergman finished his call and handed the phone back to Ed. He leaned back in his chair and rubbed his face wearily. Devlin waited, wondering what the call had been about. Finally Bergman spoke.

"Ed, the strength of the case against Major Kelly was in

the intelligence intercepts we received, right? Those intercepts presented Kelly's story as the cover an as-yet-to-be-identified American double agent would use to explain his disappearance and re-insertion into the Air Force, correct?"

"That's right, Sam. That's what everybody said."

"Yeah? Well, everybody was wrong. Including me. We fell straight into their web of deceit. There's no one on the planet who does disinformation as well as Ivan. We not only took the bait, we swallowed the whole thing, hook, line, and sinker."

"How can you say that? It wasn't just your source. We had multiple independent confirmations of the ruse Kelly was trying to pull."

"All based on intelligence intercepts, however."

"Yes, that's true."

Sam got out of his chair and began to pace about the room. "What I'm telling you cannot leave this room. One week ago today a Soviet communication intercept from one of our most sensitive and reliable sources was translated by someone in the National Security Agency. I was called in to assist with the translation by providing background on the Russians.

"The intercept consisted of three copies of what we now know as Major Kelly's cover story. It was addressed to various Soviet embassies as an FYI to the intelligence officers at those embassies. The three messages were bundled together. They were identical in all respects save one. Each had a single spelling error, but the error was in a different word in each dispatch.

"The NSA translator was uncertain what to make of this triplicate arrangement. Actually, it was one of the reasons I was sent over to help her. Normally such a thing is done—the errors, I mean—when the sender believes that his communication network has been penetrated. He sends a subtly edited version of the same message to different recipients. If the communication winds up being leaked, the sender will know who leaked it.

"But the problem with last Monday's message, so we thought, was that all three copies were bundled together. Each recipient would see the whole bundle, including the spelling errors. So I concluded that the triplicate nature of the message must *not* be an attempt to catch a leaker but just some bureaucratic screw-up." Sam fell silent, shaking his head.

"And?" Devlin asked, after a moment of silence.

Sam looked up, irritated with himself, "That phone call changed everything. An NSA technical expert analyzed the raw bits and bytes of the intercept and concluded that the triplicate nature of the message was a chance artifact of the digital communication protocol. The intercept *was* three separate messages to three separate destinations. No one should have seen those messages bundled together."

"So, you are saying that the message *was* an attempt to ferret out a leak."

"Yes."

"Well, Sam, I can see how that might have other implications, but how does it affect us?"

"Because, Ed, it means the message was prepared by the sender knowing it would be leaked or intercepted. *We were intended to see that message!* Which has to mean, Ed, the content of the message is false."

"But how could they know so precisely what Kelly was going to tell us?"

"Simple, Ed. It's so simple. They assumed he would tell us the truth."

****

"The ceiling at Cantwell is about two thousand AGL, so we should be okay, Gene. Besides, we don't have a choice anyway." Beau had just finished communicating with the Trooper Post in Cantwell.

"That we don't, son, that we don't," Gene muttered as he watched his instruments. The Beech was descending, passing out of clear air into the dense cloud layer. Minor bits of turbulence picked up, buffeting the craft. Eugene ignored the sense of disorientation as everything outside the windshield became featureless white cotton. He kept the nose up just enough to maintain eighty-five knots Indicated Air Speed (IAS). His rate of descent was just over seven hundred feet per minute. "We should be getting below this stuff in about four minutes, Beau. Let's hope we see a nice, empty, straight stretch of road when we come out of the soup. You be ready to drop the gear as soon as I say so."

"Roger that. I will be ready to drop the gear on your command." Beau also kept his eyes glued to the instrument panel. He was grateful that Eugene Martin was in the left-hand seat. If any pilot could pull them through a dead-stick landing in the rugged terrain of Alaska, it was Gene. Rather than yield to the fear eating away at the edges of his demeanor, he decided to trust his pilot.

****

The satellite phone in his briefcase rang. Jensen pulled it out and answered, "Jensen here."

"Bill, it's Roger Carson. We lost Ott."

"What?"

"I'm sorry, boss, but he must have left the Troopers HQ right after we last talked, before we had a chance to locate him. We're staking out the airport but we have no idea what his transportation plans are. I don't know if we have much of a chance of bagging him."

"Is he running? That would be proof positive of his guilt."

"No, I think we simply missed him. I don't think he's running. Certainly nothing we've done on Alpha Team would have spooked him. Except for you and Baker Team no one even knows we're here."

"Okay, Rog. Stay in place until I get back to you."

****

The King Air began passing through broken clouds and the pilots started seeing brief glimpses of the snow-covered terrain below. Fifteen seconds later they dropped out of the overcast. Stretched below them on the snowy landscape was Highway 3, winding through the rough country, connecting Fairbanks to Anchorage.

The aircraft was descending through forty-two hundred feet above Mean Sea Level (MSL), or around eighteen hundred feet AGL. Gene could see the Chulitna River Bridge dead ahead about four miles. He had hoped to get beyond the bridge to where there were several long, straight sections of road. But the aircraft lacked sufficient altitude to glide that far.

A new problem presented itself. There was still traffic on the section above the bridge where they must land. He could see it from here.

"Beau! Get on the radio NOW to the Trooper Post in Cantwell! We are setting down in little over two minutes on the highway above the bridge." Gene had not intended to speak so sharply but his palms were getting sweaty and his mouth was dry. He forced himself to loosen his death grip on the control column, and tried to relax.

Within twenty seconds he began to see results as the call was relayed to the troopers and all state vehicles on the scene. A large snow plow created a new space on the frozen ground off the highway, and several trucks followed the plow into the cleared-off space.

"Drop the wheels. We need to bleed off some altitude."

"Gear down and locked. Cantwell says the road elevation is twenty-two sixty MSL. Troopers estimate a northwest crosswind of eight knots." Beau replied. He shouted back into the cabin, "Touchdown in about a minute, boys, be ready." He had forgotten that without the roar of the engines, there was no need to shout.

"Read off my airspeed and altitude, Beau. I've got to watch out the window."

"Eighty-five and twenty-eight hundred."

"What's my rate of descent?"

"Seven hundred."

"Too fast, too fast," Gene muttered under his breath. He pulled the nose up, and started quoting the forced landing checklist from memory.

"ELT on."

"ELT on, check."

"Mixture, right and left."

"Mixture right, full lean, left, full lean. Eighty-three and twenty-six hundred."

"Fuel selector."

"Fuel selector, off. Eighty and twenty-five thirty."

"Seat belt and harness."

"Check, strapped in. How about you?"

"Good boy, Beau. I'm strapped in. Magnetos."

"Magnetos right, off, left, off. Eighty and twenty-four fifty."

"Cabin door."

"Cabin door is unlocked, checked it on my last trip back. Eighty and twenty-three fifty."

"Be ready on the flaps. Wait for my command, son. When you put them down, do it smoothly through all stops. Don't jam it."

"Roger that. Smoothly. Ready on the flaps. Eighty and twenty-three hundred."

The tops of taller trees were racing past as Eugene made minute adjustments to keep the airplane over the road.

"Power line, Gene, dead ahead."

"I see it, nothing we can do about it now." Gene eased the nose up and the stall warning began to sound.

"FULL FLAPS SMOOTHLY, BEAU!" Gene shouted over the stall warning.

The aircraft traded speed for a greatly lessened rate of descent and was set for a smooth touchdown on Highway 3 when the worst happened. The nose of the aircraft caught the lone power line crossing the road. The line readily snapped but not before the tail of the aircraft pivoted down, smacking into the road and then bouncing back up. The King Air porpoised, forcing the front end down as the Beech pitched about its center of gravity. The nose slammed hard onto the pavement, collapsing the nose wheel. Still doing seventy miles per hour, the aircraft skidded down the highway, leaving a trail of sparks. The left wing clipped a snowbank and crumpled, sending the plane spinning counter-clockwise down the road, pinballing between the mounds of snow on either shoulder. The initial impact broke Eugene Martin's back, as well as both legs. The old pilot's last thoughts were, *I hope Beau makes it . . . .*

Chapter 15

Monday, October 12, 1987: 1152 hours, local time
Anchorage, AK

Ed Devlin sat in his office staring out the window. He played out over and over in his mind the interrogations and *Snowbird* meetings. And every time he re-examined the data he came to the same conclusion: Kelly was guilty.

And yet that conclusion was evidently wrong. Other than Jesse Pierce the whole team was led to their erroneous conclusion by a crafty GRU disinformation campaign. *Like lambs to the slaughter.* What really galled him was that the men in *Snowbird* were not a bunch of wet-behind-the-ears neophytes. They were very competent men engaged in a very difficult business, and they had been snookered.

He jumped as the telephone interrupted his morose ruminations. "Devlin here."

"Sir, we just got word. The Beechcraft ran out of fuel about fifteen minutes ago. Eugene verified that he had checked the fuel levels with a dipstick during his pre-flight and the Beech had full tanks. The gauges on the instrument panel confirmed the dipstick reading. I called the fuel vendor at the airport and they checked the logs and verified that they had topped the tanks off three days ago. So we know it should have had a full load of fuel at takeoff. Both pilots indicated, however, that when the aircraft ran out of fuel the gauges still showed full, as though they had not used a drop since take-off."

Devlin nodded, "So it isn't pilot error. Somebody messed with the plane."

"That is their conclusion also, sir."

"What's their current status?"

"We don't know, sir. The last transmission we received was

a check with Anchorage Center to verify their position before they descended into the clouds over Cantwell. We've not heard anything since. I'll call the Trooper Post in Cantwell and get an update."

"Let me know as soon as you find out anything." Devlin hung up the phone. If there had been any doubt before, there was none remaining: someone was trying to silence Kelly. Devlin remembered the end of the final interrogation session earlier that morning. *I'll bet it has to do with those nine names!*

He called his secretary and asked her to track down the *Snowbird* group and have them meet in the conference room at 1600 hours.

****

"Roger, this is Bill Jensen. I want you to reel in the IDC team in Fairbanks. Do it now. You are authorized to use deadly force if necessary to prevent civilian injuries. But I want the targets alive, if possible."

"You got it, Bill. I'll contact Team Baker and we will put those bad boys in the bag."

"How about Major Ott? Any luck finding him?"

"Sir, it turns out he is on his way to Fairbanks. He boarded a commercial flight out of Anchorage right before you told us to shadow him. Bill, we cannot do both the IDC team and Ott. If we get spread too thin my guys are liable to start making mistakes."

"Gotcha covered, Rog. I'll have the Air Force handle the major."

****

The phone rang in Devlin's office. His gut told him the news would not be good. He reluctantly picked up the receiver. "Devlin here."

"Sir, I just got off the phone with Cantwell. The plane is down, sir. It was a very rough landing, both the cockpit and the tail area of the cabin are smashed up. The left wing was ripped off, the landing gear all collapsed. Witnesses say the Beech tangled with a power line at touchdown, the only line that crosses the road for miles. The pilot had no choice, sir. It was dead-stick all the way in."

"What about casualties?"

"They don't have any report yet, sir, but Cantwell said it doesn't look good. They're not holding out much hope for survivors."

Lord, have mercy. "Give me an update as soon as you can."

Devlin hung up the phone and slammed both fists down on his desk. "*NO! NO! NO!*" he shouted at the window. Most of the men on that plane were among his closest friends. One of the troopers serving as the prisoner escort was his eldest daughter's fiancé. And the lives of nine innocent men were hanging on information still locked in Kelly's brain.

****

"General Martin, that nasty citizen is back again to complain about last night's flight operations. He is very irate, sir."

Martin smiled. It sounded like Bill Jensen was enjoying his cover story a little too much. It was pretty easy to pull Cathy's chain, and apparently Jensen was giving it a couple of hard yanks just for fun.

"Send him in, Cathy. I'll try to convince the good citizen that the Air Force is not intending to be his personal irritant."

"Are you sure, sir? I could just call security and have him escorted off the base."

"No, no, don't do that. Send him in."

A moment later his door opened and a sour-looking Cathy deposited the visitor in his office and withdrew.

"Good afternoon, General."

"Hi, Jensen. If you keep razzing my secretary, you're going to need personal protection. She can be one mean lady."

"Just trying to keep up a good cover, General," Jensen chuckled. "Sir, we found the spy, and it's time to drop the hammer on him. I was wondering if I could have some help."

****

General Larry Martin, Base Commander of Eielson Air Force Base, strolled nonchalantly into the base Intelligence Section, chomping on an unlit cigar. As the men scrambled to attention, he waved them back to their seats, "As you were, men, as you were." He walked through the office and paused by Senior Master Sergeant Hank Swift's desk.

"I am looking for Major Ott. Has anyone seen him today?" he asked the room, addressing his question to no one in particular.

Swift looked up and smiled, "He's in Anchorage today, General. We expect him back this evening."

Martin grunted with disappointment. He pulled the cigar out of his mouth and said, "Got a light, son? I left mine in my office."

Swift reached into his pocket and pulled out his Zippo, handing it to the general. Martin lit his cigar and shut the lighter, surrounded in a wreath of smoke. He looked down at the two full ashtrays on Swift's desk. "You got to do something about that habit, son. They tell me smoking is bad for your health." He drew deeply on his cigar and emitted a dense cloud of smoke, still holding the lighter.

Swift chuckled. "Yes, sir. They tell me that, too, sir. I can see that you are taking that advice the same way I am, sir."

Martin grinned at Swift. "Got that right, Sergeant. But I'm a real *picture* of health, you know. A *snapshot* of the good life."

Swift blinked and swallowed. Forcing a grin, he choked out, "Yes, sir."

"Pardon the puns, son, I'm really not any good at them."

"Puns, sir?" The color was draining from Swift's face. The others in the office were staring at the general and wondering if perhaps he had a screw loose. They had no idea of what had been going on right under their noses.

"You know what I'm talking about, Sergeant. You know," the general said softly, dangerously. He was still grinning but without warmth—it was the grin of a shark closing in for the kill. "Do you see that overhead ventilator, Sergeant Swift?" he asked, pointing up at the HVAC vent in the ceiling.

"Sir?" the sergeant croaked. It was all he could manage. His mouth had suddenly gone dry.

"Well," General Martin continued mercilessly, "there's a surveillance camera in that vent. Now, it's a video camera, not a still camera—not like the one in your lighter. But we captured some very interesting footage. Would you like to see it?" Martin dropped the lighter into his pocket and puffed on his cigar. The other men in the office slowly stood to their feet as the general's meaning dawned on them.

Swift looked back toward the door, calculating how many steps it would take to get out of the room. He began to stand up. General Martin barked, "GENTLEMEN!" Six armed MPs rushed through the door, weapons drawn.

"Master Sergeant Swift? It's a mighty sorry way to end what might have been a fine career. But your career in the United States Air Force is surely at an end, and your own personal hell is about to begin." General Martin motioned to the MPs to do their duty, and then turned on his heel and left the office.

****

Until paramedics arrived the troopers on the scene would have to serve as rescuers. Thankfully, fire had not broken out in the wreckage. The men ran first to the crumpled cockpit and looked inside. The pilot's head was crooked at an odd angle, his eyes sightlessly looking up into the clouds. Both legs were broken—compound fractures—and blood was everywhere. The copilot was worse. The cockpit smashed into a sturdy sign during its out-of-control sliding spin down the highway and the copilot's position had absorbed that impact. The man was very obviously dead.

Running to the left side of the aircraft, the rescuers found the cabin door closed, largely intact, but with sufficient damage that they could not open it. They backed a snow plow up and managed to get enough of a grip with a chain to pull the door open. Fearing more carnage, they approached the opening and looked inside.

****

Skip called Mike over the radio. "What is your status, Mike?"

"Jimmy and I have been in position for the last hour and a half. I am freezing my butt off and I 'spect Jimmy is worse."

"Thanks for the weather report, Mike, but I'm more interested in the bad guys."

"You're heartless. Okay, Jimmy and I both have clear fields of fire to the IDC team. They managed to infiltrate the airport perimeter and cop an official vehicle, a pickup, and are now in the southernmost one on the flight apron, just behind the snowplows. According to what we heard last night, they're planning on waiting until they hear the Beech contact the tower for landing clearance, and then one of their guys will exit the truck and take down a plow operator so they can put their scheme into effect."

"What they don't know, however, is that the Beech isn't coming. I have been on the sat phone with Bill and the Troopers' aircraft went down on the other side of Cantwell about fifteen minutes ago. As soon as the bad guys learn the plane isn't coming, they will head back to the hotel, get their gear, and skip town."

"Do you think this is the best place to take them?" Mike asked.

"I do. They're out in the open, away from the public for the most part, and you and Jimmy can take them out if they run or cause trouble. We stand the least possibility of collateral damage if we take them down right here."

"Roger that. Okay, we're ready. How do you want to do this?"

"Randy and I will enlist airport security to secure the perimeter and serve as our backup. We will take an unused snow plow and drive out to the apron. We should be able to get close without causing suspicion. I'll ram the plow into their pickup and then Randy and I will take them. Two patrol cars filled with the local gendarmes will come out as soon as I ram them."

"Sounds like a plan. Don't forget to buckle your seatbelt. How long will it take to put this together?"

"We can be ready in ten minutes," Skip replied.

"Okay. Keep your ears on, just in case the IDC team starts to move before you are ready."

"Will do."

****

Matthew Loeb checked and rechecked the Intelligence Section duty log, comparing it with the technical printout Bill Jensen had given him of the attempt to modify the DPMO database record. There was no question about it: Major Bill Ott had not been on base when the attempt was made. But it was clearly done from the computer in his office. The IP address of the computer attempting the edit was assigned to Ott's computer.

Loeb sat back, trying to figure how it could have been done. If Sergeant Swift had gone into Ott's office everyone else would have seen it. Besides, it was a serious breach of intelligence office protocol: you never used someone else's computer and you did not share passwords. Kind of like bank tellers not using one another's cash drawers. It wasn't done; you were held accountable for your own.

Maybe I need to think like a computer geek, he considered. *After all, I really don't know squat about surveillance or intelligence.* He nodded. *Yeah, how would I do this if I were a hacker? I would need to get Ott's IP and password. The password would not be that tough. But how about the IP address? Hmmm. We are using a DHCP server with static reservations. It ladles out reserved IPs based on the requesting network card's MAC address. What if I spoofed the MAC address on my computer, to make it look like it was Ott's? Then I'd get his IP address. I bet that's how Swift did it.*

Matt rubbed his head, pondering. The more he considered it the more certain he was that he had figured it out. *Is there anything that could verify my theory? . . . Of course! The log file on the*

DHCP server would tell me exactly what happened!

He accessed the network management area and located the DHCP log file for Friday, 2 October. He scanned it for all activity pertaining to IP address 11.107.6.15.

Bingo! On that date Major Ott's computer appeared to have been booted up just once. There was only one request from his MAC address for an IP number. Loeb reviewed the log for activity just prior to the request. *This is interesting,* he thought. There was an IP RELEASE request from Sergeant Swift's computer just sixty seconds prior to Ott's computer's activity. Then Swift's own computer seemed to disappear from the network. Next, Ott's MAC address appeared, requesting an IP. Several minutes later, Ott's IP was released and Swift's computer reappeared.

Matt went through the log one more time, just to ensure he was drawing the right conclusions. Ten minutes later he was convinced: the attempt to edit the DPMO database had actually been made from Sergeant Hank Swift's computer, masquerading as Ott's, using the major's login credentials. Technical Sergeant Matthew Loeb picked up the phone. He thought Bill Jensen would be very interested in his discovery.

****

"Get in here quickly! Please!"

The trooper ducked his head and stepped into the battered cabin. The scene was indescribable. Two obvious fatalities were sprawled in the aft portion of the cabin. To his left, a man in prison garb had his hands clamped down on a trooper's leg. Part of the wreckage had lacerated the leg, damaging the femoral artery. Blood was spurting from between the prisoner's fingers as he tried to staunch the flow. Three other troopers, seated in the forward area of the cabin, appeared to be alive, though in shock.

"We have to work fast to save this man's life," the prisoner said calmly. "Got to stop the bleeding or he will die. I need something to use as a compress, and I need to maintain pressure on the wound. I cannot release my hands, so it is up to you. First, get a compress."

The trooper shouted to his companions just outside the door, "Jerry, open the medical kit and give me the biggest compress in there, stat! Al, we need a *Lifeline* helicopter: get on the horn and dial one up. Four fatalities and five souls living. Injuries look bad. Al, after you send for the chopper get those plows clearing a landing zone."

"Listen up," Jacob Kelly directed, "I need two belts. We've got to strap that compress down as tight as we can. If this doesn't work we'll have to use a tourniquet and he might lose the leg. How long before we have skilled medical help?"

"Could be as much as twenty minutes before paramedics are on the scene. We had less than eight minutes to prepare for this, I'm sorry."

When the officer unwrapped the compress, Kelly said, "When I count to three I will take my hands away. You slap the compress on and apply pressure, all in one movement, understand? Use two hands and hold it. I'll strap the belts around it while you apply pressure."

The trooper nodded, so Jake counted, "ONE, TWO, THREE, GO!" Blood spurted as soon the pressure was released but the trooper skillfully applied the compress and murmured, "Got it. We're good."

Kelly rummaged through the wreckage and found a magazine to provide a stiff backing for the dressing, then belted the whole assembly firmly in place. The blood flow slowed to a trickle, though the bandage was rapidly becoming saturated.

The three remaining passengers began groaning and stirring, fumbling with their seatbelts. "Please, stay put until we've had a chance to assess your injuries," Jacob Kelly commanded.

"What about you?" asked the trooper who was first on the scene.

"I think I'm okay. I was sitting in the middle of the cabin. All the action was pivoting around me. I don't even recall getting hit by anything. Right now I feel fine."

"You must be in shock then, because you have a nasty gash on your forehead and there is blood running down your pants."

The eyelids of the young trooper with the lacerated leg fluttered open. He began to work his mouth. Jacob Kelly leaned down to hear.

"Di—did you start to count to ten yet?" he asked, smiling weakly, "Because if you run, I don' think I can chase—" The man lapsed into unconsciousness.

"He's okay. He just fainted. If we can get some help here, he might make it. What's your name, sir?"

"Jake Kelly."

"Jerry, take Mr. Kelly to the squad car. Make sure the heater is on, I expect he'd like to warm up. Sir," he said, turning back to the major, "I'm afraid we have to cuff you, as you are still a prisoner in the custody of the Alaska State Troopers."

"Not a problem, officer. I'm just glad to be alive and on the ground."

"Jerry, see to the wounds on his head and leg as well. And call in, give the Cantwell Post an update of the situation. Al," he called out the door of the cabin, "detail someone to round up some blankets. Oh, yeah, and send officers in either direction to let folks know the highway is going to be closed for at least four hours. We don't want people sitting in their cars in this cold."

****

Stewart sat in the conference room reviewing his notes. The phone at his elbow rang, startling him. "This is Special Agent James Stewart. How can I help you?"

"Agent Stewart, this is Levi Cohen. I am a special assistant to Ambassador Keilman. I understand you have some information for us."

Keilman was the Israeli ambassador in Washington. Stewart grinned to himself. *Special assistant indeed!* Cohen was probably the ranking Mossad officer assigned to the embassy.

"I might. Am I correct in understanding that Captain Moshe Shimonah is missing?"

"I have not said that. He is on extended leave."

"I see. And where might I contact him?"

"I am afraid I can't say." Cohen was trying to divulge nothing.

"Can't say, or won't say?"

"I beg your pardon?" Cohen replied innocently.

"Do you mean you don't know where he is, or you know but you are unwilling to tell me?" Stewart inquired brusquely.

"May I ask to what purpose all these questions are leading?"

"Sure, Mr. Cohen. We know where Shimonah is, and we are trying to get you to verify that he is missing."

"Well, if you know where he is, why are you asking us?"

Stewart groaned inside. *Did Sally prompt this guy? I feel like I am talking to her all over again. Maybe it is time to play hardball.*

"Forgive me, Assistant Cohen. We thought we had some news that would be helpful to the State of Israel. Evidently we were wrong. I will take no more of your time. Good day." Stewart gently hung up the phone, and looked at his watch. *I wonder how long it will take for him to swallow his pride and then get clearance to speak with me?*

Several minutes later the phone rang again. He let it ring five times and then answered it, "This is Special Agent James Stewart. How can I help you?"

"Agent Stewart, this is Levi Cohen. I have been authorized to tell you that, yes, Captain Moshe Shimonah of the Israeli Defense Forces is missing. We have no idea of his whereabouts and would be grateful for whatever assistance you might render."

That's more like it, Stewart sighed to himself. *It also means we were wrong about Kelly. Have to deal with that later.*

"Assistant Cohen, I have a feeling you and I will be talking with each other frequently in the coming days. May I call you Levi? Please call me Jim."

"Certainly, Jim."

"Good. Now, we are not on a secure line and I understand your situation as an embassy officer. But I need to ask you some simple questions which will not in any way compromise your national security, and which will enable me to make some quick decisions."

"Very well, Jim, fire away."

"First, Levi, I understand that Shimonah is a captain in the IDF. But is he also somewhat of a scientist?"

"Not to my knowledge, no."

"Okay, then, was he working on any projects for the IDF of an, um, *sensitive* nature? I don't need to know what they were, and this is the last question. A simple yes or no will suffice."

A moment's hesitation told Stewart all he needed to know. The "yes" that was finally elicited from Cohen's lips was just confirmation of the obvious.

"Very good. Levi, we will be in contact with you through the CIA. The project name that will be used to refer to these discussions is *Thunderbird*."

"*Thunderbird*," Cohen repeated.

"Right. The Israeli government will need to appoint someone to liaise with us on this matter, someone who is competent to determine what sort of intelligence can be shared with our team. The whole affair should be held in utmost secrecy. Shimonah's location will be divulged in those meetings in a secured environment. Is this suitable to your government, Levi?"

"Yes, I can agree to these arrangements on behalf of my government. We will await your call."

In the next twenty minutes, four more of the nine people on Kelly's list were confirmed missing. The conversations were similar in each case, the representative of the host country playing close to the vest, and Jim Stewart trying to secure a spirit of cooperation. By the end of the following day, all nine contacts would be confirmed.

Kelly's information had checked out. Stewart was now convinced Major Jacob Kelly was innocent.

****

"It's really simple to understand, sir." Matthew Loeb looked across the table at the older man and tried once again to explain the mysteries of MAC addresses and DHCP servers.

Simple for you, maybe, thought Bill Jensen. Finally he said, "Stop, Matt! I am convinced! I believe you. You're telling me we have conclusive evidence Bill Ott was not the man who tried to change the DPMO record, correct?"

Loeb stopped mid-sentence and nodded.

"Great job, son, great job!" Jensen thought for a moment. The only evidence which had implicated Major William Ott was the attempt on the DPMO record. Nothing else pointed to Ott. *He must be clean*, surmised the CIA agent.

"Matthew, our task is almost finished. I need you to write up a full report containing every detail pertaining to the past week. Make sure I get a copy of it. Air Force investigators will be contacting you, probably tomorrow, to impound all of the equipment we have used. Leave it set up and allow them to take it down. I'm going to recommend you to General Martin, son, for some sort of medal or commendation. It was your work that identified the spy and cleared Major Ott from suspicion."

Loeb could not contain his wide grin, "Thank you, sir!"

"And now I have to tell you the worst part of the whole spy trade."

"What's that, Bill?"

"When you have done something great, as you have, *you can't tell anyone*. It's all confidential. You'll have to be content just knowing you've done a good job."

"No one else can know?"

"No one else."

"Not even my wife?"

"Especially not your wife. Don't burden her with something exciting she can't tell anyone else."

"Rats."

Chapter 16

"We are in position. Final check: Mike, are you and Jimmy ready?" Skip's adrenaline was surging.

"Affirmative."

"Sergeant Todd, are your men ready?" Skip queried.

"Check," crackled the reply over the radio. "We are ready to deploy as soon as you hit the pickup."

"Mr. Sykes, are the airport police ready?"

"Affirmative. The perimeter is secured."

"Okay, boys, we're going in."

Skip illuminated the flashing yellow beacon on top of his cab and pulled out of the maintenance vehicle parking area. The day was gloomy, making the runway and taxiway lights stand out. The snow was picking up in intensity again.

Randy pointed to a pickup truck on the tarmac. "There they are, Skip. It's that extended cab pickup on the left. I can see all three of them inside." Randy was nervous, anxious to make up for his mistakes in the surveillance.

"I see 'em, Randy. Listen, you don't have anything to prove because of the other night, okay? Don't be too aggressive, and don't put yourself in danger. Alright?"

"I'm okay, Skip. Let's just do this thing. I'm buckled in, how about you?"

"Snug as a bug in a rug. Here we go."

Skip floored the accelerator. The plow rammed the back of the pickup, the impact tossing the occupants around like pebbles in a tin can. None of them had been wearing their seat belts.

Skip and Randy jumped out of the plow, service revolvers drawn, and raced up on either side of the pickup.

"FEDERAL OFFICERS! GET YOUR HANDS IN SIGHT! GET YOUR HANDS IN SIGHT!" screamed Skip at the IDC team. Behind him he heard the policeman on his car PA system telling all the airport workers to stay in their vehicles and get down.

One of the IDC team members kept his hands in the air, but both the driver and the man in the rear seat came up with weapons. The area erupted in gunfire. Skip took out the driver with two shots to the head, Randy shot the thug in the right-side back seat just as Mike's sniper rifle barked into action, pumping another round into Randy's target. All the windows in the pickup not already shattered by the collision were shot out.

And suddenly it was silent, over as quickly as it had started. The only sounds came from a 727's turbines winding down half a mile away at the terminal and the small army of idling snowplows.

"Sergeant Todd!" Skip shouted back toward the police cars, without taking his gun off the ruined pickup and its occupants. "We have two shooters down and one that needs to be cuffed. Please bring your officers up and take custody."

"Gotcha covered, Skip. Coming up on your left."

The assassin on the passenger side of the front seat kept his hands on his head, but looked back at Randy and said casually, "Hey, aren't you the private investigator I ran into the other night?"

Randy grinned, "Yep."

"Who do you really work for?"

"You know the drill, sir. If I told you . . ."

"Yeah. You'd have to kill me. Okay, son."

****

Ed Devlin's phone rang. He shook his head; every time it had rung today, it had been bad news. He shut his eyes and picked it up again.

"This is Ed Devlin," he said resignedly.

"Sir, I have the casualty figures from the Beechcraft."

"Okay. Let's hear them."

"We have four dead, sir. Both pilots were killed, both from broken backs and other injuries sustained during the crash. The two officers sitting aft in the cabin, Pelty and Smithers, were also killed. Everyone else is still alive although with injuries."

"And how about Norm Denning?" Devlin asked. Norm was his daughter's fiancé. The wedding was only six weeks away.

"He's in critical but stable condition. Had a laceration near the femoral artery of his right leg. He lost a lot of blood, but I am told they expect him to pull through. Has several broken bones as well, but nothing that won't heal."

"Oh, thank God," Devlin replied. The strength left his legs and he dropped into his chair. Involuntarily he began to weep. The emotionally charged tension between the relief that he felt and the grief over losing good friends finally overcame him.

The voice on the other end of the line was silent for a moment with understanding, and then said quietly, "Sir?"

"Yes?" Devlin mumbled, when he was able to speak.

"The prisoner? Major Jacob Kelly? He saved Norm's life. It took the troopers about two minutes to get into the cabin. When they got in, the major was applying pressure to Norm's leg to stop the bleeding. The doctor in the Lifeline chopper said that Norm would have died if not for Kelly's quick actions."

"What about the major? How is he?"

"He's fine. Couple of stitches in his head, and his left leg. Nothing broken. It's amazing, really."

"Where is he?"

"They are all at Valley Hospital in Palmer. He is under guard there."

How ironic, Devlin thought to himself. *This affair with Kelly began in a hospital in Kotzebue with the major saving a Naval MP from death at the hands of an IDC assassin, and it's ending in a hospital in Palmer, the major again having saved a life that had been threatened—I'm guessing—by an IDC assassin. And this time the life he saved is my future son-in-law's. How could I have been so wrong about Kelly?* "Is he able to travel?"

"Sure. We're just holding him, awaiting further instructions."

"Have him brought here, immediately. Send a chopper for him: he is to be well treated, do you understand?"

"Yes, sir. Shall I continue to hold him under guard?"

"Yes, for now."

****

It was going on 1600 hours when Ed Devlin finally gathered all the *Snowbird* participants in the conference room of the Alaska State Troopers headquarters, except Major Ott, whom he was unable to contact, and Jesse Pierce, who joined the meeting via speaker phone from his office at Adak. Bill Jensen was also connected via speaker phone.

"Jesse, with your permission I am going to moderate this meeting," stated Ed Devlin. "It would be a little tough for you to do it over a speaker phone."

"I agree, Ed, please proceed," Jesse replied.

"First things first," Devlin said. "The Beechcraft crash-landed southwest of Cantwell. There were four fatalities, and we have four men in the hospital. Major Kelly has some stitches and bruises but is otherwise fine. He saved the life of one of my troopers. Kelly is being brought here by helicopter. I expect him any minute now."

Devlin continued, "Today's events change everything, which is why I asked you men to stay. For the benefit of the those on speaker phones, let me say who is present. Jim Stewart and Sam Bergman are here. Bill Ott has already returned to Fairbanks; we couldn't contact him. Besides Jesse, also on speaker phone is Dr. William Jensen, special assistant to the DDO, CIA. He is calling from Eielson in Fairbanks."

Sam looked up sharply and said, "Bill, it's Sam Bergman. I thought you weren't involved in this case."

"Hi, Sam. I am sorry, I couldn't spill the beans to you because you were involved in the *Snowbird* project."

"I don't understand. You are saying that you could not level with him because he was part of *Snowbird*?" Ed Devlin looked confused.

"Correct. Listen, gentlemen. I have been tracking your progress over the last week. Jacob Kelly contacted me several days after he fled from Kotzebue. That would have been, let's see . . . the 29th. He could not turn himself over to the Air Force because of his concern that there was a spy, the same spy that gave his flight path to the Soviets on 10 July a year ago."

"Then you believe his story?" Jesse Pierce asked.

"Of course. I have multiple independent corroborations of it. I'll share those in a minute."

"So do I," offered Jim Stewart.

Both Bergman and Devlin had an idea of what Stewart was talking about, but Pierce was surprised. "You're kidding? Why didn't you say so this morning, Jim?"

"Because I did not have the evidence this morning. Or more accurately, it had not been confirmed. It has now."

"And I," said Bergman, "received incontrovertible proof this afternoon that our intelligence intercepts which have been so damning to Jacob Kelly were, in fact, part of an elaborate Soviet disinformation campaign."

The room fell silent for a moment. Devlin was the first to voice the thoughts going through the *Snowbird* participants' minds, "Then those four deaths this morning were the result of our bad decision? They could have been avoided? We nearly sent not four but nine men to their deaths in that aircraft! If it hadn't been for Jensen's warning, they would've all been killed!"

Bill Jensen's voice came sharply from the phone in the center of the table, "No! No! NO! Gentlemen, these deaths were NOT caused by your decision this morning! These deaths were caused by the Soviet Union and their reckless efforts to get a leg up on military technology the easy way: by kidnapping scientists from Western countries. Do not forget it! The blood for these events rests on the heads of General Nikolai Chernikov and his patrons in the Politburo.

"Now gentlemen, please allow me to tell my tale."

"Please!" said Devlin wearily. "Please do."

"Thank you. When Jacob Kelly contacted me, I began to investigate his story. The *Snowbird* group had already been constituted. Because I had no idea who the spy was, I received permission from the DDO to pursue this independently. Since I was not on your radar, I could also keep an eye on you men in case the spy had maneuvered into your group. I believed that he had, up until just a few hours ago."

"Bill Ott!" Bergman cried.

"Right. That's why I could not talk to you, Sam. I was afraid he was dirty. But anyway, let me continue.

"I discovered another group investigating Jacob Kelly's disappearance. They had no idea Kelly was even alive, but they were making good headway establishing that his disappearance was neither pilot error nor mechanical failure, but a Soviet shootdown. General Jim Franks, who leads the *Hydra* Project, and Admiral John Bridger, CO of SPECWAR Group One, had two pieces of evidence. First, they had an eyewitness report of the shootdown. Second, they were able to locate recordings of the Soviet jamming signal which blocked Major Kelly's distress call when he was shot down. Providentially, the evidence of the jamming was contained on ELINT recordings of last year's RIMPAC exercises. Both pieces of evidence corroborated the story Jake had shared with me in his phone call.

"In my own investigations I uncovered the fact that someone attempted to modify DPMO records pertaining to the major's disappearance. Some unknown person attempted to insert the suspicion that Jake defected, the very story circulating in the intelligence intercepts we have been receiving. The initial evidence pointed to Major Ott as the one who tried to change Kelly's DPMO records."

"May I jump in here briefly, Bill? I have some additional light to shed on that," Sam Bergman requested.

"Sure, Sam, go ahead."

"Thanks. This afternoon I received a phone call from the NSA translator I've been working with. Further analysis of the intercept has shown it was sent by General Valeriy Ivanovich Patrikeyev, head of the GRU Ninth Directorate, with the express intention of finding an intelligence leak within their own communication network. In other words, he sent it knowing someone would intercept it and we would see it."

"Which means it had to be false," concluded Jesse Pierce, "because they would never put such sensitive information on a network they felt to be insecure."

"Precisely," affirmed Sam, "so we now know that the stories identifying Kelly as a spy were false—disinformation."

Devlin shook his head in amazement, and encouraged Jensen to continue.

"The person who tried to modify the DPMO record unknowingly left a digital footprint, and I was able to follow it back to Eielson. This past Wednesday I secured the assistance and support of General Larry Martin, the Eielson CO. With the help of a technical sergeant from their IT department we were able to trace the attempted breach to the Eielson Intelligence Section. Sergeant Matt Loeb and I set up video surveillance and by Saturday night we had bagged the spy, thanks to Matt's excellent work."

"So there really is a spy?" asked Pierce.

"Yes, indeed. He's already been apprehended. You may be interested to know, Commander Pierce, that the report of your sorties against Petropavlovsk-Kamchatskiy was what betrayed Master Sergeant Hank Swift. Your report was long enough that his repetitive motions photographing its many pages were obvious when the surveillance video was viewed at high speed. The evidence was conclusive. It was providential that your report came along when it did."

"Has the data in the report been compromised?"

"No. This afternoon the film was found in his basement. It hadn't been delivered to his Soviet handler."

"What about Ott?" asked Bergman.

"As it turns out, he was being framed by Swift. Swift had been setting him up the last several months with numerous actions. Through a bit of technological wizardry which I am still at a loss to understand, Swift made it appear as though the attempt to change Kelly's record was done by Ott. His mistake was doing it while Ott was away at a *Snowbird* meeting, ironically. Sergeant Loeb is writing up a complete report explaining the data, which will be entered as evidence against Swift.

"Unfortunately, this last piece was not untangled until late today. I have gone through the entire past week thinking that Ott was a traitor."

"Weren't you concerned about Kelly's safety?" Ed queried.

"Yes, but I figured there could be no attempt on his life while he was held at your facility, Ed. I expected the attempt would come, as it did, during the transfer. I hoped I could bag the spy before the transfer happened. Unfortunately, I did not know Kelly was being moved today. The situation got away from me and I've been playing catch-up all day.

"What you gentlemen undoubtedly did not realize is that two separate assassination squads from IDC have been operating in Alaska since the failed attempt at Kotzebue. I was made aware of these two squads this past Thursday. One was dispatched there, to Anchorage, the other here, to Fairbanks."

"Wait! I don't understand! Why didn't the Agency's IDC monitoring team tell me? I was checking in daily!" Sam was clearly irritated.

"I'm sorry, Sam. Barry did not tell you because I told him *not* to tell you. I could not very well have you sitting in *Snowbird* meetings talking about countermeasures to IDC when a Soviet agent was sitting in there with you, could I?" Jensen's voice was patient, but firm.

Sam grinned sheepishly, "Well, now that you put it that way, I guess not."

"I deployed two teams to keep an eye on the IDC boys. Sam, do you know Roger Carson at the Agency?" Jensen asked.

"Sure do. He is one mean man, a bad operator. He's got quite a reputation."

"Yeah," Jensen agreed, "but he plays for our team and that's what counts. Anyway, we put a team there in Anchorage and the other here in Fairbanks to shadow the IDC goons. Both teams are under Carson's command. The Fairbanks team got on top of theirs immediately, but we never did find the IDC team assigned to Anchorage."

"I know this part of the story," Devlin offered. "You called today when you heard that the Anchorage team had pulled out. That's when you had me order the Beechcraft down."

"Right," Jensen affirmed.

"What happened to the IDC goon squad in Fairbanks?" Stewart asked.

"Carson's team took them down four hours ago. Two IDC operators were killed. No injuries on our side. That pretty much wraps up my story, Ed."

Devlin turned to the FBI agent. "Thanks, Dr. Jensen. Jim, you mentioned you have some information verifying Kelly's claims. Share it with us."

"Well, at the final interrogation early this morning Jacob Kelly played his last card when he knew that *Snowbird* had decided against him. He gave Sam and me nine names of others the Soviets kidnapped. Kelly claimed they were being held at the same facility in Siberia."

"Why didn't you mention that this morning at our final meeting?" Pierce challenged.

"I decided to say nothing until I had followed up on the names. If we were wrong about Jacob Kelly—in other words, if he was right about the spy—we would be signing death warrants for these nine men. Now that the spy has been captured, I can tell you. This afternoon I have received calls regarding five of the nine names verifying that the people in question have gone mysteriously missing. A Soviet plant would hardly give us information which is so easily checked out and so seriously implicates the Soviet Union in international thuggery. When the calls began coming in verifying Kelly's information, I knew he was innocent."

Someone knocked at the conference room door. "Enter," called Devlin.

The door opened and there stood Major Jacob Kelly, still in shackles and wearing the torn and bloodied prison jumpsuit. Devlin walked over and held his hand out to the guard,

who gave him the keys. Devlin unlocked the shackles, muttering, "We don't need these anymore." He turned again to the
guard and said, "Go get his clothes. If they didn't survive the
crash, use the department account and get him several sets of
clean clothes."

Then Ed Devlin turned back to the man who'd saved the
life of his future son-in-law. He wrestled with his emotions
momentarily, lost the battle, and with tears streaming down his
face held out his hand and said hoarsely, "Welcome home,
Major."

Chapter 17

Sunday, October 25, 1987: 1300 hours, local time
Edwards AFB, CA

The T-38 Talon sat on the runway apron, waiting for take-off clearance from the tower at Edwards. Falcon was in the front seat and General James Franks the rear.

"FALCON EIGHT ONE, THIS IS EDWARDS TOWER. YOU ARE CLEAR FOR TAKEOFF RUNWAY ZERO FOUR LEFT. CONTACT OAKLAND CENTER UPON DEPARTURE. GOOD TO HAVE YOU BACK, JAKE."

"EDWARDS TOWER, THIS IS FALCON EIGHT ONE. ROGER CLEARANCE RUNWAY ZERO FOUR LEFT. THANKS, TOWER, IT'S GOOD TO BE HOME."

Jake smoothly throttled up the General Electric J85 turbojet while he stood on the brakes. As soon as the engine spun up, he released the brakes and the aircraft rocketed down the runway and climbed smoothly into the cloudless October sky. He checked in with Oakland Center ATC and was advised to climb another two thousand feet to avoid traffic. His destination was the Alameda Naval Air Station.

After Kelly had returned to Edwards from Alaska he was subjected to a lengthy series of videotaped debriefings and intelligence meetings which had finally concluded this past Friday. Jake was ready to move on to new challenges and responsibilities. Soon he would be released from Project *Hydra* and returned to a fighter wing. Toward that goal, Kelly was flying whenever he got the opportunity so he could be recertified in the F-16. When Franks had mentioned that he needed a lift to Alameda and that there was a good dinner in the bargain, Kelly jumped at the chance to log the flight hours.

"Tell me again, General, who are we having dinner with?" he queried through the aircraft's intercom as he trimmed the

Talon for straight and level.

"Roger and Susan Bates. They are dear friends. Shandra and I get together several times a year with them, usually camping. Roger is a captain in the Navy but don't hold that against him. It was Roger's boys who found the Soviet jamming signal on the RIMPAC tapes recorded the night you were shot down."

"How's Shandra getting there, General?"

"She's already there. She and Susan have been speaking at a conference of the Military Wives Christian Fellowship. You and I will be flying back this evening; Shandra will drive home later this week."

****

The day after Galya had confided her story at the church social function, Roger Bates called General Jim Franks.

"General, I did not know whom to call, and figured maybe you could give me some advice."

"I always knew you were clueless. What's up, Rog?"

"Last night our church got together with a Chinese Presbyterian church from across the Bay. Susan and I met a young woman there with an amazing story to tell. She escaped from Russia, by way of China and is seeking asylum here in America. In Russia she encountered an American—a major in the US Air Force—who was fleeing from a manhunt by the Soviet armed forces. He was trying to escape from the country. Jim, this sounds like pretty serious stuff. I want to tell someone, but I don't want to turn it into a media circus and I especially don't want to compromise this guy if he's still over there."

Franks immediately made the connection to Jacob Kelly, but decided not to let the cat out of the bag. It was becoming increasingly difficult to hide the fact that Kelly had returned, and Franks wanted to get clearance from Bill Jensen before he widened the circle of those in the know. He asked, "What's her name, Rog?"

"Galina Toporova. But Jim, you'll scare the poor girl to death if you send Air Force investigators to her door."

"Actually, I have another idea, Roger. I think I am aware of the incident to which she refers. Let me get back to you."

After discussing the matter with Jensen, Franks contacted Roger Bates and had Susan set up a dinner party for the Bates, the Franks, Galina and Jacob. Neither Galya nor Jake were to know the other would be there.

****

Susan Bates was setting the china on the table when the doorbell rang. She hollered down to the family room in their comfortable bi-level home. "RJ, get the door please."

Wiping her hands on her apron she took it off and lay it aside and went to the front door as RJ was opening it. Galina Toporova was standing on the porch.

"Come in, Galina! You're right on time. Our other guests have not arrived yet. This is my oldest son, Roger, Jr. We call him RJ."

"I am pleased to meet you, RJ."

RJ smiled, "Hello, Miss Toporova. Glad you could come over this evening. Dad and I are watching the Middies get beaten downstairs in the family room. You're welcome to join us."

"The Middies?"

"Oh, sorry! The football team at Annapolis. My dad went to school there."

"Ah. I see. Well, thank you for your very kind invitation, but I think I'll help your mother get supper ready." She smiled as the teen returned to the game, and then followed Sue back to the kitchen. "He seems like a very nice boy."

"Oh, he has his moments. As does Randy, his twin. They're so much like their dad, it's getting so I can't tell whom I am talking to on the phone. They both sound just like Roger. Randy is over at a friend's house and won't be back until late."

As work resumed in the kitchen the two women chatted happily about the Bates' twins and other family-related matters. Since meeting two weeks before, the two women were developing a close friendship. Susan was helping Galina adjust to her new life in America. The Bates had invited her over for supper and an evening of games, telling Galina they would introduce her to some new friends.

The doorbell rang again. Susan looked at the clock. *The timing could not be better*, she thought to herself. *This should be interesting.* "Galina, there is a flower arrangement back there in the dining room. I have been trying to fix it as a centerpiece, and can't seem to get it looking right. Would you mind trying your hand at it while I get the door?"

As the young woman went back into the dining room, Sue went to the front door. "Hello, Jim and Shandra! It is so good to see you! Roger," she called down the stairs, "the Franks are here!"

Roger came bounding up the stairs and said, "Howdy, General. You must have gotten lost on the way. You're late as usual!"

Franks responded, "I am not late, and we did not get lost. Your directions were terrible! What do they teach you boys at the academy, anyway? It's amazing you can even find your way home each day!"

Shandra and Susan looked at the two men, then at each other, and rolled their eyes. They knew that the more insults the two men threw at each other the happier they were to be together again.

"And this must be—" Roger managed before Susan cut him off with a vigorous shake of her head.

Practically whispering, she said, "Jacob Kelly, you are very welcome here."

"Thank you, Mrs. Bates. I hope I'm not crashing your dinner party. Any friend of the Franks is someone I will enjoy getting to know."

"Call me Susan, Jacob. Jim has told us about you, and Roger and I are looking forward to getting to know you, too. But I have a friend who is absolutely dying to meet you. I know this sounds a little odd, but would you mind introducing yourself to her? Just go up these stairs and straight back."

"I'd be glad to. Would you excuse me?" Kelly started up the steps, chuckling to himself. He guessed that the Franks had talked the Bates into inviting a single girl. Jim and Shandra were always playing cupid, trying to get him married ever since he'd gone to work for the general. *Now they are back at their conspiracies. But my heart belongs to someone else. At least, though, I can be a good dinner partner tonight.*

Susan looked at her husband and the Franks, and said firmly, "I think we *all* need to go downstairs for a few minutes."

****

A young woman was standing at the table, her back to him, when Jake entered the dining room. She was absorbed in arranging the flowers in the centerpiece and did not hear him enter. Recognizing her instantly, Jake caught his breath—he couldn't believe his eyes! *Galya? Here in America? It can't be true! How—?* The room seemed to spin and he grabbed the back of a chair to steady himself. Overcome by emotions that could not be contained, he could only manage a whisper, "Galya."

She froze. The red roses slipped from her fingers and fell to the table. Her shoulders began to tremble. "Galya," he whispered again, ever so gently.

She turned around, quivering. Tears streaming down her face, she said softly, "Jacob, can it really be you? I didn't even know if you were still ali—" She could get no farther. He gathered her into his arms as she began to cry, and she clutched him tightly. For six months she had been strong and had kept the stress, grief, fears, and loneliness at bay. All that she had bottled up now demanded expression and she could no more control her emotions than stop the tide.

Jacob Kelly said nothing but held the weeping woman in his arms, their tears mingling. What words could express the depths of emotion welling up from their souls? As Jake held her close it dawned on him, *This truly is providence. It could be nothing less.*

Two hours later the joyful young couple and their friends were pushing back from the dinner table. "Who wants coffee?" Susan asked. Shandra and Galina followed her into the kitchen, while the men moved into the living room.

"Jake, if you don't put a ring on that woman's finger within a week, you're a fool. Some big brawny sailor's liable to try and steal her. You don't let a woman like Miss Toporova get away from you, son," Franks was saying with his customary bluntness.

Kelly frowned. "There is something I have to do first, sir, before I put a ring on Galina's finger. I have one more task to accomplish."

Jacob Kelly's tone made Franks stir uncomfortably, and the general asked, "What's that, Jake? What is so important that you would set your plans aside?"

"General Nikolai Chernikov kidnapped me, detained and tortured me, and tried to hunt me down when I escaped him. He has tried to have me killed several times since. I'm afraid that no one I love will be safe until I have dealt with the man; he'll use them to get at me. Chernikov stopped being professional when I escaped. Now I believe it's personal to him. I don't think he'll ever stop trying to kill me—I represent his greatest failure. If I am to have peace and my loved ones safety, I need to find him before he finds me."

Franks asked, "Are you actually thinking of killing Chernikov? Jake, killing an enemy when we are at war is one matter. But you're talking about an assassination, a revenge killing. We're not at war with the Soviets, nor do we want to be. I cannot have you killin—"

"General, whatever I do will be done on my own time and out of uniform. I have a lot of leave coming and I've already put a request in for two weeks in January. I am not telling anyone exactly what I intend. I haven't even told you—just that I have to find him first. Nothing about my plans when I do find him. I alone will be responsible for my actions."

"Jacob, if you get in trouble over there for criminal activity you realize that we couldn't bail you out? You might spend the rest of your life in a Soviet jail cell—or worse."

"Yes, sir, I am well aware of that."

Franks came away from the evening with two thoughts:

first, somehow he had to keep Jake from going after Chernikov. And second, he was glad he wasn't in Chernikov's shoes because the general suspected that he'd be unsuccessful restraining Jake. The young man's lethal skills had been vividly displayed across the wide expanse of Siberia. Chernikov's days were numbered.

****

They were sipping coffee in the living room after playing several rounds of Scrabble when the telephone rang. Susan went into the kitchen to take the call, and came out a moment later with a curious look on her face. "It's for you, Jim." He took the call in Roger's private study.

"Franks here."

"General, it's Bill Jensen. Sorry to disturb you."

"You darn spooks! How did you track me down? With a satellite?"

"No General, it was a tracking device on your car," Jensen chuckled. "Actually, sir, I just called the Duty Officer at Edwards."

"What's up, Bill?"

"I just got a phone call ten minutes ago. The National Security Council is meeting tomorrow at 1400 hours. You and Major Kelly are to be present at that meeting."

"Oh, I see. And what about my schedule? Did anyone think of that?"

"I'm sorry, General, but your protegé has kicked over the proverbial can of worms here in DC. I've worked in this place for years, Jim, but I've never seen 'em move as fast as they are now. We're going to have to sprint to stay ahead of the politicians."

"What do you mean, Bill?"

"'Tween you and me, General, I think they are screwing up the political courage to get behind a military rescue effort. Anyway, don't forget these are the guys who set the budget for all your nice little black projects at Edwards. You might want to keep that in mind as you think about tomorrow's schedule.

I'd keep 'em happy if I were you."

"As usual, Jensen, you manage to get right to the heart of the matter," Franks grumbled. "Alright, we'll be there."

He returned to the living room and said to the group, "I've got to get Major Kelly back to Edwards before curfew. Wouldn't want him to turn into a pumpkin. Say your good-byes to your sweetie, sonny."

Shandra said, "It's early, Jim. Can't you two stay another hour or two?"

"What's up, General?" Roger asked.

"This bad boy," he said, pointing at Jake, "and I have to be in Washington tomorrow. Seems that some important people want to hear about his adventures. Sorry, folks, but I can't say any more than that."

****

"Sir, you still haven't told me where we are going or whom we are going to meet." Major Kelly was sitting next to General James Franks in a staff car that had picked them up at An-drews Air Force Base, and was now driving into Washington, DC. Both men were decked out in their dress blues, complete with service ribbons and decorations.

"That's because I don't want you to soil your trousers, Jake. Just sit tight. You'll see."

Ten minutes later the staff car pulled through the gates of the White House grounds. As the driver was parking the car, Franks turned to Kelly and said, "We are headed for the Situation Room, under the West Wing. You are going to be questioned by the President and the National Security Council. Also in attendance will be the Gang of Eight. There will be several others there you know, among them Admiral Bridger, Lieutenant Commander Jesse Pierce, and Dr. Jensen.

"You nervous?"

"No, sir."

"Quit lying, son. If you had any sense you'd be scared to death. There aren't that many people living who've even been *in* the Situation Room, and you've been invited to a meeting of the whole gang."

"Sir, you mentioned that the Gang of Eight would be here. Who are they?"

"The legislative branch of the government has a statutory responsibility for oversight of the intelligence services, Jacob. The House and the Senate each have their own Select Committee on Intelligence. The Gang of Eight is made up of the chairmen and ranking members of both those committees plus the Speaker and the Minority Leader of the House plus the Majority and Minority Leader of the Senate. *Eight* people. Gang of Eight."

"I see. But why all the legislators, General? Aren't these sorts of briefings usually confined to the intelligence community?"

"They haven't told me why, Jake, but I can speculate. I think the President is planning to make a decision today, and he wants full support of the legislative branch. He's still stinging over the shellacking he's taken on Iran-Contra. If he decides on a military action, this time it's going to be by the book. That's what I'd guess, anyway."

Franks and Kelly walked into the mahogany-paneled room, followed by Bridger and Pierce.

"How are you doing, Major Kelly? It's a pleasure to finally meet you," Bridger said enthusiastically. "Captain Kirk here has told me all about you, but I'm really pleased to meet the first Air Force major to thumb rides across Siberia."

"Bridger," Franks started in, his face red, "I swear I'm going to find the person in my command who's leaking that Star Trek nonsense to you, and drop them out of an airplane at fifty thousand feet." Bridger just grinned.

"Pleased to meet you, Admiral. Actually, sir, I stole a few aircraft along the way," admitted Kelly as he shook the admiral's hand.

"So I heard. Seems that's become something of a habit for you. I understand you lifted one from the airport in Kotzebue as well."

"Yes, sir. But I've turned over a new leaf. No more airplane thefts for me." He turned to Lieutenant Commander Pierce,

"Hey Jesse. Good to see you. How are things up in the Bering Sea?"

"Pretty boring since we reeled you in. Think I got used to all the excitement. Only thing that's changed is the Sovs have pretty much doubled their patrols. I think they are expecting some sort of retaliation."

"Jake!" Bill Jensen walked in and gave Kelly an affectionate bear hug. "How are you, son? Settling back into the routine of normal life?"

Before Kelly could answer, Howard Baker, the White House Chief of Staff, strode in and said loudly, "Gentlemen, if you could please find your seats we'll get started in a few minutes." The room gradually filled up. When all the attendees had been seated, Baker called upstairs, and a few minutes later President Reagan entered the room.

"Please, gentlemen, remain seated. Let's begin. Major Jacob Kelly, I'd like to start off by saying how proud I am of your accomplishment of escaping the USSR without any outside help. I've read the full account in the briefing packet and it's very impressive.

"And Lieutenant Commander Pierce, congratulations to you and your *Snowbird* group for your role in this. It must have been a wild ride, young man, to have managed a maritime rescue, a manhunt, and an intelligence operation all wrapped into one. Good job, son.

"Dr. Jensen, thank you for running the traitor at Eielson to ground and capturing him. That was a great service to the national security of our country.

"I can't tell you how proud you men make me feel. I thank all of you for your service to our country. And General Franks and Admiral Bridger, that goes for you, too. Thank you."

From that point, Baker ran the meeting and the President interrupted here and there with questions. Everyone's briefing packet contained a thorough account of events from the time of Kelly's capture to the crash of the King Air. For the sake of time Kelly was not asked to narrate those events in the meeting, although opportunity was given for clarifying questions.

"General Franks, what is the status of *Hydra*?"

"Mr. President, the *Hydra* project has completed all testing and the first production run of the modified PAVE ordnance has commenced. The avionics for the next production block of F-16s will be *Hydra*-capable. We now have a small team studying how to retrofit current F-16s, as well as all the other front-line strike aircraft in our inventory. Major Jacob Kelly has been officially released from the *Hydra* project, and will be returning to an active fighter wing soon."

"Dr. Jensen, what is your best estimate of the Soviets' knowledge of *Hydra*? It is my understanding they were unable to get Major Kelly to tell them anything."

"Mr. President, we have to assume they know more than we thought they did. Their effort to kidnap and interrogate Kelly means they probably know the purpose and scope of the project. If I had to guess, Mr. President, I would assume they are already working on ways to counter the weapons."

"General, your opinion?"

"I agree with Dr. Jensen, sir. But the fact that *Hydra* will not be a surprise on the battlefield does not change the fact that the tactical balance of power has shifted somewhat in our direction. *Hydra* munitions perform as promised. Although perfection is never achieved on the battlefield, theoretically a flight of four *Hydra*-equipped Falcons can take out three companies of Russian tanks. And because it's a fire-and-forget weapon system, sir, once the aircraft release their ordnance they can skedaddle."

"Mr. President, with your permission we'll move on to the big question," Baker directed, "and that is, what next? The USSR has committed a clear act of war against the United States, and it has kidnapped two citizens of this country beside Major Kelly, as well as three Brits, an Israeli, two Germans, and one of the premier mathematicians of India. All of these men were involved in highly secret projects that were either directly tied to advanced weapons systems, or have direct applicability to advanced weapons systems. So what are we going to do about it?"

A vigorous discussion followed. The Secretary of State and the Attorney General wanted to handle the matter through diplomacy. The Chairman of the Joint Chiefs suggested that the Soviet Union and its proxies be denied the use of the Panama and Suez Canals as well as the Bosporus Strait for both military and merchant use until the scientists be returned. Although the cooperation of Panama, Egypt, and Turkey would be required for such an action, both State and the Chairman thought the deal could be swung.

"Mr President, there is another option." The speaker was Paul West, Director of the CIA.

"Go ahead, Paul."

"Sir, Major Kelly is concerned that the moment we begin to agitate for the release of those scientists the Russians will kill them, dispose of the bodies, and claim no knowledge. At that point it becomes little more than a 'he said, she said.'"

"I think he's right, Mr. President," affirmed West. "If we approach this through diplomatic pressure, sanctions, or canal closures we could be signing the death warrants of those men."

"So, what do you propose?"

"A lightning raid, sir. I say we go get them and bring those men out. I believe that Admiral Bridger's SEAL teams could do the job."

The room erupted in shouts and objections. It took Baker a full minute to regain control. "Gentlemen, please! Let the Director finish!" The hubbub wound down and Baker said, "Please continue, Paul."

"Gentlemen, we are looking at this all wrong. If we do nothing those men will ultimately die in Soviet captivity. If we pursue any other sort of pressure, we hasten their deaths. A military option, therefore, is those men's best chance at life and freedom.

"Second, there is very little diplomatic risk to us. If we recover even one captive able to corroborate Major Kelly's testimony, the Soviets won't be able to *buy* a friend on the planet. No one will trust them.

"Third, we have a man who's actually been on the inside

of their prison camp. He knows their routines. He's a great source of intelligence for the raid planners."

"Paul, your first two points have merit, but not your third. Kelly's been trained as an Air Force pilot, not as a special forces operator. Unless we were planning on bombing the prison camp his usefulness to operation planners will be limited." The speaker was the Senate Minority leader, Walford Branson of Tennessee, who'd retired from the SEALs in 1968 after an injury ended his career. On his final tour he'd taken shrapnel from a mine that killed the man next to him. Branson still walked with a limp. He was respected on both sides of the aisle as a man of integrity and wisdom.

"Senator Branson, with all due respect to your experience, you are wrong on this matter." The speaker was General Jim Franks, speaking out of turn from the second tier of seats. Everyone turned and stared at him, surprised that he would speak out of turn and doubly surprised that he would disagree with a notable like Branson on military matters.

"Actually, Jim, he's right—" started Admiral Bridger, commanding officer of Navy Special Warfare Group One, but Franks cut him off.

"Please, John, let me finish. I defer to both Senator Branson's experience and wisdom and yours as well, Admiral. And Mr. President, please pardon me for speaking out of turn. But there is something about Major Kelly none of you know—in fact, no one in this room knows other than the Major and myself.

"If you were to examine the Air Force personnel files for Major Kelly, you would find that he's followed the training track of the typical USAF fighter pilot. If, however, you examine the personnel file of Major John Smith, you will discover that Major Smith is an Air Force Combat Control Team operator who's been downrange four times, engaged in firefights three times, and was decorated twice for his actions in those operations. Major Smith was the man who tested the *Hydra* Project PAVE weapons in hot-war conditions. We needed a man skilled both as a pilot delivering the ordnance and a special operator illuminating the targets in order to refine our *Hy-*

dra weapons.

"Gentlemen, let me introduce you to Major John Smith." Franks pointed to Jacob Kelly. A low murmur went around the room. Jensen raised his eyebrows and Franks realized that the CIA man had been unaware of what he had just revealed. Franks continued, "The subterfuge was done in order to preserve security for *Hydra*, and now that *Hydra* is all but over the need for that part of our security no longer exists. Kelly is an elite special operations operator, Senator Branson. The reason he was able to escape the prison camp in Siberia, Senator, is because he could examine it with an operator's eye, sir."

The room was silent for a moment as the council considered this startling revelation. Jensen could tell that momentum was swinging in the direction of the CIA director's recommendation. Then the Chairman of the Joint Chiefs raised an objection. "This is all well and good, but Siberia's a pretty big place. They're bound to have moved that prison camp, and we haven't the foggiest notion of where it's at."

"Oh, but we do, sir," Jensen replied with a smile.

"We do?"

"Yes, sir. It was spotted during a routine shipping census of Magadan, one of the harbors of the Soviet Pacific Fleet. The KH-11 satellite was programmed to roll the camera five minutes early. Providentially, the region the satellite was passing over during the early camera run included the new prison site. A pair of alert technicians at the NSA happened to see it. It was under construction at the time, and Kelly has examined the photographs of the foundations and walls of the buildings, taken before the roofs were put on, and has verified that they follow the same floor plan as those in Prison 87. The most convincing piece of evidence, however, is that Major General Nikolai Chernikov's personal helicopter was spotted on the helipad there. Chernikov is the man running the show on the kidnapping operation. A man of his rank would not be inspecting prison construction unless it was a facility under his direct command."

The group pondered this latest bit of information. Finally President Reagan spoke. "Gentlemen, history teaches that wars begin when governments believe the price of aggression is cheap. I think our obligation is to make this aggression perpetrated by the Soviet Union an expensive endeavor, so that they never try such a thing again. I want those scientists home by Christmas, gentlemen, and I think our SEALs are up to the task. What do you say, Wally?"

Branson paused before answering, "Mr. President, based on what I've just heard and the possible danger to the captives if we pursue diplomatic or economic options, I don't think we really have a choice. If we were taking a vote, sir, I'd vote for a quick strike to recover the captives. And if that's your decision, Mr. President, I'll back you to the hilt, publicly and privately. But before a strike team is inserted I think we need firm confirmation that the Magadan sighting really is the location of the new camp. Because, sir, if we don't know where they are being held, we don't *have* a military option."

After further discussion and a clarification from the Attorney General that military action would not violate either US or international law, the recommendation was unanimous and the President acted on it immediately. Operation *Thunderbird* was now officially sanctioned.

Chapter 18

"Gentlemen, if you'll take your seats we can begin." Bill Jensen waited as the men finished getting their coffee and sorting themselves out at the large conference table in one of the secure rooms at CIA headquarters. Since the decision of the President on Monday events had gone into high gear. This meeting was the first for the team that had been tasked with responsibility for Operation *Thunderbird*.

"We are here this morning to discuss a clandestine operation, designated *Thunderbird*, to be executed against the Soviet Union. The operation can be described in one sentence. We have been tasked with the rescue of hostages held by the GRU at a detention facility outside of Magadan on the southeastern coast of Siberia. It will be a multi-agency project, involving resources of the CIA, NSA, the Navy, and the Air Force. It is possible that other civilian or uniformed organizations will get involved before the job is done. Cooperation, therefore, will be essential.

"I'll start with introductions since we don't all know one another. My name is Bill Jensen, I am a special assistant to the DDO, CIA. I've been given overall authority in this endeavor, and will be reporting directly to the President. Seated to my left is Admiral John Bridger, CO of Naval Special Warfare Group One. The admiral will be doing the operational planning, and has command of the operation when boots are on the ground. Next to him is one of his staff officers, Commander Marcus Clausen, who will be assisting with the planning. At the far end of the table is Major Jacob Kelly, US Air Force. The major is recently returned from the USSR, and will be able to answer many of our questions about the target and the forces guarding it. In addition to being a pilot, Kelly is a trained CCT operator with four deployments downrange. He is here in the role of consultant.

"To my right is Sam Bergman, the CIA's top counterintelligence analyst on the Soviet Union. Sam will be coordinating the CIA's intelligence assets, doing analysis, and liaising with the NSA. Next to him is Lieutenant Commander Jesse Pierce, the intelligence officer at NAS Adak. Commander Pierce is responsible for managing naval intelligence resources operating out of Adak, and will liaise with the Office of Naval Intelligence. He will assist Admiral Bridger by coordinating all additional naval assets needed by *Thunderbird*. He's been attached to Admiral Bridger for the duration of the project.

"Besides overall leadership, my job is logistics. I'm responsible for seeing that you men receive whatever is necessary to make *Thunderbird* successful.

"Some of you are aware of the genesis of this operation, how it began as Project *Snowbird* under the excellent and capable leadership of Commander Pierce. Your briefing packets contain a précis of the events surrounding *Snowbird*. In that project, the CIA, NSA, FBI, Alaska State Troopers, US Navy, and US Air Force all worked together to bring the matter to a successful conclusion. The President expects the same high level of cooperation and professionalism in *Thunderbird*. I assured President Reagan that he would have it. I have this warning straight from his mouth: there is no room for interservice or interagency rivalries. If anyone hinders this operation because of competition or rivalry, that person will spend the remainder of their public service sorting paper clips, although the President used slightly more colorful language. Be sure the people under you are aware of that and behave accordingly.

"Let's begin by establishing the executive authority under which *Thunderbird* is proceeding. On Tuesday morning President Reagan issued Executive Order 12573, specifying that the CIA and DOD shall, in cooperation, expend whatever resources and take whatever actions are necessary to rescue all hostages from the Soviet detention facility before destroying it. The aggressive first-use of deadly force has been authorized, although the Executive Order specifies that civilian casualties be avoided insofar as possible. This will not be a covert action, gentlemen. Other than any preliminary recce operations, the assaulting force will be uniformed as American soldiers.

"I've asked Sam Bergman to provide a briefing on Magadan and the surrounding area, and then some information on General Chernikov. Sam?"

Sam Bergman stood up, and moved behind the lectern. "It's always easier to talk about something when we are looking at it, so let's get the satellite photos up on the screen, and start there. Could we have the lights down, please? . . . Thanks." He clicked a small controller and the first slide came up. "This is a wide-angle shot to help you get oriented. Here are the Koreas, this is the north coast of Japan, the Kuril Islands, and the Kamchatka Peninsula. The body of water in the middle is the Sea of Okhotsk. This area is the Magadanskaya *Oblast*, organized as a geopolitical entity in 1953 after the death of Stalin. Prior to that time, this whole area was under the general control of the Soviet *Far North Construction Trust*, whose acronym in Russian is *Dalstroi. Dalstroi* was responsible for the industrial, transportation, and economic development of the Kolyma region of the Russian Far East. The area is rich in natural resources, and particularly gold in the upper Kolyma watershed. *Dalstroi* accomplished their work with a series of some eighty-odd forced-labor gulags populated by dissidents and opponents of Stalin's rule. Prisoners and freight headed for the area were shipped by rail to Vladivostock and then conveyed by ship to the port at Magadan. Before World War II the region was considered one vast forced-labor encampment. You might think of what Australia was to Britain in the eighteenth and nineteenth centuries. The present residents of Magadan and its environs are largely the descendants of those prisoners and forced laborers. The population of the city is presently around 150,000.

"In addition to ethnic Russians, the population includes Koryaks, Yupiks, Chukchis, and several other tribes of indigenous peoples. They tend to hate the Soviet Union. However, that does not necessarily mean that they would like us any better. With the Soviet economy in the tank, their greatest loyalty is to whoever is paying the most. The bottom line here is that it may be possible to obtain assistance from some of the locals, if the price is right and the danger is minimal."

Sam clicked the controller again, and pointed to the screen. "Magadan itself is right here. It sits on the Gulf of Taui. This is the Bay of Nagaevo. You can see how the land forms an excellent, protected, natural harbor. The mouth of the bay narrows down to a little under three thousand meters wide. The water is deep enough for large containerized-cargo ships, as well as ore colliers. Numerous smaller freighters also visit the port. The economy there remains heavily dependent upon the gold mining industry. Between the coal and lignite deposits in the area, the tin mining operations in the upper Kolyma, the fishing industry, sausage and pasta factories, and a large distillery, there's quite a bit of ship traffic in the area, particularly between Magadan and Vladivostok. Since Magadan is the largest port in the northeastern USSR, they keep it open as long as possible with their own small fleet of icebreakers. The ship traffic might provide opportunities for insertion or extraction of an assaulting force.

"Now let's move on to our specific target and the Soviet officer running the operation." Sam brought a new slide up on the screen. "This photograph is actually one frame of a video sequence taken by a KH-11 on the night of 5 October. It shows what we believe is a prison facility under construction. The site is located about twenty miles north-northwest of Magadan. Notice the helo on the pad. The tail number on that chopper matches that of a helicopter assigned to General Nikolai Chernikov." Bergman clicked again, and a photo of Chernikov filled the screen. Sam looked over at Jacob Kelly out of curiosity. The pilot's face was unreadable.

Bergman continued, "Chernikov is known to be the man in charge of the Soviet kidnapping operation. We believe that Chernikov's presence is a strong indicator that this facility will receive the prisoners from the camp where Major Kelly was being held. That supposition has not been confirmed, by the way, but we are working on it. For the time being we will treat this site as the correct one for our planning purposes. The DCI has retasked satellite assets to monitor the site as well as to locate the original detention camp. We should have an update on these photos in the next seventy-two hours. That's all I've got, Bill."

"Thanks, Sam," Jensen said as he stood up. "Held at the detention facility are at least nine known scientists or military officers: two Americans, three Brits, an Israeli, two Germans, and an Indian. It's possible that there are more by now, and it's also possible that some of the nine have already died. We simply don't know. Their physical condition is liable to be very weak and they might be mentally disoriented.

"Our job is to send an assault team in, secure the hostages, grab whatever we can of intelligence value, destroy the facility, and then get everyone out safely. The President wants everyone home by Christmas."

"Christmas? You're kidding!" The agitated speaker was Admiral John Bridger. "I mean no disrespect, but the President is nuts if he thinks we can pull this off that soon! Do you have any idea how long it takes to do this kind of planning?"

Jensen affirmed coolly, "Yes, Admiral, I *do* know how long it takes, and this time it's going to take between now and 25 December to plan, execute, and complete *Thunderbird*!" Jensen locked eyes with the admiral for a brief second before continuing, "John, your long record of success as the CO of our most aggressive SEAL teams gives me tremendous respect for your opinions. But in this case the President wants us to push hard and fast, and he's right to do so. He's concerned that the longer we wait the more of these people will die. Plus, the Soviets might be putting together plans to snatch more scientists. We cannot allow that to happen.

"Our job is simplified somewhat in that we don't have to hide who we are. Our teams can use American uniforms, weapons, and munitions. Even so, I know it is a very compressed time frame," the CIA officer conceded, "but I am counting on you in particular, Admiral, to get it done. If anyone can pull this job off, it is you and your operators."

"But Bill, we haven't verified the location of the target, we don't have any idea of how insertion or extraction will be accomplished, we have no mock-up to practice the assault! For that matter, we don't even have any troops designated to assault it yet!" Bridger continued to protest.

"I know, Admiral, I know. But the construction of the mock-up begins as soon as we decide on a secure location for it. It will be done in four or five days at the most. You should be able to pick your teams today, and they can be practicing their assault while we are working out the other details."

Bridger shook his head slowly, "Jensen, I will obey my commander-in-chief and I will do my best to make it work. But I am warning you: if this gets screwed up there could be a score of American casualties on the ground on foreign soil. The whole thing could blow up in our faces. I could wind up having a lot of letters to write to newly minted widows. You understand that?"

"Yes, Admiral Bridger, I surely do. And I don't like it either. But it must be done."

Jensen briefed the group on the currently known disposition of Soviet military forces in and around Magadan. Then Kelly went over the complement of *Spetsnaz* attached to the prison where he'd been held, including weaponry, the size of the guard details, and what he had been able to determine about shift changes and force structure.

"Okay, for purposes of discussion let's grant that the reports we have so far are accurate and that the Magadan site is our target. What is it going to take, Admiral, in the way of manpower and equipment to assault this camp?" Jensen looked at Bridger with an expectant expression.

The admiral grunted, and then began. "Well, the bad news is that we are going up against over one hundred Soviet soldiers. That's going to be an awful lot of death and destruction when we haven't even got a war going on. The good news is that other than the machine guns mounted in those guard towers, they probably won't have heavy weapons. I'd be willing to bet their machine guns all face inside the camp. Their job is not to protect the place from a *coup-de-main* coming from outside the gates, but to keep the prisoners in line. That is our greatest advantage: they are going to be thinking like jailers, not like soldiers.

"We will have several other advantages, too, the most important of which is surprise. With snipers we can eliminate the guards in the towers before anyone realizes that an assault is in progress. They can keep anyone else from climbing into the towers, we won't have to worry about those machine guns. And if we can retain the initiative during the assault we'll have the advantage of knowing the plan. They'll be confused and uncertain, forced to react to our moves.

"We will have freedom of movement, but the prison structure—designed to restrict the movement of prisoners—will restrict the movement of their troops. Unless they have underground tunnels connecting their buildings—unlikely—we can post snipers or machine gunners who will keep the bad guys bottled up in place.

"Once we take out their lighting they will be operating in darkness. Our guys will have NVGs so darkness won't be a problem for us," Bridger observed, referring to Night Vision Goggles. "And finally, we have only one job: assault the prison. They have two jobs, to defend the prison and to continue acting as jailers. Some of their men will be tied up guarding the prisoners."

"So, how many men do you need, Admiral, in the assaulting force?"

Bridger was silent for a moment. Jensen could tell that the admiral was sifting through years of combat experience in his mind as he considered the question.

Finally the NAVSPECWAR Group One Commander answered, "I think we can do the job with four platoons of SEALs. That's sixty-four men, give or take a couple of officers and maybe a few others."

"SIXTY-FOUR MEN!" Bergman's irritated exclamation escaped from his mouth before he could stop himself. "Good grief, Admiral, the President is asking you to free a few hostages, not win a war! Can't that be cut down, somehow?

How on earth are we going to insert a force of sixty four, and then extract them with nine additional people?"

Bridger's response was an icy, silent glare. Bergman and Bridger both took note of the fact that Jensen did not jump in to moderate. *He's not going to play nanny or throw his weight around,* Bridger thought. *He's a good choice to run this operation.*

The admiral waited until his anger was under control before responding, "Sam, there are several things you might want to think about. First, an assault on a defensive position held by one hundred-plus men on their home turf is not in any way a covert or clandestine action. It's basic warfare. An assaulting force ought to be numerically superior to the defenders, as it is easier to defend than it is to assault. So even with sixty-four shooters, we are going in undermanned—if I were to make the assaulting element even smaller I'd be guaranteeing failure. No, I can't cut it any further. Second, these are *Spetsnaz* we're going up against—Ivan's special ops guys— not second-rate bush-leaguers. Third, our men will have no reserves, no means of resupply, no lines of retreat, and no means of extraction if they are not completely and overwhelmingly successful. They must conclusively win every firefight in which they engage, and they must ensure that none of the enemy escapes to raise the alarm. If we send too few men we may well be sending them *all* to death or capture. The only reason I don't double my estimate is because we are sending Navy SEALs, the best warfighters on the planet. But I will not waste my mens' lives by sending in too few! Besides, once mission requirements exceed fifteen or twenty men that takes us to a whole new level of difficulty anyway, with all sorts of new logistical demands on insertion and extraction. I could send in sixty-four or forty-four men, and it would not much change the requirements for getting them in and out of there."

"Sorry, Admiral, for my outburst," apologized the chastened analyst, "Of course you are correct. I guess I was foolishly hoping that we could do the job with a much smaller team. It would make getting them into position so much simpler."

"Not really."

"What? Why not?" Jensen asked with genuine surprise.

"Insertion is not the problem, Bill. *Extraction* is the problem. We will be bringing back with us a minimum of nine people whose physical condition is questionable at best. They certainly aren't going to be able to take a swim with my frogmen. In all likelihood, we would probably be moving them with *ambulances* if we could. Which means our extraction plans must take their disabilities into account. If we solve that problem, then the insertion or extraction of a larger force is probably not going to be much of an issue. Besides, during the insertion phase no one knows we are coming. During extraction, depending on what has gone wrong, there may be a whole lot of people who know we're leaving."

For a few minutes the group was silent, mulling over what had been said so far. Finally Jensen spoke up again. "Okay, guys. We need some ideas. How are we going to get our people in and out of the country?" More silence greeted him. Jensen had known this would be the toughest part of the whole assignment.

"Well," Bridger started slowly, "the SEALs have several different methods of insertion for normal operations. There are good reasons why SEALs are referred to as 'frogmen.' But in this case landing a large force from the sea undetected would be impossible, since Okhotsk is virtually a Soviet lake. Plus, we could conceivably lose an entire submarine going in that way. In any case, we couldn't extract frail or injured people by sea.

"Or, we could somehow airdrop. But that is extremely unlikely this far inside Soviet territory, especially if you consider that Okhotsk is under constant surveillance. Besides, we can't extract by air.

"We could infiltrate on the ground, except that Magadan is too far from any border and the border countries are not friendly to us anyway. A force of sixty-four men would eventually be spotted and captured. Even if we did get all the way to Magadan by land, there is still the problem of getting everyone out. We might move twenty or even thirty miles, but

not any more than that, especially if we have disabled people."
Bridger sat back and massaged his temples. This job was not
going to be easy.

"Sea, air, land. That pretty much covers the possibilities.
And none of them look good," admitted Jensen, sitting back
in his chair with his eyes shut.

"Sam, can you get me sat photos of the whole area around
the camp, and every inch of the terrain between there and
Magadan?" asked Bridger.

"Yep. I'll get them to you in the next couple of days. Anything else you need?"

"Hmm. I'd like to see a detailed analysis of all the shipping
in and out of Magadan, including the ports of origin and how
the ships are flagged."

"I'll put a team right on it, Admiral."

"Thanks. Commander Pierce, could you put together a report on all the Soviet naval assets in Okhotsk, as well as those
patrolling the blue-water approaches? It would be helpful to
know as much as possible about what their subs are doing."

"Yes, sir." Pierce looked at Jensen. "Sir, I am not sure how
good my clearance will be for obtaining that kind of data."

"Don't worry, son. If anyone says 'no,' you just call me."
Jensen stood up. "Let's meet back here in a week. Admiral, I
will be in touch regarding a mock-up where your teams can
practice their assault in secrecy. For now, your men should
plan on having only the weaponry they can carry in with them
for the assault. Any further questions?" Jensen waited, and
looked around the room. No questions were forthcoming. He
concluded, "Thank you, gentlemen. I will meet you here next
Thursday, at nine o'clock sharp."

Chapter 19

Bridger strapped himself in as the engines began to spin up. He and Commander Clausen were catching a military transport back to Coronado. As the CO of NAVSPECWAR-GRU One he avoided commercial travel, wanting to keep the bad guys guessing as to his whereabouts. They were the only passengers on the military aircraft, and were kept company by numerous shrink-wrapped pallets full of cargo, secured with nylon webbing. As the noise level increased, their conversation turned into somewhat of a friendly shouting match.

"So, what do you think, Marcus?" Bridger shouted, keeping his expression neutral.

"About what, sir?" replied the commander, trying to match his boss's poker face.

"About *Thunderbird*. What do you think about *Thunderbird?*"

"I think it's nuts, sir, nuts! Absolute unqualified lunacy," Clausen shouted gravely, pausing before he continued with a grin, "Can *I* go?"

Bridger smiled, "Be careful what you ask for, sailor!"

As the transport bumped over the joints between old concrete sections of the taxiway, Clausen became serious and shouted over the whine of the engines, "How are we going to train for this, sir? We're not the only people with spy satellites. The moment we build a mock-up of that camp, the Russians will recognize it and know we are coming. You know that Ivan watches every square inch of ground where SEALs train, sir!"

Admiral Bridger nodded and shouted back, "I know. I have been wondering the same thing all afternoon. We need to think outside the box for this one, Marcus."

"How about northern Canada, Admiral? Somewhere we

don't usually go. Maybe we can locate some area that has nothing of intelligence value around it, where they're not likely to be watching."

"No good, Marcus," Bridger shouted back, shaking his head. "If we take four platoons of SEALs out of country there will be too much support activity on the base to hide it. It would telegraph our actions. They would find out our destination, and then simply task a bird to watch us."

The problem was that the detention center mock-up would be too identifiable, too distinct when viewed from the air. One look from a satellite and the Soviets would be forewarned. Bridger's men would walk into an ambush and Operation *Thunderbird* would go down in history as a tragedy exceeding Operation *Eagle Claw*, the ill-fated attempt to rescue the Iranian hostages seven years earlier. *Eagle Claw* had been a Delta Force operation that left a bitter taste in the mouth of the whole SPECOPS community.

Bridger pulled his flight jacket closer around him, zipping it up against the cold in the transport. He relaxed, determined to ponder both the insertion problem and the need for a secret mock-up where his men could practice their assault. Instead, lulled by the drone of the engines, the exhausted officer fell asleep and did not awaken until the wheels touched down hours later in Southern California.

****

The only lights in the facility came from the black and white displays and the various indicators winking on the control panels. The reels on the video recorders turned silently, capturing every frame. As the satellite made its pass three hundred miles above the Siberian *taiga*, the monitors revealed an undifferentiated mountainous landscape, punctuated here and there by the occasional road, shack, logging camp, or mining operation. The ground was covered by snow, although there were bare spots where the wind or sun had cleared it off.

"It's a real shame, Al, an insulting waste of our incredible talent."

"How's that, Karl?"

"We *never* get to watch the KH-11 in real-time, it's always on tape delay. Until today. Our first day watching live feed and what do we get? This!" Karl carped, motioning with disgust to the monitors. "Pass after pass, and all we see are pictures of Ivan's national forest."

"Ivan doesn't *have* national forests, genius."

"How do *you* know they don't have national forests?" Karl Randolph challenged petulantly.

"I just do."

"Whatever. But you've got to agree, Al, a commando strike would have been a lot more interesting to watch."

"Yeah, right, dingbat. Nobody but the President and the brass get to watch those. Now shut up and watch the show. You always talk when we watch a movie. Pass the popcorn." Al Mercer had brought a large, celebratory bucket of buttered popcorn to mark the occasion of watching the Key Hole's output in real-time.

When the bird finally began passing over the ocean Al stopped recording the live feed. "Well, that's it for another hour and a half. Let's replay this thing and catalog what we see while we are waiting on the next pass."

Karl repositioned the tape to the beginning and pressed *Play*. The men got down to the work of measuring and cataloging the relevant features and noting the frames for which they would request high-resolution still photographs.

"Okay, this is the main road that goes by the turn-off to the construction site we discovered on 5 October. We should be able to see the site itself on the next flyover."

They watched in silence as the landscape scrolled by. Several times the road snaked out and then back in to the picture. In the spots where it was not snow-packed, the road appeared to be some sort of macadam surface in very poor condition.

"Whoa! What's this? Stop it here, Karl, and let's go back about thirty frames." Al shoved another handful of popcorn into his mouth and wiped his hands on his jeans. He was glad his wife was not in the room to see him do it.

Karl reversed the tape as requested and started it again in

slow speed. Several long, low buildings scrolled onto the scene.

"Okay, freeze it . . . what do you think?"

"Looks like a lumber operation. These are stacks of logs. Those over there look like piles of something, probably sawdust. My uncle has a lumber mill east of Portland. I've seen it from the air several times. Looks just like this." Karl made some notes on their catalog, and began determining the sizes of the buildings, as well as describing them.

"Uh-huh, I agree. It's surprising, though, that they are still in operation this far into the cold weather. Must say something about the desperate state of the economy down there. Let's roll several more frames," Al requested. As the satellite's view panned across the scene, the monitor displayed several people clustered around a large fork-truck that was hefting logs off a flatbed truck.

"Look at the cab on that truck, will ya? I'll bet that baby was old back when Uncle Joseph was still running around murdering people."

"Really! Somebody down there must have a world-class mechanic to keep that fossil running. Ho! What's this? A shipping container, forty foot. Write it down."

Fifty minutes later, the recorded video was displaying undifferentiated wilderness once again. Mercer looked at the clock. Still ten minutes to go before the next live pass started. He looked at his buddy and requested, "Ten minutes until showtime. Keep an eye on things, will ya, Karl? I've got to go talk to a man about a horse."

Karl loaded fresh tapes on the dual recorders and got everything prepared for the KH-11's next pass over the target area. The men had calculated in which pass the presumed detention camp would show up, and this was the one. Bill Jensen of the CIA had stressed the importance of getting another look at the facility. It had been early October since they had last seen it, and then it had been under construction. The layout and exposed foundations had caused the two technicians to identify it as a detention facility. They were expecting to see it in a late stage of construction, based upon their earlier sighting.

Al Mercer and Karl Randolph had scored a coveted internal NSA award for their work when they had spotted Chernikov's chopper on the helipad on 5 October. Chernikov had dropped from the intelligence community's radar several years earlier; finding him again was a significant coup. But the stinky thing about getting an award in the NSA was that you could never tell anyone what you had done.

The level of interest in these few frozen acres of Siberian wilderness had spiked in the last several days, however, and the two technicians felt as though they had kicked over a can of bees. The attention shown by people way above Al's and Karl's pay grade made the two technicians wonder what was going down. In any case, when that construction site scrolled by in a few minutes they wanted to be at the top of their game. If there was so much as a new beaver dam on one of the streams criss-crossing the terrain, the two men were determined to spot it.

Al stepped back in the darkened control center with two cold soft drinks.

"Took you long enough. I was afraid you'd miss the cartoons."

"Never! I knew exactly what time it was . . . Four, three, two, roll it, Karl."

Karl started the recorders, shaking his head at his friend's uncanny sense of timing. As the video feed wound its way through ultra-high frequency receivers, demodulators, decryption circuitry, and finally video amplifiers, a rugged but somewhat featureless terrain again splashed onto the video displays. There was no cloud cover and the picture was crystal clear. Thirty seconds into the pass, a series of parallel roads carved through the wilderness began to show up.

"Okay, Al, we pegged this earlier. These roads have got to be concentric security perimeters. After this live pass is done, let's get stills of the whole sequence. Mr. Jensen is going to want all this stuff."

The satellite continued to sweep over the *taiga* as the men watched. Within several seconds a clearing in the forest opened and the two NSA technicians found themselves staring at a fully functional prison facility. Tiny figures of men could be seen walking about the area and smoke was coming out of one of the buildings, presumably the heating plant. There appeared to be well-worn tracks in the snow around the inside of the innermost fence, tracks that would be consistent with prisoners making an endless circuit around the compound during their exercise period. Several vehicles were parked within the presumed administrative area of the compound. The helipad was empty. The two technicians were silent as the view panned back into featureless Siberian wilderness.

Al spoke first. "Wow. I guess we did *not* peg that back on 5 October. According to the estimate we gave in our report to the CIA, that camp was still supposed to be under construction right now. But what I just observed was a fully operational prison camp, and I don't recall seeing a single stack of construction materials."

"Me neither, Al. Man alive, someone must have had a king-size burr under their saddle to get from where they were on the 5th to what we just saw. Frankly, Al, I think the evident speed of the construction is in itself a valuable piece of intelligence. Soviet workers rarely show that sort of motivation unless someone is holding a gun to their heads."

"Maybe they were."

"Huh?"

"Maybe someone *was* holding a gun to their heads."

Chapter 20

Friday, October 30, 1987: 1215 hours, local time
Washington, DC

"Hello, Zvi. It's been a long time," said Bill Jensen, warmly embracing his friend, Zvi Sharon. "Thanks for meeting with me on such short notice."

Zvi laughed in his infectious way. When Zvi laughed, everyone around wanted to laugh with him. You couldn't explain it; it was just Zvi. He had a friendly, charismatic personality that sucked everyone around into its orbit.

"Shalom, Professor Jensen," he said with a twinkle in his eye, subtly emphasizing 'professor' as though it were a private joke. "How is my favorite political science scholar, eh?"

"Oh, you know," Jensen replied evasively as he slid into the booth at Zvi's favorite DC restaurant, Taverna the Greek Islands. His Jewish friend was exceedingly fond of Taverna's lamb dishes, particularly the *Arni Kapama*. "I've been dabbling about in this and that."

"Oh, yes, I *do* know!" exclaimed Zvi with almost childish delight, clapping his hands, "I've been watching. The *Snowbird* affair, for instance. That was a close thing—you nearly lost the son of your favorite friend, may he rest in peace. I am pleased that Major Kelly is well."

Bill closed his eyes and shook his head. Somehow the Mossad officer always seemed to have an inside line to the CIA. "Zvi, one of these days I am going to find your source, give him a medal, and then fire him! How on earth did you find out about *Snowbird*?"

Zvi chuckled, and then said in his thickest Jewish accent, spreading his hands as he shrugged his shoulders, "We're the Israelis! We know everything! You should be glad that we are friends, eh?"

It was Jensen's turn to laugh, "Yes, Zvi. I am *very* glad we are friends."

The two men ordered their meals and engaged in small talk for the next fifteen minutes. Zvi Sharon was a people person, and Jensen, with his typical western sense of efficiency had to discipline himself to not talk business until his friend broached the subject.

Sharon was the Mossad station chief in Israel's Washington, DC embassy. He was a first-rate spy and an implacable foe for those who earned the enmity of his country. Officially, it was a violation of protocol for any embassy to harbor spies. But in the duplicitous world of diplomacy every embassy in the world contains an intelligence section and every embassy in the world denies it. The people in the spy business eventually learn who their counterparts are.

Sharon and Jensen were indeed true friends. They had known each other (and their real occupations) for years. From time to time they had acted as an "authorized" back-channel for information flow between the Mossad and the CIA. "Authorized" meant that the two governments officially looked the other way while permission to communicate was subtly and informally given. It was useful for friendly governments to have unofficial conduits: denials of cooperation could be made publicly in the press and on the diplomatic front while in a back room somewhere necessary information was exchanged. Everybody does it. Everybody denies doing it. In the elaborate dance of diplomacy, such public dissimulation preserves a cosmic balance of some sort.

"So what's up, Bill?" Sharon asked as he carefully wiped his mouth with his napkin. "How can my country be of service to your country?"

"You mean you don't already know? You are the Israelis!" teased Jensen.

Zvi grinned and replied, "Do I know? I'll never tell . . . But come, my friend, what can I do for you?"

"Zvi, I need Ma and Pa Kettle. Are they still in business?"

****

In the early morning of 10 November, 1938, a horrible wave of violence overtook Germany's cities and towns. A Jew had killed a German diplomat in Paris several days earlier. That action ignited the fuse of emotional explosives that had been carefully and purposefully laid in Hitler's Germany. Since 1933, Joseph Goebbels, Minister of Propaganda, had been publicly establishing an intellectual basis on which the Jews could be attacked. The plan was to blame them for the ruination of Germany and tie them to the Bolshevik Revolution that had handed power to Stalin in Russia.

Enraged Germans, having been inculcated with a suspicion that Jews were undermining their country, engaged in massive mob actions against the Jews and anything Jewish. Over one thousand synagogues were ransacked, tens of thousands of Jews rounded up, and scores of Jews were killed. The night of devastation became known as *Kristallnacht*, a reference to the broken glass that littered the streets during that early-morning pogrom. It was the beginning of terrors for the Jewish people in Nazi Germany.

Many Jews fled while they still could. One such family managed to escape to Moscow. They were allowed into the country because Herr Daniel Klausowitz was a highly regarded materials scientist, and Stalin's Soviet Union was desperate for technology. The family had secreted their considerable wealth in a Swiss account when Germany's situation began to deteriorate several years earlier, and in their exile they managed to keep their wealth intact (and secret). As the years passed, one of the three Klausowitz children, Benjamin, eventually found himself serving as a high-ranking official in the Moscow local government. Though early on he was an avid disciple of Karl Marx, age, experience, and a cold-eyed comparison of the Western standard of living with that of the average Muscovite had produced a gradual transformation. By the time Benjamin Klausowitz was fifty he was a closet capitalist. By the time he was fifty-five both he and his wife had secretly adopted Zionist loyalties and were subsequently recruited by the Mossad.

Because his personal fortune was sufficient to provide for

his wife Katerina and himself, Klausowitz retired from government service and the couple began traveling the Soviet Union. Their handlers in the Mossad did not use them to gather highly sensitive data, but employed them as "boots on the ground," able to give immediate, first-person situation reports wherever Israeli intelligence needed them. Benjamin's former high position in the Moscow government, plus the network of government contacts he had developed over the years, opened the USSR to him for virtually unlimited travel. Because he was careful to never travel outside the Soviet republics, he never aroused suspicion.

On one of their trips they rendered a service to the CIA, mediated through the Mossad. The contact name provided to the American DDO was "Ma and Pa Kettle." In late December of 1979 the USSR invaded Afghanistan. On 27 December the Soviet 103rd Airborne Division, based in Vitebsk, landed at and secured the airport in Bagram, Afghanistan. Several weeks later, when the United States desperately required on-site information to get an idea of Soviet intentions in Afghanistan, Benjamin and Katerina had traveled to Vitebsk, Belarus under the operational control of the Mossad. Their mission was to nose around in the bars and other haunts of the military to try to pick up information on the ultimate goals of the Soviet invasion.

The information was passed along to the CIA and wound up being extraordinarily helpful. Since that time Bill Jensen had learned (in part) the story of a Russian couple he knew only as Ma and Pa Kettle. Jensen knew that they were mobile and financially independent, had significant political clout, and were completely committed to the State of Israel.

****

Zvi's normally friendly eyes narrowed and his grin disappeared. Jensen sensed the man's protective spirit. After a moment of silence the large Israeli queried coolly, "And why, may I ask, do you need them?"

Bill sensed they were approaching a potential impasse. He

was loath to speak of any of the operational details of *Thunderbird*, but he knew that it could not be avoided. The Israeli clearly felt a personal sense of responsibility for the couple. Jensen realized that Sharon would have to know the stakes involved before he budged.

The professor evaded the question and asked instead, "Are you done? I think we need to take a walk."

Instantly the joy returned to his friend's face and Zvi replied happily, "Without dessert? You are kidding, right? We must try their *Galaktoboureko*, no? Have you had it? Oh, William, you will love this." Zvi motioned to a waiter and ordered two with coffee. "We will go on your walk, my friend. But first, a taste of something sweet."

****

Bridger yielded to the pleas of Commander Marcus Clausen and selected him as the overall mission commander for *Thunderbird*. Clausen was a skilled, proven operator and highly respected among all the teams. He was an intimidating figure: six-foot-three, superbly conditioned, with steely grey eyes. Bald as a baby's bottom and sporting a scar from his left ear to his mouth—a memento of his first SEAL deployment—Clausen was dubbed Mr. Clean by his fellow shooters.

Admiral Bridger spent the first part of his day with Clausen, reviewing the commander's selections for his operators for *Thunderbird* and writing the necessary orders to attach the men to Clausen's command. Marcus had cherry-picked the best of the best from among all the SEAL teams based at Coronado.

After lunch Bridger sat at his desk and worked through a mound of papers that had been piling up. *Bureaucracy,* he silently cursed to himself, *is the bane of all combat officers!* Several hours later the stack was almost gone. He was down to returning phone calls. The last call on his list was one to Universal Studios. His secretary's neat printing on the note simply said, *Universal needs some SEAL consultants for a current movie production. Please call Anthony Petroli.*

Bridger looked at the note with exasperation. He did not have time for this sort of foolishness. He threw the note in the trash and pulled out the *Thunderbird* file. It was time to think about his insertion/extraction problem. After setting the file on his desk, he buzzed his secretary on the intercom.

"Mabel, I need a map set of the Sea of Okhotsk and surrounding area. I also need the latest map set of Magadan, USSR and surrounding area. Would you locate those and bring them in?"

"Yes, sir. You must have worked your way through that mountain of trivia I built on your desk this morning."

"I have. I am surprised that you would be so heartless to an old gentleman such as myself, young lady," Bridger teased.

"Hey, sir, I don't make the work, I just pass it on to you."

"I know. Just kidding, Mabe."

"Were you able to contact Mr. Petroli? He really wanted to talk to you and was so disappointed to learn that you were not available."

Bridger looked guiltily at the note in the trash, and answered, "Uh, no, not yet anyway. I'm not sure I'm going to have time to get back to him, Mabel."

"That's too bad, sir. He was really interesting on the phone. He was looking forward to talking to you. He told me he was with the 82nd Airborne Division in World War II when they jumped into Normandy. I think he was hoping to talk shop."

After hanging up, Bridger reached down into the trash and picked up the note. When Mabel entered with the requested maps, he was sitting in his chair looking out the window, lost in thought. She knew better than to interrupt him and quietly set the maps on the table and withdrew.

Bridger's father had been a replacement trooper with the 82nd in *Overlord*, at Normandy in 1944. As part of Operation *Boston*, the 507th Parachute Infantry Regiment had been assigned to capture and secure the Merderet River crossings. Heavy flak had resulted in the pilots of Sergeant Jack Bridger's transport losing their nerve and their bearings. The pilots simply turned the green light on, clueless as to their actual location. The entire stick jumped into the darkness. All but two drowned in the Merderet, each man weighted down with one hundred pounds of combat gear. Seconds after the jump, the German anti-aircraft gunners found their mark and the transport was transformed into a fiery comet, plunging to the ground. None of the aircrew survived.

The day after Sally Bridger had given birth to her first and only child, she received the telegram. Unable to cope with the loss, she turned to the bottle. She was dead before little John's third birthday, killed in a car crash. Bridger had been raised by his uncle.

Admiral John Bridger, CO of NAVSPECWARGRU One, roused himself from his thoughts and stared at the note in his hand. He nodded to himself and picked up the phone. He was busy. But not too busy for a man who had parachuted into the hell that was Normandy.

****

The small talk continued after dessert and during the drive to Great Falls, Maryland. The leaves had fallen as the calendar wound toward winter and the beautiful park was deserted. Wrapped up in their coats, the two spy masters began walking down the picturesque C & O Canal towpath.

"Well, Zvi, you do have a knack for choosing remote locations."

"Yes, William, and a knack for picking great restaurants, too! Don't forget that!"

"That too, my friend, that too." Looking about him at the deserted towpath and the fading light of the grey sky, Jensen continued, "This feels a little melodramatic, like a scene from *The President's Analyst*, or something out of *Get Smart*. But we can talk safely here."

"Yes. Now, why are you interested in Ma and Pa Kettle?"

"Does the name 'Moshe Shimonah' mean anything to you?"

Zvi stopped and slapped his hands together for warmth. "Ah, so that's it? *Thunderbird*."

Jensen affirmed, "Yes, *Thunderbird.*" The two resumed walking down the towpath. Jensen could see that Zvi was wrapped up in his thoughts, and fell silent.

Finally the Israeli spoke, "I was wondering when we would be contacted again about *Thunderbird.* An FBI agent in Seattle made contact with one of my people, oh, it must have been early October—"

"It was 12 October."

"Yes. You know about this? Ah! This has something to do with *Snowbird,* doesn't it?"

"Yes, Zvi. We learned through Major Kelly that Shimonah and eight others are being held by the Soviets."

Zvi was silent again as they continued to walk. Finally the Israeli spy said, "Captain Moshe Shimonah was a key player in the oversight of Israel's developing nuclear capability—"

"A captain?" Jensen asked incredulously.

"Yes, and you have just demonstrated why a captain was chosen for this task. We thought a lowly captain would never be suspected of being the military liaison between the nuclear weapons development teams and the prime minister. His job was to keep the PM fully briefed on all the happenings down at Dimona."

"So capturing Shimonah gives Ivan complete, up-to-date knowledge of Israel's nuclear capabilities."

"Precisely. If Shimonah has talked."

"That is information Syria, Iran, and Iraq would dearly love to get their hands on."

"Quite, and half a dozen other Arab countries as well. Shimonah simply evaporated from a vacation in Bermuda. No sign of struggle. No blood. He went out for a morning run and never returned. When Agent Stewart contacted us a couple of weeks ago, that was the first indication that anyone knew what happened. Do you think he is still alive, Bill?"

"Honestly, I don't know, my friend. But we're going to find out. We are going in after him and the others. That's what *Thunderbird* is, Zvi. It is not an intelligence operation. It is a military rescue operation. We're going to get those men and bring them home."

"Come, come, Dr. Jensen. Your President will never go for that! Look at Iran-Contra!"

"He will and he has. Everyone who needs to be is on board, including the gang of eight. The presidential finding has already been issued. Frankly, I am surprised you don't know this—you are, after all, the Israelis." Jensen couldn't resist that jab. "I'm surprised it hasn't made the front page of the *New York Times* by now. You know how it is, Zvi, if you want to lose control of a secret just tell a politician."

Zvi shook his head in disbelief. "Let me get this straight. You're telling me that the *US*, for crying out loud, is going to mount a clandestine military operation and rescue hostages held deep within enemy territory? My word, you sound like us! This sounds like the raid on Entebbe!"

"Wait just a moment, my Israeli friend! Don't underestimate the US! We don't care for conflict. And it might take us a while to make a decision. But whatever Uncle Sam finally lays a hand to usually moves."

They walked another hundred yards in silence and then the Mossad agent stopped again. "How can we help? I know that this will require approval at higher levels, but what can Israel do to assist the United States in this operation?"

"I need Ma and Pa Kettle to go to Magadan. I need eyeballs on the situation. And I need two-way communication with them. If you will not permit the United States to have direct contact with them, then I need an Israeli representative in our Op Center twenty-four seven until this job is done. And if it is at all possible, I would like that rep to be you, Zvi."

By 2100 hours Zvi Sharon was setting up shop in the CIA's Operations Center, and the opening round of *Thunderbird* was set to begin.

****

Bridger changed into civilian clothes, complete with sunglasses and an LA Lakers ball cap. One of his SEAL pilots flew him in an unmarked helicopter to the helipad on top of 10 Universal City Plaza, the thirty-six-story office building housing the nerve center of Universal Studios. The chopper was met by four security guards and Bridger was escorted into the spacious penthouse office of Anthony Petroli, CEO of Universal Studios.

When he entered the office a thin man in a well-tailored (and very expensive) grey suit was standing, leaning on a cane, looking out the window at the city below. Bridger estimated the man to be in his mid- to upper sixties. Other than the cane he appeared to be remarkably fit, tanned to the color of old leather. The old man continued to stare out the window, either unaware of or ignoring Bridger's arrival.

Standing respectfully, the admiral looked down sheepishly at his jeans and tennis shoes and shook his head. He removed his cap and sunglasses, then looked up sharply as the thin figure at the window spoke, still with his back turned.

"Do not take care for your appearance, Admiral. I am honored that you would take the time to meet with me."

Bridger then realized that the man had been studying him through the reflection in the window. Petroli turned around and Bridger knew immediately that he had seen the man before, though he could not place him.

Petroli observed the flash of recognition followed by uncertainty. "Please, Admiral Bridger, be seated. You recognize me." It was a statement, not a question.

"Yes, sir, I do but I don't know why."

"Perhaps that picture will explain." Petroli gestured to a large black and white print on the wall behind Bridger. It was a picture of B Company of the 507th PIR, 82nd Airborne. Bridger had studied the picture many times before—a smaller version of it was hanging in his own office in Coronado. His dad had been one of the sergeants in B Company. Standing next to his father in the photo was a man he now realized was Anthony Petroli. The years had had their effect on the old man, but the fire in the eyes was the same.

"You knew my dad?" Bridger was incredulous.

"I should say I did! Jack and I worked hard collecting an exhaustive knowledge of every brig, jail, and detention center in southern England. We did time in most of them—and usually together. You know the drill, Admiral. Couple of young, proud Airborne punks—full of more salt and vinegar than common sense—go out on the town on a twelve-hour pass and get plastered. You pick a fight with the regular army because some mere infantryman is blousing his boots, and then you spend the rest of your leave in jail playing cards with the same gents with whom you had just previously been practicing the fine and manly art of fisticuffs. We had great fun, busted up a few bars along the way.

"The training was tough. Oh, it was awful! Of course, you SEALs know all about that. But it produced a unit cohesion that was beyond description. We just knew as soon as we put boots on the ground in Normandy, B Company would take Paris inside of a week, all by itself."

He smiled, and then a shadow passed over his face and his voice got husky, "Never had a chance to find out how good we were. Pilots dropped us right into the river. The whole stick. What a waste, a terrible, terrible waste." He paused, struggling to control his emotions. "Your dad and I jumped together, but he landed in a deep spot in the river and I landed in the mud on the bank. Nothing I could do. We had surprised a German patrol and they started firing when the first guy splashed into the river. I went after Jack because I had seen where he went into the water, but the Germans were pouring it on so hot and heavy I couldn't move until they withdrew. By the time I reached your dad he was already dead—drowned."

Bridger said nothing, watching as the tears streamed down Petroli's face. He had seen it before. Men who were as tough as nails and who'd held together through the worst of firefights like killing machines, while death and destruction piled up all around them. But to a man, when the action was over and they were remembering their buddies who did not make it, the tears would come. Did not matter if it was three years ago, or thirty, or forty-three. Some things the passage of time would never erase.

Petroli cleared his throat and continued, "Well, they put me and Jimmy—he was the only other B Company survivor —in F Company. And that's where we both finished the war.

"Your dad was a fine man, Admiral, and a good friend. May he rest in peace."

The two men sat and swapped war stories for another ten minutes and then Bridger asked how the SEALs could help the film magnate.

"We are shooting a feature-length film on the actions of SEAL Team One in Vietnam. I need some SEALs as consultants to work with the actors on everything from how they carry themselves to how they run into action, behave under fire, etc."

"Why don't you contact some retired SEALs, Mr. Petroli? I am sure you could find a number that would be glad to do the job and probably not a few that need the work."

"That would be fine, but finding genuine retired Navy SEALs is not easy, Admiral. They don't generally advertise themselves and the ones that do often are not the real McCoy."

Bridger chuckled, "I guess you are right, sir. If all the guys who claim to have been SEALs actually were we would be able to muster several divisions' worth. I'll be glad to put you in contact with five or ten who are the real deal." Admiral Bridger stood up and picked up his cap and glasses. "Mr. Petroli, it has been a great honor to meet you, sir. I have the highest respect and admiration for all the men of the 82nd, and I'm so thankful to have met someone who knew my dad. You can't know how much this has meant to me."

"Thank you, Admiral. It has been a pleasure to meet the son of a dear friend. Until my secretary contacted the base at Coronado I had no idea that you were even alive. After the war I tried to find Sally, but she had already died. Not knowing the whole tale, I assumed you were also dead."

As the two men walked to the door Bridger inquired about the film Petroli was shooting. The movie maker was eager to talk about it. "We are almost ready to begin shooting. Most of it is being filmed in Ecuador, as the vegetation is similar to that of Vietnam, but we also have rented three thousand acres northeast of LA. We have a full-scale mock-up of a Vietnamese village in which some of the fiercest fighting took place. Seems a shame to build a village only to blow it all up, but, that's the nature of the business."

He shook Bridger's hand and began to turn back into his office but the look on Bridger's face stopped him in his tracks. "Admiral, you look like you've seen a ghost. Are you feeling well?"

"Mr. Petroli, I just had the most amazing thought. May I ask for ten minutes more of your time? Please sir, it is very important."

Immediately the movie maker looked around at his secretary and said, "Cindy, whatever is on my schedule this afternoon, reschedule it." He looked at Bridger and said, "Come right in, Admiral. And please, call me Tony. Don't call me sir. I never got above the rank of sergeant. I feel like I should be saluting you."

Bridger smiled and replied, "Fine, but only if you call me John."

They settled into Anthony Petroli's spacious office once again and the mogul ordered some refreshments to be brought to them.

Bridger hesitated and then began, "Is this office, uh—"

"Secure?" Petroli asked with a smile. "This office has better security than the US Capitol Building does. There they are just dealing with piddling matters like national security, you see, but here? We are dealing with *MONEY!*" Petroli laughed at his own remark, then continued, "Admiral—John, I mean —every movie company wants to know what every *other* movie company is doing. The movie-going audience is pretty well defined and we are all fighting for the same piece of the pie. The safest direction for a producer to go is the same direction everyone else is going, but just beat them to the punch. That's why when you see one disaster flick there are three or four more just about to be released. There are *four* other war movies to be released within two months of the one I'm working on.

"All of which is to say that Universal Studios takes security very seriously, because we don't want to help the competition. I don't know how often your office is swept for bugs, John, but this entire floor, every room, including the bathrooms and the maintenance and mechanical closets, is swept twice a day, every day, seven days a week, and at random times. The encryption technology built into the telephones used by our executives is probably better than what you use at Coronado, no offense intended.

"So the only possible security leak in this office is me. And I can be pretty tight-lipped when I decide to be. So if you can trust me, you can speak freely."

Admiral Bridger searched the man's face but already knew what he would find, and so he decided to plunge ahead. "I'll be blunt and brief. Everything I am telling you is classified at the highest level, and if it were to leak a lot of very good men, men like yourself and my father, will pay for that indiscretion with their lives.

"Four platoons of Navy SEALs will be putting their lives on the line to rescue a handful of hostages, very soon. We need a place to build our mock-up to practice our assault. We cannot do it in normal SEAL training areas because the target has a distinctive look from the air. Our enemy is able to spy on our normal training areas and if we were to build the mock-up in one of those we would telegraph our intentions. Our team will be murdered as soon as they hit the beach."

Petroli nodded slowly, absorbing the words and anticipating what was coming. "Sure," he said, "that makes sense. What you are saying is you need a place to practice where the enemy will never think of looking. What you need is a place to train right out in the open. And what better place to practice an assault than on the set of a war movie?"

"Exactly."

Petroli grinned. "OH, I LOVE IT! I love it! How much space do you need?"

"Six hundred acres."

Petroli nodded, excited. "Okay, here is what I need from you. The government must pay for everything that happens on that six hundred acres, both construction and cleanup. It is Universal's policy that when we leave a site we restore it to its original condition, so you will need to pay for a team to clean up, reseed, etc. Furthermore, if you will pay the bill I will provide you with a complete film production staff so that it looks to everyone, from the air or the ground, as though you really are shooting a movie. And John, my top people are accustomed to secure projects. I'll flat out guarantee the secrecy of this project."

Admiral John Bridger grinned and stuck out his hand and said, "It's a deal, Tony. Can you get me one of those neat little black director's berets? I've always wanted to wear one of those."

Within twelve hours heavy equipment was on site, turning several acres of California into Siberia. Within one week the site would be ready for use.

Chapter 21

Tuesday, November 3, 1987: 0700 hours, local time
Moscow, USSR

"Sir, General Chernikov is on the line for you."

Patrikeyev put down the reports he was reading and picked up the phone. "*Dobroye utro*, Comrade General."

"*Zdravstvuitye*, sir. Please go secure. Code of the day."

Patrikeyev adjusted his encryption device, waited for the whistling to stop and then said, more curtly than he intended, "Report."

"General, Project *Krasnyy Voskhod* is proceeding in its new location. The move has been accomplished with very little disruption to our routines. Our interrogations have resumed. Most of the scientists are cooperating freely now."

"*Molodets*, Nikolai."

"*Spasibo*, Valeriy Ivanovich. Sir, the reason for my call is that I would like to urge you to terminate Jacob Kelly. Now that he has re-entered the US and is no longer being detained, he is a much softer target—easier to locate, easier to get close to. And he may still be going through debriefings and interrogations and sharing damaging information. Killing him would put a stop to that."

"But General Chernikov, the damage has been done. I see little point in ordering his termination."

"Respectfully, sir, I disagree. Killing him might still be a worthwhile exercise in damage control. And it will rob the Americans of their star witness if they try to expose our operations."

"*Pravda.*"

"Sir, at great expense we have taken the trouble to relocate the prison facility. Don't you think we should go one step further and put Kelly away, once and for all?"

Patrikeyev weighed his subordinate's arguments and conceded that he had a point. From every respect it would be helpful if Jacob Kelly simply disappeared. Perhaps an accident could be arranged.

"*Da*, General, I think you are right. But I will arrange things—I don't want you involved."

****

Benjamin Klausowitz put his suitcase down on the lumpy bed. The accommodations were not fancy, but adequate. They had paid for a two-month voucher in Moscow for a government *dacha* in Magadan, reserved for high government officials. The accommodations came with the use of a vehicle although the customary driver was not provided, which didn't bother Ben as he preferred to drive himself anyway. After arriving at the airport in Sokol at midday, they had located the little bungalow overlooking the harbor. The urgent message from his Mossad handler three days ago instructed him and Katerina to travel to Magadan for an indeterminate stay, instructions to follow. They brought a large supply of rubles and were prepared for the long haul.

"Kat, dear, let's drive around town a bit. I want to get the lay of the land. I'm really looking forward to relaxing after the hustle and bustle of Moscow."

Most of their chat was for the benefit of presumed listeners, consequently their conversation was guarded. Ben surmised that both the *dacha* and the car were likely bugged. The KGB maintained a professional interest in the affairs of comrades who were sufficiently wealthy to travel. Even if their activities were found to be legitimate they might still be fruitful targets for blackmail by the local agents. Alternatively, the local agents could make themselves sufficiently obnoxious that wealthy "benefactors" would bribe them to keep the gumshoes off their backs. Sort of like *paparazzi*, only they were chasing the targets around for ostensible intelligence reasons, not for photographs.

Ben wanted to check in with his controller and they needed to get away from the house and the car in order to do it. Communication with the Mossad was actually the easiest part of this job. The Klausowitzes were well heeled and owned a fully licensed sat phone which they carried openly, making no attempt to conceal it. As a retired, high-ranking official in the Moscow local government, Ben had had no problem getting the necessary permits and purchasing the phone. They surmised, correctly, that the phone had circuitry permitting the KGB to listen in on all their calls. Until that problem had been dealt with the phone could not be used to make contact with the Israelis.

One snowy afternoon in Moscow Benjamin and Katerina had found the battery in their automobile dead, which was unfortunate as they had tickets to that evening's performance at the Bolshoi. Ben called a taxi. On the way to the theatre, the taxi driver—a Mossad agent—provided Ben with a plan for fixing his sat phone. The next day his car battery had miraculously recovered.

As instructed, they established a predictable pattern of sat phone usage over the space of eighteen months, knowing that the KGB would be monitoring their usage. While in Moscow they *never* used the sat phone—only when traveling away from home. Ben wanted whatever listeners might be tracking him to become accustomed to the phone being turned off and unused when they were in residence in Moscow.

After the usage pattern had been well established the phone was passed secretly to a Mossad agent. It was flown to Tel Aviv under diplomatic cover, where a team of electronics experts analyzed it and modified the circuitry, even to the point of fabricating duplicate integrated circuit chips. When the technicians completed their wizardry, the phone operated exactly as it always had unless a certain ten-digit number was prefixed to a call. The prefix temporarily disabled the KGB eavesdropping circuitry and the phone would use frequencies and encryptions that connected it to any one of a quartet of super-secret American satellites parked in stationary orbits over the breadth of the Soviet Union. Several channels on the birds were leased to Israel by the National Security Agency.

The Israelis assumed—correctly—that the Americans were helping themselves to the Israeli communications traffic passing through the satellites. But what the Israelis did not know was that the spooks at the NSA were unable to crack the Israeli encryption schemes, though it was not for lack of trying. When the phone was returned to the Klausowitzes, who had refrained from travel while the phone was out of their hands, it was ready for dual use: normal calls, to which the KGB would be privy, and secure communications to their Mossad handler.

Ben and Katerina purchased a bottle of wine, some cheese, sausage, and good black bread, and drove to a rocky overlook on the east side of the peninsula. The town with its harbor and all the shipping were on the west side; here a barren landscape on an empty sea stretched before them. Aside from the plaintive cries of seagulls as they wheeled about overhead, there was no sound but the crash of the surf and the rustle of the wind in the larch trees that extended almost down to the shoreline.

They bundled up against the cold November sea breeze and took their picnic lunch to a sheltered place in the rocks overlooking the sea. After they finished lunch Ben pulled out the phone and dialed his special code.

"Lion," said a terse voice on the other end.

"Of Judah," Ben replied and then said, "Oscar one seven oh."

"Go," the voice said.

"Requesting instructions."

"First objective: you are to verify the presence of a GRU prison facility, code-named *Rabbit Hutch*, located about 20 miles north-northwest of Magadan. Confirm that *Rabbit Hutch* is a GRU facility holding foreign prisoners.

"Second objective: if *Rabbit Hutch* is confirmed, survey the road access to the site and report.

"Third objective: if *Rabbit Hutch* is confirmed, provide daily situation report on harbor facilities, shipping, disposition of all observed military and intelligence assets, and all signs of activity indicating a heightened state of alert. Go."

Ben repeated the instructions. After terminating the phone call, Ben looked at his shivering wife and said, "Katerina, it's too cold for a picnic. Let's go back to the car."

****

Jake laced up his running shoes and left the duplex, locking the door behind him. The sun had not yet made its appearance, though the eastern sky was grey. A brisk north wind was pushing dry leaves ahead of it, making them rattle and rustle as they tumbled down the street. Falcon set a brisk seven-minute-mile pace for his morning run, a ten-mile jaunt that took him from the north side of Vienna, Virginia to the Potomac River and back via any one of a dozen back roads.

He'd been training aggressively, running and using the weight machines in the gym at Langley, trying to rebuild his conditioning to the point it was before the Soviets captured him. He'd also been spending as much time as possible on the shooting range, honing his skills. Though he had not mentioned it to anyone, Kelly was determined to be part of the assault team that took down Chernikov's operation. At the moment he was on temporary duty, seconded to Dr. William Jensen at the CIA as a special consultant for Operation *Thunderbird*. As soon as his TDY was over he'd be back in an operational fighter wing.

As he trotted along the county roads he kept a wary eye for anyone who might be paying too much attention to him. He was convinced that the Soviets were not ready to call it quits, and he wasn't going to make it easy on them. The pilot was wearing a zippered running jacket. Inside the jacket, out of view, was a shoulder-holster packing his Air Force-issued Beretta M9. If someone wanted a piece of him it was going to be an expensive venture.

Having been trained as a CCT operator with four down-range deployments, Kelly had a finely developed sense of caution. He mixed up the driving routes he used to get to the Firm, he never went to the same restaurants or grocery stores twice in a row, and he always varied his running routes. Jake's situational awareness was on high alert at all times. But no matter how he varied his routines, running or driving, there was only one way in and out of the subdivision where his government-leased quarters were located.

His run was uneventful and ninety minutes later he was showering and getting ready for his day.

****

Bridger walked wearily from the map table to his office windows. They had been talking fruitlessly for three hours, trying to dream up a means of getting in and out of Magadan with an assault force of sixty-four shooters. He looked longingly out the window to the west. He could see the Pacific Ocean with its endless swells crashing onto North Island's white beach about a quarter mile distant. The flag outside the administration building was snapping smartly at the flagstaff in a steady fifteen-knot breeze. It would have been a great day to go sailing.

He looked up at the clock. It was after five. Coronado traffic would be approaching its typical rush-hour gridlock. He swung around and faced the other men in his office with a look of exasperation. "We're getting nowhere! Forget insertion and extraction! We'll come back to it, maybe early next week. Let's talk about the assault itself. Perhaps we can get some traction with that." The other officers nodded.

Clausen's planning and targeting specialist for *Thunderbird* was Lieutenant Commander Tom Rainer. Rainer was a veteran of seven highly secret (and highly successful) operations, and was recognized by both his superiors and subordinates as being a first-class planner.

Lieutenant Commander Ed Bausch would lead the First Platoon. Bausch had seen action in Nicaragua as well as in Southeast Asia and was the most experienced of all the platoon leaders. The other officers present were Lieutenants Paul Pascoe, Jerry Auld, and Kerry Davis, assigned to lead the Second through the Fourth Platoons, respectively. Of these, Davis was the least experienced.

"The overall mission objective is to free the hostages and get them back safely on friendly soil. Pursuant to that, besides a successful insertion and extraction, we have three mission-critical objectives." Bridger took his seat again at the head of the table. "First, we have to shut off all contact between *Rabbit Hutch* and the outside world. It is essential to interdict all communications. If we fail in this objective we might as well have our people carry their own personal body bags, because they'll need 'em.

"Second, no hostile can be allowed to leave the camp alive, and if any third party stumbles on the operation they cannot be permitted to compromise it. An airtight perimeter must be maintained around the facility at all times once the action begins."

"What about the surrenders, Admiral?" asked Lieutenant Auld. "Are you saying we double-tap 'em?"

"No, Jerry, that's not what I mean. Leave one of the cellblocks intact. Anyone who surrenders—and any third parties who stumble onto the action—will be locked in that cellblock when you pull out. You can't take them with you, and we sure can't leave them to their own devices. Whatever form the extraction takes, it will require some time to pull off. We need those men locked up so they can't blow the whistle." The other officers nodded. Bridger rubbed his head and then added, "This is a military operation, not a cold-blooded massacre. All the same, a lot of people are going to die and I don't want even one of them to be ours. If it's us or them, gonna be them. Remember what General Patton said."

"What did Patton say, sir?" asked Paul Pascoe.

"You don't know? What on earth they teaching you kids nowadays? Patton said that a good soldier doesn't die for his country, he makes the other guy die for *his* country. It's good advice.

"The third mission-critical objective is to keep the Sovs from killing or harming the prisoners. We have to take out the guards in each cellblock before they can shoot the scientists to prevent their rescue. That probably won't be too hard, because none of their standing orders are going to include instructions on what to do if the prison is assaulted by a large force of Navy SEALs." More nods and a few chuckles greeted this statement.

"So, gentlemen, how do we do it?" Admiral Bridger leaned back in his chair at the head of the map table.

Every head turned simultaneously to Rainer, who was lost in thought and focused on something only he could see on the ceiling. When the silence became obvious he snapped out of his reverie and looked around the table in surprise. "What?" he said to all the stares. "What? Did I miss something?"

"We are waiting," replied Marcus patiently, "for you to tell us how we are going to assault *Rabbit Hutch* and accomplish the three mission-critical objectives the admiral has spelled out."

"Marcus, don't you think we ought to give Kerry first shot at this? It would be a good experience for him," Tom suggested.

"Good thinking, Tom. All right, Kerry—you're in the hot seat. How would you assault this site?" Marcus asked, looking at the leader of the Fourth Platoon. Kerry Davis had been recently promoted to platoon commander. He'd returned a month ago from his second trip downrange, and had demonstrated good judgment and bold initiative. Lean and wiry, the compactly built lieutenant was the best marksman in the group. Seeing that all the men in Bridger's office were rated expert—including Bridger—it was quite a distinction.

Davis studied the satellite photos carefully. Techs at the NSA had generated a topographical contour map of the area from data acquired by a satellite-based radar altimeter.

"The target is sitting in a wooded, shallow valley running east to west, with a very low ridge to the south, a higher bald ridge to the north, and climbing to a gentle summit to the east. It appears that the land has been cleared to about fifty meters out from the perimeter fence on all sides. I'm assuming that entire area is illuminated at night, so once we get closer than fifty meters we might as well ring the doorbell." He paused, thinking; drawing on the photos with his finger, he continued. "Step one is to take out all the guard towers and the guardhouse at the main gate with silenced sniper rifles, using coordinated, simultaneous fire. Step two is to take out their power. In preparation for the assault, we'll need to wire the power pole down the valley with enough explosives to bring it down, along with the telephone land line."

"Why not do the power first, Kerry, then the guard towers?" Marcus asked, testing him.

"Because our snipers' eyes will already be adjusted to the lighting as it is. They can pop the tower guards using the camp's ambient light. The enemy will be trying to process what just happened, and then they lose their lights. By doing it this way we'll add to the confusion. More confusion, more surprise.

"Once the lights go out, we go to NVGs. The snipers will take out the dogs next. At some point their power is restored by the emergency generator. When that happens the snipers are tasked with shooting out all the yard lights. Once the yard lights are extinguished again, we begin breaching. I'd breach along the narrow axis of the camp, because it will make the angles more difficult for their shooters—they won't have as many windows to fire from.

"The main assault group will come from the west, breaching into the administrative compound, taking the fence down with explosives. They will face the most opposition because the barracks and the arms are on that side. They'll need support from several machine gunners who'll be laying down suppressing fire. We've got to figure the angles and fire lanes just right to avoid getting caught in our own crossfire.

"A second, smaller assault group infiltrates from the east, breaching their way into the prison side of the compound with wirecutters, using the cellblocks to block the line of sight from the barracks. If things go well, no hostile will even be aware that the second group is there, because all the fun is happening on the the other side of the camp. The main assault force is functioning as a diversion and enabling us to accomplish objective three—securing the safety of the hostages. In order to seal off the prison side of the compound, I'd put shooters here and here," Kerry suggested, pointing to either side of the compound where the access between the prison and administrative sections was located, "armed with M60s to interdict anyone who tries to move to the prison side of the compound."

He fell silent for a moment, chewing his lip as he continued to examine the photos and sketches, and then he added, "We've got to destroy the generator in the physical plant ASAP so we can deny power to their comm gear, and turn out the lights. Once it's dark, we've got a distinct advantage." He traced a few more lines on the satellite photos of the camp, pondering. "I almost wonder if we need a third assaulting group to breach here," he suggested, pointing at the fence on the north side of the compound next to the physical plant, "because I can see our frogmen getting pinned down trying to cross this space right here, between the main gate and the physical plant building. By this time, we're going to have about eighty fully armed and angry *Spetsnaz* shooting back at us. And they are going to know where we are headed—they know we're wanting to turn off the power. So if we have a third assault group breaching behind the cover of the physical plant, with machine gun support making the bad guys in barracks RH5 keep their heads down, we might get to the generator more quickly and with fewer casualties.

"If we do it that way, then the main assault group stays on its side of the compound and blows a hole in the side of the admin building, clears it, blows a hole into the next building, that's um," he paused, consulting the sketch of the camp layout, "RH2, and clears it. We should have enough fire pouring through the windows of RH3 to suppress anyone inside. Chuck a big satchel charge against its wall, blow a hole in it, then double-tap anyone still trying to resist.

"The group that breaches the physical plant can handle barracks RH5 the same way. The hostiles in the center barracks will have to surrender or face a massacre from both sides."

"You know, Kerry" Marcus said, "their guys aren't going to stay put and get slaughtered. They will try to retake the initiative. They'll be moving around as soon as they get over the surprise. How are you going to handle the hostiles shifting position, massing for a counter-attack, or trying to retake the guard towers?"

"Our snipers and machine gunners will keep everyone bottled up inside their buildings."

Tom Rainer nodded. "Okay, but you put too many machine gunners sprinkled around a small target on fairly flat land like this, and it's going to be hard to avoid friendly-fire casualties."

Kerry agreed, "We'll have to figure the angles and the fields of fire carefully, and we'll need good coordination and communication between the supporting and assaulting elements. Our mock-up will have to be exact, and we'll have to practice until we get it perfect. But, Tom, we're going to need lots of machine gun support laying down suppressing fire in multiple places. It's the only way a small force like ours can take a larger defending force—we've got to outgun them."

"That's a good first look, Kerry," Marcus approved. He stared at the drawings and photos for a moment, and then offered, "That fence is going to be a pain in the butt. We've got to get into the admin building quickly to keep them from sending out the alarm, and the fence slows us down. Our guys will be exposed while breaching it. The best way to breach it would be with explosives, or to drive right through it. But we won't have a vehicle, and we need the element of surprise. If we don't cut off their communications within sixty seconds, we'll be compromised."

"Sixty seconds isn't going to happen, Marcus," Lieutenant Auld replied. Auld would be commanding the Third Platoon. "The same flechettes in a breaching charge that cut the wire will turn anyone close by into hamburger. Somebody will have to run from cover to the fence, place the explosive, and run back before detonating it. And since the fence is doubled, that sequence has to happen twice."

"Do you suppose the area between the fences is mined?" asked Bausch, the First Platoon leader.

"No," responded Bridger quickly. "Satellite surveillance

shows dog kennels inside the wire, so it must not be mined. And remember, men: *Rabbit Hutch* was not designed to withstand an assault coming from outside the fence. So some of these problems may not be severe as we think."

"Everything is too close to risk using mortars, we could wind up hitting the cellblocks with the first round or two. And RPGs aren't exactly reliable when it comes to clearing wire obstacles. We could shoot at that fence all day with M72s, and most of them would just go right through it without detonating. So we are down to wirecutters or explosive breaching," affirmed Rainer.

The group fell silent for a few minutes, thinking. Then Commander Clausen suggested, "To buy a little more time we could use an RF jammer man-pack. Since this is a prison operation and not a combat headquarters they won't have the latest and greatest electronics. In fact, we could take two separate jammers: one keyed to Soviet conventional military radio frequencies, and the other keyed to their military sat phone frequencies. All we have to do is keep them out of contact long enough to get through the fence."

"If there's anyone monitoring the military comm nets when we do this, using a jammer would be like ringing the doorbell and giving the butler our business card," claimed Second Platoon commander Paul Pascoe.

"That's true, Paul, but we have to risk it," replied Admiral Bridger. "If they raise the alarm the entire operation will fail."

"With all due respect, Admiral, if they see a jamming signal we'll be raising the alarm *for* them. We'll be announcing our presence and they'll be all over us in no time."

"Looks like that fence is almost as bad as insertion and extraction," said Bridger, shaking his head. "Go home to your families, boys. We'll pick this up again tomorrow."

****

The *Kolymaskaya trassa,* or Kolyma Trace, was the product of an ambitious highway project taken on by *Dalstroi* in 1932. It was an attempt to connect Yakutsk to Magadan by road and it winds through two thousand kilometers of some of the most challenging and beautiful terrain on earth. The highway is officially designated as the M56, but is known to locals as the *Road of Bones* because the bones of the slave laborers who died during its construction were allegedly combined into the road surface materials. The Kolyma Trace connects not one but *two* towns each of which claims the distinction of being the coldest continually inhabited spot on the surface of the planet outside of Antarctica. Temperatures drop as low as ninety degrees below zero, Fahrenheit.

Benjamin Klausowitz pulled on to the Kolyma, and headed north for Sokol, seventy kilometers north of Magadan. On the east side of the Sokol Airport he turned left on the gravel road to the little village of Splavnaya. It was a beautiful drive. To their south the heavily forested land rose to a high ridge, bald and rocky in places. North of the road, the land gradually dropped, with forests and open meadows crisscrossed by frozen creeks and streams. He sighed. It would have been a beautiful place to visit in the summer.

Between patches of snowpack and the generally bad condition of the road, he had to drive slowly. Three kilometers after passing a closed quarry operation on the right, they came upon a broken-down military vehicle. Ben recognized it as a big Ural 375-D, a four-and-a-half-ton military truck configured to carry cargo. The hood was up and two soldiers were standing on the front bumper, peering into the engine space.

"Katerina, let's stop and see if they need help." Ben knew that there were no military facilities in the area, except for *Rabbit Hutch*. He guessed that these men were probably based at the secret prison camp. *This may be the opening we need*, he thought to himself.

He maneuvered the car to the shoulder and parked. The two young soldiers were engaged in a heated disagreement and did not notice his approach.

"It is the fuel pump, you nitwit!"

"*Nyet!* It's only a clogged filter, Sergei. When you were cranking the engine there was plenty of fuel coming out of the hose."

"Oh! Now you tell me! Why didn't you say so the first time, Boris?"

"You wouldn't shut up long enough to let me!"

Ben discreetly cleared his throat and both men whipped around, startled. "Having a little difficulty with this beast, boys?" he asked in a friendly way.

The man identified as Boris grinned and jumped down to the ground. "*Da*. It just quit on us, the piece of junk! We are supposed to be picking up supplies in Magadan, and we have a two-day pass. Looks like we will be using our time off to fix this stinking truck." He said the last with a bit of disappointment.

Ben spread his hands and said, "I don't know anything about mechanics, but I have a warm car and my wife and I can take you where you need to go. Is your base near by? Shall I take you there?"

Sergei shot his friend a glance and with a subtle shake of his head indicated no.

Boris smiled and replied, "Ah, um, *nyet, spasibo*. We don't have any repair parts there anyway. I'm afraid that what we need to fix this truck is located in Magadan."

Ben smiled grandly, bowed low, and sweeping his hand toward the old East German Wartburg 311 he was driving, said, "Comrades, it is my pleasure to drive you to Magadan. My wife and I are here on holiday and we would be pleased to render you assistance."

Sergei glanced at Boris, who shrugged, and then looked back at Ben. "*Bol'shoye spasibo*, comrade. We accept your kind offer."

The young men clambered into the back seat, and Ben turned the car around. He had noticed the black bat shoulder patch—an emblem of GRU forces—and he felt certain that these men must be based at his assigned target. He guessed that they were part of a Ministry of Internal Affairs (MVD) special police detachment connected with the GRU. As he drove, he and Katerina chatted casually with the soldiers.

"I am Ben Klausowitz and this is my wife Katerina. I am retired from the Moscow Directorate of Central Planning. We get away from Moscow whenever we have the opportunity. Kat and I have always wanted to tour the Kolyma River country. We have a small *dacha* on the outskirts of Magadan. I tried to tell Kat we should wait till next summer, but she loves snow so here we are. Brrr! I think we should have gone to the Black Sea instead! And who might you young men be?"

Sergei spoke first. "I am Sergei. My home is in Leningrad. My parents are factory workers."

"My name is Boris. I'm actually not very far from home; well, at least not as far as Sergei. I was raised in Khabarovsk."

Ben noted that neither man indicated to what military unit he was attached, nor even their last names. He smiled to himself. Everyone working for the GRU was pretty tight-lipped about their work. *Still*, Ben thought, *warm motherly hospitality from Katerina along with her tasty home cooking plus liberal quantities of vodka has been known to loosen tongues before. It will probably work again.*

They chatted all the way to Magadan, where Boris secured the proper fuel filter. Ben and Katerina invited the two young men to stay overnight at their *dacha* and to enjoy their hospitality, which the boys were only too glad to do. He promised to drive them back to their truck first thing in the morning.

Six hours and two bottles of vodka later, he had all the verification that he needed. Objective one had been accomplished.

The next morning good news from Bill Jensen at the CIA was waiting in Admiral Bridger's secure email, "*Rabbit Hutch* location is confirmed. Proceed with all dispatch."

Chapter 22

Monday, November 9, 1987: 1000 hours, local time
Coronado, CA

"Admiral, this is impossible! We've *got* to have better information. There are too many unknowns! The whole operation will go south right out of the box unless we can get some meaningful intelligence about what we're facing. Our butts are on the line, and we're making plans based on guesswork. I don't like it, sir."

Bridger threw his pencil on the desk in frustration and got up and walked to the window. "I know, Marcus, I know. Add to the lack of good intel the compressed schedule and we've got a budding disaster on our hands. We need another forty-five days for planning and training. But Jensen is standing firm: 'Everybody's got to be home by Christmas.' Says that the President is leaning on him, so he's leaning on us."

Davis, Pascoe, and Auld were not present at this meeting. They were dressed in civvies at the mock-up facility, pretending to be film construction coordinators, directing the final phases of construction. The remainder of Clausen's shooters were training in the base Kill House, keeping their skills honed. Practice at the mock-up wouldn't begin until Wednesday.

Problems and challenges were cropping up faster than they were being solved, and the group was getting a little antsy. They had put off figuring the fastest way to breach the fence until they could see the problem at the training site. Nobody had solved the insertion/extraction dilemma. Tom Rainer and Ed Bausch looked on with gloomy expressions as they considered the need for better intelligence.

Marcus tried again, "Admiral Bridger, wherever the Firm is getting this intel, it's not from a military source. Their data is *generally* useful but *specifically* worthless for our needs. We've got to have a military eye evaluating *Rabbit Hutch*. We can't send an assault team in with nothing more to go on than photographs and general statements about the port facility." Commander Clausen rubbed his temples with his hands. No one responded, but it was clear that everyone agreed.

Bausch listened to the silence for several minutes and then suggested quietly, "Let's send in a recon team."

"Huh?" queried Rainer, startled out of his thoughts.

"Let's land a four-man recon squad," repeated Ed, "and get some good SEAL eyeballs on this thing. I know that the Sea of Okhotsk is not a favorable setting for landing guys from a sub. We definitely could not offload sixty-plus frogmen, but we could do just four."

Bridger shook his head and replied adamantly, "No! Too risky! Way too risky. We might lose more than the team; we could lose a whole submarine and crew. That's a risk I'm not prepared to accept."

Bausch persisted, "But sir, if we *don't* get some good recon on this target we are risking not only the loss of dozens of good men, but total mission failure as well. I submit that the value of the mission itself justifies the risk."

"No, it doesn't! Look, Ed, if we sent a *Los Angeles* class attack boat in there to drop off your recon squad, and if that boat was captured, we would lose more than a very expensive piece of United States government property, not to mention its crew and the secrets they hold in their heads. We would also compromise dozens of technologies ranging from the electronics to the sonar signal-processing software to the very shape of the screws. It would be a massive, incalculable loss. We would be creating a national security problem of immense proportions. We aren't going to risk it."

"Perhaps we can insert them by some other means. What if they deployed off a civilian freighter while it was still several miles out of Magadan?" Ed persisted.

Clausen nodded in agreement, "Perhaps Bill Jensen has some Agency assets, sir. Maybe a freighter. We could drop a Zodiac over the side at night and motor to shore. It's worth a phone call, anyway."

Bridger sighed. *Too many people cutting too many corners, including me. I knew from the start that the intel was helpful, but not really what we need. So why didn't I demand something better immediately? Answer? Because we are talking about the friggin' Soviets, that's why! Not some South American banana republic! I don't want to lose my men in the USSR, because there'd be no getting them back. A recce squad could just vanish and we'd never know what happened. These boys don't worry about that because they think they're invincible. But then, to be an operator, you've got to think that way. But I worry about it, because they're my men—and I'm responsible for them. Stop it, John! You can't command the SEALs if you're going to worry about casualties. Everyone knows the risks when they sign up. But if this mission goes belly up they'll need to come up with a new definition of headache.*

Bridger relented. "Okay, I'll ask. Why don't you three take a coffee break, and give me a few minutes? I'll call him right now."

****

Galina Toporova was all smiles as she left the INS offices clutching her green card. Though she was unaware of it, Bill Jensen had spoken to the Director of the CIA and asked him to put her on the fast track for permanent status. The director was on excellent personal terms with the head of the INS, consequently Galina's application sailed through the process with lightning speed, which, in the labyrinthine bureaucracy of the US government, qualified as a miracle.

She could now seek employment, her own apartment, a driver's license, and pretty much anything else she wanted. The freedom she enjoyed in America was intoxicating. Had she the resources she could go anywhere in the US without fear and without permission. Many from Soviet bloc countries found the freedom intimidating and frightening; in the US it was the responsibility of the citizens—not the government— to provide for themselves. But Galina was exhilarated, not intimidated, by this. As one of the founders of a black-market timber cooperative in Siberia, she was used to assuming responsibility, taking risks, and making decisions to which great consequences attached.

Jake, she knew, was on temporary duty in DC. He'd not been allowed to give her his phone number, but would contact her through the Bates when his current assignment was finished. She was not sure where he would be transferred when he rejoined a fighter squadron, but wherever it was she intended to move to be close to him.

She decided to find a job immediately and stay put for several months, building up some financial strength before she moved to join Jacob. Her host family had promised that she could remain with them, rent-free, until she moved. Susan Bates had assured her that with a Masters in Mathematics, teaching experience, and fluency in both Russian and English she'd have no trouble landing a good job.

Permanent residency in the United States! It was worth celebrating. She was walking past Caffé Trieste on Vallejo Street, and decided a good cup of coffee and a pastry would do the trick.

****

"Bill, it's John Bridger. Got a minute?"

"Sure. Are you calling from a secure line?"

"Yeah, we're good. How's things going on your end? You're teaching at Georgetown, aren't you? How do you manage that? Have you even left your office at the Agency in the last two weeks?"

"Hardly. The semester is a total loss. My TAs have been teaching everything. Thank the Lord for tenure, or they'd have kicked me out a long time ago. I keep promising the department chair that I'll make up for it in the winter term. We'll see.

"So, what's up, John? How's the planning going?"

"Bill, we need to insert a recon squad into Magadan, yesterday. The Sea of Okhotsk is too closely patrolled to use a sub. Does the Agency have any assets like, perhaps, freighters we could use to drop a few frogmen off eight or ten miles out of the port?" Bridger came to the point quickly, anticipating the objection he knew was coming.

"John, you've already got all the recon you need. I've called in some favors and we have an asset right in Magadan. The good intel I've been sending you comes straight from them."

"It's not enough, Bill. We need one of our own, and preferably someone we can talk to realtime."

"Can't do it! They don't even let me talk to this asset. Look, John, write out a list of questions. I'll get you whatever you need, I promise."

"Bill, with all due respect, I've read the reports you have been forwarding and I can tell you several things about your asset. First, I know that they are native, meaning they are Soviet and not someone who's been inserted. This means their training is minimal and their familiarity with SEAL tactics and weapons is non-existent. Second, I know that they are a civilian asset, not military, so their knowledge of Soviet weaponry will be little better. That's not adequate. I need trained SEALs on site looking at the situation and I need them there now." Despite his best effort to control himself, Bridger was becoming combative and insistent.

"Admiral, I beg to disagree. I've personally read every report forwarded to you from our source. They've contained intelligence of the highest value, including good information about the disposition and make-up of local military units. I am familiar with this particular source from several years back. They have always been highly accurate with respect to military information."

Bridger paused, dreading what he had to say. "You were never in the military, were you, sir." It was a statement, not a question.

"No. But I had a great deal of interaction with the military in southeast Asia some years back."

"Vietnam?"

"Yes, and other places of which I am not at liberty to speak. Why?"

"Bill, have you ever planned a full military assault?"

"No, Admiral, I have not. But I expect you knew that before you asked." Jensen sounded irritated, defensive.

"Yes, sir, I did," admitted Bridger quietly.

"Then what's your point, Admiral?"

Bridger paused again, knowing that he was running the risk of ruining their working relationship. But it had to be done, so he continued carefully, "May I respectfully submit, sir, that *you* probably don't know what sort of intelligence we need, and may I gently suggest that you're not qualified to pass judgment on the quality or kind of intelligence necessary to successfully plan a clandestine operation involving a full-scale assault with sixty-plus boots on the ground."

Holding his anger in check with great difficulty, Jensen fought for a moment with his pride. His own reputation in the Firm was near legendary. He considered himself a competent warrior. But he knew that Admiral Bridger had raised an indisputable point. CIA field officers of Jensen's background were expert at planning and executing small, isolated actions, but unless they were former military they did not have the training or experience for larger, multi-platoon, coordinated assault operations.

"Bill? Hello?" The silence made Bridger wonder if the connection had been broken.

"Yeah, I'm here. Admiral, what you just said took a lot of courage."

"Uh-huh. Yes, sir, it did." Bridger wiped his sweaty brow with his handkerchief, and sat down heavily in his chair.

"But you're right, John. I've been treating this as a CIA game, and it's not. Our asset on site is very valuable for standard intelligence and limited minor field work. But they have no military skill or training."

"Yes, sir."

"It's funny, y'know, John," Jensen admitted.

"What's funny?"

"Well, I told the entire *Thunderbird* group that interservice rivalry would not be tolerated, and here I myself caused the first problem with it. *You* are our covert military operations expert, not me. Okay, John, tell me what you have in mind."

Bridger breathed a silent sigh of relief, and then said, "Bill, I need a four-man SEAL recon squad on site as soon as I can get them there. Yesterday, if possible. We need eyeballs on *Rabbit Hutch*, and I need to have interactive communications with them. They will be tasked for various surveillance jobs, by me, as needed. I know there is some risk of detection involved with two-way communication, but it's a risk I can accept.

"We can't insert them through any of our normal means. We can't risk a HALO jump, there's too much military air traffic and active radar between Vladivostok and the installations at Kamchatka Petropavlovsk. There's no overland route we can use to get them in, and in my judgment it's entirely too risky to use a submarine for the job."

"Yes, I concur. Do you need extraction capability for this squad?"

"Probably not, John, but I'd like to leave the option open. I plan to bring them out with everybody else. So, does the Agency have any maritime assets we can use to insert them?"

"Give me a day to ask around, and I'll get back to you. Don't worry, Admiral—you've convinced me. If we can make it happen, we will."

****

The road from the subdivision where Kelly was quartered intersected with a larger boulevard. To the left Kelly could pick up a network of county roads leading to the Potomac, five miles distant. The right led into Vienna. Kelly trotted to the left, running on the shoulder against traffic. The morning was dark and grey with lowering clouds and falling temperatures. The forecast was predicting a cold, rainy day with temperatures dipping into the high thirties.

Though Jake was associated with *Thunderbird* as a consultant, his life was returning to something approaching normalcy. No one was trying to arrest him, he was sleeping and eating on a normal schedule, and soon would be returning to the life of an Air Force fighter pilot.

Last night he'd gotten a call from Roger Bates informing him that Galena received her permanent residency status.

Things were stable enough to begin thinking about the future, he decided. As soon as he could ensure that Chernikov was no longer in the picture, he was going to marry Galya. *Can't wait!*

He did not notice the cobalt blue Jeep Cherokee that came through the intersection from the Vienna side. The driver was patient. He allowed Kelly to jog out of sight before moving forward, only driving far enough to regain a visual on the runner before pulling off onto the shoulder. This time of the morning there was plenty of traffic on the roads. The further out in the country the target got, the less the traffic. The driver was counting on that.

Kelly was perspiring slightly as he fell into his running cadence. The moisture evaporating from his sweats helped cool him down. He loved running on dark, cool mornings. He wished he hadn't missed the leaves changing—he was in California when the fall colors were at their peak in northern Virginia.

Kelly reached an intersection and decided to take the road on the right. There were no residences on it—only farm fields. Because the road traced the boundaries between the fields, it meandered, with plenty of sharp right-angle turns. The average northern Virginia driver was not interested in scenic beauty at 0700 hours, he just wanted to get to work fast. This road wasn't fast, hence it had little traffic. Kelly loved it.

The tail saw him take the farm road and consulted his map. There were no intersections on the road for the next two miles. *Perfect.* He let Kelly get out of sight, and waited an extra three minutes. The Jeep had been rented in Ohio, one-way with unlimited mileage, to be returned to Denver, Colorado. Its license plates had been stolen in Tennessee. All transactions, hotel, restaurant, air travel, vehicle rental, were done with cash—no credit cards, no checks. A hit-and-run accident with no witnesses would be untraceable, with no reason to suspect foul play. It was just a tragic reality. Runners sometimes got run over on dark mornings, and the drivers sometimes didn't stick around to get charged with involuntary manslaughter. *Sad.*

As Kelly rounded one of the right-angle curves, he saw a

dark blue Jeep coming up behind him. There was no other traffic in sight. He heard the car accelerate as it came out of the curve, one hundred feet or so behind him. Jake looked over his shoulder. The vehicle seemed to be taking up a lot of the road, so Kelly moved further onto the shoulder, out of the way. The driver veered sharply and headed right for him, forcing Kelly to dive headfirst over a deep, narrow, drainage ditch and into the stubble of the harvested corn field.

"HEY! Watch where you're going, buddy!" Jake shouted.

The driver tried to whip the vehicle back onto the road, but his momentum on the graveled shoulder was too great. He lost control and the Jeep careened into the ditch, sliding to a stop, high-centered by the edge of the ditch.

Still angry, Kelly picked himself up. He put his right hand inside his running jacket and gripped the butt of his gun, but did not draw it. He approached the vehicle warily, intending to see if the driver was hurt. The man was unable to open his door, as it was pinioned against the side of the ditch. The tinted window rolled down and Kelly was surprised to see the driver was grasping a pistol with an attached silencer. The man was squirming as he tried to untangle himself from the seat belt, steering column, and pedals, seeking to reposition himself for a better shot. The few seconds of delay was all that Jake needed. He drew his Beretta—there was already a round in the chamber—and put four rounds into the driver before the man was able to fire.

The whole thing happened so quickly Jacob didn't even have time to think—he just reacted. Still flush with adrenaline and holding the pistol with a two-handed grip, he looked about. No traffic, no witnesses. A quick check verified that his assailant was dead. Kelly rapidly searched the body and the vehicle, finding the original license plates under the seat and a little under two thousand dollars cash on the body. Grabbing the man's pen and a Burger King bag he found on the floor of the car, he wrote down both license plate numbers, quickly copied the information from the dead man's driver's license, as well as the transaction number and rental car agency phone number from the lease agreement in the glove compartment.

Kelly looked around again. Not a soul in sight. Grabbing a napkin from the fast-food bag, he carefully wiped down everything he had touched. Jake rolled all the windows up, locked the vehicle, and sprinted across the field to a narrow strip of woods bordering the field on the opposite side. After crossing two more fields he came to a road, jogged home, and called Bill Jensen.

"Bill, somebody just tried to take me out."

"What are you talking about, Jake?"

"I was just doing my morning run on a country road between Vienna and the river, and a guy tried to run me down with his car. He missed, and went into the ditch. Next thing I know he's rolled down his window and is snaking out a hogleg with an attached silencer."

"A silencer?"

"Yeah, I thought that was odd, too. Not something your average joe carries around with him. Not unless he's a hit man. When I saw the silencer I went for my gun. He got tangled up in his seat belt and I got my piece in action before he did. I wiped the car down to get rid of my fingerprints and left it locked with the windows up. What should I do?"

"Did you pick up all your brass?"

"Yes, sir."

"Good. Don't call the police. Get a shower and get in here as fast as you can. But first give me a description of the car and its location. I'll get an Agency clean-up crew with a flatbed over there immediately."

Chapter 23

"Got him!" Erin Masters was standing in Bill Jensen's doorway with a look of satisfaction on her face. Masters was a top analyst who had a small group of hackers under her command, former black hats who'd come over to the light—or who had betrayed the underground hacking community and come over to the dark side of the force, depending on one's perspective. In any case, there weren't many networks that could keep her boys out for long. Masters was an ad hoc analyst: she was not assigned to long-term projects, rather, she specialized in solving puzzles and Jensen had put her on the case to identify the gunman in the Jeep.

"Good work, Erin! Who is he?"

"Pyotr Orlov. He arrived five days ago as Gennady Abramov on a diplomatic passport, in the company of another individual. According to his cover story he's a special envoy to the Soviet Embassy's deputy attaché for cultural affairs. He and his friend came over to arrange bookings for a Russian ballet troupe touring the States next summer. The guy he arrived with checks out legit and has been booking major venues today. But Orlov is known to be with the GRU and specializes in wet work."

"An assassin."

"Right. He's shown up on our radar in several places starting seven years ago. We managed to get fingerprints on him in Brussels a year ago but were never able to get a visual. When the Brits turned the top KGB agent in London four years ago, Orlov was the guy Moscow sent to eliminate him. He's very good. We've been able to tie him to three killings with fingerprints, but all the targets were Sovs gone bad. Today's attempt marks the first time we know of that he's been tasked to kill the citizen of another country. It also marks the first time he's failed, according to our contact in MI6."

Jensen turned in his chair and stared out the window. He mused aloud, half to himself, "If he's that good, how did he fail today?"

"Sir? I'd file Orlov's screw-up under the 'stuff happens' rubric."

"No, Erin, I disagree," the professor said, turning his chair once again to face her, "I'd file it under Providence."

She shrugged, "Whatever. Orlov had fake identity documents on his person. He was traveling as an American citizen. We're still working on reconstructing his movements, but I expect to get that sewn up in the next twenty-four hours."

"You're the best, Masters, glad you're on my team," said Jensen with grin.

She smiled, "Thank you, sir," and disappeared down the hall.

Jensen got up and paced for a few minutes, thinking. *This is an unnecessary complication to an already difficult situation, but I do believe it has a simple, elegant solution.* He picked up his phone, punched a few numbers, and commanded, "Bring Major Kelly to my office now."

****

"He's been lying to us, lying to us all along," spat the chief scientist responsible for microcircuitry research at the Academy of Sciences in Moscow. He'd come to the prison facility to meet with Oswald Simmons, and had requested to speak with Chernikov before he returned to Moscow.

Dr. Oswald Simmons had been kidnapped in early July the year before. A scientist considered by many to be a genius, Simmons had done his undergrad work in Geology at Colorado State University, and completed his doctorate in Electrical Engineering at MIT. Chernikov kidnapped him to gain advantage of the man's research in sub-micron integrated circuit structures, a field crucial to miniaturizing weapons. Having the physique of an athlete, Simmons held black belts in five martial arts disciplines and had nearly turned the tables on the agents sent to capture him. A fluent speaker of Russian, Oz—as he was known to his friends—escaped with Major Kelly from the Soviet interrogation facility, but was recaptured after getting shot during a raid on Chernikov's apartment.

"I don't understand, Dr. Budnikov. For the last eleven months you've been telling me how valuable Dr. Simmon's contributions to your research have been," objected General Chernikov. Although it was disingenuous, he'd learned that the scientists who were working with his prisoners preferred to speak of the data the captives provided under threats and torture as contributions—as though they were colleagues. It was a matter of academic pride, Chernikov supposed.

"Frequently in advanced research, General, we follow leads that initially appear promising but wind up being dead ends," Budnikov explained carefully and with no small degree of condescension. "Dr. Simmons has enabled us to push processor speeds to twenty-five megahertz—double what we achieved in the past. It did appear to be a breakthrough and we built an entire semiconductor manufacturing facility based on his research and methods. But what was not apparent at the time was that the thermal energy—the heat, General—generated by the chip would not allow it to run in continuous duty without destroying itself."

"So why do you say he's been lying? It sounds as though you simply have a new problem to overcome, Dr. Budnikov."

"*Nyet*, Comrade General. Simmons displayed a thirty-two-megahertz processor at COMDEX in Las Vegas two years ago. It ran a stress test—nonstop—during the entire three days. He knows how to conquer the heat problem, General. He's led us on a wild goose chase and he's done it intentionally. Not only have my scientists not been working on their own research the last eleven months, they've been working on something that Simmons knew would fail."

Chernikov felt rage rising in his chest and choked back the bile. "You are telling me, Doctor, that not only has Simmons' data *not* advanced your work, it has actually hindered it?" he asked, barely able to control his fury.

"*Pravda*, Comrade General."

"GET OUT, Budnikov!" Chernikov shouted, standing so suddenly he upset his chair.

"What? I don't underst—" sputtered the scientist, face growing pale.

"YOU FOOL! You allowed Simmons to pull the wool over your eyes and only now do you see it? What are you, some sort of KGB stooge? GET OUT!" Chernikov was outraged, ready to shoot the hapless little man on the spot.

"But, General! The initial results! The scie—"

"Get out of my sight! Perhaps we need a new chief scientist at the Academy?" Chernikov suggested between clenched teeth.

Major Nikitin, Chernikov's second-in-command, rushed into the room and dragged the diminutive scientist from the room. Nikitin was accustomed to his boss's explosions and knew the only way to get Chernikov back on an even keel was to remove the provocateur.

The general righted his chair and sat, burying his face in his hands. If word of this got out it could kill *Krasnyy Voskhod*. And he knew—word would get out.

Even though the door was still open to the outer office where his assistant worked, he picked up the phone and dialed him. "GET SIMMONS IN HERE, NOW!" he shouted into the receiver. Slamming down the phone, he turned to the cabinet behind him and removed his soldering pencil and plugged it in. Simmons would pay.

****

"It appears, Jacob, that you were right about Chernikov trying to eliminate you. The guy who tried to pop you this morning is a known GRU assassin. While the Sovs typically use IDC to do this kind of work, I think somebody over there felt they had to bump the job up several pay grades."

"How is this going to work with the police and everything, Mr. Jensen? I killed a man this morning."

"It was in self-defense."

"Yes, sir, but that does not change the brute facts. I killed a man. Do I need to turn myself into the police?"

"No." Jensen got out of his chair and walked to his office window. Jake sensed a heaviness, a world-weariness in his friend. "That's part of the downside of working for the CIA, Jake. We don't always do things according to domestic law. It's a part of the job I hate, but I believe it is a necessary evil. We are not above the law. We try to protect the nation and stay within the spirit of the law at the same time. But there are times we do not keep the letter of the law.

"No, we aren't going to tell the police about this. Hopefully they will never find out about it. Nor will we tell the Soviets. They already know they'll be out of contact with their man for the next week or so. It will be some time before they start wondering what happened to him. The Jeep will be repaired and sanitized, and early next week it will be dropped off in Denver at the rental agency in the middle of the night. The keys—with his fingerprints on them—will be put in the drop box."

Jensen turned and faced Kelly. "And you, Jake, are going to disappear."

"Disappear?"

Jensen nodded. "Gone. We will put out a story that Major Jacob Kelly is nowhere to be found. The Sovs will assume that the hit was successful. They will know the Jeep has been returned. They'll probably figure their man went underground for a while to allow things to cool off."

Kelly didn't respond for a moment. The CIA agent allowed the pregnant silence to hang in the air undisturbed. Finally Jake asked quietly, "And what about Galina?"

"She can't know the truth. In order to sell this, we will have to deceive her, too."

"NO WAY, Bill!" It was the first time Jensen could remember that Jacob had called him by his first name. "I will *not* do that to her! And I won't let you or anyone else do it to her."

Jensen didn't answer, but turned back to the window. Over his shoulder he advised, "Think it through, son. Stop thinking with your heart and use your head instead. You tell me why this is a good move, a smart move."

Jake got up and moved around the room, working off the energy of his anger. He tried to analyze the situation dispassionately. In a few minutes he stopped pacing and stood by his father's best friend, looking out the window with him. It was raining, and a cold, foggy mist had settled over the landscape. "It would put an end to the assassination attempts, if they thought I was dead."

"Exactly. Does Galina want a live husband or a dead memory? And how many more times do you think you'll dodge a bullet before your luck runs out, Jake? If you were a cat, you'd be working on life number thirteen right now."

"But—what if she does something foolish when she hears the news? What if she hurts herself, or worse?"

"I've already talked to Roger Bates. You know that the Bates have drawn close to Galina in the last month and have taken her under their wing, so to speak. They are going to move Galina into their home where they can keep an eye on her until all this is over. She'll get plenty of support and she won't have an opportunity to hurt herself. And Jake, from everything you've told me about her, that gal is made of pretty stern stuff. She'll grieve, to be sure, but she'll be okay."

"Will Mrs. Bates know the truth?"

"No. Roger will, but Susan won't. We can't risk that she'd spill the beans in a moment of sympathy."

"How do you do this, Bill? Is there no honor in this place? And you're supposed to be a Christian!"

Kelly's bitterness cut him like a knife. He walked back to his desk, sat down, and put his head in his hands. "I wrestle with that question constantly, Jake. Frankly, there are times when my faith and my actions are contradictory. It's not just that I don't have an answer for you—I don't have an answer for me, for my own conscience. The Agency is filled with its own corruption, Jacob. It's a fallen organization tasked with protecting a fallen nation in a world ruled by violence—what more can I say? There are no good solutions, and there won't be until the Lord returns. For my part, I try to do my job in such a way as to honor my God by honorably fulfilling my mission. Sometimes I fail. All I can do is fall upon God's grace."

Jake returned to his chair and sighed. "So what do I do now?"

"Since Major Jacob Kelly is going to drop off the face of the world temporarily, we are going to resurrect Major John Smith. How would you like an all-expenses-paid trip back to Siberia?"

Kelly brightened, "Really?" He'd been wanting a means of revenge and now it was being offered on a silver platter.

"Bridger has called for a recon team to be inserted as soon as possible. I want you on it. What do you say?"

"When do we leave?"

"Good boy. Go home. Call Galina on the phone and tell her how much you love her. Then pack everything you want to take with you and leave the suitcases in your bedroom. Our boys will pick them up before I file the missing persons report. Make sure things in your apartment look as if you were expecting to be back momentarily. Tomorrow morning I want the neighbors to see you leave for your morning run. You won't return."

****

"John, about your recon team: you get your squad and their gear to Misawa Air Base in Japan by next Wednesday and I'll get them to the waters off Magadan. Figure that they will need to travel up to fifteen miles on the water after deploying. They will have the use of a cargo winch to launch a small submersible or water craft, if desired. But it's going to cost you."

"Cost me? How much?"

"I want to name the commander of your recon team. He'll report to you, of course. I just want to pick him."

"Bill, you probably can't even tell me the names of my platoon commanders. You don't know anything about my guys. You've only met Marcus, and he's not going on the recce team. What gives you the idea that you know enough about my people to pick one to lead the team?"

"Of course, you're right. But it's not going to be one of your people. I want Major Kelly to lead the team."

"Kelly? Why?"

"I've got a whole lot of reasons, and all of them are good. Kelly is a trained CCT operator and recon is their bread and butter. He's led four deployments downrange, all successful, three of which involved firefights. He speaks Russian like a native. He's just come from fifteen months behind the lines, so to speak, so he knows the culture and the terrain. He's an expert regarding the prison facility itself and their schedules. And most importantly, as an officer he's got the brains to let your NCOs run the show.

"Plus, Admiral, the Sovs are still trying to assassinate him. He survived an attempt just this morning."

"Was he injured?"

"No, but the Soviet Embassy here is going to need to find themselves a new assistant cultural attaché."

Bridger chuckled, "Caught in the act, huh? He's being deported for bad behavior?"

"No, he's found a new home in a pine box, six feet down. Jake doesn't mess around. Look, Admiral, all of this is on the QT. We are not going to tell Ivan what happened to their bad boy; he's just disappeared as far as they know. But Jake's going to disappear, too. I want everyone to think the hit was successful—even his girlfriend. So Kelly is living for the next month or two under a false identity, one that General Franks created for him when he signed on to the *Hydra* project several years back: he's now Major John Smith, and that's the name we'll use in all future communications.

"So, Admiral: are you going to play ball? Do I get Smith as the CO of your recce team?"

"It's a deal, Jensen. I can't promise that Major Smith won't have to endure a little hazing by the teams. He'll have to prove himself. But I agree: given his recent history, he'll be a great asset to have on site."

Chapter 24

"Gentlemen, this is Major John Smith, USAF. He thinks he's going to be tagging along with us on *Thunderbird*. You men have earned a spot on the operation. He has not. The spooks at the Agency threw him at us, but as far as I'm concerned he's got to earn his spot—if he can. Today begins three days of get-acquainted time, where we see what our Air Force major is capable of. So we're going to start this morning by taking our sweet little eight-mile run in the sand. Let's go." Marcus Clausen led his sixty-plus frogmen off at a trot.

Major Kelly, aka Major Smith, aka Falcon, sprinted to the front of the pack until he reached Clausen. Running along side of him, he asked the SEAL, "So, what's on tap for today, Commander?"

Clausen responded gruffly, "Well, Major Smith, I intend to do my dead-level best over the next three days to make you regret you volunteered for this operation. If we don't manage to kill you, we're going to try to wash you out. If we don't succeed, I reckon we'll resume training for *Thunderbird*."

Falcon replied wryly, "Ah, southern California hospitality. Nothing like it in the world."

"Right. There's a bell in front of the admin building. Anytime you want the pain to stop, Major, you just go ring that bell. Then you can fly back to DC or where ever you came from, and let us do our job. As far as the details of today, if you survive this run you'll find out when everyone else does."

Kelly didn't respond. He thought to himself, *Either this guy hasn't a clue what CCT training is like, or he's just a hard-case trying to get under my skin. Good luck with that, swabbie! Ah, well, if I am to be tortured there's not a more beautiful setting for it.*

Falcon ran, reveling in his surroundings. Other than the labored breathing of the men around him, the soft crunch of the sand, and the steady crash of the surf there were no sounds. It was too early for the eastern horizon to betray the approach of sunrise. A stiff off-shore breeze carried the tangy aroma of the ocean. A light drizzle was falling, and the low clouds reflected the lights of San Diego, providing faint illumination. Off to his right, the sea was obscured in blackness, its presence made known only by the dimly visible white foam of breakers crashing onto the sand.

There was a little straggle to the bunch seventy minutes later as they jogged down the street to the firing range. Special operators had to learn accuracy under the worst of conditions, when their chests were heaving and they were exhausted from physical exertion. Earning a marksman's badge was not of much use if the only time you could shoot straight was in perfect, controlled conditions. Clausen noted with approval that Falcon's scores were in the top third of all his frogmen.

After two brutal hours of calisthenics, the group practiced combat shooting techniques. Shooting at a target while loping across uneven terrain, burdened down with eighty pounds of gear, was not an easy skill to master but the SEALs had re duced it to a science. Once again, Major John Smith demonstrated that he was equal to the task.

They spent the rest of the day practicing close quarters battle (CQB) in the Kill House. Though he did passably well, it was evident that Falcon needed to be brought up to speed with SEAL tactics, for his own safety as well as that of men he would be deploying with.

For two more days Kelly felt as if he was in the early days of CCT training and that if he screwed up once he'd be washed out. He never pulled rank even though his worst tormentors were the NCOs. He knew he was being tested so he swallowed his pride and adopted a simple mindset: suit up, show up, and shut up. He passed every challenge they threw at him and even asked for extra hours in the Kill House. Though he'd received CQB training, it was not something that Air Force CCT operators had honed to the same sharpness as the

SEALs. Over the three-day period, what started as malicious hazing slowly changed into the salty insults and harassment borne of grudging respect.

The turn-around began at the end of the second day when Lieutenant Jerry Auld cornered Commander Clausen privately at the end of an exhausting day.

"Marcus, I don't trust that guy. I think we need to wash him out." Leader of the Third Platoon, Auld was a muscular six foot four, a skilled and deadly warrior. There wasn't much that bothered him, but Clausen could see he was provoked.

"Who, Jerry? John Smith?" Clausen asked.

"Yeah, him."

"Why? He's been taking all the punishment we can give him, his times and conditioning are great, his shooting is outstanding. What's your beef?"

"Have you seen his shoulders, Marcus? The left one has a heart with the name Lenin under it. The right one has the same thing, except it says Stalin. Somehow I don't think those are the names of his girlfriends. I asked him about it and he just laughed and said, 'What's the matter, sailor? You got a problem with my politics?'

"He's a nutcase, Marcus. Some guys get tattoos, Smith had it *burned* into his shoulders. And, yeah, I've got a big problem with his politics, especially since we're headed for Uncle Joe's backyard. The other guys don't like it, either. You know I'm not given to complaining or bucking your authority, Marcus, but he's gotta go."

"You haven't heard his story, have you?" replied Clausen. When Jerry shrugged, Marcus said, "Sit down, Jerry. Major John Smith is not his real name but you don't need to know what it is. Falcon is his code name and that's what we'll call him. Anyway, July a year ago Falcon was flying an F-16 over the Bering Sea—yes, he is a pilot, don't ask how he came to be trained for spec ops. Anyway, he was shot down by a Soviet fighter. They captured him and took him to a detention camp in Sibera, a camp that was the prototype for *Rabbit Hutch*, which we will be attacking in just a few weeks. Falcon was tortured for some secret info that Ivan wanted, and part of the torture was having what you describe as his politics burned onto his shoulders with a soldering pencil. Not only did he not break, he actually escaped from the camp. For fifteen months the Red Army chased him across thousands of miles of Siberia, never caught him. He made it back to Alaska in a kayak. I understand he left quite a body count behind him."

"Wow! Had no idea. And a pilot, too, eh? So, I'm guessing he really doesn't have a place in his heart for Uncle Vladimir and Uncle Joe?"

"No. And *he's* not going to tell the story, either. That's just not who he is. So Jerry, you need to tell the story for him, privately. Spread the word. Make sure the guys know. I'm giving Falcon a hard time, but it's just because I'm such a mean and nasty hard-nosed son of gun. He's going to be a real asset to our team."

"Will do, Marcus. Thanks for telling me—it makes a lot of little things add up."

"Now, Lieutenant Auld, I want you and everyone else who has been gossiping about our pet airdale to do one hundred push-ups before our sand run in the morning. It's your job to get 'em up early, gather them, tell them the story, and lead them in their push-ups. Better be ready to run at 0500."

"Aye-aye, Commander."

At the end of Falcon's third day at Coronado it was Jerry who assigned him his equipment cage and helped him gear up. The next day the whole group resumed practice at the mock-up.

****

Galina took off her shoes and stretched out on her bed. It had been a long day of job-hunting, but she already had some decent leads. Two private secondary schools had expressed great interest in having her teach algebra. One had already scheduled her for next Monday to teach a demonstration class on solving quadratic equations.

The next thing she knew her Chinese host was shaking her shoulder and saying that she had a visitor. Galina looked at the clock and was surprised to see that she'd slept for an hour. She put on her shoes, ran a brush through her hair, and walked out into the living room. Susan Bates was sitting in one of the armchairs.

"Hello, Susan! What a pleasant surprise." Then she noticed Susan's eyes were red-rimmed, as though she'd been weeping. "Susan, what's wrong? What has happened? Can I help you?"

"You'd better sit down, Galya. I've got some bad news." She waited until the girl was seated, and then continued, "Roger called me an hour ago. Jacob is missing."

"Missing? What do you mean?" Galina's heart began to pound.

"Four days ago Jacob failed to report for work at CIA headquarters in Langley, Virginia. After waiting several hours to see if he'd show up, Bill Jensen sent some men to Jake's apartment. It looks like he went out for his morning run, and ne—" she choked on her words as a tear trickled down her cheek, "and never returned. He's not been heard from since."

Galina felt her own eyes filling with tears as she asked, "But why? What could have happened? This is America," she protested in a small voice.

"Oh, dear Galina," Susan said, as she moved to sit next to Galina on the couch, "bad things happen in America, too. It wasn't that the police or some government agency picked up Jake. The CIA has already looked into that. No one knows what happened to him, or where he is."

Galina clenched her jaw, determined not to fall apart. Her shoulders shook once as she suppressed a sob. But it was no use. Her chin quivered, her eyes filled up, and she began to cry. She felt as though the joy of life had been stolen from her. To have found Jacob in Siberia and fallen in love with him, then to have to turn him loose as he completed his es-cape was painful enough. But to find him in America, reviving her hopes and dreams, only to lose him again—it was just too much. She finally lost all control and began to sob uncontrol-lably. Susan gathered the girl in her arms and cried with her. There was nothing else to be done.

Finally the young woman pulled away from Susan. Her

eyes were red and puffy, and she dabbed them with a tissue. Her tear-streaked face was turned to the floor and she was sniffling, twisting a tissue in her hands. Susan gave her another few minutes with her thoughts and then said gently, "Galina, Roger and I have talked about this. We'd like you to move into our home for the next several months. I'd like to help you work your way through this. And we have an extra car you'd be welcome to use once you get your driver's license, while you are settling in to life here in America. Would you be willing to move in with us?"

"Yes, thank you." And she burst into tears again.

****

Lieutenant General Valeriy Ivanovich Patrikeyev studied the decoded cable that had just arrived from the Soviet Embassy in Washington, DC. He took another sip of his tea, uncertain whether to celebrate or worry.

Pyotr Orlov had been dispatched from his normal lair in Sevastopol, through Moscow where he picked up fake identity papers, to Washington. He had one mission: kill Major Kelly. Orlov was one of the GRU's top assassins. He was fearless, smart, and meticulous in caring for the little details of a hit. An incredibly skilled operator culled from the best of the *Spetsnaz*, he'd been trained to a fine edge. Normally used to sanction traitors and to deal with the rising threat of Muslim jihadis in Central Asia, Orlov was tasked to eliminate Kelly. And now he'd not been heard from in five days.

Patrikeyev quelled the rising anger in his gut. Kelly had become a nemesis, a one-man wrecking ball for the GRU's best operations. *Nyet, Valeriy, don't give him more credit than he's due. Kelly's just had a string of good luck while we've had a run of bad luck. It's nothing more than that.*

He read the cable again. Orlov was not the only one missing. So was Kelly. A missing person report had been filed in Vienna, Virginia. The men assigned to watch his apartment reported that he left the house in a jogging suit, ran down the street, and never came back. Later in the day the place had been crawling with police and FBI agents.

So, Pyotr, did you rack up another kill and you're just waiting for things to calm down before reporting in? Or did the chase take you both off the grid? Or did you manage to kill him, but he killed you, too? Or worse, Pyotr, did you defect?

Patrikeyev tapped his finger absentmindedly on the cable as he considered the possibilities. *Pyotr is too good for me to assume something bad. I'll give him a couple more days before I raise the alarm.*

Chapter 25

The Panamanian-flagged *Krystal Gail* was a small, general-purpose freighter, gross tonnage just under three thousand. Built in 1976, for the past seven years she had been plying a lucrative trade route between various Japanese, South Korean, Chinese, and Russian ports. Ownership of the *Gail* was nearly impossible to determine. The company it was listed under, East Orient Shipping, was itself owned by multiple layers of offshore holding companies that seemed to change regularly. But in fact, the *Krystal Gail* was owned and operated by the CIA. It was an illegal profit center buried in the part of the Agency's budget no one ever saw. Profits from the shipping concern funded various black operations, all well within American interests but of dubious legality. It was easier than asking Congress for the money.

The ship's master, chief officer, second officer, and chief steward knew the score, but the remainder of the crew had no idea. In order to secure a tight-lipped and loyal crew EOS paid very, very well, much better than other merchant marine operations. But it also operated as close to the fuzzy borders of maritime legality as possible, and sometimes a bit beyond the borders. No one wanted to mess with a good thing so everyone on the *Gail* learned to keep their mouths shut. It was an effective tactic to get the crew to keep secrets without raising suspicions by telling them to do so.

When four tough-looking men boarded with several pallets of gear and a large Zodiac in Otaru in the evening gloom, nobody asked any questions. The men all spoke Russian and were dressed like common seamen. Their freight was stored in the forward hold on top of cargo bound for Magadan. None of the four had produced a manifest, at least not that the crew had seen. Most of the *Gail's* crew assumed the men were connected with some sort of Russian smuggling operation. If the Otaru harbor master wasn't concerned about it, well, neither were they. They would be paid well, and they figured he had been paid well, too, so they simply looked the other way.

****

Anatoly Geredin found it difficult to stay warm. The old spy master had taken to wearing his great coat, even when sitting at his desk. Not even his hot tea, laced with a liberal dose of vodka, warmed him anymore. He sighed to himself, *It must be age catching up to me. It's a pity that I am at the peak of power and influence just when my body is yielding to the ravages of age. There is no justice in that. . . . Actually,* the old man mused, considering his life, *perhaps that is justice. Maybe justice has finally caught me. . . . Nyet, we won't go there. For years, Anatoly, you have fought the knowledge of God and denied the existence of Him to whom you will eventually answer, that One who dispenses final justice. Don't go soft-headed now as the end approaches. What is it the British say? Keep a stiff upper lip? If my atheism does not deal with nagging, ultimate questions, it does render me one great advantage: I answer to no one—I am my own authority, my own judge, a law unto myself. It is . . . useful.*

He slurped his steaming hot tea and considered his duty to the *Rodina*, to Mother Russia. General Patrikeyev and his lackey Chernikov had thoroughly bungled the operation to retrieve the American major. Their latest assassination attempt appeared to have failed, at least it seemed so, if his sources were to be trusted. Their entire scientist-kidnapping scheme threatened to publicly dishonor his beloved Russia. If word of what they had done leaked out, it would be a public-relations debacle. The useful idiots of the United Nations would offer gaseous condemnations, full of pious fury, but they would ultimately do nothing more than preen and posture before the cameras and pass meaningless resolutions that no one intended to enforce. No real damage there.

No, the damage would not come from the UN. It would

come from the Third World—all those client states that the USSR was cultivating in the Middle East, Africa, and South America. The fools would have no stomach to treat with a nation, even one as powerful as the Soviet Union, that committed such reckless, dangerous acts against America and their pitiful NATO partners. *Paper tigers all. Oh, for the iron fist of Stalin. Where have the real men gone?*

Chernikov must be executed. Maybe his patron, too. Geredin decided to let the program have a few more weeks to squeeze the last few drops of information out of the captives, and then he would have the prisoners eliminated at the same time that General Chernikov was killed. The GRU units assigned to the facility would simply be reassigned. *No sense in killing them. They're good men. With proper leadership, they will again be useful to Mother Russia.*

He picked up the phone and began to call in favors, assembling the team that would stanch the flow of blood Chernikov had caused. He smiled to himself. *A little more bloodshed should stop the flow quite neatly. Isn't that the way it always works?*

****

"Snipers, report," Clausen whispered, his throat mic catching his words clearly.

"Sierra one, green."

"Sierra two, green."

"Sierra three, red, repeat red. No shot."

The other three snipers reported in, all green. Clausen waited for sniper position three to report back.

SEAL sniper three waited patiently for his target to reappear. The man had bent down to do something and was obscured by the guard tower wall. Suddenly the man straightened up. The sniper triggered his infrared laser designator and immediately saw a small green dot through his scope. He centered the dot on the middle of the man's head and whispered into his mic, "Sierra three, green, green, green."

Marcus responded with a string of terse commands, "Snipers, engage. Demolition, engage."

Muffled reports from six suppressed M21s coalesced into a single sound an instant before an explosion from several hundred yards behind Clausen's position put an end to the stillness of the night. The compound's lights went dark immediately. The rattle of six M60 machine guns commenced, laying down suppressing fire on the three troop barracks and the other administrative buildings of *Rabbit Hutch*. The snipers, now firing independently, sought and shot the second soldier occupying each of the six guard towers and then began seeking targets of opportunity.

Under heavy covering fire two breaching teams raced to the chain-link fence—one at the front gate, the other behind the physical plant building, and attached explosives with timers. They raced back to the woods, and hit the dirt just as the charges went off.

Clausen spoke into his mic, "Hold your fire! Hold your fire! Abort! Abort!" He waited as the sounds died down and then said into his mic again, "Okay, people, we are down to forty seconds. That is much better, but not nearly good enough. Everyone meet at the compound gate for debrief. Judges, you come in, too, and give us a casualty count."

Five minutes later the assault team, judges, and defenders assembled at the main gate. Wisps of smoke from the explosive charges hung low in the chill nighttime air. There was a quiet muttering of men comparing notes and stories, as Marcus climbed into the bed of a pickup truck brought up for the purpose.

"Good job, people. I think this one went better. What's the score, Barry?" he asked, addressing the head judge. The judges were composed of a mix of officers from other SEAL teams and Army Ranger units. Colonel Barry Jeffords of the Rangers was the head judge. The Rangers had been brought in to play the part of defenders in the mock-up facility. They were all wearing hastily assembled GRU uniforms and carried Russian-issue weapons.

"It was a lot better, Marcus, than the last two run-throughs. You're way ahead of where you were two days ago. This time only two of the guard towers got into action at all, and neither of them was firing for more than five or six seconds. There was return fire from the Admin building, however, and you actually lost four guys from your breaching squads who were setting charges at the main gate, all from Squad One. The three barracks buildings were fully suppressed, but we only ran forty seconds of the scenario." Colonel Jeffords glanced over at a tough-looking character and asked, "How much longer before your guys would have been on-line, Marv?"

The officer, a young lieutenant, responded with a scowl, "About another ten seconds, sir. I think these squids are shutting it down just so they don't have to take a little return fire."

The comment started a grumble of assent among the other Rangers, who were miffed at not being able to bring their own weapons to bear, especially since they had overwhelming numerical superiority over the SEALs.

Marcus grinned and said, "Save it for the shooting, men. You'll get your chance. I know you boys are good. Once we figure out how to breach this thing we'll let it play out a little longer, and you guys can strut your stuff."

Mollified, the officer grinned back, "Yes, sir. And we'll be ready for you, believe me. Rangers own the night."

Jeffords continued, "One other thing all of your guys missed, Marcus, as far as I could tell. You were getting pistol fire from both RH2 and RH6, the physical plant building. It appeared that your team was completely unaware of this." Colonel Jeffords frowned.

"What about it, guys? Any of you notice action from those two buildings?" No one spoke up. Commander Clausen admonished, "Listen, people, we've got to be better than that. I know this is just practice and we're all firing blanks, but maybe you or your buddy gets picked off during the real thing. Be aware, people!"

"Commander?" The query was coming from Commander Tom Rainer, the resident planner for *Thunderbird.*

"Yeah, Tom, whatcha got?"

"I don't like the way we're breaching the fence. We're using C4, trying to bring it down, but that just creates a new problem—one that's not apparent since in our practice runs we aren't really blowing it up and it isn't actually falling down. We don't *want* to bring the fence down, Marcus."

"No? Why not?"

"Because it's topped with that concertina wire. We bring that fence down, the razor wire comes down with it. We still have the inner fence to eliminate, and we've just created a new obstacle for ourselves with that wire before we can even get to the inner fence."

Clausen nodded, "Yeah, Tom, you're right." Marcus turned to the group, "Listen to him, people! This is why we are training." He turned back to Rainer and asked, "Are you thinking what I'm thinking? TH3?"

"Uh-huh. Let's use thermate cord on the fence and just cut a hole in it, not blow it down. That way the wire stays on top and doesn't get in our way. It also solves another problem—timing. With C4, the men have to run nearly thirty yards from cover to the fence, plant the explosives, and then run back to cover so they are not injured by the blast. Then they have to run thirty yards back and climb through the debris, before they can get to the inner fence and repeat the process.

"But using TH3 they can just drop back five or ten yards and hit the dirt. We'll cut out some forty yards of running around and shave at least ten seconds off the time. And we get the same savings, better really, with the inner fence."

"Good call, Tom, let's do it. Jerry," he said, addressing Lieutenant Jerry Auld, "send several men down to the supply shacks and bring up enough thermate to run through this another five or six times."

"Okay, switching gears, how were the fire lanes? Did any of the breaching teams stray into the M60 fire lanes?"

"Yeah," Chief Petty Officer Tim Secrist responded, "Breaching Team Two ran all over our lane. We had to cease fire twice. That might be why someone from the physical plant was able to return fire. Sir, I have studied the sat photos thoroughly, and I know that we can move to our left another ten yards and still be in good cover. If Breaching Team Two started from ten yards further to their right, I think we'd be

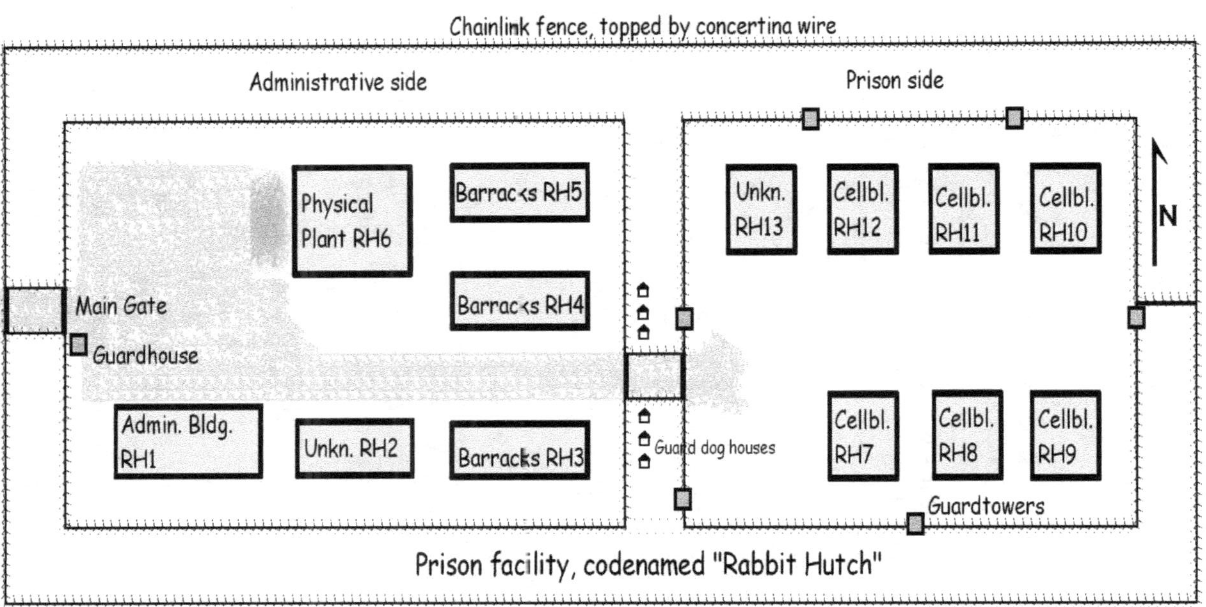

Chainlink fence, topped by concertina wire
Administrative side
Prison side
N
Physical Plant RH6
Barracks RH5
Barracks RH4
Unkn. RH13
Cellbl. RH12
Cellbl. RH11
Cellbl. RH10
Main Gate
Guardhouse
Admin. Bldg. RH1
Unkn. RH2
Barracks RH3
Guard dog houses
Cellbl. RH7
Cellbl. RH8
Cellbl. RH9
Guardtowers
Prison facility, codenamed "Rabbit Hutch"

okay."

"Okay, Chief, make it so. You got that, Breaching Two? Okay, we're good. Anybody else got something to say? No? Alright, it is 0130. We are going to make these adjustments, and restart the scenario at 0215. In the meantime, clean your weapons. Lieutenant Davis, I want to see you for a minute."

Although Pascoe commanded the Second Platoon, he was away on emergency leave for a week. Marcus had temporarily given Davis command of the platoon in order to give him more experience. In Pascoe's absence, Davis had set up the assault vector, fire lanes, and positions for the platoon.

As the men filtered away Lieutenant Davis moved up. "Yes, sir?"

Clausen did not respond until the men were out of earshot. When he turned to Davis, he was angry. "Those are *your* men, Kerry! The machine gun squad and Breaching Team Two! What the devil are you doing, putting your machine gunners where the breaching team is going to run through their fire lane? What if we'd been doing a live-fire exercise? Worse, what if we were in Magadan right now? What were you thinking, mister?"

Davis turned red. "Sorry, sir. It won't happen again."

"You mess up again, I'm replacing you. You better sit your butt down with the photographs and the scale model and go back through all your assignments, placements, fire lanes, everything! Don't you *ever* screw up like that again. You risked the lives of your men needlessly and you've damaged their confidence in your leadership. You can bet Secrist knew *exactly* what you had done, three days ago. He's been giving you the opportunity to discover it yourself, but you didn't. He *had* to speak up."

Davis nodded, but said nothing.

Clausen relented. "Listen, Kerry. One of these days I will tell you about my first screw-up as a SEAL platoon commander. But you need to understand something. When one of your men is killed on a mission, you never forget it. And if he is killed because you screwed up, it is almost impossible to live with that knowledge. It haunts you all your days. I know. So don't screw up!"

****

Clausen walked back to the canteen trailer. It was parked near the office trailers used by the faux film crew that had been supplied by Anthony Petroli as part of the ruse to keep the practice facility secret. The symbiotic relationship was working to everyone's profit. Petroli's director was filming the SEAL training exercise for stock battle sequence shots in Petroli's movie. With a little scene-rewriting, and film- and sound-editing, the practice assaults would fit well in the film.

"Hey, Buzzy, how's it going?" Marcus asked, as he poured a cup of coffee and sank gratefully into one of the chairs in the canteen trailer. Buzzy Reardon was the head armorer for Universal Studios. He stayed on the site whenever the SEALs were there to learn more about weaponry from watching real warriors in action.

"Hi, Commander. It's going great, just great! I can't tell you how excited I am to watch what you people do."

"Want some real excitement, Buzzy? Come with us when it's for real. That'll get your blood moving! The bad guys fire real bullets."

"I expect it gets pretty scary at times."

"Darn right it does. Being scared is one of the best ways to stay alive, as long as you don't let fear take over." Marcus looked around, seeming to see the inside of the trailer for the first time. "You got some pretty nice digs here, Buzzy. Does it take you movie guys a long time to get set up on site?"

"Not at all, Commander. We just haul these trailers wherever we are shooting and we are ready to roll. Instant office! They've each been customized exactly like we need 'em, so it works out really well."

"What about when you shoot a film overseas. What do you do then?"

"Same thing, sir. These office trailers are actually containerized cargo shipping containers. We just took a welding torch and some carpentry and made 'em like we want 'em on the inside. But they are designed to be transported. The containers come off these wheels and can be loaded on-ship in a matter of minutes. When we get to the destination port, we put 'em back on wheels and drive 'em to wherever we need 'em. The transportation infrastructure in just about every country in the world is designed to handle containerized cargo by road, rail, ship, and even air. Makes it easy as pie. All of our stuff is designed to go in either twenty- or forty-foot containers. The only thing we can't ship in 'em are the actors," Buzzy chuckled.

Marcus finished his coffee and walked back to the staging area where the next scenario would begin with a silent, stealthy infiltration of the SEALs around the *Rabbit Hutch* mock-up. He was thinking his way through the alterations to their assault, but in another corner of his mind an elusive idea was trying to take shape. Something Buzzy said was important to Operation *Thunderbird*, but he just couldn't grab hold of it.

****

Commander Marcus Clausen sat bolt upright in bed, sweating. The dream had been coming to him for five days straight, as the tensions caused by the unsolved problems of Operation *Thunderbird* mounted. The dream was always the same: despite the dangers they had decided to try for a submarine insertion using one of the boomers whose missiles had been removed and the spaces converted to bunks. Always, in his dream, the submarine was detected just after the SEALs had deployed from it in rubber boats. They would be quietly motoring to shore and a huge underwater explosion would erupt several miles behind them, out to sea. He knew that the sub had been found, tracked, and killed by one of the many *Kilos* that patrolled the Sea of Okhotsk. He always woke up just after the explosion, nauseous.

Like most Special Operations commandos, when he was training for a mission Clausen's days and nights were swapped. Despite the tightly drawn blinds keeping out the daylight, he knew the horror of the dream would keep him awake. It was futile to go back to bed with the destruction of the submarine lingering in his mind.

He padded silently to the kitchen and brewed a pot of coffee, his thoughts wandering aimlessly. As the pot percolated, the aroma of coffee filling the kitchen, Marcus' conversation with Buzzy percolated to the surface of his awareness. *Hmm, those movie people are really creative. Who would think to use shipping containers as mobile offices? What a great idea.*

The coffee pot sent up a few final gasps of steam, and he started to pour himself a cup. The thought hit him with the force of a sledge hammer: *Magadan has a container-handling facility. We can do insertion and extraction from three or four specially modified forty-foot containers! THAT'S IT! It's perfect!*

"OUCH!" he shouted as hot coffee, overflowing from the cup he was still mindlessly filling, puddled on the floor and found its way to his bare feet. Startled, he dropped the pot and it shattered on the counter, the rest of the coffee flooding from countertop to floor along with bits of broken glass.

"YOWWW!" he bawled.

"*What* are you doing?" his wife asked, running into the kitchen from the baby's room where she had been changing a diaper. "Are you okay?" she asked dubiously, surveying the disaster her husband stood in the middle of, grinning stupidly. If he made a single move in any direction he would cut his bare feet on the glass.

"Ouch!" he repeated, chuckling in spite of himself. "Oh, babe," Marcus replied happily without a hint of sarcasm, "I'm *fine*. I'm doing *just great*."

Chapter 26

Two nights previously Benjamin Klausowitz had been instructed by his Mossad controller to locate a business north of Magadan, preferably in a remote location, utilizing containerized cargo. This sort of thing was where Ben really excelled as a spy. He was an expert at mining the bars for information. He didn't talk much—patrons probably would not remember anything he said—but he had a way of provoking conversation and keeping it rolling with a comment here, a joke there. He'd learned that by making an erroneous statement—purposefully—there were plenty of gregarious souls who would straighten him out. "Oh, I heard that the 9th Guards Motorized Division is bivouacking in town—I hope there's enough vodka for all of us!" "*Nyet, nyet*, it's not the 9th, it's the 4th." "Ah, my mistake." Listening rather than talking enabled him to ferret out most of the gossip going around town, and the gossip often led to good intelligence.

The regulars at the local watering hole had accepted his presence upon learning that he was visiting on holiday from Moscow. He'd been a regular at the bar most nights since the beginning of November, listening to the talk and occasionally adding a friendly comment. Tonight, however, he had an agenda. The conversation was already focused on the economy when he arrived at the tavern. Ben nudged it towards shipping.

"It's too bad no one is using Magadan's container facility. Why, in Moscow, you see many containers on the road. It's a good, cheap means of shipping," Ben said, knowing that someone would correct him.

"What do you mean? We have many businesses in Magadan using containers!" replied a man who Ben guessed was a longshoreman.

"*Da*, perhaps in town here, but not north. It would be a great opportunity for Sokol, or even farther north, to cut their shipping expenses," Ben observed.

"But you are wrong, comrade. Cooperatives throughout the region use our container facility. Why, there's a sawmill just west of Sokol that ships lumber frequently through our port, and the mines along the Kolyma are always shipping and receiving with containers."

"You don't say? Is the port open throughout the winter, then?"

"May through December, *da*. But after the first week or two of January, the shipping stops until late April or early May. The ice is just too thick."

By the time he left the bar late in the evening, Ben had five solid leads on cooperatives north of Magadan that shipped their goods in containers.

****

Benjamin Klausowitz was traveling without Katerina today, wanting to project a formidable image of personal political power and strength. It was a look not quite achieved if you appeared to be a tourist on vacation with your family.

The sawmill he was visiting was four kilometers beyond Splavnaya, just off the main road—if one could call it that, for all the roads were rough gravel or macadam affairs and mostly snow-covered this time of the year. The longshoreman Ben had befriended the night before had filled his ear with gossip about this particular mill and the curmudgeon who operated it. The fellow had a reputation as a disagreeable drunk.

A small sign where a heavily rutted gravel trail met the main road indicated Ben had reached his destination. The mill itself could not be seen from the road. He drove up the washboarded road and pulled into the sawmill lot, clambered out of the old Wartburg, and looked about. The mill was surrounded by a thick forest of fir trees with a smattering of larch, plus piles of sawdust and neat stacks of logs.

The sawmill was the fourth of five leads he'd gotten at the bar. The other locations he had explored were not suitable for one reason or another, but this one was perfect. As an added bonus, it was only a little over three kilometers from *Rabbit Hutch*, separated by a river and a forest-clad, granite-capped ridge to the south, three hundred meters higher than his present elevation.

As he walked about the deserted mill yard, snow crunching beneath his feet, he discovered two forty-foot containers partially loaded with rough-cut lumber.

"*CHEGO TEBYE!* What do you think you're doing here? Who are you?"

The gruff, angry voice sounded from behind and to his left. Ben turned. A mountain of a man, features as rough hewn as the timber in the yard, was approaching angrily with a club in his fist.

Though Ben was frightened he did not show it. He put his hands on his hips and assumed the air of the important and powerful Party figure that he once was. The expression on his face conveyed haughty disdain. He ignored the man and his threatening approach, and made as if he was inspecting the yard and its condition.

The effect was immediate. The man stopped and lowered his club uncertainly, and then quietly stood by until Ben deigned to speak to him. It pained Ben to know that the government was so feared by its citizens that they could not defend even their homes or businesses in the face of government intrusion. Nonetheless, that fear was useful to him now.

"*Dobryy dyen'*, comrade. You are the night watchman of this, this—facility?" Benjamin's tone was intentionally insulting.

"Why, no, good comrade. I am the owner of this mill."

"There is no private ownership in the Soviet Union, comrade. You know that, and so do I."

"Ah, yes, but of course, good comrade. I have made, er, arrangements that permit me to, ah, act as the owner of this mill."

"*Blat?*"

"*Da*, good comrade."

"You are a criminal," Ben said harshly.

"Oh, no, comrade, no indeed!"

"Can you explain these containers? Do you have licenses for export?"

"But of course. The local Party, they have provided my import/export licenses. I am held in favor within this district by all the Party officials. It is a profitable relationship, comrade," said the man, shrewdly examining Ben, "*mutually* profitable, yes?"

Ben softened his harsh tone, "Ah. I see. Perhaps we, too, may do business, comrade?"

"Certainly, comrade. Let us go in from the cold and talk."

Ben followed the now docile man into the shed that served as his office. A potbellied stove fed from a large pile of scrap lumber kept the chill from the room. He motioned Ben to a chair after wiping a thin layer of sawdust off of it. As the fellow was about to speak Ben seized the initiative, interrupting him.

"Your name, comrade?"

The slightest hint of fear crept back into the man's eyes. "Golinskiy, Edvard Stepanovich, comrade."

Ben smiled and replied, "Mendel, Igor Zorinovich. Golinskiy, with whom do you trade in your export business?"

Golinskiy relaxed and replied, "Japan. Port of Sapporo—Takayoshi Industries. They take as much lumber as I can ship to them."

"What do they ship to you?"

"Empty containers."

Ben saw his eyes flicker and move off to the side as he answered. *He's lying. He's getting duty-free shipments. I'll bet the rascal has more money than I do, or will someday.*

"And what sort of—arrangements—do you have with the local *apparatchiki?*"

The man smiled slyly, "Sometimes the containers do not come back completely empty, comrade."

Uh-huh. Just what I thought. I expect the containers never come back empty. Aloud, Ben said with a condescending smile, "I think you and I can do business after all, Golinskiy."

At that, Golinskiy appeared to rediscover his courage. "Perhaps you can tell me what you want, Igor Zorinovich, and I will tell you whether we can do business. After all, I know nothing at all about you. Why should I trust you?"

Ben pulled a fat roll of American dollars out of his briefcase and placed it on the desk. "Perhaps, comrade, I can buy your trust?"

Golinskiy's eyes narrowed, and he asked suspiciously, "Who are you, Igor Zorinovich? What is your business here?"

"Does the name Mikhael Alekseyevich Promyslov mean anything to you?"

"Of course. He was the mayor of Moscow up until last year."

"*Da*, and he is now retired. Comrade Promyslov is weary of Moscow. He desires to build for himself a place of rest in the Kolyma region. He is drawn by the beauty of this place. Mikhael Alekseyevich has had a plan drawn up by an architect from Cincinnati, Ohio—in the USA, of all places. I have been commissioned by him to see to the construction of his *dacha*.

"I have a source of western-style building materials in Japan. I will be receiving them in cargo containers and I need a site for unloading them. This mill yard would be perfect. Comrade Promyslov would like to, shall we say, bypass the normal channels in the purchase of his materials."

"*Blat?*" queried Edvard with an innocent expression.

"Exactly."

Golinskiy grinned, "Then I guess we can do business, Igor Zorinovich. What are you expecting of me?"

"You will order four 'empty' forty-foot shipping containers from Eastern Exports in Japan, to be shipped from Otaru. There is a container vessel, the *Lady of Singapore*, arriving in Magadan from Otaru on Sunday morning, 20 December. Have your drivers at the port at noon to move the containers here as soon as they are unloaded from the ship. The containers are not to be inspected by any port authority, nor are their shipping seals to be broken. They are to be brought to this mill, and left in the yard. Leave the truck cabs connected to the trailers, with the keys in the ignition.

"The ship will remain in port for about thirty-eight hours. You are to have your drivers pick up the unloaded containers here at precisely 9:00 AM on Monday the 21st, and return them to the port. They will be sealed once again, and the seals are not to be tampered with nor are the containers to be inspected at the port. They are to be immediately reloaded on the *Lady* before she sails."

"What about the billing?"

"Trust me, my friend, no bills will come to you. They will go straight to Promyslov. Eastern Exports is simply waiting on a destination to which they may ship the containers."

Golinskiy shrugged, "I can do this. No problem. And what will you give me if I do?"

"A great deal of money. I will pay you very well, but you must listen closely, my friend. Do not let the thought of cheating me enter your mind. Do not let the thought of failure enter your mind. You had better pray that your truck drivers are sober and on time going in both directions. You'd better pray that the seals on the containers are not tampered with, incoming or outgoing, and that the containers are not inspected in either direction. If your trucks break down you'd better have a backup plan. Promyslov does not accept failure. If you fail, I promise you that you will be strapped to one of those logs in your yard, and run through the mill feet first and very, very slowly. Do you understand me?"

Golinski's face was white and sweat beaded on his forehead. He licked his lips and managed to croak, "*Da*. I understand, comrade. I will not fail."

"Good. If you want to contact Promyslov you talk to me —only me. His good name must never be associated with this business. If you tell anyone who you are doing business with, your life will have a very violent, very unpleasant end. Do you understand?"

Golinskiy nodded, eyes wide.

"Still interested?"

Golinskiy nodded again.

Ben grinned and slapped the man on the back in a show of conviviality. "Good! I knew we could do business when I first saw you, Golinskiy. Now, here are the arrangements. If you agree to do business with Comrade Promyslov, when you say *Da*, you will get ten thousand American dollars. Any expenses you incur convincing the harbor master to let the containers through without inspection are your own affair and must be taken out of what we pay you.

"If your truckers are at the port and ready to go at noon on 20 December, and if they bring the containers here without inspection and with the seals unbroken, you get another ten thousand American dollars. If your truckers pick up the containers here at 9:00 AM on the 21st and take them directly to the port, and they are loaded without inspection on the *Lady of Singapore*, that's worth another fifteen thousand.

"There is one additional requirement. You must shut down the mill by noon on 20 December, and you are not to reopen it until 25 December. I don't want to see even one person—not even you—on this site after the containers are brought here on the 20th. That will be worth another ten thousand wonderful American dollars.

"The whole deal is worth forty-five thousand American dollars to you. Now, Golinskiy, what do you say?"

Golinskiy's eyes gleamed at the thought of all that beautiful money. He looked Ben squarely in the eye and nodded vigorously, "I say *Da*, Comrade Igor Zorinovich! Now, where is my ten thousand?"

****

The *Krystal Gail* dropped the recon squad—one CCT member and three SEALs—eleven miles from the Magadan Harbor. The Zodiac was heavily loaded, but Falcon wasn't worried. The water was almost bathtub-calm, a fact that made the deep cold even more penetrating. The outboard had special silencers fitted to its exhaust, and made little more noise than a barely perceptible mutter, though on these calm waters even that sound would travel far.

The four passengers had fooled the deck crew of the *Gail*. The entire time aboard ship they had spoken only Russian, pretended not to understand English, and even their conversation in Russian had been designed to be overheard, in case any of the crew spoke the language. Their cover as Russian smugglers was secure.

As the island of Zarechnyy came up on his port bow, Chief Petty Officer Arlen Moses changed course from due north to northeast. Two miles later they were retrieving their gear from the boat, just before hiding the Zodiac under a camouflage tarp in thick brush about two hundred yards from shore. There was little risk anyone would stumble upon it by chance; the beach looked uninhabited for miles in both directions, displaying no hint of human activity.

Each man worked quickly, silently, and efficiently. When they spoke at all, it was in whispered Russian. Now on enemy soil, their lives and mission hung upon remaining undetected. When they were ready to begin their eighteen-mile trek, Falcon radioed the code word, *Baby Ruth*, with a satellite burst transmission.

There wasn't much snow on the coast, which was unusual for this time of year. The men had cross-country skis strapped to their eighty-five-pound rucksacks. Further inland —closer to *Rabbit Hutch*—the skis would become necessary. The march to their target would take two days, as they were heavily loaded with supplies and could only travel at night. Besides that, the terrain was very rough, but no worse than what Falcon had experienced during his escape trek in the summer.

The SEALs chosen for the recon squad, designated Alpha Squad in the *Thunderbird* Order of Battle, were the best of the best under Marcus Clausen's command. They had participated in multiple covert operations and had been battle-tested in firefights.

Major John Smith, USAF, was the designated commander of Alpha Squad. Smith—Jacob Kelly's secret identity, manufactured for Project *Hydra*—had seen action all around the world in unnamed places, and was completely unflappable. But he was Air Force, and he knew that the real experts in this operation were the three SEALs under his command. As a consequence he relied heavily on the experience and leadership of Chief Petty Officer Arlen Moses. Short, wiry, and tough as an old boot, Moses had been a SEAL for fifteen of his forty years. His size was deceptive; dwarfed by some of the young giants in the SEALs, Moses was nonetheless one of the most lethal men in hand-to-hand combat on SEAL Team Three.

Petty Officer Andy Litchfield was thirty-three, a veteran of eight years on the teams. He was Moses' best friend, and the two were constantly together. Six four and tipping the scales at two hundred forty, Litchfield was a bull in search of a china shop. He and Moses had been thrown in the various hoosegows surrounding Coronado so many times—for busting up bars—that they were on a friendly first-name basis with most of the desk sergeants.

Petty Officer Wayne "Annie" Williams rounded out the squad. A SEAL for ten years, Williams tended to be reserved. He was the top sniper under Clausen's command. Part way through sniper training, he'd been saddled with the nickname Annie Oakley. It stuck, and Annie became his official code name.

The squad shouldered their rucksacks and began ghosting through the night, flitting soundlessly from one dark shadow to another. After an hour they came to a gravel road cutting across their direction of travel. Communicating with hand signals, the men sank into the brush, becoming invisible in the gloom. After five minutes of listening to a silent night and examining the deserted landscape before them with NVGs, they crept across the road and disappeared into the dark woods on the other side. Their passage was undetected save by a sharp-eyed owl who swept above them on soundless wings, prowling for an unwary rodent.

****

Thousands of miles away in Coronado, California the simple expression *Baby Ruth* coming clearly over the sat link caused a great deal of relief. It was the code word Kelly had picked for a successful insertion. Admiral Bridger and Commanders Clausen and Rainer were on hand in the secured communications center, awaiting word. They had been hanging out for two hours in anticipation of the planned landing time on the coast west of Magadan.

"They're in, Marcus!" Bridger exulted, smiling at his second.

"Yes, sir," Clausen replied, without expression.

"You don't seem to want to celebrate," observed the admiral. He knew what Clausen's response would be, for he, too, had sat in that chair many times himself.

"I'll save my celebrating for when Alpha Squad gets out, sir."

Chapter 27

"Snipers, engage!" Marcus Clausen whispered into his throat mic. He counted to ten slowly, then whispered, "Demolition, engage!" A hollow boom sounded behind him, and the compound lights went out, plunging the scene before him into darkness. He pulled on his NVGs as he whispered into his mic, "Goggle, goggle! Commence Objective Alpha. Go, go, go!"

The early morning stillness was interrupted by a rapidly growing cascade of semi-automatic and automatic weapons fire. The guard towers were all knocked out immediately. All eight machine gun teams—two had been added as the practice assaults had been analyzed—commenced hosing down the barracks, administration building, and physical plant.

The defenders were caught completely off guard by the additional M60s. Contrary to the rules of the scenario, the defending Rangers had placed two ready fire teams in both the physical plant and the administration building. The Rangers, however, had no idea that tonight's assault would be carried out with added firepower. All illegal Ranger teams were quickly annihilated.

A four-man fire team raced forward to the main gate in a carefully defined lane, M4s clattering as they engaged the defenders. When they drew near to the fence each man chucked a Model 308-1 smoke grenade over the fence into the compound. The breachers were close on their heels, and rapidly snapped the thermate cord to the fence, using snaps fabricated specially for *Thunderbird* at China Lake.

"Fire in the hole, fire in the hole! Degoggle, degoggle!" shouted the lead breacher. It was a warning—the attackers had three seconds to shut their eyes or remove their NVGs before the thermate was detonated, briefly illuminating the scene with near sunlight brightness. The breachers and their fire team dove for cover, while the M60s kept up a withering covering fire.

The night was lit up by bright muzzle flashes, and the clattering reports of the defenders' AK-47s produced a staccato cacophony. It seemed that every window of the admin compound buildings was spitting fire and sound. But with the defenders' view obscured by billowing clouds of smoke the return fire was increasingly ineffective.

Springing up from the ground, the forward fire team led the breachers through the hole in the outer fence and raced to the inner fence. The remainder of the assault team, including operators armed with M72 LAWs, broke cover and sprinted from the woods, passing through the outer breach and diving for cover between the fences as they waited for the inner fence to be breached. The crews manning the M60s kept up a relentless suppressing fire wherever they saw the muzzle flashes of defenders.

A SEAL scanning enemy radio frequencies picked up activity on the spectrum used by Soviet military communications. He immediately hit the red button on the front of the jammer man-pack, and then calmly spoke into his throat mic, "Engaging the Buzzer. Comjam initiated." He started a stopwatch, knowing that the goal of the exercise was to eliminate the radio tower within twenty-five seconds.

Clausen also started a stopwatch, and then resumed observation of the assault from his hidden command post. "Come on, guys!" he muttered under his breath.

The breachers hit the dirt again and Clausen heard the brevity code barked over the comm link, "Degoggle, degoggle!" Three seconds later thermate was slicing through the inner fence. Before the destroyed sections finished falling to the ground, the LAW operators were up on one knee taking careful aim at their assigned targets through the gaps in the fence. The movements of the men during this phase of the assault had been very carefully choreographed so that no one was in the danger zone of the back-blast from the rocket-powered charges. Since this was a training exercise the warheads had been removed, leaving only a paint-splotch where they hit.

Suddenly, Clausen saw three of his six LAW operators drop, followed in quick succession by four more members of the assault team. The assault, which had been working like a well-oiled machine, began to falter. Then other shooters from the assault team rushed forward and took up the M72s dropped by their fallen buddies, found their targets and pulled the trigger. Lieutenant Commander Bausch's voice came through his earbud, "Objective Alpha One complete!" Seconds later, Lieutenant Pascoe, whose Second Platoon had been breaching behind the physical plant building, reported "Objective Alpha Two complete!"

Clausen spoke into his mic tersely, "Cease jamming, cease jamming. Shift to Objective Bravo, Objective Bravo!"

Their objective obtained, each breacher unslung the M4 from his shoulder and added his firepower to the assault, as did the remaining M72 operators. The squads moved further into the compound, engaging the defenders at close range. One by one the outlying machine guns fell silent as their fire lanes were occupied by the assaulting forces. As rehearsed, some of the machine gunners grabbed their M60s and raced to new, preplanned positions to resume support of the assault as it penetrated deeper within the compound.

However, the pause of suppressing fire had an immediate effect. Seven more SEALs fell. But several operators had gotten close enough to start chucking grenades through the building windows, and the advantage turned decisively back to the attacking force as the defenders were overwhelmed.

One by one the compound's administrative buildings were secured, until finally the southern California early morning was silent once more. The butcher-bill weighed in at a much greater cost than Marcus wanted to pay, but for the first time in all their practices all objectives were accomplished. He was confident that further refinement would reduce their losses significantly.

****

Petty Officer Andy Litchfield slowly stretched, and with nearly imperceptible movements, tensed and then relaxed various muscle groups in his legs and arms. The SEAL arctic gear and camouflage kept him alive and hidden, but not necessarily comfortable.

A small guard hut that had somehow been missed in the satellite photography sat below him, about sixty meters away. The hut commanded the only approach road into *Rabbit Hutch*, and was itself about one kilometer from the compound. Well situated, it could not be seen from the compound but it had an excellent view of the approach road. Any visitors to the facility would be spotted and identified and a welcome prepared well before they arrived at the main compound gate.

He looked behind him at the snow cave he and the chief had dug out, back in the larch forest about ten meters behind his concealed observation point. CPO Amos had another hour to sleep before his turn to watch came up. The SEAL grinned at the inert form buried in his mummy bag. He was a good friend. *'Amos and Andy'*, he thought, *I like it.* The two had been inseparable since they had found themselves on the same SEAL team. Both single, they enjoyed the same sports and hobbies and shared a dry, cynical sense of humor. They were more like brothers than friends.

Chief Petty Officer Arlen Moses was his buddy's real name. Smitty—Major Smith—had christened the chief with the nickname *A-Moss* on the flight from Coronado to Japan. It quickly contracted to just *Amos*, and the handle stuck. Now the pair were labeled Amos and Andy.

Alpha Squad had arrived at *Rabbit Hutch* on Monday evening. They spent the next two days performing a clandestine survey of all the road and trail approaches to the facility, as well as the routing of the electric and telephone wires. It was during this survey that they had discovered the guard post. Next, using infrared reflective dots they marked three different routes that could be traveled under cover from several hundred meters past the guard shack to the planned assault positions surrounding *Rabbit Hutch*, and they disabled the boo-by traps along the routes. Then Falcon divided them into two teams, one that surveilled the camp and the other the guard post. Both teams cataloged the patterns in the shift changes for the guard post, guard towers, and cellblocks, as well as procedures and movements about the compound.

The teams were each equipped with a sensitive tripod-mounted parabolic microphone that could pick up conversations from hundreds of meters away. Simply listening to the chatter of the men at their posts yielded valuable intelligence about the running of the camp, the locations of targets, and the calendar of events for December. After five days the two teams traded places on the theory that a new set of eyes on the target might spot something overlooked by the other.

One of the most valuable pieces of intelligence they discovered was that the camp had a big Ural 375-D truck that made at least one trip per week into Magadan. The schedule was not precise, although the vehicle generally left for town each Sunday morning and returned the same evening filled with supplies. No password was used at the outlying guard post; the truck was just waved through without any interaction between driver and guard. The guard then called the watch officer in the compound to let them know the truck was approaching. From what Amos and Andy had been able to discern there were no passwords used in that telephone call either. The watch officer notified the main gate and the Ural just drove straight in.

The sound of a telephone ringing in his earbuds startled Litchfield. He made a minor adjustment to the parabolic microphone and continued to listen. He was able to hear only one side of the conversation.

"Guard post, Sergei speaking . . . Tomorrow? . . . Do we know what time? . . . *Da*, got it. We are to expect a lignite delivery for the boiler tomorrow afternoon. I'll write it in the log. *Spasibo*."

****

Admiral Bridger watched the platoon commanders file into his office. Over the past week he sensed growing confidence as they solved one by one the difficult problems of the insertion and extraction and the assault itself. But he also knew that they were training hard—too hard—burning the candle on both ends. Assaulting by night, refining the plans by day, no one was getting enough sleep. He glanced at his desk calendar. *There's enough time. If they keep working like this they are going to make mistakes, and we can't afford any mistakes.*

Once they had gotten coffee and arranged themselves around the conference table Bridger started the briefing. "Gentlemen, good afternoon. I like what I've been hearing about the operation. The major commanding the Ranger unit was in to see me this morning. He was furious. He was so steamed I wondered if the paint would peel from the walls. Evidently you men are doing a real good job," Bridger chuckled. "Marcus, why don't you fill me in?" Bridger tipped his chair back and took a swig of coffee.

Commander Clausen grinned, unable to contain himself. "Admiral, early this morning we achieved both objectives Alpha and Bravo within the required time constraints. First time we've done it. And that was despite the fact that the Rangers cheated, using four additional, fully armed and ready fire teams—two in the physical plant, two in the admin building."

Bridger laughed out loud. "*They* cheated? The major was accusing *you* of cheating. Said that you increased the number of machine gun teams and began using smoke grenades without warning him."

"Sir!" Lieutenant Davis interjected, agitated. "The scenario rules allow us to make any changes we want without telling the defenders. We won fair and square! But they cheated! Not only did they deploy the extra fire teams, but they also had the weapons lockers unlocked and opened in advance, so the Rangers could arm up immediately!"

"At ease, son! Anytime Army plays Navy you get this sort of thing. If there is one thing both services agree on, it's this: *it's not cheating unless you get caught.*"

"But we didn't cheat, Admiral!" insisted Davis. Kerry

Davis was the commanding officer of Fourth Platoon.

"Well, actually, Kerry, we kind of did," admitted Tom Rainer, Clausen's executive officer.

Everyone turned to Rainer, surprised expressions on their faces.

"Really?" asked Clausen.

"We did?" asked Ed Bausch, incredulous. "None of us knew that!"

"Yeah—we did. I've been monitoring the frequencies the Rangers are using to communicate," Rainer said.

"But that's not cheating. We are *supposed* to be monitoring their comm frequencies," objected Clausen.

"Right, skipper. And we *are* monitoring the frequencies the Soviets use, and the Rangers are indeed using the Soviet-made radios we supplied them with. But they also snuck in their own comm gear, which is another instance of cheating, technically. So I've been listening in on the Ranger frequencies for the last five assaults. That's how I found out about the extra teams. I warned Machine Gun Team Four about them just before the scenario started. Team Four just chewed 'em up."

"Well, I'll be jiggered. I had no idea," chuckled Clausen, "and you never told me!"

"You have enough on your plate, Marcus. Our time is getting short and we need a good run-through. I knew if those teams were not taken out it would screw up the assault and our planning by introducing an unrealistic element to the scenario. So I decided on my own that we would neutralize them so we could have a truer evaluation of where we really are in our training. The Russkies are not going to be expecting us. If they are, no amount of planning or training will help us."

Bridger listened silently, impressed, and decided that the next time that recommendations for promotion came up Tom Rainer's name was going to be on the list. He was ready to become a full commander.

"Tom, I'm glad you're on our side," Marcus laughed. "Admiral, last night we breached both fences in thirty-four seconds. The jammer was on for only twenty-two seconds before the radio tower was destroyed. The LAWs did the trick quite

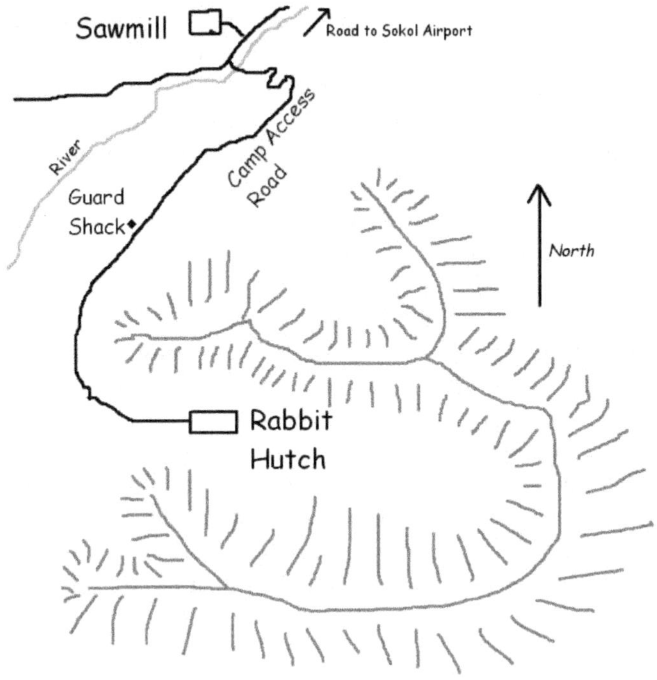

handily once the fence was down. Within seventeen minutes we had complete control of the administrative side of the compound. Unfortunately, it took another twenty minutes to secure the prisoners and the cellblocks. Guards in three of the cellblocks fought to the death, and we were limited in that part of the assault out of fear that we might harm the prisoners."

"Marcus, that's something else I heard on the Ranger frequencies," Rainer admitted. "The major radioed those cellblocks—after he was supposed to be dead—and told them not to surrender but to fight to the death."

"Actually, that's a good thing, Tom," asserted Admiral Bridger.

"How's that, Admiral?" asked Lieutenant Pascoe, leader of Second Platoon.

"Remember, you boys won't be facing military police

forces, but *Spetsnaz*. They probably *will* fight to the death in some of the buildings, if not all. Your shooters will have to use lethal force at all times with these people. They are going to be good—very good. Don't underestimate them."

Clausen nodded soberly. "That's what worries me, Admiral. Our force of sixty against one hundred or so regular army is not bad. But sixty of us against one hundred of their crack special forces, well, that's another matter."

A moment of silence followed, each officer wrestling with his own thoughts. Then Ed Bausch spoke up, "We still have surprise. We'll have the edge in equipment. We will have the advantage of a good plan, which forces them to respond to our initiative. Ivan is probably cycling units through *Rabbit Hutch*, considering it a safe place for rest and refit—meaning that their mindset won't be on combat. They will be facing an enemy who has both maneuverability and lethal fields of fire, while they are forced into fixed defensive positions—a death trap for them, an advantage for us. Once their electrical power is taken out, they won't be able to see us but we will see them."

Rainer nodded, "I agree, Ed. Those advantages are decisive. But let's add a margin of safety. What if we added two more snipers, two more M60s, and two more M72s? We could pull them from Third Platoon and put them in First, making them available for the frontal assault. The extra snipers could be weapons-free for targets of opportunity. The additional M60s would give us better suppressing fire. And the extra LAWs could be used to put down any defensive strong points that develop."

"Good idea, Tom," agreed Clausen. "Let's do it. I also noticed this morning during the assault that most of our casualties happened when the covering fire from the machine guns lapsed. I talked to the teams afterwards, and it turns out that they were coincidently replacing ammo belts at the same time. We could team the two extra machine gunners with two others, and make them work together so that when one has to change ammunition, the other cuts loose. No lapse in covering fire. Use the same loader for both guns." All the men nodded.

Marcus looked at Bridger, "Do you have any new intel for us, Admiral?"

"In fact I do. Smitty reports that *Rabbit Hutch* sends a big Ural 375-D down to Magadan every Sunday morning. It comes back on Sunday night. When the truck driver gets to the guard post he is simply waved through, no passwords, no checking what's in the truck, no interaction with the guards. The guard post then calls the camp duty officer, who contacts the main gate. The truck drives right through and parks in front of the admin building. Men from each of the barracks turn out to carry the food and supplies into the mess hall which, by the way, is what our unknown building RH2 is."

Bridger turned to Rainer and said, "Tom, I think that gives us a new option for getting in the compound. Plan A would be to hijack the truck before it gets to the guard post. You could load part of your assaulting team into it, and your boys could drive it right through the main gate. Your shooters could take out the generator and radio tower in the opening seconds of the assault. You can task those two extra snipers to take out the men on the gate before they have a chance to close it. Everybody else can come through the gate.

"We need to keep working on Plan B in case the truck doesn't go for supplies, or gets back before you are ready. But Marcus, now you'll want to plan and practice both options."

Bridger passed around a manila folder to each officer. "This contains a detailed report that we received today from Alpha Squad. It includes a survey of all roads and trails within five kilometers of *Rabbit Hutch*, routes from your insertion point to the target, and a host of miscellaneous intelligence they are picking up. Study it carefully. Something in this folder could make the difference between success and failure."

Bridger turned back to the *Thunderbird* CO, and asked, "Marcus, what are your final platoon assignments?"

"They haven't changed, sir, from when you and I talked about them a few weeks ago. First, Second, and Third Platoon will all provide snipers and machine gunners that will be under my control for Objective Alpha, the initial breaching. At that point command of those guys will return to their platoon leaders for the support of their platoons. Ed will take First Platoon, code-named *Long Shot*, and assault the main gate. Their assignment is to secure the admin building, take out the radio room, and then continue through the mess hall to barracks RH3.

"Second Platoon, code-named *Bad Man* is under Paul's command and will breach the fence on the north side, behind the physical plant. Their immediate objective is to clear the physical plant building and destroy the generator. Having done that they will then take down barracks RH5. First and Second Platoon will combine to clear barracks RH4.

"While all this chaos is breaking loose on the administrative side, Jerry's Third Platoon, code-named *Sneak Thief*, will be doing what we hope is a very quiet, very peaceful breach of the fence on the northeast side of the prison compound. They'll be using wire cutters out of the enemy's field of view. Our goal is for everyone's attention to be fixed on the firefight in the admin compound, and no one will even know the Third has infiltrated the prison side. Jerry's boys will then secure the prisoners, I hope with minimal resistance from the guards. Alpha Squad will be attached to the Third, making up for their loss of personnel.

"Kerry Davis commands the Fourth Platoon, code-named *Point Guard*. They provide perimeter security. They are watching the main road by the sawmill, the containers, and the *Rabbit Hutch* access road.

"The basic assault time-line looks like this, Admiral, assuming we have to use Plan B:

> H-HOUR + 0:00.00: SNIPERS TAKE OUT TOWER
>   AND GATE GUARDS.
>
> H-HOUR + 0:00.15: ALPHA SQUAD BLOWS
>   POWER/PHONE LINES. FIRST AND
>   SECOND PLATOON BREACHERS
>   AND FORWARD FIRE TEAMS
>   ADVANCE UNDER COVER OF
>   DARKNESS, PLACE SMOKE
>   GRENADES, BEGIN BREACHING.
>
> H-HOUR + 0:00.30: EMERGENCY GENERATOR

KICKS IN, LIGHTS RESTORED. MACHINE GUN TEAMS AND FORWARD FIRE TEAMS PROVIDE SUPPRESSING FIRE FOR BREACHERS.

H-HOUR + 0:01.00: OUTER FENCE BREACHED BY FIRST AND SECOND PLATOONS. BREACHERS AND FORWARD FIRE TEAMS ADVANCE TO INNER FENCE. REMAINDER OF FIRST AND SECOND PLATOON ASSAULT TEAMS ADVANCE INTO BREACH.

H-HOUR + 0:01:30: INNER FENCE BREACHED. FIRST PLATOON AND SECOND PLATOON ASSAULT ADMIN BUILDING AND PHYSICAL PLANT, RESPECTIVELY. SNIPERS SHOOT LIGHTS OUT.

H-HOUR + 0:02:00: FIRST PLATOON DESTROYS RADIO ROOM. CEASE JAMMING. SNIPERS AND MACHINE GUNNERS SHIFT TO TARGETS OF OPPORTUNITY.

H-HOUR + 0:03:00: SECOND PLATOON DESTROYS GENERATOR. ALL TEAMS GOGGLE. THIRD PLATOON BEGINS SILENT BREACH OF PRISONER COMPOUND.

H-HOUR + 0:06:00: ADMIN AND PHYSICAL PLANT BUILDINGS SECURED. PRISONER COMPOUND BREACHED, THIRD PLATOON BEGINS SECURING HOSTAGES. HQ TRANSFERS TO ADMIN BUILDING.

H-HOUR + 0:10:00: ADMIN COMPOUND SECURED.

H-HOUR + 0:12:00: RABBIT HUTCH SECURED, HOSTAGES SECURED. MAIN

> OBJECTIVES COMPLETE. GATHER
> ALL AVAILABLE INTELLIGENCE
> INFO. LOCK SURVIVING
> DEFENDERS INTO CELLBLOCK.
> H-HOUR + 0:30:00: DESTROY THE REMAINING
> BUILDINGS OF RABBIT HUTCH,
> RETURN TO THE CONTAINERS TO
> AWAIT EXTRACTION.

"If everything goes according to plan, sir, the shooting will be over in about twelve minutes."

"Good. Shifting gears, what's the status of the shipping containers?"

"Well, Admiral, I checked them over just before getting here. Each container has been outfitted with two concealed, internally operated hatches to allow unassisted egress. One is on the bottom, the other is on the opposite end of the container from the cargo doors. Several peep holes have been fabricated on each side, providing the ability to observe a full three hundred sixty degrees. Air scrubbers have been installed to eliminate carbon dioxide from the container atmosphere. We debated heating the containers, but have decided against it. Each bunk will be equipped with an arctic-rated sleeping bag, and we'll have a supply of chemical heat sticks in each container. We are palletizing our gear in boxes marked as building supplies, and the gear pallets will be stacked and lashed on the cargo door side of the container, behind one row of actual building supplies. If someone happens to inspect the container we should be okay, as long as he's not too thorough.

"They still have to build the bunks and install a toilet and small septic tank in each container. Our weapons and equipment inventory needs to be finalized, collected, and palletized. Then it can be lashed into place. I'd say they'll be ready in a week."

"Good," Bridger affirmed. "There is one more piece of the puzzle I am putting into place. The USS *Carl Vinson* will be involved in exercises off the Kuril Islands in a few weeks. I'm petitioning the head of Naval Operations to have the carrier group stick around until the first of the year. I am also asking that they carry four Super Stallion CH53Es, just in case we need to speed extraction along. The Soviets could stop and board the *Lady of Singapore* anywhere in the Sea of Okhotsk. If we see that situation developing, I want the option of reeling you guys in with the choppers, pronto."

"Sir, I request that we change that to eight Super Stallions. If we were to develop problems with just two aircraft, that means we'd have to leave someone behind."

"One is none, two is one," murmured Bridger, considering the request.

"Right. Those choppers are crucial to the success of the extraction if Ivan figures out what we're up to. Please, sir, don't put me in the position of having to choose who goes and who gets left behind."

Bridger nodded, "You're right. Eight choppers it is. Now, back to the containers. See that they are outfitted so that we can pick 'em up from the air if need be. And I want you to prepare a complete second set of containers, painted, marked, numbered just like the first set, duplicates right down to the rust marks, bar codes, everything. Don't customize their interiors. I want just standard, empty containers. Clean 'em out, and then have them taken to a lumber mill and loaded to the gills —and unloaded—about three times with green, rough-cut lumber. Don't clean them a second time. The more bark and litter left in them the better. Understand?"

"Yes, sir. Will do."

"Okay, good. One last thing, gentlemen. I want you and your men to stand down for the next forty-eight hours. Get some rest, all of you. Spend time with your family. That's an order. Dismissed."

Chapter 28

Saturday, December 12, 1987: 0630 hours, local time
Somewhere in the western Pacific

"Message for you, sir, from CINCPACFLT."

Captain Arthur Young, CO of CVN 70, the *Carl Vinson*, took the decrypted dispatch and read it carefully. He looked at his executive officer and shook his head. "Well, well, well. Steve, we've been assigned to play chicken with the Russians around the Kuril Islands, through Christmas—another fleet presence exercise. Seems I recall that the last time we did this, the *Vinson* was bait to draw in Ivan's *Kilos* while our 688s played *catch me if you can* around all the approaches to Okhotsk.

"But this time there's a bit of a twist. Some genius behind a desk seems to think we need a flight of eight Super Stallions and four forty-foot cargo containers. Hmm. Think I smell a black operation coming on."

He stared at the dispatch for another moment and decided that the Carrier Air Group (CAG) commander needed to be notified. The complement of aircraft the *Vinson* carried would have to be shuffled around, and Young was loath to lose any of his Anti-Submarine Warfare (ASW) assets this close to the Soviet coast. "Steve, tell CAG that we need to make room for the Stallions and the containers below. If we have to ferry a few Tomcats over to Misawa to make room, so be it. I'd rather give up a few fighters rather than my ASW capability. If CAG agrees, see that he has everything he needs to make it happen. And by the way, this is top secret. Make sure he keeps it under his hat."

****

Bridger was alone in his office, staring at his map table, when his intercom buzzed. He walked to his desk and picked up the phone, "What is it, Mabel?"

"Sir, Commander Clausen has arrived."

"Very good. Send him in." A moment later his office door opened and Clausen walked in, shutting the door behind him.

"Take a seat, Marcus. How's your preparation going?"

Clausen sat down at the corner of the map table and rubbed his face with both hands before responding. "Sir, it's going so well it's scary. Frankly, I'd rather have our problems on this side of the puddle than on the other. Training is complete. The men all know their assignments, and they all know each other's as well. They've had two days to rest. The gear is being gathered by our logistics people and will be delivered to the hangar you designated tomorrow night. My team will start rechecking it Monday morning. We will be ready on time, sir. Easy."

Bridger nodded. He'd been keeping an eye on Clausen for the last year or two. The man was a born leader and a very intelligent warrior—bold and innovative but not reckless. The admiral knew that he'd picked the right man to lead this mission and each time he met with Clausen that conviction strengthened. He decided it was time to let Clausen in on a slight change of plans. Now that the Japanese Air Self-Defense Force (JASDF) had decided to play ball it was going to make it a little easier to get the containers to the docks at Otaru, with the added benefit of confusing anyone trying to spy on the operation.

"Marcus, you have done well—very well. I have complete confidence in you."

"Thank you, sir."

"There has been a change in plans, but no one is to know about this but the two of us. No one. Not even Tom."

"Sir?"

"Bill Jensen worked a little magic with the JASDF. They are going to let us land the containers and the Skytrain at Chitose Air Base. There is sufficient hangar capacity there to let each of the Herks off-load the containers under roof. I have taken the liberty of adjusting the flight plans so that the Hercules, as well as the C-9, will be able to land and leave again without any Soviet spy satellites overhead."

"You mean we are not going to Misawa?"

"No. Everybody thinks you are and we are going to let them think that for security's sake, just in case the Russians have caught wind of something and have extra eyes on Misawa. When the C-130s load up on Tuesday, you will give each pilot an envelope they are not to open until after their *final* refueling. It will contain last minute flight plan changes that will redirect the last leg from Misawa Air Base to Chitose. You will have a similar envelope for the pilot of your C-9."

"What about ATC? Won't they start asking questions?"

"It will be handled real-time."

Clausen nodded, and Bridger continued, "No one except you and I and Bill Jensen knows that this is going to happen. The folks at Misawa will be expecting the inbound aircraft. When the planes don't show up and Misawa inquires, they will be told the flights were canceled. At that point—if we are fortunate—you and your team will have dropped off everyone's radar, so to speak. By the time the Soviets pick up the scent again it will be too late."

"What have we told the Japanese?"

"Only that we are shipping some new parts for one of our radar installations and that it was easier to land on Hokkaido than to take a ferry from the Japanese mainland. Your team is being passed off as civilian contractors and test engineers. Your men will have to fly over in civilian clothes and change into uniform at the warehouse in Otaru."

"Does this impact any other parts of our schedule?"

"No. None of it. You'll be waiting several extra hours in the warehouse at Otaru. That's the only change."

"Sounds good to me, sir. Do you have the envelopes for me?"

"You'll have them on Tuesday morning."

"How about the four empties?" Clausen asked.

"They are already at Misawa. I'll see that they get out to the *Vinson*."

****

Captain Moshe Shimonah lay on his bed, groaning. His face was bloody and battered. He was certain that at least four ribs were broken. His left kneecap had been shattered a month earlier, and only minimal medical attention provided. Two years ago he'd been a runner, a trim one hundred eighty pounds, topping out at six feet even. Now he weighed all of one hundred twenty pounds, and could hardly walk. He carried enough injuries to keep multiple teams of medical specialists busy for months.

Shimonah was an officer in the IDF. He had served as the liaison between the prime minister of Israel and the nuclear weapons development effort going on near Dimona, southeast of Beersheba. He'd been chosen for the job for two reasons: he had an undergrad degree in nuclear physics, and Israeli military intelligence believed that no foreign intelligence service would suspect a lowly captain of carrying military secrets of such strategic import to the nation.

But the GRU had stumbled upon the true nature of Shimonah's work through a mole in the prime minister's office. On July 5, 1986, when Moshe and his American wife Erin were vacationing in Bermuda, Shimonah had been abducted and brought to Chernikov. For the last eighteen months he'd been interrogated and tortured. General Chernikov knew that Shimonah had Israel's most sensitive military secrets locked up in his head: the capability, number, and disposition of the country's nuclear weapons. But the IDF had chosen its man well. Shimonah had not broken under torture, which was the only reason he was still alive. General Chernikov still hoped to squeeze something useful out of the battered, broken scarecrow of a man.

The torture Chernikov inflicted on Shimonah had long since lost any hint of subtlety or sophistication. Now it was just endless brutality. They would beat him to within an inch of his life, and drag his trembling body back to his cell. Sometimes they would wait for the worst of his wounds to heal before doing it again, sometimes they wouldn't.

Shimonah lay on his bloody, dirty mattress and groaned. On nights when he was physically capable of it he would stand in front of his cell door and send silent Morse Code signals to Oswald Simmons, a prisoner in the cell across the hall, with hand gestures. It was a technique Simmons and Jacob Kelly had used to communicate when Kelly was imprisoned. But tonight Shimonah could not move. His body was a mass of outraged nerve endings.

Ah, well, he thought philosophically, *my injuries are throbbing because my heart is still beating. My heart is still beating because I am still alive. And as long as I am alive, there is hope. Although, I think now that I will be a cripple the rest of my life.* He'd not seen his beautiful wife since he kissed her good-bye before going out for his morning run. She was pregnant—which meant he had a child by now, a child he'd never seen. *Might never see. I don't even know if it's a boy or girl.* A tear escaped from the corner of his eye, and mingled with the drying blood on his cheekbone.

Across the hall, Oswald Simmons—Oz to his friends— was praying for his fellow prisoners. Over the last eighteen months he'd memorized their names along with the names of their spouses and children. Every night he went through his mental list, praying for each prisoner and their families. He prayed for their captors, including Chernikov. Most of all he prayed for Jacob Kelly, that he would be able to lead some sort of rescue effort to free them from this nightmare.

It had been about seventeen months ago that Kelly and Simmons escaped together. Several days after the escape Simmons was brought down by a bullet and had encouraged Kelly to go on without him. Though his friend had been reluctant to abandon him, finally at Simmons' urging Kelly ran off into the night. Oz had been recaptured and returned to the prison camp. About four months ago he'd overheard Chernikov shouting in one of his rages, and learned that Kelly had finally escaped the country. The hope of eventual rescue was rekindled, and Simmons renewed his prayers with a new fervency. Sometimes he wondered if the Lord had in fact left him in this prison, prevented his escape, so that he might intercede for his fellows. He'd also obtained permission to carry Shimonah to the prisoners' mess for each meal time. It was a concession on Chernikov's part that Oz had not expected. *Perhaps God is answering my prayers that Shimonah survive this experience and one day be reunited with his wife.*

Chernikov relied less on brutality and more on persuasion when it came to interrogating his captured scientists and securing their cooperation. He hoped they would eventually accept their fate and resume their research in a Soviet laboratory. But that restraint had ended for Oswald Simmons.

Simmons' was America's leading researcher on miniaturizing electronics. This was the holy grail of weapons builders. The smaller the electronics the more intelligence could be packed into a warhead. It was an advance every bit as crucial as the transition from vacuum tubes to semiconductors had been. Whoever won the race for compact intelligent weapons with very low power requirements won it all.

Simmons had taken his Soviet counterparts down a path that showed good initial results but which ultimately failed. He bought time for himself, appearing to be cooperating—which ended the torture and interrogation—even while his researchers were effectively chasing their tails. The chief scientist at the Academy of Science in Moscow had finally caught on to what Oz was doing and ratted on him to Chernikov.

It was then that Oz discovered—to his dismay—that soldering pencils could be used for something other than electronics. Something extremely painful.

Chapter 29

Monday, December 14, 1987; 1300 hours, Washington, DC
Tuesday, December 15, 1987; 0300 hours, Otaru, Japan
Tuesday, December 15, 1987; 0500 hours, Magadan, USSR

"Welcome gentlemen. This is Bill Jensen, in the War Room at Langley. I'll be moderating our meeting today. I won't keep you any longer than necessary. With me is Sam Bergman, CIA analyst, Soviet Department, and Zvi Sharon, Mossad. Could everyone else please report in?" Jensen asked. It was a final conference call of the major players before Operation *Thunderbird* commenced the next day with the transport of the SEALs and their containers to Japan.

"Jesse Pierce at Adak, NAS."

"John Bridger here, at Coronado. I have Commanders Marcus Clausen and Tom Rainer with me."

"Arthur Young, of the USS *Carl Vinson*. I'm plugged in and ready to go."

"Hey, Art! Long time no see!" said Admiral Bridger warmly. "We must have gotten you out of bed for this one."

"Hi, John. We haven't seen each other in a while, have we? You know why that is, don't you? Real navy men are out here at sea—on ships—not sitting behind a desk. Anytime you want a kind word at CINCPACFLT, let me know. I might be able to get you into a rowboat or something. Oh, wait! You're an *admiral*—I forgot. For you maybe there will be a fleet of rowboats."

"Indeed. You are very kind, *Captain*." Bridger rejoined dryly, emphasizing Young's rank.

"Since we're all ready, I'll get right to the point," Jensen interjected. "Everything is set for Operation *Thunderbird*. Captain Young, I know this operation is not something you are familiar with. It has been held very close to the vest for reasons that shall become obvious. Briefly, *Thunderbird* is a covert SEAL operation to rescue nine hostages being held by the Soviet Union in a prison camp just north of Magadan. We are inserting the assault team and extracting everybody using specially modified cargo containers. Your flattop will be supporting the extraction phase of the mission in case an emergency arises and we need to pluck the containers from the cargo vessel while it is still in transit. You should be prepared for things to get hot in your neck of the woods."

"Define hot," Young requested.

"Captain, this is straight from the President: you are clear to use deadly force—whatever is required for a successful extraction—if we call upon you for assistance. You must be prepared to do so. You will be receiving PRIORITY traffic from the Chief of Naval Operations in several hours providing the specific authorization, including the presidential directive pertaining to this operation. That message will also contain detailed information about *Thunderbird*, including the mission timeline.

"I must emphasize that this is strictly need-to-know; you may inform CAG and your XO, but the rest of your crew should be told that your carrier group is on an ASW exercise. Not even CINCPACFLT is aware of the true nature of the mission. The CNO asked them to place your carrier group on an unplanned ASW exercise through 25 December. That's all they know. On the morning of 21 December, you may inform your crew of your actual mission.

"Now, gentlemen, it's time to move the chess pieces on the board to set up our final gambit. I'll go over the schedule and then tell each of you where I need you.

"The containers will arrive at Magadan on a container ship sometime after 1300 hours Zulu on the 19th, or midnight local Magadan time. The assault will take place sometime after 0700 Zulu on the 20th, 1800 hours local. The containers will be picked up at 2200 Zulu, or 0900 local the morning of the 21st, hopefully with everyone tucked safely inside. They will be loaded on the ship at 0100 Zulu, 1200 local—same day—and hopefully depart soon after. The ship will return to Otaru by 2300, Otaru time, on the night of the 24th, if all goes well."

"What ships are involved?" asked Captain Young.

"Ship," Jensen corrected, "it is the *Lady of Singapore*, and we are catching a ride both ways."

"How did you manage that? Container ships don't spend that much time in port."

"Correct, Captain. But the *Lady* is going to experience a failure of her steering hydraulics that will unfortunately detain it at Magadan. Those hydraulics will be repaired in time to pick up the containers the following day before leaving."

"How did you arrange that, Mr. Jensen?"

"Come, come, Captain, we must keep a few secrets!" Everyone chuckled. Jensen continued, "When the party begins on the 20th each of you men will need to be in a secured communications center for the duration of the mission. You'd better just go ahead and set up a cot in it, because when we need to talk to you, more likely than not it is going to be an emergency. Zvi will provide us with communication to Mossad assets in Magadan. Sam will be standing by to bring any available CIA assets to bear, and to report on NSA intercepts. Commander Pierce, I need you at Adak in close contact with Captain Young. We need to know if the Soviet command in the Far Eastern District so much as sneezes. I'd like plots of every ship and aircraft in and over the Sea of Okhotsk, the Sea of Japan, and the Tartar Strait. You men will need to blanket the area with as much airborne SIGINT hardware as you can—just don't make it obvious. Admiral Bridger, you'll be in the Combat Direction Center of the *Vinson* with Captain Young. Everyone should route all communications to that location—they will provide us with a real-time feed, so anything you send to the *Vinson* we'll receive at the Agency. I will be in the War Room here, with Sam and Zvi.

"Captain, I assume you have heard about the new helicopters you are acquiring?"

"Yes, sir, I have. Eight CH53Es are headed my way and

they are bringing four empty containers with them."

"That is correct. I want you to turn the choppers into flying gas tanks."

"Who are they refueling?"

"No one. We'll only need them if the wheels fall off during the extraction. In that case they are going to have to find the *Lady* in the Sea of Okhotsk, leave the four decoy containers, and return to the carrier with the real ones, each of which will weigh about ten tons. It will take every drop of fuel they can carry. Send all eight choppers; that way we can sustain a fifty-percent failure rate on the whirly birds but still pull off the extraction."

"So the Master of the *Lady* is in on this?" queried Captain Young.

"Actually, no. The poor man hasn't a clue. If all goes well, those Sea Stallions stay on the *Vinson* and the *Lady* unloads as scheduled at Otaru. With luck, he'll never find out that his ship was the key to extracting our SEAL team and hostages," answered Jensen.

"Hmm. And suppose our luck does *not* hold? What if he is *not* inclined to let us stop him on the high seas and fly off with four of his containers, what then?"

"When Admiral Bridger comes to see you, Captain, he's bringing some of his buddies. We figure that twelve armed SEALs will be sufficient to enable the good captain to see the light. And besides, we'll let him know that the Soviets are hot on our heels, and that he definitely does not want them to board the *Lady* while those four containers are anywhere on his ship. If this operation is detected before the *Lady* is back in Japanese waters, the Soviets will be in a very surly mood.

"Any more questions? No? Okay, this is the command structure for the op. I have overall command. When boots are on the ground in Magadan, Admiral Bridger has complete operational control. Commander Marcus Clausen is commanding the assaulting force and Tom Rainer is his XO. For the extraction phase Admiral Bridger has absolute authority over all assets attached to this operation, including, Captain, the air assets of your carrier group. Captain Young, you of course retain total authority over your ship at all times. The PRIORITY message from the CNO will clarify these arrangements for you, Captain."

"Thank you, sir. You shall have my complete cooperation, Mr. Jensen. I am quite comfortable with the command structure and I look forward to collaborating with Admiral Bridger again. *Someone*, for crying out loud, needs to keep the man out of trouble—I suppose it is my turn."

****

The *Lady of Singapore* had paid off its crew a month earlier, just before going into the Kawasaki Heavy Industries shipyard in Kobe, Japan. Normal maintenance on its hull had been scheduled, as well as an overhaul of its engines and steering gears. As was typical in merchant marine situations many of the seamen had gone home to their families for a stay of several months before returning to the sea. Several of the officers did as well.

Since it was due to resume container operations in the Pacific within the week, the *Lady's* company offices were busy filling out the crew complement. It raised no eyebrows when the new second engineer, wiper, and three able seamen all hailed from ships operated by the East Orient Shipping Company. Then again, no one knew they were all CIA field agents, either.

****

Galina sat on her bed in the Bates' spare bedroom and stared dully at the wall, a small pile of used tissues at her feet. Her eyes were rimmed with red. It had been a month since Jake had disappeared, and there was no word of his whereabouts. No body had been found. There was no trail left behind. The police report indicated that his apartment bore all the signs of a man who expected to go out for a run and return. Dr. Jensen had spoken to her several times and tried to offer her words of encouragement. But what could he say? What could anyone say? For the second time the love of her life had been taken from her—and this time she felt in her heart that he was not coming back.

Galina had been hired by a private high school to teach advanced mathematics, replacing a teacher who would be going on maternity leave over the Christmas break. Until then she was serving as the woman's aide. In January she would take the class for the remainder of the school year. She loved the students although she was disturbed by the lack of discipline in American classrooms and the general lack of respect the students showed their teachers.

There was a light tap at the door and she heard Susan Bates call out softly, "Galina, may I come in?"

"Yes, come in," she answered.

Susan sat down next to Galina and put her arm around her. They sat that way for several moments without speaking. Then Susan asked, "How are you doing, Galya? What can I do for you?"

"Oh, I'm doing better," the young woman answered. "I'm down to using up just one box of tissues every two or three days. That's better than it was," she offered with a small smile.

"I have been praying for you, Galina, asking the Lord to help you through this."

"Thank you, Susan," she replied, squeezing the older woman's hand. "You and Roger have been very kind."

"Galina, I've learned that when I don't understand why bad things happen, I can still trust that God is in control, and I know that He is good. He has promised that He will work all things together for my good. If you ever place your faith in Christ, that promise from Romans 8:28 will be yours as well."

"If only I could believe that were true! I know it would be a great comfort. But Susan, I just can't bring myself to believe in your God. Not yet. I have too many questions, and some of them I don't even know how to ask. One of my biggest problems with your God, though, is this: if he is so good, why does he let all this suffering go on? Why doesn't he put a stop to it?"

"That is one of the most difficult questions of all, Galina. The problem of evil and suffering has bothered philosophers and theologians of all religions from the very beginning. Even atheists aren't agreed on how to handle it. Some deny that evil as a reality exists. Some deny that meaning itself exists, saying that the brain is nothing more than the product of blind evolution and that thought and consciousness are nothing more than the random firing of nerve synapses. Other religions say that suffering is but an illusion. It's a daunting question."

"So Christianity doesn't have an answer either?"

"We do. We have an answer, but not one that resembles a formal logical proof. It's an answer that can be accepted only by faith—and since faith is the area in which you are struggling, I doubt you will find my answer very satisfactory."

"Susan, it seems to me you are always speaking of faith when you speak of Christianity. Can't you people prove anything?" As she heard her own words Galina realized how harsh she sounded. "I'm sorry, Susan. I didn't mean to offend you."

"No worries, you haven't offended. You've put your finger on the very center of what Christianity is from man's perspective: it is a response of faith to what God has done in history and to His *explanation* of what He has done, as found in the Bible. Faith is complete, unreserved, unqualified personal trust in Him.

"The Bible has two statements about faith you might find helpful. In Hebrews 11:1, the Bible says, 'Now faith is the assurance of things hoped for, the conviction of things not seen.' You're not going to be able to pull proofs out of that. In Hebrews 11:6, it says, 'And without faith it is impossible to please Him, for he who comes to God must believe that He is, and that He is a rewarder of those who seek Him.' Your observation is correct: Christianity is all about faith, because our God will not reveal Himself to anyone on any other basis. I guess that's something you should know about being a Christian—it's either an all-in or all-out affair. There are no partial Christians as far as the Bible is concerned."

"So, what *is* the Christian answer to evil and suffering?"

"The first part of the answer involves the natures of both man and God: We are finite, limited. God is God and we are not. He is all-wise and all-knowing. He dwells in eternity—above time, outside of time. He sees the end from the beginning; we only see what is directly in front of us. So we aren't even competent to make ultimate judgments about whether suffering is good, because we can't see what it will finally produce. He can, and He guides all events to His ends.

"God is also perfectly just and holy. He always enacts justice. He will judge all evil—sometimes in this life, but mostly in eternity. Part—but not all—of suffering involves His righteous judgment against sin. Sometimes God allows His people to suffer to build their character, or to help them see their dependence upon Him. Sometimes God uses a suffering Christian as a signpost to the world that He is able to grant perfect contentment even to those who suffer. We should never assume that any particular case of suffering is some sort of punishment. In the Bible Job suffered because he was righteous, not because he had sinned.

"But in the bigger picture, the existence of suffering is ultimately a consequence of the world's rebellion against God. Christians know from the Bible that the cosmos as God created it was without evil or suffering. Those aberrations came in only when mankind rebelled against God's authority. So really, it is man and not God who is behind suffering and evil. God permitted it, yes, but it was not within His moral will.

"But why doesn't God take it away? Why doesn't he put a stop to it?"

"Oh, but Galina, that's exactly what He *is* doing. He sent His perfect Son Jesus Christ to die on the cross, to pay the righteous penalty for sin, so that we might be forgiven. God is at work through his Son to reconcile the world to Himself, according to 2 Corinthians 5:19. One day Jesus will return with a final judgment, and evil, sin, and suffering will be forever banished."

"But why is faith so important? Why can't He just send us a telegram telling us what He is doing? Why can't He come

Himself and tell us?"

"Faith is important, dear Galina, because that is the condition He has placed on forgiveness. Only those who believe Him will be forgiven. Those who do not believe demonstrate that they want nothing to do with Him. He will allow them to have their way even though that way leads to eternal judgment. And He *has* sent us a telegram, if you will— it's the Bible. And He *did* come Himself and tell us. That's who Jesus Christ is. He's God. He told His disciples in John 14:9, 'He who has seen me has seen the Father.'"

"I'm sorry. I just can't get past the faith part, Susan. I *don't* believe Him."

"I have given you more than enough to think about tonight, let's let it go for now. I want you to know, dear Galina, no matter whether you ever believe or not, Roger and I love you and you can count on us as your friends. We will be here for you. Before I go, would it be okay if I prayed for you and for Jacob? He could be still alive and in need of prayers."

"Please do."

Susan bowed her head and prayed aloud for several minutes before quietly leaving the room and shutting the door behind her. The simple prayer profoundly moved Galina— more than anything Susan had tried to explain to her—for it seemed to the young woman as if Susan was talking to Someone she actually knew.

Chapter 30

It was a tough morning in Coronado. It was just ten days before Christmas and elements of SEAL Team Three were kissing wives and children goodbye. The hardest part was not being able to tell weeping family members that they'd actually be home for Christmas if everything worked right. Operational security forbade discussing the mission with anyone not part of *Thunderbird*. SEALs knew that the quickest way to endanger their families and themselves was to talk about their work. So secrets remained secret.

By 0730, sixty-four tough, battle-hardened men were completing the final check of their gear in a secured and tightly guarded hangar at NAS North Island. Logistics teams several days earlier had checked the munitions, weapons, and supplies, which were palletized and ready for loading into the containers, but SEALs were big into checking and rechecking their stuff while still in a position to fix mistakes or oversights. They have a saying learned from the school of hard knocks: "One is none, two is one." Whenever possible, they double up on mission-critical supplies, knowing that when Mr. Murphy strikes—he of "whatever can go wrong, will" fame—he always strikes at the worst possible time.

SPECOPS missions do not provide the opportunity to run back to a supply depot so you can pick up something you forgot. A covert insertion deep inside enemy territory provides terrific motivation to take the right stuff with you the first time, because there is no redo. You go to war with the stuff you brought, not with something you left back in a warehouse or a gear locker.

The lists were endless. At least three sets of eyes verified every item on every list individually, checking weapons, radios, ammunition, explosives, arctic weather gear, food, medical supplies, batteries, and more. There were even several teams of men who cross-checked things that ought to be obvious, such as insuring they had the correct ammunition for their weapons and the proper batteries for the electronic equipment. Other men were testing the electronics, verifying that everything was functioning properly.

The United States military has gradually become one of the best self-correcting organizations in existence. The rear-echelon types still buy six-hundred-dollar toilet seats, but not the men with combat responsibility. There is no military organization in existence better at learning from its mistakes. Two hundred years of US military history have been studied and used to develop tactics, procedures, and equipment to minimize errors. After-action reports are scoured, mined for data. Mistakes and failures in combat are relentlessly examined. Postmortems of the worst screw-ups are analyzed to see what went wrong and why, and the lessons are taken to heart. Consequently, the lives of many servicemen have been saved.

There's no lack of material for that sort of study. Some of the failures are real jaw-droppers. The North African campaign in World War II was half over before some genius found that the rounds American tank crews were being issued were training rounds rather than armor-piercing high explosives. During early infantry tangles with German armor it was discovered that the guys on the front lines did not have any of America's new bazookas; they were all hundred of miles behind the lines being used for training.

In Operation *Market Garden*, some clown forgot to give the ground troops radios or frequencies that would enable them to talk to the air crews responsible for the all-important supply drops. The troops involved in the Battle of the Bulge during one of France's coldest winters were without winter gear and clothing because some rear-echelon type warming his buns in a French chateau back in Normandy and thinking the war would be over before winter never shipped the winter gear forward.

The lists were pored over that morning in the hangar at North Island NAS, and not just once.

****

"How's it going, Chief? Are they going to fit?" asked Tom Rainer. He marveled at the sight. It looked like the huge C-130 Hercules had literally been built around the forty-foot cargo container.

"Like a glove, Commander—as long as no one inhales. We have a total of four inches of clearance fore and aft. You can see for yourself how close we are in height and width. We can barely shut the door, but yes, it does fit."

The loading operation was taking place inside the giant hangar at the Naval Air Station, hiding it from Soviet "eyes in the skies." The containers had been driven to the base and parked in the cavernous hangar between passes of unfriendly spy satellites. Likewise, the giant C-130s landed and taxied into the hangar where they were loaded out of sight of spying eyes, and held until they could taxi and take off unobserved.

Each plane had been ordered to Japan by a different route. Everyone except Bridger and Clausen believed the transports were routed to Misawa. In fact, they would be going to Chitose Air Base. From there the containers would be attached to truck bodies and driven to Otaru where they would disappear into a warehouse close to the wharves, waiting for the SEALs' arrival. By noon, the last of the four C-130 Hercules was in the air. Behind them they left a hangar littered with discarded remnants of packaging, and pallets half-filled with unneeded munitions and supplies.

The SEALs were standing inside a roped-off area in the hangar, clumped in little groups, talking quietly. The far hangar door opened just enough to admit a pickup truck loaded with folding chairs. Commander Marcus Clausen and Admiral John Bridger exited the truck and stood before the men.

Marcus called out, raising his voice so as to be heard in the large hangar, "Hey, guys, get these chairs set up, please. Admiral Bridger has a few words for you. Our ride outta here leaves at 1500, a C-9B Skytrain to Misawa, and we've got a bit of ground to cover between now and then, so let's get to it." Everyone turned to and in no time the truck was empty and the chairs were set up in a neat eight-by-eight square, with an aisle down the middle.

Bridger noticed that men sat with their assigned platoons rather than according to prior friendships. He nodded with approval; the intense training had produced the bonds necessary for smooth-functioning units. Bridger had known most of these men for several years, had practically memorized the personnel files on them. It was a tough, competent group.

He stood in the bed of the pickup, savoring the moment. There were no men he would rather be with, no company in which he sensed greater honor. Each was prepared to do anything necessary—including dying—in order to accomplish the mission they had been assigned. They were as well-trained as warriors could be and supremely confident in what they could do. The track record of the SEALs demonstrated time and time again that their self-confidence was well-placed.

"Men, I am completely disgusted! Never in my life have I been so ashamed," Bridger barked. There were sharp intakes of breath and a murmur of disappointment rippled through the men. Clausen's eyes were big as saucers; he had no idea the admiral was displeased. Bridger looked positively angry.

"Never have I led a bunch of men who have caused me so much trouble. Do you know what you have done? No, of course not! Well, let me tell you. You have ruined the fine training relationship we had with the Army Rangers!" The hint of a grin flickered at the corner of Bridger's mouth, but only for an instant.

"The major leading the Rangers we borrowed for our practice assaults stormed into my office earlier this week and accused me of being everything but a gentleman. I had no idea my ancestry was so colorful until that man informed me of it. You know what his problem was? You men beat the living snot out of the best Ranger units he had, and not once, not twice, not three times, but in every single engagement. And that was with *Rangers as judges*!" Bridger looked over at

Tom Rainer and muttered as an aside, loud enough for all to hear, "At least they do have integrity, anyway. Gotta hand that to 'em."

The admiral paused for a moment and then emphasized slowly, carefully enunciating every word, "And you were outnumbered every time! And you beat the snot out of them anyway!"

Clausen watched his platoons closely and saw relieved grins breaking out everywhere. *Bridger really had 'em going there for a moment. Had me going, too!*

"Now, you men have done me wrong and I don't know what to do about it. I worked a long time to convince one of the other Armed Services to come and spar with my SEALs, and you fellows just scared away the best group I could find. They don't *ever* want to come back and go up against you boys again." Bridger paused again and finally laughed, "But that's my problem and not yours. When that major was having his meltdown in my office I could have burst with pride for the outstanding job you fine men have done. And those Rangers are all tough men, good men. But you frogmen . . . well, you're just better."

A roar of approval came up from the seated group. Bridger waited for it to subside and then continued, "Gentlemen, it is *my honor* to speak to you this afternoon. You have accomplished your training with excellence. I have every expectation that you will accomplish Operation *Thunderbird* with the same skill, courage, and overwhelming success as you have every other mission that has been assigned to you."

Bridger always gave a good motivational speech to his SEALs before he sent them downrange, but Marcus knew the admiral was stretching the truth a bit. The Rangers had given them a real run for their money but had never been able to overcome the deficits of fighting from a fixed position. If both teams had been in the open field with room for maneuver, Marcus wondered if the contest would have been so lopsided. In any case, he was glad he wasn't leading his team against the Rangers in actual combat. Clausen set aside his thoughts and resumed listening.

"You know most of the story behind this mission, but there are a few things you may not know. You've been told that you are rescuing hostages held by the Soviets. This is true. What you don't know is who these hostages are, nor how we found out about them. Perhaps it will be helpful to you to know exactly why this mission is so critical.

"For the last several years the Soviet Union has been kidnapping top scientists and military officers from around the world. They are snatching people who know basic and applied sciences in areas in which Soviet scientists have not made progress. You might think of it as doing science on the cheap. If they can't figure out some knotty problem they simply kidnap people who already have.

"So not only are you rescuing hostages who have been kidnapped and are, as we speak, suffering the worst kinds of interrogation, but you are preserving the lead the West has enjoyed in the military sciences. The big picture of your mission, then, is huge—critical! You are fighting for security on a global scale.

"With a few possible exceptions, the men you are rescuing have never been trained to withstand interrogation. These are very good people, very intelligent people, but they are not tough people. Some will probably be in bad physical condition. But they are very important to their families and to their countries—make every effort to bring them back alive. You are rescuing two scientists from the US, three from Britain, two from Germany, one from India, and an Israeli military officer.

"The second thing you should know is that Major John Smith, the man who is leading our recon squad, was captured by the Soviets through this kidnapping scheme. In an almost legendary act of heroism, he escaped from their interrogation facility and ultimately from the Soviet Union, even though half the Red Army was pursuing him. He knows their operational procedures as well as the layout of the camp and the buildings. So you men are going into battle with the advantage of intelligence from someone who's been on the inside of the prison camp.

"The camp was relocated after Smith escaped, but we managed to find the new location. Don't ask me how—that's a matter I am not permitted to go into. It was, I am told, an act of divine providence that we even found it. Well, I wouldn't know anything about that but I can say this: we know where they are, and we are coming!

"You men today are writing the end of this tale yourselves. You are going over there, you will rescue those hostages, and you will turn *Rabbit Hutch* into a pile of smoking rubble.

"This flag," Bridger held up a package, "is the flag that flew over the Tomb of the Unknown Soldier last Memorial Day. The President of the United States gave me this flag last week when I was in Washington. Commander Clausen," he said as he passed the package to Marcus, "by order of the President of the United States, you are directed to ensure that this flag is properly displayed on a flag pole or what's left of the fence at *Rabbit Hutch*, when you depart from there."

The whole group of SEALs jumped to their feet with a roar, cheering and clapping. Operation *Thunderbird* was different from all their previous missions: normally on a SEAL mission if the frogmen leave any sign at all of their presence it is disinformation that will point to some other country. For *Thunderbird*, however, they could finally show their colors. The mission was to be carried out in uniform—with a few exceptions, of course.

Bridger held up his hands to restore order. Gradually the men quieted down and took their seats again. "Gentlemen, I simply cannot begin to express the love and pride I feel for you, or the gratitude I have for the privilege of leading the finest warriors on the planet. I will wait and hope for your safe return. Godspeed and good luck."

With that he snapped to the military stance of attention. All the men responded, standing at attention and raising their right hands in salute. Admiral Bridger gave a crisp salute in response, shook Commander Clausen's hand, and walked out of the hangar to his waiting staff car.

Chapter 31

The warehouse was unheated and dimly lit. The smells permeating the area were strong and familiar—creosote from the pilings and beams of the nearby wharf, marine diesel fuel, the oily smell of heavy equipment, and the lighter aroma of the sea. Sixty-four men moved quietly in the gloom, preparing to enter the containers for their long and boring trip to the port of Magadan. *At least*, Marcus thought, *I hope it is boring.*

An unseen team of CIA agents was providing a force security perimeter around the warehouse. No one would get close. Everything depended upon stealth. Detection here in Japan would mean that the mission was endangered, but not necessarily compromised. Detection once they were off-loaded in Magadan would mean certain death.

The variables and what-ifs were innumerable—some were catastrophic. What if the CIA or SPECOPS had been penetrated by enemy agents, and the Soviets were lying in wait? What if the drivers for the containers did not show up? What if the containers were opened for inspection? What if the defenders of *Rabbit Hutch* were able to transmit a message that they were under attack? What if the defenders of *Rabbit Hutch* were stronger than previously thought? What if the *Lady of Singapore* was not delayed at Magadan and sailed away without them?

Marcus, you have always wanted an exciting life. Congratulations. Looks like your wish has been fulfilled. In spades.

****

The *Lady of Singapore* was maintaining steerage way, but not much more. Her master, Kim Choson, watched from the wing of the bridge as the pilot boat approached. In a few minutes it had drawn alongside, and the pilot made the precarious climb to the deck on Jacob's ladder without incident. Kim returned inside the bridge, knowing that the first mate would escort the man up.

Kim loved this time of the morning. The rim of the sea to the southeast was taking on the color of a tiger lily as the disc of the sun approached the watery edge of the world. Clouds far to the east caught the orange and red colors and magnified them. He was enthralled with the sight and did not notice the steps of the men approaching him.

"Captain Kim?"

"Ah, yes, Yun Su. Good morning."

"Good morning. This is our pilot, Captain Shima Nasaki." The man he indicated was short and wiry with skin the color of old leather. His hair was white with age. Shima's eyes had crow's feet wrinkles from much smiling, and his face now creased naturally into a grin as he bowed slightly. His was an air of calm and friendly self-assurance.

Kim returned the traditional gesture and then said expansively, "Captain Shima Nasaki, how are you on this fine December day? A great day to be at sea, *ne-e*?"

"Indeed, Captain, it is truly beautiful. There is no place I would rather be at sunrise than on the deck of a ship. Are you prepared for port, Captain?"

"Yes, Captain. The first mate can provide the details of the anchorage to which we have been assigned by the harbor master, although I do think the dock is ready for us. We will probably be directed straight to it."

"What's your draft at present?"

"Six meters. You have the bridge, Captain."

"Aye, I have the bridge."

The *Lady* was a small feeder ship of six thousand tons, providing container service for small ports throughout the littoral regions of the Orient. It was well equipped to handle ice, and due to its unusually powerful engines it was capable of maintaining a sailing speed of twenty-two knots, giving it an edge over competitors.

Shima skillfully guided the small ship southward through the main shipping channel. It was a quiet morning without much commercial traffic. As the master had suspected, the *Lady of Singapore* was directed to their wharf without going to the anchorage.

There they would be unloaded by the small port's cargo crane before taking on containers to be delivered to Magadan. Winter was drawing on, and ice would soon choke that northern port. The *Lady* was one of the last freighters of the season bound for Magadan. She would return to Otaru from the Soviet port practically empty and then take on a fresh load of containers bound for southern waters.

****

Falcon trained the camouflaged parabolic mic on the guards at the front gate to see if he could pick up any new gossip. Falcon's partner Annie Oakley, also known as Petty Officer Wayne Williams, was making a circuit of the interrogation camp perimeter, well back in the woods, putting tiny reflective push pins in trees to mark the initial firing positions for the snipers and machine gunners of the assault team. The pins would reflect infrared light that could be seen in the assault team's night vision goggles. Tomorrow the two men would trade places, and Falcon would check Williams' selections, while Williams kept the camp under surveillance.

Wayne Williams had come by his nickname honestly, though the reserved SEAL didn't much care for it. He was the top-ranked sniper on SEAL Team Three. He'd put on a shooting exhibition one day on the firing range, and one of the frogmen had said that Williams "might even give Annie Oakley a run for her money." Some of the guys heard only "Annie Oakley," and much to Williams' chagrin the nickname stuck.

Falcon had already picked up some disappointing intel: General Chernikov was not scheduled to be at the camp again until after their assault. Chernikov maintained his staff office in Magadan, and sometimes came to the camp only once or twice a week. Falcon had been hoping the man would be at the camp during the attack. If Chernikov was on the grounds during the assault, Falcon had already decided that the general would not survive it.

Something was going on down at the camp. A pair of soldiers had come out of the administration building and fired up the big Ural 375. Falcon grabbed his binoculars, and watched. In a few moments troopers were leading the six guard dogs to the truck, and putting them in the back. The truck pulled out of the compound and disappeared down the access road.

The guards at the gate were grumbling after the truck disappeared, and Falcon managed to pick up much of the conversation. Major Aleksei Promokov, acting commandant in Chernikov's absence, had sent the dogs back to Magadan. Falcon was not able to make out the reason, although he could tell the soldiers at the front gate were plenty disgusted with the captain.

****

The trip to Magadan was cold, dark, and boring for the men packed into the shipping containers. It was like being taken aboard ship in a dank, steel coffin, an unfortunate connection more than one man made. There were twenty-two bunks in each container. Unsure of how many prisoners they would be rescuing, and knowing that Alpha Squad as well as the Kettles would be extracting with them, the planners ensured there would be plenty of space available for the ride home.

Riding in a container was dangerous. Since you could not see what was going on outside you could not brace yourself for the jostling, bumping, swinging, or quick trips up or down when the container was being handled by a crane. Consequently, Marcus established a hard and fast rule: when the containers were being handled the men were to be strapped into their bunks. The bunks were designed to protect the men from rough handling, and were equipped with what amounted to seat belts, complete with shoulder harnesses. As long as the crane operator did not drop them into the drink, they would be safe.

Once aboard ship they were able to unstrap from their beds and get up. Each container had space to allow four men to stretch and exercise at a time, so the officers divided their men into shifts that allowed them to stretch their legs and do some calisthenics.

All told, the men were inside the containers for about three days straight without heat. It was miserably cold, although they had chemical heat sticks they could place in their sleeping bags, which helped a great deal. However, the moisture generated by twenty men condensed on the sides of the containers and greatly added to the discomfort. The air was kept fresh enough by the scrubbers, but it became very humid and uncomfortable.

It was a great relief to hear the activity outside indicating they had reached Magadan. Once again they strapped into their bunks and within several hours felt the obvious motions of handling by a crane. Their containers were immediately mated to truck bodies and moved out of the way; then all motion and most sound stopped.

In Container Two, occupied by Third Platoon, Lieutenant Jerry Auld commanding, a SEAL murmured softly into the darkness that surrounded him, "Well, boys, it's almost show time. Let's get it over with."

Another voice, one with authority, hissed, "Shut up, Jackson, unless you fancy spending the rest of your days in some Soviet gulag!"

Another several voices chuckled in the darkness. Lieutenant Auld leaned over and whispered almost imperceptibly into the ear of the man next to him, "Pass the word. No noise! None! That's an order!"

They had made it to Magadan undetected. *It's a start*, Auld thought. Several hours later they could feel a truck being hitched to the container trailer. He looked at his watch in the darkness. *Noon, Magadan time. Well within mission parameters. So far, so good.*

They felt the driver swerving right, then left, then right, at slow speed. More than one wondered what the driver was doing until with a bone-jarring thud the whole container dropped, then bounced up again.

Ah, potholes. Just like home. This feels like the Pennsylvania Turnpike, Auld thought wryly.

****

Master Kim Choson watched the unloading of his ship proceeding smoothly. He glanced down from the bridge wing to the black, oily water. There was a thin skim of ice on the water under the wharf. *Give it another two weeks and this port will be closed. No matter. In another six hours, I'll be underway, headed south.* It was possible, he thought, that they could have one more visit to Magadan before spring, but he strongly doubted it.

Kim turned up the collar of his sea coat. The temperature was dropping and the sky was lowering, with the forecast calling for a severe winter storm. The sea would be rough and cold. *Better have the deck crew recheck all the cargo lashings and tie-downs,* he thought. *It would not do to have something clattering around loose in one of the holds. It could punch a hole in the hull.*

A voice on the intercom interrupted his thoughts. "Captain, we have a problem." It was the voice of his new second engineer. Kim had been impressed by the man: he seemed thoroughly competent and completely unflappable.

"What is it, Mr. Boles?"

"The steering hydraulics have died. Not sure what it is. The first engineer and I are going over everything right now. But for the moment, sir, the rudder will not answer the helm. We can't go anywhere until we get this fixed."

Kim thought for a moment, then said, mystified, "We have just come out of dry dock, Boles. The steering hydraulics were completely overhauled. Surely nothing serious could have gone wrong this soon! Perhaps you are mistaken?"

"No, sir. Sad to say, but I am not mistaken. Unless you can

turn this ship by the force of your will alone, Captain, I recommend you work out a deal with the harbor master that will
allow us to stay tied up tonight."

There was no choice; he must extend his stay in Magadan.
At least, he thought philosophically, *this time of year it won't put
me behind schedule. And there's no ship waiting to use the wharf. We
should be good.* He had a day or two to give. Master Kim gave
the lowering sky a baleful glare, then turned on his heel and
headed for the radio room.

Chapter 32

Sunday, December 20, 1987: 1215 hours, local time
Magadan, USSR

Benjamin Klausowitz watched as the four container trucks pulled past him onto the *Kolyma Trace*, headed north. He knew from the markings on the containers that they were headed for Golinskiy's lumber mill. The man had been as good as his word—so far. Whether that would continue only time would tell.

Ben stepped out of his Wartburg 311 and crunched through the snow toward the harbor overlook where there were some trees that would shield him from prying eyes. Examining the sky as he walked, he could see that the clouds were lowering. The snow could start any moment—his handler would want to know.

Once he gained the privacy of the trees he opened his satellite phone and dialed the number. The voice on the other end answered, "Simon."

"Maccabeus," Ben responded.

"Go," the voice commanded. Unknown to Ben the voice was that of Zvi Sharon; all Ben knew was that it was his controller, his handler.

"They have arrived and are on their way. Everything looks good."

"Excellent. Wait thirty minutes, then drive to the yard. When you get there, leave the car running. Open all the car doors and the trunk, then shut them all loudly."

"Got it. Leave the car running, open all the doors and the trunk, then slam 'em shut."

"Right. You will be contacted by someone there. His challenge will be *Mars Bar*. Your response is *Reese's Cup*."

"*Da*. Mars Bar and Reese's Cup."

"Right. If there is anyone else on the premises your contact will not appear. You may need to order any observers to leave. If you must, leave yourself and come back an hour later and repeat the signal. Your contact will not risk himself until there's no one but you in the area. He will have further instructions for you. Consider that his instructions have my authority."

"Got it. One more thing. There is a significant winter storm predicted, twelve to sixteen inches of snow over the next twenty-four hours. Looking at the sky, I'd say that it could start anytime."

"I'll pass that along. Now listen to me. You must pack your bags quickly and bring Ma Kettle with you to the lumber mill."

"I . . . I don't understand."

"I am bringing you both home. This is your last assignment. If you remain behind you will not survive the investigation that results from this operation. Your contact is your ride home."

Ben was silent. He was struggling with what he was hearing. All he'd ever known was the *Rodina*. But now it was really going to happen—he and Katerina were really going to flee the country. He didn't know if he could do it. He didn't want to do it. He loved Russia—not its government, but its people, its culture, its . . . .

His handler said gently, "Mr. Kettle, you always knew the day would come when you would have to leave your country for your own safety. That day is today. You and your wife must allow us to bring you home, today, now, before you are arrested. I know you both love your country. Now you must love your own lives. There is no other way. Do you follow?"

"*Da*," said Ben softly, a few tears sneaking out of the corner of his eye. He truly loved Mother Russia, but he could no longer stay. His work was done.

"Mr. Kettle, one more thing. When this conversation is over you must remove the batteries from your satellite phone. Is that clear? It is very important. You *must* remove those batteries. Otherwise you could endanger yourself and the entire operation. Be sure to bring the batteries and the sat phone with you. Do you understand?"

"*Da*, I understand."

****

Staff Sergeant Yuri Slavin placed Chernikov's bags in the trunk and then walked around the car and slid into the front seat. He could see that the general was in no mood to talk, so he remained silent as he started the car and picked his way carefully out of the Sokol Airport parking lot and headed south to Magadan.

Chernikov was returning from a trip to Moscow where he had made a full report on the moving of the prisoners and the occupation of the new detention facility. While away he'd decided to move his office from the rented space in Magadan to the prison itself, to be closer to the interrogations. The following morning was moving day.

Chernikov felt like a bridge had been crossed—finally. The events of the last sixteen months were now safely behind him. Somehow General Patrikeyev had managed not only to save his life from those who were calling for his execution, he had even managed to preserve the program and Chernikov's oversight of it. It was time to move on. *Tomorrow morning I will bury the past. There are four rounds in my sidearm that have been spoken for: two for Captain Moshe Shimonah, and two for Dr. Oswald Simmons. I will execute them in front of all the prisoners. They will be useful one more time—as examples of what happens to those who thwart my will. No more patience!*

Nikolai Pavlovich Chernikov knew, however, that Anatoly Geredin's thugs were keeping a close eye on him, and he guessed that the old bear did not have them on a particularly short leash. One more major mistake and there would be no meeting at the Politburo to decide his fate. Geredin's assassins would see to the matter, and when the Politburo met it would be a *fait accompli*.

****

By the time Ben and Katerina pulled into the sawmill yard the snow was falling and already four inches deep. The yard was deserted. Parked off to the side near two other containers that had been closed against the weather were four trucks with the containers still attached. He inspected the cabs and verified that the keys were still inside. All was according to the arrangements that he had made with Edvard Golinskiy. *Money works wonders*, he thought.

He walked back to his vehicle and pulled out a small package containing ten thousand dollars, then entered the mill office. Ben hid the money in the location that he and Golinskiy had decided upon. The package also contained a note that Golinskiy would get the following morning:

> *Molodets, Golinskiy! Here you will find ten thousand dollars, US. If your drivers return the containers to the port on time as discussed, I will drop off another fifteen thousand. As long as no one comes today and none but the drivers tomorrow, there will be another ten thousand.*
> *I. M.*

There would be no further payments, but Ben needed to dangle the expectation in order to keep Golinskiy out of their hair until the operation was complete. The Mossad agent was confident that the man's greed would overpower his curiosity, and that no one would come snooping.

Ben trudged around the yard through the snow, walking between piles of logs and sawdust. He saw no one, not even any tracks in the snow. The entire mill operation appeared to be quite deserted. He walked back to the car and opened the trunk and all the doors. He walked around the car several times wanting to give any hidden observer plenty of time to notice, then slammed the doors and trunk. Katerina remained in the car, but he stood in the snow, waiting. For ten minutes nothing happened. Just as he turned to get back into the car he heard a voice call softly from behind a stack of logs, "*Mars Bar?*"

He stopped and called nervously, "*Reese's Cup.*"

The tension was broken as the voice behind the logs broke into a tirade in English, complete with a drawl that must have been born on the plains of West Texas. "You must be loco for thinkin' up these loopy passwords. *Mars Bar, Baby Ruth, Hershey Bar!* I'm 'bout to have a conniption—been up in this neck o' the woods for half of forever, and ever'time I say one of your passwords I get a hankerin' for chocolate. That's a downright mean, nasty, an' ugly thing to do to a hungry boy like m'self. Least you could do was pack a couple candy bars for me in your kit."

"I am *quite* sorry, bu—" Thinking he was being addressed, Ben started to apologize when he was cut off by another voice coming from somewhere behind him. The second speaker had an unmistakable New Jersey accent.

"Yo, quit your complaining, Amos. Besides, what makes you think I didn't pack some candy bars in my kit?"

"Really? You gonna share 'em?"

"You're dreamin', cowboy. I hauled 'em in, I eat 'em. You want candy bars, you carry 'em yourself. Besides, only brought one of each. Each time we use a password for the first time, I treat myself to a celebratory candy bar."

By this time the first speaker had ambled into sight; he was a tall man with a month's growth of beard on his face. Clothed in a typical Russian worker's winter clothing, including a well-worn fur cap, the man cradled an M4A1 in his arms. Ben turned around and saw a similarly clad fellow, albeit a good deal shorter, trudging through the snow from the other side of the yard. He, too, was carrying an automatic weapon.

"Pleased to meet you, Mr. Kettle," said the tall man. "I'm Amos, and this here short feller is Andy, and we are here," he waved his arms expansively, grinning, "to *save the world!*"

"Indeed!" Ben replied dubiously.

"Please, Mr. Kettle," said the second man, "please ignore my friend's delusions of grandeur. He has had a long, um, day, and is not quite himself."

"I am so," insisted Amos.

"No, you are not and you haven't been ever since I knew you, but that is quite beside the point."

"GENTLEMEN, please!" barked Ben.

"Sir!" they said in unison, snapping to attention.

Ben shook his head, and then said, "Apparently you two are my contacts. I was told you would have instructions for me."

"Yes, sir. If you and the missus would kindly step into the office and make yourselves warm and comfy, Andy and I will dispose of your automobile."

Ben was surprised, "Dispose of the car? Why?"

"Well, sir, we want to make sure that nothing ties you or your car to us and those shipping containers. It could result in some unwanted attention before we get outta Dodge. So Andy and I will drive your car back to the town several miles up the road, and park it somewhere."

"But how will you get back?" Katerina asked.

Andy replied, "We'll walk, ma'am. Not a problem. Please return to the office and stay inside. Come on, Chief. We've got a car to ditch."

****

Falcon and Petty Officer Wayne Williams watched the scene below in the sawmill yard without giving away their presence. Had anyone unexpected shown up that person would not have lived long. Both men were equipped with silenced M21 sniper weapons. The task of Alpha Squad was now to watch over the containers and the Klausowitzes and ensure that no harm came to either.

Falcon reported in with a burst transmission directed to a satellite in stationary orbit above Korea, and then resumed watch. Until darkness fell, there would be no more action.

****

"Everything has arrived safe and sound," Bridger announced to the others via a secure comm-link. He was on the bridge of the *Vinson* as it cruised on the southeast side of the

Kuril Islands. "All the pieces are in place, people. The insertion was successful. Now it's just a matter of time."

Jensen spoke from the CIA War Room in DC. "Jesse, Arthur, have either of you picked up any signs of a heightened state of alert with any Soviet units? None of the Firm's assets have reported anything unusual."

"This is Jesse. We have received no SIGINT suggesting anything abnormal, other than the fact that Captain Young's flattop is twisting Ivan's tail a little bit."

"This is Art, and I agree with Jesse. There is a Soviet Ilyushin IL-38 operating out of Vladivostok shadowing us, but that's normal. The ASW screen has picked up two Kilos, but we expected them, too. We have detected no suspicious activities."

"Art, won't that May be a problem if we have to launch the choppers?" asked Jensen.

Art shook his head. He'd already given orders to have two of the CH53Es outfitted with Electronic Counter Warfare (ECW) equipment. "Negative, Bill. In addition to the EA-6B Prowlers we'll be launching, two of the Super Stallions are being fitted with ECW pods. If we have to use the choppers, we'll jam the spectrum with enough ECW noise to confuse anything they've got. I think we'll be okay."

Bridger spoke up again. "If anybody needs to catch a few winks, this is a good time to do it. Things won't get started for another three hours or so. I'm not a praying man myself, but I understand you are, Bill."

"That's right."

"Well, if you could send up some prayers for these boys, I wouldn't object in the slightest."

"Been doing that already, Admiral, and I promise I'll keep it up."

"Much obliged."

****

Captain Arthur Young took his cup and Admiral Bridger's and handed them to a steward for refills. He looked at Bridger and asked with curiosity, "You're not a praying man, Admiral?"

"Nope. Seen too much to be a believer, Art."

"That's funny."

"Why's that?"

"I've seen too much *not* to be."

Chapter 33

Amos poked his head into the sawmill office. "Mr. Kettle, the cavalry has arrived. You want to see 'em?"

"Cavalry?" Ben looked confused.

"Sure! You know, cowboys and Indians? The good guys?"

"I'm afraid I don't follow."

"Huh? Oh, right, you're Russian, I guess you wouldn't be familiar with that little bit of Americana. Well, follow me anyway. Want to show you why we needed you to find a place for those cargo containers."

The two men stepped outside into the dark. Snow was falling steadily, although the temperature had risen somewhat. Amos guessed that it was at least fifteen degrees Fahrenheit. If it were not for the little bit of light coming from the dirty office windows and reflecting off the snow he could not have seen his hand in front of his face.

Ben and Kat had spent the last four hours sitting in the sawmill office. Nothing seemed to be happening outside, and Ben had begun to wonder exactly what kind of operation this was. His Mossad controller had given him no information about the mission other than the requirements for the site, and that the containers were not to be inspected. He assumed the operation was related to the early requests for information he had received pertaining to a secret military prison facility. Perhaps these two crazy Americans, Amos and Andy, comprised the entire operation? Though never formally trained as a spy Ben realized that being kept in the dark was the norm, not the exception, for intelligence work. For security's sake everything was compartmentalized, based on the "need to know," and Ben didn't need to know.

The tall American with the Texas twang led him around one of the containers to the cargo door. He looked at Ben and then said, "Watch this."

Breaking the seal on the shipping container, he released the latch and opened the door. He swept a flashlight around the front of the container. All Ben could see were pallets with boxes strapped to them. A particularly unpleasant, ripe odor wafted from the container.

Amos wrinkled his nose and with disgust called out in English, "Aw, man! Y'all stink! This is awful." He looked at Ben and winked, waiting silently. They stood there in the snow for fully thirty seconds and nothing happened. Then Andy explained reproachfully to Ben in Russian, "This is silly. No Soviet soldier would have said what I just said. The boys in the back of this container could have said 'hello' or 'glad to see you' or something. But *no*! *Security*! Oh, brother! Now watch this." Switching to English he called into the back of the container, "Milk Duds."

"Oreo cookies," came the muffled reply from inside the container.

Amos put on a mournful expression. "See? Do you see how cruel Andy is? He is the one who set up the challenges and respon—" Amos immediately straightened up and listened. In the glow of the flashlight Ben noticed a small wire going up to the soldier's ear and realized for the first time that the man was wearing earbuds.

The silly humor vanished immediately and Amos was suddenly all business. He shouted into the back of the container, "STAY PUT! WE GOT TRAFFIC COMING!" He shut and locked the container doors and then directed Ben firmly, "Get back in the office now!" Grabbing his weapon, Amos disappeared into the snowy gloom. As he ran back to the office Ben realized that the repartee he'd witnessed between the two soldiers was just an act; underneath they were pure professionals. Though he still did not know what the events of the night would bring, the realization gave him confidence.

After contact had been made with the Klausowitzes earlier in the day, Alpha Squad had repositioned itself. Amos remained in the sawmill yard, watching over the Klausowitzes and the containers. Falcon took up a position several miles east of the mill watching the road from Sokol. Petty Officer Williams, hidden halfway between the guard shack and the Sokol road, was watching the access road to *Rabbit Hutch*. Andy Litchfield was also keeping an eye on the Sokol road from two miles west of the mill. Between the three hidden observation posts, no vehicle could approach the sawmill un-detected.

From his hiding place between the mill and the road Amos saw the headlights of the big Ural 375 as it labored past, headed for *Rabbit Hutch*. *Well*, he thought philosophically, *there goes assault Plan A. We just missed our ride into the gate. Nuts! I guess we'll have to go to assault Plan B*. Williams radioed the all-clear once the truck had passed his position on the access road.

Thirty minutes later, the assault force was spread over the mill yard, gearing up. Amos had relieved Falcon at his obser-vation post, and the pilot came to the mill seeking Comman-der Clausen.

"Well, well, well, look who showed up! It's Mr. Clean him-self," Falcon said warmly. Mr. Clean was Clausen's nickname, earned by virtue of his billiard-ball bald head. "Marcus, wel-come to Siberia, man! Great to see you."

"Ditto, Falcon. Is the weather here always this nice?"

"No, bro. This is special—just for you boys."

"Thanks a heap. We're going to leave tracks everywhere. That's a problem."

"I don't think so. The snow is fillin' 'em in just as fast as we make 'em. But the drivers might have a problem getting these trucks back to the port. The forecast is calling for up to sixteen inches. The roads may not be clear enough to get the trucks back to Magadan tomorrow."

"One thing at a time, Falcon, one thing at a time. Okay, fill me in. What's the situation at *Rabbit Hutch*?"

"Well, you just missed the easy way in. The Ural went past just before you guys came out of the containers, so instead of getting a ride through the fence in a nice big truck, we have to fight our way in."

Clausen nodded, "Drat! Plan B. Well, okay, we're prepared for it. We can do it. What else you got?"

"About the approach: we have to stay to the road until three hundred meters past the guard shack. The woods are booby trapped with trip wires connected to air horns. We nearly set one off ourselves two weeks ago. Did not even know they were there until Amos almost put his foot down on one."

Clausen chuckled, "Amos is one of the best there is, but he does have big feet."

"He really fooled me, Marcus. Watching him and Andy back at Coronado—well, I wondered if he was just a big clown. He's proved me wrong—the man's a tough, competent operator."

"He's a clown, alright. Sometimes it gets on your nerves. But I've never met a tougher SEAL. If you ever find yourself in a tight spot, like maybe, oh, Siberia, you'll want him watch-ing your back, because he's good. Real good."

"Yeah, like when would I ever find myself in *Siberia* of all places? That's crazy!" Falcon said dryly.

"Maybe you are crazy, 'cause this is your *second* trip, bro. You must like the food here, or something," Clausen grinned. "Tell me the latest about the schedule at *Rabbit Hutch*."

"They are running on a rotating shift. This is, uh, Sunday, so they will change guards at the gate, guard shack, and towers at 2200 hours. That's just two hours from now. The guards on duty at the guard shack have started checking in by telephone every hour, on the hour, with the watch officer. That gives us about forty minutes from the time we wax the guards to begin the general assault, if we leave a ten-minute margin of safety on either side."

Clausen pulled out his sketch of *Rabbit Hutch*. Falcon pointed out the north barracks and said, "Second Platoon is in luck for their breaching operation. Barracks RH5, on the north side, will be empty because their people are going on duty at 2200 hours. The troops in RH4 were on the day shift earlier today; they rotated off at 1400 hours so most of them will probably be asleep. The guys in RH3, on the south side, are the ones being relieved at 2200—when we begin our assault they should have just turned in."

"Okay, good. What about the admin building and the physical plant?"

"Normally there's no one in the physical plant at all, not unless something is broken and they are fixing it. No guards, no nothing. The admin building, RH1 on your map, has a skeleton complement on the graveyard shift. There is a watch officer, someone manning the radio, and anywhere from two to three others. The officer's mess is in there, too, so sometimes you've got off-duty officers in there until fairly late. It's unpredictable. Total hostiles could be as many as ten in the admin building. The mess hall, RH2, doubles as a recreation building and is often packed until midnight or so and then it empties out pretty quickly."

"What about vehicles?"

"I checked earlier today. There is a front-end loader parked inside the compound which they use as a snow plow, and to handle the lignite for their boiler. Plus, there's a jeep, a civilian two-door sedan, and the Ural. They will be parked right here," he said, pointing at the end of the physical plant building. "Unless you have changed the assault vectors since Alpha deployed, that loader will be blocking part of First Platoon's fire lane to the physical plant. It's no big deal, but it does mean that the First won't be able to support Second Platoon if they start taking fire from the end of the physical plant."

"Not a problem. We added some machine gunners to the plan after you left. They will still have a clear field of fire. Besides, it's First Platoon that will be facing the worst opposition. Now, what about these containers, Falcon? In your opinion, can we drive one of these trucks closer without alerting the Sovs in the guard shack?" asked Marcus, motioning to one of the containerized cargo rigs.

"Absolutely not. The guard shack has too good of a view down the road, and besides, if we got the truck stuck up there in this snow it would really ruin our day, exposing the whole extraction plan."

"Good point. Anything else?"

"Yeah, a really big bonus!"

"What's that?"

"No dogs! Chernikov has been absent this week, and the idiot he left in charge decided he didn't like all the racket the dogs were making. I think they must have smelled us, because they've been barking nearly every night. The guards would holler at them constantly, but they just kept barking. We were listening with our parabolic mics, and it was getting hilarious hearing those guys grumble about their dogs. Earlier in the week Andy picked up an officer begging the commandant to allow him to send out a patrol, saying that the dogs were barking because they were picking up a scent. The commandant scoffed at the idea. 'We're in the middle of Siberia,' he said, 'why do we need a patrol? The stupid dogs are barking at rabbits!'"

"What a moron. I'll bet *that* guy is not *Spetsnaz*. They'd never make such an idiotic mistake."

"You're right, but it does reinforce the fact that these guys are thinking like jailers, not soldiers. A few days ago the commandant got fed up with the noise, and sent the dogs away. Chernikov would have never done that."

"That's providential, Falcon."

"Funny. I've been hearing that word *providential* more and more. I'm starting to believe it."

The munitions in the containers were quickly divided among the platoons. In addition to the ammunition for their own weapons, everyone took two hundred-round belts of M60 ammo. Nobody wanted the machine guns to run dry. In addition to the normal spare barrel per gun each platoon took several extras.

At 2100 hours Kerry Davis' Fourth Platoon deployed in a force protection configuration, setting up positions to guard the containers, keep the Sokol road under surveillance, and guard the entrance to the *Rabbit Hutch* access road. They were loaded heavily with M72 LAWs at each position, plus two heavy fifty-caliber machine guns defending the intersection where the access road met the Sokol road. The SEALs of

Fourth Platoon would remain hidden, allowing any non-threatening, normal traffic to pass through between Sokol and points west. Any military traffic that tried to turn into the access road, however, would meet with an expertly-sited, lethal ambush.

Alpha Squad was assigned to take out the guards at the guard shack and sabotage the telephone and electrical wires leading into the prison camp. At 2130 hours Falcon led his three men, all of whom were outfitted with night vision equipment, up the access road. Three hundred meters shy of the guard shack the four men verified their comm links with Commander Clausen, and then Amos and Andy peeled off to wire the utility pole with explosives. Falcon and Annie Oakley Williams disappeared into the woods on opposite sides of the road, each taking a trail that had been cleared of booby traps and was marked with IR reflective dots from earlier in the week. The paths led to their sniper positions on either side of the outlying guard shack.

Twenty minutes later Williams whispered into his throat mic, "I'm in position, Falcon. I have clear shots at both hostiles. How about you?"

"I can only see the guy sitting at the desk. I don't see anyone else."

"Okay, I got the other guy targetted."

"Good. Shift change is in ten minutes. We'll give them an hour to get settled in. I'll talk to you again at 2300."

A little after 2230 hours First, Second, and Third Platoons began slogging up the snowy access road, burdened under by their heavy gear. By 2300 hours the assault force was hidden along the access road, just below the guard shack.

****

"Point Guard, this is Big Daddy. Report," Commander Clausen whispered into his mic.

"Green and clean, Big Daddy, we are go," Kerry Davis replied. Fourth Platoon was set and ready.

"Alpha Squad, report."

"We are green, Big Daddy," Falcon reported, "the big bang is set and we are ready to commence."

"Roger that. Okay, boys, this is it. Alpha Squad, you may engage at will."

"Alpha Squad engaging, Big Daddy. Annie, I've got the hostile at the desk. Do you have a clear shot at the other target?"

"Affirmative, Falcon."

"Fire on my mark. Three, two, one, mark!"

The sounds of the silenced M21s were absorbed into the snowy world around them, but the sound of breaking glass in the windows of the guard shack seemed amplified. It sounded horrendously loud to Falcon though he knew it couldn't be heard from more than fifty meters away. The two snipers cautiously advanced on the little shack and double-tapped the unmoving forms of the guards.

"Clear," affirmed Williams.

"Clear," repeated Falcon. "Big Daddy, Alpha Squad objective one is complete." Soon the three platoons were trudging past the guard shack. Over the next thirty minutes they moved stealthily into their assigned positions for the assault, using trails previously marked by tiny IR reflective dots.

Chapter 34

Although he had been hoping to use the Ural to breach the fence, Marcus was confident that his men could take *Rabbit Hutch* in short order, even with Plan B. He considered his SEALs to be the best operators on the face of the planet, and harbored no doubts as to the success of the mission.

The order of battle was straightforward. Once Alpha Squad had completed its preliminary objectives, eliminating the guards at the guard shack and destroying the utility pole, Alpha would be absorbed into First Platoon for the remainder of the mission. Though Falcon was the ranking officer, Lieutenant Ed Bausch would command. As Clausen quipped, Falcon would have command of all Air Force personnel on site. Both First and Second Platoons—the main assault forces— were further strengthened by pulling four men each out of the Third and Fourth.

First Platoon ("Long Shot") was attacking from the west side of the camp, at the main gate. Their objectives included securing the admin building and destroying the radio room. Second Platoon ("Bad Man," Lieutenant Paul Pascoe, commanding) was attacking from the north side of *Rabbit Hutch*. Their objective was to capture the physical plant and destroy the emergency generator. Third Platoon ("Sneak Thief," Lieutenant Jerry Auld, commanding) would remain hidden until the generator was destroyed and then would breach the east end of the compound, using wire cutters, under the cover of darkness. If things went according to plan, the defenders would be unaware of this third thrust into the compound. Third's primary objective after breaching was to secure and protect the hostages. Fourth Platoon ("Point Guard," Lieutenant Kerry Davis, commanding) would provide force protection and serve as emergency reserve.

****

It's show time, Marcus decided, *let's get this thing rolling.*

He spoke into his throat mic, "Point Guard, report."

"We are in position and there is no traffic on the roads, Big Daddy. Ready and waiting for you to rock and roll."

"Copy. Apha Squad, report."

"The big bang is ready, Commander, standing by."

"Roger that, Alpha. Long Shot, report."

"Long Shot is in position and ready."

"Copy. Bad Man, report."

"Bad Man is ready, Big Daddy."

"Copy that. Sneak Thief, what's your status?"

"Sneak Thief is ready to commence."

"Roger that, Sneak Thief. All platoons, we are shifting to assault objectives, Plan B. Stand by to commence."

****

The watch officer on the late shift, Lieutenant Victor Andropov, stirred his coffee absentmindedly as he sat at his desk reading a magazine. His office was on the northwest corner of the administration building. Something caused him to look up, he was unsure what. He stood up and walked to the north window. The snow had briefly abated and he could see the dark green of the forest some thirty meters beyond the fence, illuminated by the perimeter floodlights. He looked out the west window. He could see the two soldiers sitting in the guard shack at the main gate. Everything appeared to be normal. He shook his head, puzzled.

The peaceful scene belied the disquiet Andropov felt. The absence of the guard dogs' barking was thunderous to his ears. Three days ago, when the dogs were sent away because their barking *disturbed* the major, the specialized canines had been trying to raise the alarm. Victor had worked with military dogs in Afghanistan and knew that trained dogs don't bark at night creatures. They don't bark at all unless detecting an explosive or picking up the scent of a hostile.

In vain had Andropov gone to the camp's acting commandant, Major Aleksei Promokov, begging him to send patrols to investigate the perimeter. The obstinate major had not earned his rank in the GRU by prowess in combat. In fact the battlefield was unfamiliar territory for the rear-echelon man—he'd advanced to his rank through police work. Never under fire from skilled and motivated adversaries, he was instead accustomed to exercising control over a cowed populace. Promokov was competent enough at police matters, but he thought too much of himself and was unimaginative. His decision about the dogs was arrived at thusly: "We are in Siberia, there are no enemies in Siberia, therefore the dogs cannot be barking at enemies." Whereas Andropov, as a member of the *Spetsnaz*—the Soviet Union's elite special forces—was accustomed to popping up in unexpected places behind enemy lines. In his thinking if the dogs were barking there must be a good reason for it, and no possibility should be dismissed. But dismiss it is exactly what Major Promokov did with Andropov's warnings. The dogs were sent away and the soldiers were not dispatched to patrol the camp's perimeter.

Stymied by his superior, Victor did his best to work around him. No firearms were permitted on the prisoner side of the compound, but he ordered his men to be fully armed at every other duty station. The commandant had been inquisitive but was satisfied when Victor lied to him, explaining that he was trying to bolster the morale and readiness of a finely trained combat unit. Indeed, Promokov had enjoyed the sight and ordered the other two shifts to do the same, though he required all weapons to be returned to the lockers and locked up between shifts. *Promokov thinks I am playing "army,"* sighed Victor, *and he has decided to join in the fun. At least he doesn't have us marching around in parade formation.*

So it was that roughly one third of the camp was fully armed, even if not exactly battle-ready.

****

Commander Clausen polled the snipers, waiting until each had their hostile targeted. "All platoons, H-hour commences on my mark; snipers, execute on my mark. Three, two, one, mark."

Between the silenced sniper weapons and the sound-deadening effect of the snow, there was little shock and awe when the battle commenced. The guards in the towers saw their comrades fall but had no time to react before they themselves were killed. No one raised an alarm and no one inside the buildings had any idea that they were under attack.

"All platoons, when the power goes out you may pursue your objectives under local command. Alpha Squad, execute."

"Copy that, Big Daddy. Fire in the hole!"

Amos triggered the detonator and the top of the utility pole blew off, severing the telephone and electrical wires. The power lines on the grid side crossed each other and continuously arced with loud, snapping pops and mighty showers of blue-white sparks before the circuit upstream finally failed. The utility pole was separated from *Rabbit Hutch* by a high ridge and about one thousand meters of snow-covered forest. No sound of the explosion made it to the camp.

The lights went out and pitch-black darkness covered the camp like a blanket. The SEALs put on their NVGs, and the First and Second Platoon breachers and forward fire teams broke cover and raced to their planned spots at the outer fence. The defenders of *Rabbit Hutch* still did not realize they were under attack, so there was no firing of weapons at all, neither from the defenders nor the assaulters. The opening stages of the breaching proceeded without the defenders becoming aware of their danger.

In the physical plant building the automated startup sequence for the generator kicked in as soon as utility power had ceased. The heavy batteries of the backup generator were fully charged, and the unit as a whole had been well maintained. For several seconds power was applied to the glow plugs. The whir of a fuel pump began and then the heavy starter kicked in, turning the crankshaft of the large engine. The compression built in the cylinders until finally the pressure was sufficient and the diesel vapors detonated. After two throaty coughs, the diesel rattled into life. When the crankshaft reached its prescribed RPMs the centrifugal clutch engaged and the rotor of the heavy generator began to spin. A pronounced hum signaled the generation of electricity. The system gagged as the startup demand for power bogged the generator down for the first three or four seconds, then it settled into its operating groove and the lights of *Rabbit Hutch* flickered back on.

****

His cup was to his lips when the lights went out. Victor froze. *I hope this means a tree has fallen across our power lines, but my bones tell me that's not what it is. Instead, I think we are just about to pay the piper for Major Promokov's galactic stupidity.*

Two things happened next in such quick succession that Lieutenant Andropov barely had time to swallow his coffee. The compound lights came back on and he saw through the north window a bright yellow light winking in a rapid stutter at the edge of the forest. Years of combat experience identified it immediately—the muzzle flash of a machine gun! He threw himself onto the floor even as he heard windows shattering. The gunner stitched a pattern across the side of the admin building. Andropov's quick reaction saved his life—for the moment anyway.

Time slowed to a crawl. Lying amidst the broken glass on the floor he sorted out the sounds. The snow deadened much of the noise but he could distinguish multiple machine guns firing. Soft pops and tinkling glass told him that the attackers were systematically shooting out the compound lights. He shut his eyes in despair, thinking, *if they have night vision equipment, we are finished. This camp has only ten sets, and I am not sure we have enough batteries.* Cries of alarm sounded within the camp, but he heard no return fire. Lighter automatic weapons began firing on the west side—M4s from the sound of them. The western window shattered. Four sharp bangs told him that someone was using smoke grenades somewhere close. *The machine gun to my north is providing covering fire. My west window did not break at first, because the assault team must have been in the fire lane. So the assault axis is coming from the west. Better get busy and rally the troops. This is no drill.*

It felt like an eternity before Victor grabbed his AK-47 and crawled out of the room, but only three seconds had elapsed since the firing began. He crawled past the radio room—a room with no windows, fortunately. The soldier manning the radio was sending a distress call. "*Magadan, Magadan, Magadan,* come in please!" No answer. The radio operator repeated the call—still no answer. Suddenly the receiver was filled with a sound that could best be described as a circular saw ripping through plywood.

"They're jamming us, sir. I'll never get through that. Phones are dead, too."

"Okay, soldier. Get your weapon. They are hitting us on the west fence. Either we hold them off or the next thing we see is grenades coming through the windows. Listen to me: run to the east door. Wait until you hear me open fire, then dash across to the mess hall. Send me ten men; I have weapons for them here. Understand? Now go!"

"Vasiliy! Georgiy! Come here!" Andropov shouted down the hall. Last he knew the two officers were having a nightcap in the officers' mess. He crawled into the commandant's secretary's office, and got to the weapons locker. Two pairs of NVGs, a dozen grenades, fifteen AK-47s, and one hundred magazines, plus the most precious item—a small radio transceiver. Its range was inadequate for contacting anyone beyond the camp perimeter, but they would be able to coordinate their defense with troops in the other buildings. The radio was on a different, much higher frequency than the base radio. He doubted the jammer would affect it. He donned the earbuds and throat mic and slipped the unit into his pocket. No one else was on the air, but he expected they would be soon.

The two men ran up, crouching to stay below window level. "Grab a weapon and ammo. Grenades, too." Victor

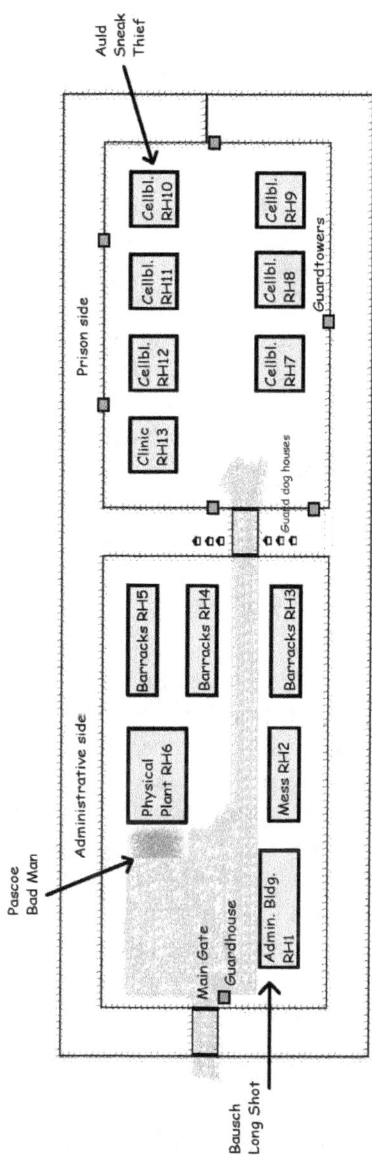

grabbed several grenades and as many spare magazines as he could stuff in his pockets.

"Follow me!" Doubled over, the three men crept to the west end of the hall. He took the watch office on the north side and sent the other two into the commandant's office on the south.

"When there's a pause, I'll return fire. That will attract their covering fire to my window. As soon as that happens, chuck some grenades. We've got to stop them right here." His comrades nodded and disappeared into the other room.

The lull he was waiting for came and Victor popped up, spraying bullets. It was the first sight he'd had of the enemy. They had breached the outer fence by the main gate and were working on the inner one. In the split second he had before ducking back to safety, Andropov emptied his magazine in the general direction of the attackers. He dove to the floor as a fusillade of return fire blasted through the window.

"Two away!" called one of the men from the next room, just before the fire shifted to their window.

****

Ed Bausch observed the return fire from the admin building. A member of the forward fire team dropped, then two breachers. One of his machine gunners was about ten meters to his right, and he heard the operator swear as he started pumping bullets through the window. Two grenades came sailing out of the adjacent window and the gunner swore again.

"Long Shot, grenade, grenade, get down!"

He saw his men dive to the ground and cover their heads. One grenade fell harmlessly far from the mark, but the other sprayed his men with lethal shrapnel, kicking up a cloud of snow and momentarily obscuring his view of the battle.

"This is Long Shot, I want those two windows hosed down, and grenades through each at the first opportunity."

Frogmen from the assault team leaped forward to replace the breachers lying bloody in the snow. A fiery duel between the defenders and assaulters was slowing the breachers down. Bullets were zipping around like angry bees. It was apparent that the fighters in the admin building had been reinforced.

Finally the cry "Fire in the hole" came, and the inner fence was breached in a brilliant flash of light. The assault team raced through the hole in the fence.

"Long Shot, RPGs now! Covering fire, covering fire!" Bausch directed.

Four operators, each with an M72 Light Antitank Weapon (LAW), knelt in the snow and uncapped, extended, and locked the extension tubes of the weapon. After checking that the back-blast area was clear, the four took aim at the corners of an imaginary square below the south window at the end of the admin building and fired simultaneously. With a blaze of fire that lit up the night, the sixty-six-millimeter, high-explosive warheads rocketed out of their tubes, traveling just shy of one hundred fifty meters per second. They hit the concrete wall at their maximum velocity and detonated, the shockwave from the shaped charges pulverizing the concrete for two feet around each point of impact. The concussion blew out all the remaining windows on the west end of the building and stunned the defenders, killing several. Two more RPGs brought down the radio tower. The dust had not even begun to clear when Long Shot's assault team raced through the jagged hole into the building and began clearing it, room by room, shouting *Sdavaysya! Sdavaysya!*—Surrender! Surrender! The defenders who surrendered were herded or carried into the officers' mess and placed in binders. Those who did not were quickly put out of action. Lieutenant Victor Andropov was carried into the mess alive but unconscious, blood coming from his nose and ears. The equipment in the radio room was destroyed with a couple of grenades.

"Big Daddy, this is Long Shot. Objective is complete. RH1 is secure and the radio is destroyed. Shifting to secondary objectives."

****

While the First Platoon was engaged with the defenders in the admin building, Paul Pascoe's Second Platoon was breaching the fence on the north side of the compound, just west of the physical plant. The night lit up with blazing brilliance as the thermate did its work on the inner fence.

"Big Daddy, this is Bad Man, we are inside. Shifting to RH6." Pascoe's main assault force raced through the holes in the fence and took up positions behind the lignite pile and amongst the vehicles in the parking area. As soon as they had reached cover Pascoe radioed, "Bad Man, Bad Man, machine gunners, snipers, engage targets of opportunity."

The assault team kicked in the west door of the physical plant, hurled in three grenades, and dove to the ground. The blast tore the door off its hinges, and the assault force advanced swiftly into the building, clearing it room by room. The forward fire team took up positions around the lignite pile, and waited.

"Bad Man, RH6 is clear. Wiring generator." The operators attached small blocks of C4 explosive to the generator and the diesel engine, and withdrew to the lignite pile.

As they exited the building on the west end, the outside door on the east side was kicked open and a team of four *Spetsnaz* jumped in, sweeping the area with their weapons. Twenty seconds later the timed charges blew, killing all four Soviet soldiers and plunging the entire camp back into darkness once again. Tendrils of flame tentatively licked the diesel fuel spilling on to the floor, but it did not catch.

"All platoons, this is Big Daddy. Goggle, goggle, goggle."

Bad Man's whole assault force re-entered the physical plant and prepared to advance to the barracks.

****

Once the generator was destroyed, Sneak Thief went into action. Lieutenant Jerry Auld examined the prison side of the compound carefully through his NVGs. Other than a few cell-block guards peering out of their doors there was no sign of Soviet activity on the east side. The guards possessed only batons for weapons—no firearms. The lieutenant also guessed that on the prison side of the compound the Soviets had no night vision equipment.

Auld watched from the cover of the forest as two squads of *Spetsnaz* charged from the barracks to the passage between the compounds. The carefully sited machine gunners cut them down, beating back the attempt and effectively interdicting the passage between the two sides.

The danger for Sneak Thief was not personal safety—it was the well-being of the hostages. The breaching would be easy; everyone's attention was riveted on the raging firefight to the west. The breaching party would be virtually invisible in the thick darkness, and out of the line of fire of practically every Soviet soldier with a gun. As long as his men remained undetected, Auld assumed the guards would not harm their prisoners. The key to freeing them would be hitting the occupied cellblocks simultaneously. This is where Alpha Squad's surveillance paid off in spades: of the six cellblocks at Rabbit Hutch, only four were occupied. The two easternmost units were known to be empty.

Using hand signals, Auld waved his team forward. Three breachers ran to the fence and immediately went to work with heavy-duty fence cutters, slicing a hole in the outer fence. In ninety seconds they were through. They raced to the inner fence and started snipping away, while the rest of Sneak Thief's assault force poured through the outer breach. In another ninety seconds the whole force was lined up on the east wall of the empty cellblock RH10. Assignments had been made weeks ago back at Coronado, and the men needed no instructions now. Auld pointed to the cellblocks on the south side, and his chief petty officer (CPO) nodded. The four men detailed to clear the cellbocks crawled across the open space, accompanied by their fire support team and the CPO. They reached the empty cellblock on the south side undetected. A similar team deployed around the back side of the buildings on the north side. Lieutenant Auld waited for the message in his earbud that all the players were in position.

Chapter 35

Dr. Oswald Simmons lay on his bunk. He was bruised from head to toe; no position was comfortable. Burn spots on his hands were inflamed and weeping. His face was covered with scabs and dried blood. His nose was broken, both arms and most of his fingers had been broken. It wasn't from interrogation—his days of interrogation had come to an end. Now they were simply punishing him for having misled their scientists. Everyday at lunch he was beaten before the entire prison population as a warning of what others would suffer if they failed to cooperate with their interrogators.

That evening at dinner he and Captain Moshe Shimonah had been informed by their guards that they were "scheduled for termination" the next morning. Both men were in such pain from the beatings they had endured that they welcomed the message as the promise of an end to their torment. Simmons spent the rest of the evening witnessing to the Israeli, arguing from Isaiah chapter 53 and Jeremiah chapters 31 and 33 that Jesus Christ was indeed the promised Jewish Messiah. Simmons sought to convince Shimonah that it was Jesus who perfectly fulfilled the Law of Moses and offered Jeremiah's New Covenant promises of the forgiveness of sins to all who would believe in Him. In the end the captain had repented of his sins and placed his faith in Christ.

Up until this point Oz had wondered why the Lord was allowing such a nightmare in his life. It would have been one thing if he'd been tortured for his faith—that he could have handled. But what was going on at the prison camp, in his mind, was little more than senseless, pointless brutality. He had wrestled nightly with God in prayer, seeking to find some larger purpose in his suffering. Now he understood. God had placed him there so that Moshe Shimonah would hear and believe the message of Christ, the Messiah of both Jews and non-Jews alike. The memory of the man's simple prayer made Simmons smile. Knowing God had used him to bring the Israeli to faith provided an eternal perspective for the whole experience.

The lights in the cellblock flickered and went out. Thirty seconds later they came back on, and Oz heard the rattling sounds of machine gun fire. Several minutes later the lights went out for good, and the sound of gunfire and grenades exploding rose to a crescendo. *It's gotta be Jake! He's come back with his buddies, just like he promised. Lord, You used me there, too, helping Jake escape. Thank You! All in all, it was worth it.*

A blood clot was forming in Oz's carotid artery, a consequence of the brutal beating earlier in the day. When he turned his head, trying to get comfortable, the movement dislodged it. The blood flow pushed it straight to his brain and the scientist had a massive, fatal stroke. He was finally free.

****

The sound of machine gun fire instantly yanked Sergeant Pyotr Soldoy from a sound sleep to full alert. A veteran of numerous special operations in Afghanistan, no one needed to tell him that they were under assault, nor did he allow the incongruity of being attacked in his homeland paralyze him. He sprang up from his bunk and ran for the weapons locker, shouting as he went, "UP, UP, UP, EVERYBODY UP, WE ARE UNDER ATTACK." All over the barracks men stumbled sleepily out of their bunks. The replacements, those who'd not seen battle in Afghanistan, began pulling on clothes. He shouted as he passed them, "You don't need clothes yet, fools, you need weapons! To the weapons locker!"

The locker was secured with a heavy padlock. A young soldier, new to the unit and quite green, asked loudly, "Who's got the key?"

"I do, moron," snapped Soldoy as he shouldered past the

man and grabbed a fire axe off of the wall. In one swing he swept the lock, hasp and all, off the locker and threw it open.

The grizzled veteran turned and faced the men behind him. "LISTEN TO ME, all of you. You will need your flashlights in a matter of minutes. The power will go out and the people attacking us will be using night vision equipment. You must be armed, dressed, and ready!"

"How do you know these things? Is this a drill?" asked the young soldier.

"No, son, this is no drill," responded Soldoy as he passed out assault rifles, grenades, and ammunition. "I know these things because that's how I would do it if I were assaulting this camp. These guys are good—how else do you think they could penetrate our homeland? Whoever they are, tonight we have to be better.

"Grab a weapon, load it, then find your flashlight. Only then should you get dressed. Put on your cold weather gear," he instructed the room at large, "and fill the pockets with ammo and several grenades. No screwing around. This is no drill! You screw up and we could all be dead in ten minutes. Stay away from the windows and below window level. Now MOVE!"

Most of the men in Soldoy's barracks were fully clothed and ready to fight when an explosion echoed around the compound and all the lights died. They were in the middle barracks, between the others, and so their side windows were spared the murderous fire from the machine gun positions north and south of the camp.

Pyotr Soldoy had no idea how to begin fighting back. He positioned his best friend, a sergeant by the name of Kharlov, at the east door with a pair of NVGs to get a careful look around and try to see what was happening. He grabbed the radio unit out of the weapons locker, put on the headset, and headed for the west door with his own NVGs.

Kharlov was back in a moment. "There's no activity I can see. I don't think anyone has penetrated the east side of the compound."

"Well, there will be. We've got to beat them to the punch

and arm the guards. Kharlov, form up two squads of five men each. Load them up with extra ammo, and each man with a spare rifle on his shoulder. Lead them to the other side and arm all the guards. Now!"

Soldoy turned his attention back to the firefight at the main gate. He observed two machine guns set up to the west, beyond the fence. They were hosing down the compound and anything that moved. To his immediate right, he saw two gaping holes in the physical plant building, and black oily smoke pouring out of it. Movement caught his eye, and he could see hostiles through the holes and windows. They appeared to be massing for an assault on the barracks just north of him. He turned back to his comrades, and whispered, "Can we see the east door on the physical plant from any of the windows on the north side of this barracks?"

One man nodded, "*Da*! The last three windows in the common area."

"Okay," Soldoy responded, "get some men at those windows. The enemy is about to cross over to the north barracks from the physical plant. When you see them come out the door, rip 'em to shreds. If you can't see anything, just fire when I do. Understand?"

The men nodded and got in position.

Pyotr Soldoy eased the west door on the end of the barracks open, trying not to attract attention. He side-armed a grenade through one of the windows in the physical plant and then opened fire, spraying the holes with his assault rifle. Though they could not see their targets, the men at the barracks windows opened up with their AK-47s, firing into the doors, windows, and holes in the physical plant.

****

"Listen up! Soon as our machine guns stop, we haul out of this door and into RH5! Got it? We're coordinating with our machine gunners, understand? I want split second timing." Pascoe looked at his men, and they nodded.

"Scott, Howie, lay heavy fire on the windows and doors of

RH5," Pascoe said into his throat mic, speaking to his machine gunners, "then when I give the word, hold your fire because we'll be moving in."

Seconds later, the men of Bad Man—Second Platoon—heard the ripping bark of M60s positioned on the north side of the compound as the gunners fired short bursts into the windows of RH5. Just as Pascoe was about to tell the gunners to hold their fire, Soldoy's grenade sailed through the window, careened off the opposite wall, and bounced to Paul Pascoe's feet, spinning on the floor. Before anyone could react, it detonated.

Pascoe was killed instantly, along with two members of his forward fire team. The other two men were shielded by the bodies of their less fortunate buddies, but were blown ten feet back down the hall. Shrapnel and ricochets made the space lethal to anyone not lying on the floor.

CPO Julio Gonzales, Bad Man's second-in-command, was further down the hall firing through a window in the maintenance room. He heard the explosion and stepped out to look down the hall. Seeing the carnage, he cursed in dismay.

"Big Daddy, this is Bad Man. Pascoe just bought it, plus Peters and Smith. This is CPO Gonzales, looks like I'm in command. I need fire support on the west door of RH4, and our machine gunners don't have the right angle for it. We are getting heavy resistance from that building."

"This is Big Daddy. Copy that, Julio. Pascoe, Peters, and Smith are down. Gonzales, you have Bad Man. Fire support is coming up."

Clausen raised Ed Bausch on the radio. "Ed, give me heavy fire on the west door of RH4. We have resistance in that area. They just took out Pascoe and two of his men."

Clausen heard an angry expletive. Bausch said sternly, "Copy that, Big Daddy. You got it." In the next instant, Long Shot's machine gunners were pouring a flood of lead and death into the west door of RH4.

Gonzales gathered up the six remaining members of his team, and led them past their fallen buddies to the east door, preparing to assault the north barracks building, RH5.

Through his NVGs he saw more movement in the windows of RH4. He turned back behind the safety of the wall, and said, "Sam, when I give the word, you and Billy go through the door and hose down the windows on RH4. Mike and I will be right behind you. We'll chuck a couple of grenades through them. Then everybody gets back behind this wall again so we can reload before doing RH5. Got it?"

The other three nodded. Sam and Billy ejected their mags and slammed fresh ones in place. Mike and Julio pulled grenades from their harnesses.

"Ready?" he asked, and received several nods of affirmation.

"Scott, Howie, hold your fire, hold your fire!" he said into his throat mic.

"Copy that, holding fire," came the reply.

"NOW!"

Sam and Billy stepped through the door, taking a kneeling position while they fired suppressing bursts through the windows. Julio and Mike lobbed their grenades and all four jumped back into the cover of the ruined physical plant building.

They slammed fresh magazines into their M4s. Julio slung his M4 to his shoulder, then grabbed Pascoe's MP5, which was laying on the floor. He fired a test burst out the door. The weapon was still functioning. He searched Pascoe's blood-soaked pockets and retrieved the magazines for the submachine gun. He rammed a fresh thirty-round magazine into place.

Looking around, he asked, "Is everybody ready?" His men nodded. "Let's do RH5." Gonzales spoke into his mic, "Scott, Howie, give me five seconds of fire on RH5, then hold your fire because we are coming through."

"Copy that. Here we go." The M60s spoke their staccato syllables of death, then fell silent.

"Bad Man is moving, Bad Man is moving!" Gonzalez spoke into his mic, "NOW!" Sam and Billy thrust through the door, dropped into the snow and began unloading their ammunition through the windows of RH4 to suppress its defenders.

Gonzales, followed by the rest of the platoon, raced across the gap between the buildings and kicked in the barracks door. He stepped left and crouched low while spraying the room with his MP5. His platoon followed him in, diving to the floor. The room was crisscrossed with fire and jagged ricochets for several seconds. But the SEALS were wearing NVGs, and the Soviets were not. It was no contest. Within thirty seconds all resistance was crushed. Gonzales heard his men slap in fresh magazines even as he himself reloaded.

"Scott and Howie, hold your fire. We are moving through the building. That's us you're seeing through the windows. For goodness' sake, don't shoot!" The platoon advanced through the building, carefully stepping around bodies, double tapping the dead and those playing dead.

The building was a charnel house. Many had dropped to the floor when the M60s began pouring lead through the windows. Most had been hit by ricochets as bullets bounced between the concrete walls. The survivors lay on the floor spread-eagled—not offering resistance—obviously figuring it was better to survive to fight another day when the odds were not so decisively stacked against them.

"Clear!"

"Clear!"

"Clear!"

The SEALS went through the building, disarming the living and placing plastic binders on their wrists. Those still able to move were herded into the barracks shower room and forced to lie on the floor. One last sweep of the building revealed no living soul other than the prisoners in the shower room and the Navy SEALs themselves.

"Big Daddy, this is Bad Man. RH6 and RH5 are secure," Julio reported. *The building is secure,* he thought, *but the price was way too high. Can't believe Pascoe is gone. Can't think about it now, though.*

****

After hurling the grenade, Soldoy crouched over and carefully worked his way back through the barracks, admonishing the men at the windows to keep up their fire on the east door of the physical plant. Using a flashlight, he found Kharlov at the east end, sitting propped up against the wall. He was bleeding from the thigh and chest, and had taken a slug that went in one side of his face and out the other, taking most of his teeth with it. With a cry of rage stuck in his throat, Soldoy sank to the floor and held his comrade in his arms.

Kharlov struggled to talk, blood bubbling out of his mouth. "Couldn't make it. Machine guns everywhere. Men, all cut down. Slaughter." Even as he spoke the life drained from his body. Soldoy lowered the body to the floor and gently shut the lifeless eyes. *Grieve later. Fight now*, he told himself.

He grabbed his weapon and stood up. At that moment a stream of M60 fire came from Long Shot's machine gunners. They had an angle that allowed them to cover nearly the entire length of the building through the splintered door and broken windows on the west side. Soldoy's ears filled with the angry buzz of slugs and ricochets as the M80 ball ammunition impacted the interior concrete walls, sending jagged shards of lead whizzing through the barracks. The surviving defenders hit the floor. The lead was immediately followed by grenades coming through the windows of the common area. Resistance from the middle barracks ceased.

The fighters of Long Shot swept in the west door as the men of Bad Man came diving through the east door.

"Clear!"

"Clear!"

"Big Daddy, this is Long Shot. All barracks are secure."

****

As the sounds of the assault coming from the administrative side of the compound approached a crescendo, Sneak Thief silently infiltrated the cellblock side, undetected. After verifying that the two easternmost cellblocks were indeed empty, the men fanned out to the occupied units.

Three SEALs materialized in the dark around RH11, the middle cellblock on the north side of the compound. Two assumed an assault stance on either side of the cellblock outer door and the third quietly taped a small shaped charge to the door handle, and then took up a position behind his buddies. The leader nodded, and he detonated the charge. With a soft "whoomp" the door blew open, and the SEALs darted in. In less than three seconds the guards inside were dead.

"Clear."

"Clear."

One of the men searched the pockets of the guards and came up with a key. They unlocked but did not open the cellblock door. Taking up assault positions again on either side of the interior door, the one nodded to his buddy. He kicked the door open, the other darted in, and he followed. It was an empty concrete hallway, with three cell doors on either side. The men stealthily advanced down the hall and cautiously inspected each cell.

****

Captain Moshe Shimonah of the IDF listened to the commotion going on outside as he lay on his bunk shivering. Like Simmons, he had been aggressively tortured for the past week. Even the subtle muscle movements of shivering produced agony in the bruised tissue. The explosions, automatic weapons fire, and occasional shouts had told him that the camp was indeed under attack, and the defenders were losing. He wondered who the aggressor was. *The Brits would never do it, they lack the capability. The Americans have the capability but not the resolve*, he thought. *Unless it's an internal insurgency, it must be the Israelis. Except those weapons don't sound like ours. Of course*, he thought, *if it is my people, they'll make it appear as though someone else did it.*

He heard and felt the concussion of the charge that blew open the outer door of his cellblock, and heard the sharp *cracks* as the guards were double-tapped. He backed into the corner of his cell in case more explosives were used. He heard the sound of a key rattling in a lock. There was a pause for perhaps five seconds, and then the sound of the inner hall door being kicked open. Then the cell across from his was opened.

It was time. He called out in Hebrew, "Hello! I am Captain Moshe Shimonah of the IDF. Who is there?"

He heard a response in English from out in the hall, "Hey, Bubba! What language is that, man?"

"Got me, ace," a second voice responded, "Yo! Voice in the dark! Spikka da English, or whatever?"

Moshe would have smiled if it didn't hurt so much. *Typical American cockiness*, he thought. He called back in English, "Yeah, I *spikka da English*, and pretty well, too. I gather you don't speak Hebrew?"

"Nah," said the second voice carelessly, "never took it up. Who are you?"

"I am Captain Moshe Shimonah of the Israeli Defense Forces."

"Hey, buddy, ain't you a long way from home?" asked the first voice.

"Wow! I didn't know that the IDF maintained a base in Siberia! Are you the commandant?" asked the second.

Shimonah groaned a chuckle, couldn't help himself. "Very funny. *Verrry* funny. My presence here is most unintentional, I assure you. Who are you fellows?"

"United States Navy SEALs, at your service. Like a ride home? We just happen to be going in your direction."

He heard his cell door swing open. One of the men turned on a flashlight and in its glow he could see two SEALs standing in front of him, clothed in arctic camouflage and wearing large grins.

"About time you guys got here. I was scheduled for execution later this morning. That was really going to mess up my day. Across the hall you'll find Dr. Oswald Simmons, he's an American scientist from Colorado."

"Sorry, buddy. I guess we're a little late for him. He's dead."

"Dead?" It was more than he could take. Shimonah sank

to his bunk weakly.

****

Sneak Thief found that the troops in the cellblocks were armed only with batons. All of the buildings on the cellblock side of the compound were taken without incident. In three of the buildings the Soviet guards surrendered, saving their own lives.

Within another five minutes all resistance ceased and *Rabbit Hutch* was secure.

Chapter 36

"All platoon commanders meet me in the administration building in ten minutes," Marcus Clausen ordered over his radio.

All over *Rabbit Hutch* men from both sides were dealing with the aftereffects of the battle as the adrenaline slowly ebbed away. Some were discovering cuts, bruises, broken bones, and even bullet and shrapnel wounds that during the intensity of battle had gone unnoticed. Attackers and defenders alike were checking to see if buddies made it through the firefight. The Soviet soldiers were still trying to grasp the idea that an American assault team was in their country—on their turf—and were wondering exactly how that state of affairs had come to be.

Men from Sneak Thief occupied the prison's guard towers, manning the mounted machine guns in case there was an unexpected renewal of hostilities. The doors and locks of cellblocks RH9 and RH10 were still intact, so Clausen designated those buildings to hold Soviet survivors. Injuries, both American and Soviet, were being treated in the small clinic on the prison side of the compound. Thankfully the building was undamaged. As the Soviet soldiers were locked in the cellblocks, Tom Rainer, *Thunderbird's* executive officer, saw that they were provided with adequate medical supplies to continue caring for their wounded until their own people arrived to release them. The Soviet fatalities of the battle were placed in cellblock RH11.

The snow continued to fall. The ugly scenes of combat were giving way to a concealing robe of pure, white snow.

****

Falcon shouldered past the members of Sneak Thief as Moshe Shimonah was strapped to a stretcher they had found in the clinic building. He looked down at the Israeli and grinned.

"Hey, Moshe! How's it goin'?"

"Hey Jake!" Shimonah replied. The men of *Thunderbird* looked at each other with quizzical expressions. Except for Rainer and Clausen none of them knew Kelly by his real name.

"Great to see you again, buddy," Shimonah said. "I was wonderin' if you were mixed up with this bunch. Sure took you long enough to get here. You've been gone for, what, seventeen months?"

"Yeah, I ran into minor problem here, a delay there. You know how it is when the whole Red Army is on your heels and everyone wants to shoot you, right? Funny how that can slow you down, eh?"

The soldier grimaced as a jolt of pain shot through him, then smiled and replied weakly, "Yeah, guess that might slow you up a bit."

"So how are you, really?"

"Not so good, Jake. Chernikov's been taking his anger out on Oz and me. Been pretty ugly. I'm not sure I've got a bone above the waist that's not broken. Have you been across the hall yet?"

"No, why?"

"Oz didn't make it, Jacob. Died some time in the last hour or so. The Sovs beat him to a pulp every night in the mess hall, in front of the rest of us. I'd guess he died of internal injuries, I don't know. We were both scheduled to be shot at breakfast tomorrow, or today, anyway."

Kelly swallowed hard, and waited for the lump in his throat to subside before he answered hoarsely, "I'm so sorry, Moshe. I'm so sorry we didn't get here sooner."

"Not your fault, Kelly. Not anyone's fault, except the Sovs', I guess. Oz always knew you would come back. He was sitting outside Chernikov's office when the report of your escape came through. Laughed his head off. Cherny didn't take that too kindly, and made him pay for it, but Oz didn't care."

The soldiers attending the Israeli finished their work and gave a slight nod to Falcon. He stepped out of the way and the men picked up the stretcher.

"Take care of yourself, Moshe. I'll be around. We'll talk more after the extraction."

"See you later, Jake. Thanks for stopping by."

****

"First things first. What's the casualty count, Tom?" Clausen asked.

"We lost ten men, five from Long Shot and five from Bad Man. I've got a list for you. There are other injuries but all minor. Both Sneak Thief and Point Guard got off without a scratch."

"Ed, what is the report from the prison compound? How are the hostages?" asked Clausen as he rubbed his face with his hands.

Bausch looked up wearily. "We have recovered nine hostages, but one of them died shortly before we got to him. Another has multiple broken bones, bruises, contusions, and possible internal injuries. The rest are very weak, but I think they will all make it. We've got them wrapped in blankets with heat sticks."

"What about the Russians?" Marcus asked. Clausen was constantly amazed by his XO. Tom Rainer was one of the most organized, detailed men that he knew. He was a superb warrior, a first-class planner, and still somehow managed to have all the details at his fingertips.

"As far as the enlisted men go, forty-two are dead, and another twenty-five are wounded with something more than just cuts and bruises. Some of those won't make it until dawn. There's another thirty men without much more than a scrape or two."

"Officers?"

"The commandant is dead, as are most of the officers. The camp doctor is unscathed, and he is attending to their wounded. I made sure he has all the supplies he needs. The senior officer still alive is a Lieutenant Andropov. Ed's boys pulled him out from under some rubble in the administration building." Tom stood by impassively and pulled out a candy bar.

"Is he in any condition to talk?"

"Oh, yeah. He's a little bloody, but he'll live to fight another day," replied Tom, munching as he spoke.

"Okay, have him brought to me under guard.

"Now listen up! Gonzales, you take what's left of Bad Man and wire these buildings for demolition. Amos, you take all of Long Shot's machine gun teams and strengthen Point Guard's position below the guard shack on the entry road. Take what's left of the M72s with you.

"Ed, take the rest of your platoon and make sure we don't have any problem from the prisoners. I want 'em locked up, but situated properly with blankets and water and food. You can also give 'em the two kerosene heaters you found in the mess hall, so they don't freeze to death. Then, Ed, deal with the fatalities. Stack the bad guys in RH11—and Julio, don't wire that one—then take the bodies of our men down to the containers and prepare them for transport.

"Jerry, take Sneak Thief and transport the hostages and all of our wounded down to the sawmill. See if you can dig up the keys of that *Ural* somewhere, and give them a ride down. Make sure you leave it parked up here when you're done. We don't want anything to connect what happened here with that logging operation. We still need to get home!

"Tom, take Falcon, Andy, and Annie Oakley and scour this camp for all the intelligence info you can find. If any of these scientists broke under interrogation, maybe the transcripts are still here and we can reel them in."

****

"Lieutenant Andropov. That's your name, correct?" Marcus asked, harshly.

"*Da.* I will tell you nothing else." The man's uniform was bloodstained and he had a bandage on his head. His eyes sparked with defiance.

"Are your men being properly cared for?" Marcus queried, a little more gently.

"*Da, spasibo.*"

"Very good. Your commanding officer is General Nikolai Chern—"

Andropov cut him off, angrily insisting, "I am not required to tell you anything!"

"*Shut up*, Lieutenant! I am *telling* you that Chernikov is your commanding officer, not asking you! We already know everything we need to know. I won't be interrogating you or any of your men. Is that clear?"

"*Da*, Commander," Andropov replied grudgingly.

"Okay. I have an officer who wants a private word with you, wants you to deliver a personal message to Chernikov. Will you consent to do that?"

Andropov looked confused. "I don't understand."

"Join the crowd. I don't understand either. Will you talk to him? Yes or no?"

After a pause, Andropov nodded. "*Da*, Commander, I will talk to this officer and deliver the message to the general."

"Good. I'll send for him. You and your men will be locked in the cellblocks with blankets, water, and food. You will not be harmed. But anyone who resists will be shot without mercy. Do you understand?"

"*Da.*"

"We are going to demolish the rest of the camp before we leave. You and your men will hear explosions. You do not need to fear, no harm will come to you. If we were of a mind to kill you we'd do it right now. Understand?"

"*Da.*"

"Our ambassador will notify your people that you men are here, so that your people can come up here and release you."

"May I ask you a question, sir?"

"You can ask. I may not answer."

"This is our homeland. We are not at war with the US. Why have you done this? Why have you attacked us in our homeland? Do you have any idea of the hornet's nest you have just kicked over?"

"Your command of English, Lieutenant, is quite good. I compliment you. But I am going to answer your question with a question of my own," Clausen replied. Then he raised his voice and got in Andropov's face, all the anger and bitterness of his losses surfacing, "What in the name of God's green earth were you friggin' people thinking when you committed acts of war against five nations by kidnapping their citizens? None of *us* were at war with *you*! What did you expect us to do, abandon our own?"

With some effort, Marcus Clausen controlled his anger and backed off. He said quietly between gritted teeth, "No, Lieutenant, there will be no war. If your country so much as raises a *finger* in retaliation for this raid, these hostages your country kidnapped will be paraded before the cameras of the world and they will tell their story. If that happens, the USSR will not be able to *buy* a friend on the planet.

"Now, mister, I am done with you and your people. Wait here. One of my men wants to talk to you."

A moment later Jacob Kelly walked in the door. In his hand was General Chernikov's soldering pencil. "Lieutenant Andropov, I want you to deliver a message to General Chernikov. Tell him that Major Jacob Kelly sends his regards. Tell him that I will be visiting him soon, and I will have his soldering pencil with me. Ask him on which of his shoulders he wants me to burn these words: *I love Uncle Sam*. Tell him that after I have burnt it onto his shoulder, I will kill him."

Chapter 37

Monday, December 21, 1987: 0815 hours, local time
Magadan, USSR

Major General Nikolai Chernikov sat at his desk looking at the mound of paperwork requiring his attention. He grimaced. *When did I let soldiering turn into signing requisition slips? Think I'd like a do-over on that decision.* He took a long sip of tea and looked out the window. *Can't wait until spring. I hate winter —especially here in northern nowhere.*

Sighing, he picked up the first stack, a boring mix of supply requisitions and bureaucratic demands from Moscow for more reports. Riffling through the papers quickly, he came across the prison camp duty log for the prior week. The general leafed through it, skimming it for anything of significance. Among the routine notations of shift changes, ill soldiers reporting to the clinic, and the coming and going of vehicles and such, there were entries for three evenings noting that the guard dogs were barking *"frantically."* Brow furrowed, Chernikov put down the other papers and began reading carefully.

The log recorded that on each of the first two nights that the dogs were barking, the watch officer had written, *"Requested permission to send out a patrol to investigate. Permission denied."* The watch officer had been Victor Andropov, an experienced combat veteran whose judgment Chernikov trusted.

Major Aleksei Promokov, the acting commandant who had shot down Andropov's requests was, on the other hand, a toady of some powerful patron back in Moscow. Promokov had no combat experience and even less wisdom. Chernikov suspected that he was a spy of Anatoly Geredin. In any case the orders had come from above leaving Chernikov no choice but to appoint the man as his second-in-command and the acting camp commandant whenever Chernikov himself was absent.

When Chernikov read the entry written by the watch officer on Friday the 18th, he slammed his fist down on the desk and roared for his secretary. "Olga Anatolyevna! Come in here NOW!" He was shaking with rage. The offending entry read:

> *18.12.1987:0930 Sgts Titov and Mikhailov dispatched to Magadan for supplies and to return dogs. Dogs being returned to kennel for more training, by order of Commandant.*

"General, my goodness, what is it?" the worried woman asked as she ran into the room.

Barely able to contain his fury, Chernikov asked through clenched teeth, "Did they *really* send the dogs back on Friday?"

"Why, yes, sir! They did! Sergeant Titov mentioned to me that the commandant had grown weary of their barking. Is anything wrong?"

Chernikov picked up his mug and hurled it into the corner of the room, shattering it. "THE FOOL!" he shouted, "THE MAN IS A FOOL! HE IS NOT FIT TO POLISH HIS OWN BOOTS!"

His secretary was speechless. She had seen Chernikov angry, but never like this.

He sat down, trembling, his face crimson with rage. With great effort he controlled himself and offered stiffly, "I am sorry, Olga Anatolyevna, forgive me. I am outraged, but not at you. Please get the commandant on the phone for me while I try to calm down."

She hurried back to her office. Returning a moment later, she said "They are not answering, sir."

"What?"

"They are not answering the phone. It just rings and rings."

"The line is probably down because of the snowstorm. Have Leonid raise them on the radio."

He looked with regret at his favorite mug, now shattered, and the pool of tea on the floor. Ever since the problem with

Jacob Kelly, Chernikov had found himself giving in to uncontrolled outbursts of anger. He shook his head and rebuked himself. *You are a professional, Nikolai, you must not indulge your anger! Get hold of yourself! There's too much at stake!*

His secretary walked in again, puzzled.

"What is it, Olga Anatolyevna?"

"They are not answering the radio either, General. That's very unusual."

His mouth went dry. On a hunch, he picked up his phone and got a connection to the GRU office in Vladivostok.

"*Dobroye utro*, Sergei. This is Nikolai in Magadan. Have you seen the morning intelligence briefing? Good. Is there any unusual military activity in our area? What? The *Vinson* is parked off the Kurils? Why? Hmm. Let's hope it really is for ASW exercises. *Spasibo*, Sergei."

He barked at his secretary, who was still standing in his doorway, "Olga Anatolyevna, round up as many of my men as you can locate. Make sure they bring their weapons and ammunition. Find enough vehicles to transport them. I want to leave for the camp within the hour."

"Sir! The snowstorm! You can't get through."

"You'll just have to find a couple of snowplows to go ahead of us. Commandeer whatever the city's got, on my authority. Now hurry, there is no time to lose!"

****

The *Kolymskaya trassa*, the M56, was completely snowed in —at least twelve inches deep. The snow had stopped falling, but the howling wind was whipping it up and creating near whiteout conditions, piling up deep drifts. Only large trucks with chains on their tires were on the road—nothing else was moving. Chernikov's small convoy of three vehicles and two snowplows moved slowly but steadily north up the highway. Halfway to Sokol they passed four container trucks going in the opposite direction. As soon as they passed, the southbound trucks pulled into the lane cleared by Chernikov's northbound snowplows. There was little other traffic on the road.

At Sokol, Chernikov's group turned west and drove past Molochnaya, headed for the turnoff to the detention camp. The road condition steadily worsened, but the two big plows created a double-lane width of driveable roadway.

What Chernikov did not realize was that his snowplows were obliterating the record left in the snow of Operation *Thunderbird*. The plows scooped aside footprints and tire tracks alike, and the fact that Marcus Clausen had confined his men to the road on the way up to the camp now worked greatly in the Americans' favor.

At the entrance to the facility's access road the plows turned in and began laboring up the rough, rocky track to the prison camp. The first five hundred meters climbed steeply, but the drivers had attached chains before leaving Magadan and they gamely fishtailed up the road behind the plows. Intent upon their work the plow drivers moved right past the guard shack and continued up the road, not noticing anything amiss.

But Chernikov halted his small convoy of vehicles. He spotted the broken windows immediately and with a sinking heart knew what he would find. Drawing his pistol, he exited the car and waded through the deep snow to the shack. The lights were out and the glass that remained unbroken was frosted over. He opened the door, and stared.

Blood had spattered the walls and was puddled, frozen, on the floor, but the small shack was otherwise empty—the bodies had been removed. Chernikov studied the bullet holes in the glass windows. "Snipers," he muttered. He stepped out of the shack. Leading off into the woods was the merest hint of a depression in the snow, where the attacker or attackers had approached to inspect their handiwork. Trying to follow that trail would be virtually impossible.

The radio bleeped on his belt. He unclipped it, and said, "Yes?"

"Comrade General, you need to see this." It was one the plow operators. The man's strained tone, apparent even over the scratchy radio transmission, propelled Chernikov into action.

"Back to the cars! Hurry!"

****

Kim Choson heard the radio crackle in the small radio room of the *Lady of Singapore*. His first mate brought the message. Four more containers bound for Otaru had just entered the terminal. Would the *Lady* care to deliver them?

"Yes, signal that we will take them on," replied Kim Choson. Perhaps the profit of the delivery would offset the extra time they had had to spend in port repairing the steering system.

Oddly enough, a fault had also been discovered in the hydraulic lifts on the hatch covers, so the four containers had to be lashed onto the deck, rather than placed in the hold.

Twenty minutes after the containers came aboard the second engineer located the problems in the steering hydraulics. An hour later the *Lady* slipped her moorings at Magadan and steamed out of the harbor, bound for Otaru. Two hours out, the engineering department reported that the balky hatch covers had also been repaired.

****

The scent of cordite assaulted his nostrils before they arrived at the camp. Ahead he could see the two large snow-plows idling in the middle of the forest track. The drivers were standing together in the snow, hands on their hips, shaking their heads.

"Yuri, pull up behind them," he snapped impatiently. *Be calm, Nikolai, remain calm.*

Chernikov climbed out of the car and waded through the snow toward the drivers. When he passed the plow he could finally see what they were so disturbed about. Though the surrounding fence appeared to be largely intact, the camp within looked like a war zone. Black smoke was billowing out of what used to be the physical plant building. Only part of one wall remained standing. Where the administration building had been was now little more than a snow-covered ruin. Here and there fires still smoldered under the blackened rubble, tendrils of smoke rising into the frigid air. Little remained of the barracks. Three of the prisoner cellblocks and the clinic appeared to be untouched, but the other structures were demolished. The guard towers were gone, jumbled mounds of snow with twisted shards of steel the only evidence of where they had once stood. The smell of death was strong. Affixed to the front gate was a large American flag.

Chernikov stumbled, and sat down in the snow. A silent crowd of men gathered behind him, stunned at the sight. No one said anything for several minutes.

"Sir? We'd better report this," said an aide, finally finding his voice.

Chernikov came to himself. He wrestled through the snow to his feet, turned around and glared at the unfortunate, rage coursing through his face. The gathered men shrank back. He drew his pistol and pointed it in the face of the man who had dared to speak, snarling venomously, "It is not your job, *Efreitor*, to report *anything*. Is that clear? I will make my report when I am good and ready! Understood?"

Trembling before Chernikov's rage, the soldier hoarsely replied, "*Da*, Comrade General! Of course, sir."

Chernikov blinked. With great effort he got himself under control and holstered his pistol. He ordered, "Search the camp! All of you. And Yuri, get that—that—flag off the fence and *BURN IT*!"

Five minutes later, Yuri Slavin shouted across the compound, "General Chernikov, survivors!"

Every man began running toward Slavin, who was standing outside one of the intact cellblocks. Chernikov slogged through the snow and entered the building. The outer door had been blown off its hinges, but the inner door was locked. Within the inner door the cellblock was packed with shivering soldiers, looking on in dazed silence. A key was sitting on top of the desk in the tiny outer room, with a note under it.

Chernikov picked up the key and examined the note.

> *Dear General Chernikov,*
>
> *This cellblock and the next one contain survivors. The one beyond that contains your dead. We tried to handle them with respect. We did not want to demolish the structures with the bodies still in them. Your men put up a valiant and courageous fight. You should be proud of them.*
>
> *Lieutenant Andropov has a message for you from Major Jacob Kelly, USAF. I believe you have met him. Kelly wanted to deliver the message personally, but we were unable to wait for your arrival. I'm sure you understand.*
>
> *Sincerely yours,*
>
> *Cdr. Marcus Clausen, USN, SEAL Team Three*

****

Over the next half hour Chernikov demonstrated why he'd been such an outstanding combat commander. He began issuing orders immediately. His men turned to, relieved that someone was taking charge. An empty room in the clinic was pressed into service as a temporary headquarters for Chernikov. Before long the plows had cleared the camp parking lot. Buses and medical personnel were following a new set of plows from Magadan and would arrive in the next hour. The Ural had been left undamaged with the keys in it—a courtesy of the Americans—and Chernikov detailed men to begin ferrying the injured to Sokol where they would be airlifted to the hospital in Vladivostok.

One of the survivors had heard the Americans talking about the airport at Sokol. *Perhaps that is how they intend to extract the SEALs,* Chernikov thought. Gathering all his men—including those without serious injury from the prison camp itself—Chernikov armed a force of forty-eight and positioned them around the Sokol Airport lest the SEALs try to secure it by force and extract via air. He also ordered up a pair of fighters from Petropavlosk-Kamchatskiy to orbit the airfield, just in case.

The snowstorm finally blew itself north into the Chukchi

Sea. The sky cleared, though the wind was picking up and the temperature dropping.

****

"Victor, I am relieved to see you alive. How are you feeling?" Chernikov's warmth toward the lieutenant was genuine. Andropov's *Spetsnaz* unit had been rotated into the prison camp a month earlier, and his demeanor and the way in which he led his men had earned the general's respect.

"Comrade General, I am furious—outraged! Permission to speak freely?"

"Please."

"This is all the fault of the acting commandant, the late Major Aleksei Promokov. I tried to warn him last week, sir, that the guard dogs were detecting intruders. He dismissed my concerns, saying that he himself owned a German Shepherd and that he knew how to read a dog's bark. The guard dogs were detecting deer, he said, sir."

"Go on."

"After several nights of barking, he had the dogs returned to Magadan. I tried to get him to send out patrols, but he refused. *'Intruders?'* he said, *'nonsense, Andropov! We are in Siberia. We don't get intruders in Siberia!'* That's what he said, sir. I don't mean to speak ill of the dead, but he was a *fool*, Comrade General. And because he was a fool, forty-nine *Spetsnaz* are dead. *My* comrades! That is inexcusable, sir!"

Chernikov waved him to a chair, slopped some vodka into a mug and gave it to the distraught lieutenant. "*Da*, Victor, I know. I agree. He was a fool. But I was given no choice. I was told by people I cannot disobey that Promokov was to be my second-in-command and the commandant in my absence."

Andropov nodded, but said nothing, not trusting his voice. Chernikov waited a few minutes, and then said quietly, "Tell me about the assault, Victor."

Andropov wiped his eyes on his sleeve and knocked back the vodka, then said hoarsely, "We were on a rotating shift, but I think they must have had us under surveillance for several weeks and picked up the pattern. The shift changed at 2200 hours, the attack came at midnight. They blew our power and phone lines just before the assault.

"The attack vectors were flawless. Surely they had satellite photography of the camp to plan as well as they did. Even if we had been awake and expecting them, the groups that hit us from the west and northwest were mostly shielded from our fire by the buildings themselves. The windows and doors from which we could have fought back were covered by well-sited machine guns. It was a slaughter, General.

"One thing I realized, Comrade General, after the assault began," Andropov said with frustration, "this camp was not designed to withstand an assault from the outside. It was not designed with defense in mind."

Chernikov nodded, "*Pravda*. Go on."

Andropov continued, "We tried to send out a distress call with the main radio, but they were jamming us. They came through the fence in two places and destroyed the generator and the radio. Once the generator was out of action we had no lights. *All* their men had NVGs. We had ten sets. Ten," he repeated bitterly, shaking his head.

"What about the guard towers?"

"All of them taken out by snipers, first thing. I talked to one of the tower guards. He took a round through the neck, nearly bled to death. Lucky to be alive. He said he was shot before the power went out the first time. They must have used silenced weapons.

"Sir, it was a well-planned, professional assault. They had just the right amount of firepower, and knew exactly where to place it. We were trapped in the buildings. Anyone who exited was immediately cut down by their machine guns. We didn't have a chance, sir, not a chance."

"I was told that you had a message for me."

"It was nothing, Comrade General. Just some taunting from the winners to the losers." Andropov looked at the floor, would not face Chernikov.

"You are reluctant, Lieutenant."

"It was nothing, sir. Nothing I should bother you with,

General. A little bravado, nothing more."

"Tell me, Lieutenant. That's an order."

"One of their officers came to me after it was all over. He said to tell you that Major Kelly sends his regards, and that he will be visiting you soon. He was holding your soldering pencil, sir. 'Tell him I will have his soldering pencil with me.' I am to ask you on which shoulder you wish him to burn, 'I love Uncle Sam.'"

"Is that all?"

"*Nyet*, Comrade General. He said that after he burnt those words on your shoulder, he would kill you."

When Chernikov did not respond, Victor looked up. The general was staring at him but the faraway look in his eyes told Victor he was seeing someone else. Chernikov blinked twice, and then said softly, "That is all, Lieutenant. You may go. *Spasibo.*"

After the lieutenant left the room, Chernikov reached for the bottle and had another shot of vodka. Things were, he reflected, spinning out of control. With a sour smile he thought, *If Kelly doesn't hurry back he's going to have to stand in line. After this, there will be many who want my scalp.*

Chapter 38

Tuesday, December 22, 1987: 1410 hours, local time
Sokol, USSR

Chernikov set up an operations center in a deserted hangar at the Sokol Airport. The force guarding the airport had been replaced overnight by two companies of infantry from Vladivostok. Having been released from military duties around the airport, Chernikov's *Spetsnaz* troops were now conducting house-to-house searches in Magadan and Sokol.

The general was puzzled. By all accounts it had been a large force that assaulted the camp. Estimates by the surviving officers ranged from eighty to one hundred twenty attackers. Such a force with all its equipment could hardly infiltrate the country by a rubber boat launched from a submarine. *How did they get here? Where are they now? How are they planning to exfil? Have they already been extracted?*

The hangar door banged open and one of his agents came in. "We have a lead, sir. We just located a Wartburg 311 automobile in the airport parking lot that no one can account for. Our men are going over it now. We are trying to find the owner. The keys were left in the ignition, sir."

"In the ignition?"

"Yes, sir."

Such a thing was highly unlikely in a place where even windshield wipers on an unattended car tended to disappear. Perhaps the owner was nearby. Or perhaps the car had been abandoned?

"We are researching the license plates now, Comrade General. I'll let you know as soon as we have anything."

****

Admiral Bridger paced anxiously on the bridge of the *Carl Vinson*. He watched as two S-3 Vikings were catapulted off the flight deck. The Vikings were maintaining an ASW screen around the carrier, in concert with a pair of attack submarines and four destroyers. The Soviets appeared to have bitten hard on the story that the carrier group was in the area for an ASW exercise. An Ilyushin IL-38 May was shadowing the carrier group. Meanwhile, two of the carrier's own EA-3A Skywarriors were orbiting, doing a little snooping for the good guys. While they were gathering ELINT their pilots knew that their missions might change to electronic warfare (EW) at any moment.

"John, just got word—we've picked up the tracking beacon. The containers must have been delivered on time. They're on the *Lady* and it's underway." Captain Arthur Young put a fresh mug of hot coffee in Bridger's hand.

Bridger exhaled a sigh of relief. The last word they had had from Operation *Thunderbird* was early yesterday morning. The team had signaled that the assault had been successful. But once they re-entered the containers, communication was no longer possible.

Once the *Lady of Singapore* was two hundred miles out of Magadan, one of the CIA plants on board had placed a tracking beacon on all four containers. About every sixty minutes (the period varied), the beacons would send a burst that was picked up by satellites. The brief transmission enabled the trackers to triangulate the position.

"How many more hours before they are within range of us, Art?"

"Sixteen. Not much we can do to help until then. Not unless we plan to start a war."

"Let's hope that's not necessary."

"We're good so far, Admiral. None of my electronic snoops have picked up anything threatening. I checked with Jesse Pierce five minutes ago, and they aren't detecting anything either. Your CIA buddies haven't intercepted any unusual message traffic. If we can just hang in there another sixteen hours, we're almost home free. At that point your boys will be within range of my choppers."

****

"Comrade General, the Wartburg is attached to a Party *dacha* in Magadan, and is available to whoever the occupants are. The *dacha* is presently signed out to Benjamin and Katerina Klausowitz. The Klausowitzes are retired Party officials who were serving in Moscow at the time of their retirement. They arrived in the Magadan *Oblast* via the Sokol Airport on 3 November. Our men searched the *dacha*; there's no sign of the Klausowitzes nor their belongings. It appears they have vacated the premises. They were last seen at a bar on Saturday night."

Chernikov nodded. "Good work. But it does not sound related to our situation. They arrived by plane—now they have flown home to Moscow. They must have left the auto here by agreement."

"Respectfully, *nyet*, sir. We've already checked all flight manifests. They weren't listed on any flight. Besides, the airport was shut down from midmorning Sunday until yesterday morning because of the weather. And judging from the depth of the snow on it, the car was parked here during the storm."

"You think the car is related to what happened at the prison camp?"

"*Da*, Comrade General. I'd say it's likely. It's also our only lead."

"*Pravda*. Okay, keep on it. Meanwhile, perhaps something else will turn up."

Something else did. Chernikov's GRU agents circulated through the bars in Sokol and Magadan and every other nearby town with pictures of the Wartburg. At 1830 they located a patron who claimed to have seen the car in the lot of Edvard Golinskiy's sawmill.

A search of the sawmill turned up several things. In the mill yard, there were four different sets of tire tracks leading to the main road. Judging from their size and depth, they were made by heavily loaded trucks. The vehicles had departed at some point not long after the snow stopped. Because the main road had been plowed, it was impossible to follow the tracks. Splotches of blood stained the snow here and there.

At Chernikov's instructions the picture of the Wartburg was also circulated among the survivors of the assault. Two young soldiers identified the car as belonging to a couple who gave them a ride to Magadan when the Ural had broken down, and who had kindly invited them to their *dacha* for a home-cooked meal.

The net was beginning to close.

****

The pounding on the door finally penetrated his alcohol-soaked brain, and a very hung-over Edvard Golinskiy dragged himself reluctantly from bed, threw on a robe, and stumbled to the door.

"Who is it?" he called thickly through the closed door.

"Military police. Open the door immediately or we will break it down."

Military police? he thought, *What could they possibly want with me?* As was true of most of the locals, he knew nothing of the prison camp.

"Okay," he said, opening the door, "*Pozhaluysta.*"

Mikhail Udovin, the GRU investigator, noting his bleary appearance, said, "We have a missing couple and we need help locating them. Have you ever seen this car?"

Fear can make the drunkest individual sober up in a hurry. Golinskiy paled and remained silent for a moment, thinking. Honesty, he decided, would be the only way he could emerge from this with his life intact. Despite the casualness of the question Golinskiy figured that something, some piece of evidence, had led the officer to his door. *Igor, ol' buddy, it's every man for himself.*

"Yes, I have. A fellow named Igor Mendel visited my sawmill in that car a month or so ago."

"What did he want?"

"He claimed to be representing Mikhail Alekseyevich

Promyslov, the former mayor of Moscow. He saw that my yard is equipped to handle containers, and said that Promyslov was building a *dacha* in the area, importing his building materials from Japan in four containers. He hired me to pick up the containers from the port."

The investigator watched Golinskiy closely, and was surprised by his cooperation. He was convinced that the man was being truthful.

"And how about the inspections of the containers, import fees, and so on?"

Here Edvard lied as slyly as he could. "He told me he would take care of that. He needed my import and export connections to bring the containers in and send them out again, and my equipment to handle them."

"Send them out? Why would he need to send them out?"

"I do not know, I am just telling you what he told me."

The investigator stared at him for a long moment. Golinskiy felt sweat breaking out on his forehead.

"Why are you sweating?"

"Because I am frightened," Edvard replied truthfully.

"Why? Have you done something wrong?"

"Pardon, comrade, *nyet*, I have not. But from what I have heard it doesn't much matter whether one has done wrong or not when the military police or the KGB is involved. I have done nothing wrong and I have answered everything you asked truthfully. But, *da*, you do frighten me," Edvard admitted.

"When do the containers come in, and when do they leave?"

"They already came in. They came in on Sunday and left on Monday."

"Why so quickly?"

"It's the nature of containerized cargo. Time is money. They keep everything moving," said Golinskiy, shrugging his shoulders and holding up his hands.

"What ship?"

"*The Lady of Singapore.*"

"Take him into custody," Mikhail ordered despite Golin-

skiy's howls of protest. "After all, we must maintain our reputation," he said dryly.

****

The phone rang in the hangar. Chernikov jumped. The
hour was drawing late on a busy day, and he'd been dozing in
his chair. He picked up the receiver.

"Chernikov," he said shortly.

"It's Udovin, Nikolai Pavlovich. I think I know how the
Americans got here and left again—containerized cargo. The
sawmill right below the camp received four containers midday
Sunday and shipped them out again yesterday. The assault was
Sunday night. If I am correct they shipped out on the *Lady of
Singapore*, between noon and 1300 hours yesterday."

"*Molodets*, Mikhail! It makes sense: four containers would
be plenty big enough for their assault force. I think you are
right! Listen, get down to the port, wake up the harbor master
and verify as much of the story as you can. Get back to me as
soon as you can. In the meantime, I've got a ship to stop."

The general hung up the phone and held his head in his
hands. From the discovery of the raid until this moment he
had managed to avoid calling GRU headquarters. The extra
troops and assets he had obtained to search for the attackers
—even the two fighters—he had received on the basis of his
own clout within the Far East Military District. He'd hoped to
recover the situation before reporting it. It was beyond that
now. He required the support of the Red Banner Pacific Fleet,
extensive air assets, and permission to board and search a ship
on the high seas—all beyond his paygrade to engineer, manip-
ulate, or cajole. It was time to call General Patrikeyev. Only he
possessed connections sufficient to reel in that freighter.
Chernikov knew the remainder of his career could be mea-
sured in days, maybe hours—but it had to be done. He picked
up the phone and dialed the number.

"Patrikeyev."

"General, this is Chernikov. Could you go secure, please,
sir?"

"Certainly, Nikolai." Both men adjusted their scramblers to the code of the day. When the whistling ceased, Patrikeyev continued, *"Dobryy dyen'*, Nikolai. What do you have to report?"

"Comrade General, there's no easy way to say this so I won't attempt to sugar-coat it. About forty-eight hours ago our new prison facility for Project *Krasnyy Voskhod* suffered a powerful attack by American special forces—SEALs, sir. They overwhelmed the troops at the facility, rescued the scientists, and destroyed the compound. We've conducted a massive search effort, trying to locate the assaulting force before they can get away. Our initial leads indicated that they intended to extract through the airport at Sokol, so we secured the area to deny that option. But we've just received intelligence, sir, indicating they extracted yesterday morning through the port of Magadan in cargo containers. The freighter, the *Lady of Singapore*, is still within reach, sir, but I need your authority to seize it."

Silence greeted him. Finally General Patrikeyev responded icily, "General Chernikov, you say this assault happened two days ago. Why am I not hearing about it until now?"

"Comrade General, I myself did not learn of the attack until about thirty six hours ago. I—I thought I could recover the situation. The assaulting force was large enough that I believed we would detect their movement before they could exfiltrate, sir." Chernikov sighed with resignation, and then added, "Frankly, sir, it would have been easier to report the attack if I had also been able to report the recapture of the scientists and the defeat of the American forces."

"YOU ARE A FOOL, NIKOLAI!" Patrikeyev shouted into the telephone. "This attack has grave international implications. The entire Far East Military District and the Red Banner Pacific Fleet should have been placed on high alert immediately. We could have stopped all shipping in the area, interdicted all aircraft. Now they have gotten away and YOU ARE RESPONSIBLE! Because of your pride you have ruined not only your own career, comrade, you have ruined mine and you have put the *Rodina* in grave danger!"

"Sir, they haven't gotten away! I know right where they are! If you will provide the necessary authorizations, we can stop the ship and capture them."

"Nikolai, how could this happen? Did you have no warning?"

"We did, sir. The guard dogs detected the intruders several days before the assault. I was in Moscow, Promokov was serving as acting commandant. That idiot decided he didn't like the racket the dogs were raising and instead of sending out patrols to investigate he sent the dogs back to Magadan. He did not report any of this to me. I did not know of it until reading the camp duty logs yesterday morning. I investigated and found the camp a smoking wreck. Sir, you know I *vigorously* objected when Promokov was attached to my command. He was a policeman, not a soldier, sir."

"Was?"

"*Da*, Comrade General, *was*. The glorious Promokov died hiding under a bed during the assault," Chernikov responded bitterly.

The two men discussed the assault and the intelligence pointing to the *Lady of Singapore*, and then Patrikeyev said, "Nikolai, you are not responsible for the assault, but you grievously erred when you failed to report it to me immediately. You allowed your own ambition to outweigh the need of the Soviet Union, and you have placed the nation in danger. You are relieved, comrade, as of this moment. You are to report to me here in Moscow within twenty-four hours. I will handle the remainder of this situation."

Major General Nikolai Pavlovich Chernikov slowly hung up the phone and stared at it for several moments. His illustrious career was finished. An overwhelming sense of weariness and defeat came over him. He looked at his aide, Staff Sergeant Yuri Slavin, who was doubling as the night desk duty officer. Slavin had been eavesdropping on Chernikov's side of the conversation while studiously trying to appear as if he was ignoring it.

"Yuri, bring Lieutenant Andropov to me—immediately. And get someone else to handle tonight's watch. Take the

Ural." Andropov and his men were bivouacked in an empty hangar a kilometer away. Slavin grabbed the keys and stepped out into the frigid night. He returned fifteen minutes later with the lieutenant in tow and a sergeant to handle watch duty.

"Lieutenant, have a seat. I have been relieved of command. You are now the senior officer of our *Spetsnaz* troops here in the *oblast*. Tomorrow morning you are to shut this operation down and prepare the troops to be airlifted to Vladivostok. If anyone has anything to report, make sure that it gets immediately to GRU, Vladivostok. If Mikhail Udovin calls tell him to report directly to Vladivostok, but then have him call me at my apartment. I'm going home to get several hours of sleep. In the morning I will return to Moscow.

"Yuri, soon as I can put Andropov's orders in writing, turn the duty desk over to your relief, and drive me home."

****

Phones started ringing all at once in the Combat Direction Center of the *Vinson*.

"Captain, it's Dr. Jensen," said a young lieutenant, holding a red phone.

Another officer reported, "Captain, Commander Santini is reporting increased radio traffic around Vladivostok on the military channels."

Young nodded, then took the red receiver. "Young here," he said brusquely.

"Art, this is Bill Jensen. Just got a message from Sam Bergman. Apparently Ivan has figured it out. The NSA intercepted several signals from Moscow's GRU HQ to Vladivostok, putting the Red Banner Pacific Fleet on high alert, and directing that the *Lady of Singapore* be stopped on the high seas, searched, and seized if necessary. I was afraid this would happen. Art, you've got to get there first and get our people out of there.

"I probably don't need to draw a picture for you, Captain, but listen. If we don't get those scientists back, the US is in deep trouble. We've engaged in a military action on their homeland, killing fifty-some-odd people and destroying a facility. Getting those scientists back is the only way we can justify our actions to the world. If the Soviets get there first they will direct the ship into a Soviet port and remove the containers. The scientists will be killed, our SEALs will be executed, and *we* will be held over precisely the same barrel in the United Nations that we were planning on holding them over. We will be turned into international pariahs.

"So, Art, you've got to grab those containers before they do. Whatever it takes."

****

The eight Super Stallions had been fueled and moved to the flight deck several hours ago. They were outfitted with extra-large drop tanks, plus a large fuel bladder lashed into the cargo hold. Two of the choppers each held a force of five SEALs. The SEALs would fast rope down to the *Lady of Singapore*—one group on the bow, another on the stern—and secure the master's cooperation. They would handle the container swap, hopefully with the help of the freighter's deck crew.

Trying to make himself heard above the roar of the powerful General Electric T64-GE-416 turbo-shaft engines, Admiral Bridger shouted into the ear of the lead officer, "Commander, bring 'em home safe. We are counting on you, and so are they."

"Don't worry, Admiral," the commander shouted back, "we'll bring 'em back!"

Bridger left the tight cockpit of the helicopter and, crouching down, ran through the prop wash back to the carrier's island. He turned before entering the companionway. The commander was saluting him through the windshield. He returned the salute and gave the man a thumbs up.

The sharp whap-whap-whapping of the seven-bladed prop increased in intensity, and the eight helicopters took off in succession and formed up about a quarter mile off the starboard bow. One by one, four of the Stallions flew back to the ship. Each was mated with an empty container. After all four decoys had been picked up the Super Stallions disappeared over the horizon to the northwest. They stayed low on the water, trying to fly beneath the radar and forestalling detection until the last possible minute. Captain Young was watching from the bridge. *Vaya con Dios*, he murmured as the choppers flew out of sight.

Twenty minutes later, four EA-6B Prowlers from the famous VAQ-138 Yellow Jackets squadron were launched in succession by the *Vinson's* catapults. Each aircraft was carrying external ECM pods. Their mission was to render the Super Stallions invisible to Soviet radar by generating dozens of false targets.

One Prowler flew at wave-skimming height north-north-east. Its track took it at extremely low altitude through the Boussole Strait, between the islands of Urup and Simushir, and then off to the northwest to take up a position about one hundred fifty miles due east of where the Stallions would intercept the *Lady*. A second EA-6B screamed off to the southwest, and would navigate the gap between Kunashir and Itrup, reappearing about one hundred miles south of the *Lady*. The remaining two Prowlers cruised at medium altitude through the Vries Strait to the northwest of the *Vinson*, all lit up like electronic Christmas trees. Their job was to draw attention to themselves and to provide enough distraction that the faint radar signatures of the CH53-E Super Stallions would be lost in the electronic noise.

Adding to the overall effect, the Skywarriors that had been launched several hours ago had been refueled, and then split up. One was orbiting fifty miles northeast of Hokkaido, and the other twenty miles inboard of the Black Brothers, a pair of volcanic islands. Both aircraft were in aggressive positions but not to such a degree so as to provoke a lethal response.

The Prowler and Skywarrior pilots had been instructed to recalculate their bingo fuel destination as the Chitose Air Base in case the carrier's flight deck became too cluttered with choppers and containers. The *Vinson's* CAG was taking no chances.

****

One of the purposes of electronic warfare is to hide in-bound attackers by confusing the enemy's radar. This is usually done by mimicking the enemy's radar signals and returning them to the sender distorted in some very precise ways. As a result the inbound aircraft's apparent position on the enemy's radar is significantly shifted from its actual position. Another counter-measure is to disguise the attacking aircraft with a clutter of electronically generated false targets. The defender's air defense system chases the false targets and the attacker is able to carry out his attack unimpeded. Of course, the *Vinson* was not attacking, but trying to conceal the presence of the eight Super Stallions long enough for them to do the container swap and get back to the ship.

The problem which Captain Young now faced was this: all that electronics warfare gear flying over the Sea of Okhotsk made it quite obvious that the Americans were trying to hide *something*. The natural response of the Soviet forces in the area would be to start looking for what was being hidden. In other words, the attempt to hide the choppers could wind up giving them away.

So the *Vinson* launched something for the Soviets to find, something that would hopefully distract them from the real thing. Captain Young had read Jesse Pierce's report on the penetration of the Petropavlovsk-Kamchatskiy airspace about a month earlier, and had taken a page out of his playbook. An hour and a half after the Prowlers took off, six heavily-armed F-14 Tomcats were launched. Their mission was to make a stealth approach to Dolinsk-Sokol, the airbase just south of Dolinsk on the island of Sakhalin. At the outer range of the air-defense system, they would flare up. The Soviet radar would pick them up and the air defenses would be activated. As the Tomcats fled in retreat the Prowlers and the Skywarriors would light up to protect them, and the Soviets would think they had located the hidden mission that accounted for all the hardware the *Vinson* launched. That was the plan, anyway.

Fifteen minutes later yet another four flights of four F-14s each were shot off the *Vinson's* catapults. One flight served as a combat air patrol on the axis of greatest threat, the northwest. The other three snuck through the various gaps in the Kuril Islands at extremely low altitude in a strict EMCON condition, and managed to position themselves undetected in useful spots to offer something a little more substantial than moral support, in case the worst happened.

****

"Captain Kim, may I trouble you for a moment of your time?" The Korean second engineer had proven his worth many times over in the short time he had been aboard the *Lady of Singapore*. Kim liked the man's soft-spoken but confident demeanor.

"Certainly, Park Chin Ho. What can I do for you?"

Park looked embarrassed, staring at the floor and not raising his eyes. Kim thought he understood and graciously suggested, "Perhaps we should enjoy some of the fresh night air. Let's step out on the bridge wing."

The two men went through the companionway and opened the hatch to the wing. Other than the lights on the freighter itself, the night was black, heavily overcast. It was now just after 2300 hours. Stepping out into the cold night air Kim said kindly, "Now, Mr. Park, how may I help you?"

"Captain, I must explain to you what is about to happen—there's not much time."

"I don't understand, Mr. Park. Is something about to happen?"

"Yes, sir. In about forty-five minutes we will be stopped and boarded by a Soviet missile boat. They are looking for those four containers." Park Chin Ho pointed to the four forty-foot containers lashed to the deck just forward of the after cargo hatch. "They must not find them. If they do, we will be seized and taken to a Soviet port."

Kim Choson stared at his second engineer for a moment without responding. Then he demanded suspiciously, "And how do you know this?"

"I knew this might happen before I came aboard, sir. But I assure you, I am not the cause of it nor am I involved in any way."

"Then how can you know about it?" asked Kim.

"I am afraid I cannot disclose that to you, sir. But please hear me out. In less than three minutes we will be met by eight US Navy helicopters. We must have a deck crew ready, sir. The helicopters will pick up those four containers and leave us four identical but empty ones.

"The Soviets are looking for those containers. We must allow them to inspect them—they will find them to be quite empty. The Russians will let us go and we will have lost maybe an hour." Park Chin Ho spoke so earnestly that Kim Choson was intrigued. What was happening on his ship? What was he carrying?

The master looked down on the four containers for a moment before asking the question that was being shouted out in his brain. "*What* is in those containers, Mister Park?"

"People. Hostages that the Soviets illegally captured and brought to Magadan. And the men that freed them."

"How did they get away?"

"It would be better if you knew as little as possible, sir."

In a flash, Kim made the connection. "The steering hydraulics? In Magadan?"

Park looked at his feet again. "The steering was fine, sir. I temporarily disabled it until these containers arrived. The company will be paid a large bonus if we deliver the four empties to Otaru, a bonus that will more than compensate for our lost time."

Kim came to a decision. "I will cooperate. We will trade containers. All of the off-duty men will be kept below-decks, so they do not see the transfer. But when we reach Otaru, Park Chin Ho, you will leave my ship and you will never sail with me again. Is that clear?"

"Yes, Captain. Thank you, Captain."

As he wheeled about to return to the bridge, the master picked up the distinct sound of approaching helicopters. He strode swiftly onto the bridge and began barking orders.

"Turn on all the deck lights, immediately! Engine room, all stop. Helmsman, turn the ship into the wind.

"Mr. Smith," he said to the third officer, "assemble a deck crew and prepare for cargo operations. We are about to have visitors. They are going to swap us four empty containers for the ones lashed forward of the after cargo hatch. You are to cooperate fully and do exactly what they ask. When our visitors leave you will warn your deck crew to forget what they have seen. They are never to mention it to anyone! Soon after we will be boarded again, this time by the Soviet Navy. They are going to inspect those four containers. We will not hinder them. But I will want the deck crew out of sight, and no one is to say anything of the helicopters! Understand?"

Bill Smith was an American working his way up through the Merchant Marine. He was nearly ready to take the second officer's exam. He had proven to be a thoroughly competent officer. But this request really caught him off-guard.

"What's happening, sir? What's going on?"

"I am afraid I cannot answer that. Please, do exactly as you are told."

"Yes, sir."

****

Two minutes after the choppers arrived over the *Lady of Singapore*, the Tomcats arrived at Dolinsk-Sokol. The six powerful fighters climbed in a tight turn. They appeared out of nowhere so far as the Soviet radar operators were concerned. The air-defense systems were activated, but by the time the targeting radar came online the F-14s had streaked out of range. The ECM pods on the Prowlers and Skywarriors lit up, filling the airwaves with masses of confusing targets. Lost in the clutter of the dozens of targets, the Tomcats returned safely to the carrier. Also lost in the clutter were the eight Super Stallions. The diversion was outstandingly successful.

****

The Soviet officer used a bullhorn to address the freighter off his port beam. "*Lady of Singapore*," he called in heavily accented English, "please heave-to immediately and prepare to be boarded."

"What ship? What reason?" came the reply.

"Soviet frigate *Revnostniy*. You are to be searched on the suspicion of carrying contraband."

"And if I refuse?" Captain Kim called back through his hailer.

There was no response from the Soviet vessel. In the reflected glow of his own deck lights he could see the twin one-hundred-millimeter gun mounts aft of the superstructure rotating. The barrels depressed until they were aiming at the *Lady's* hull.

"All stop," he said into the engine room telephone.

The boarding party searched all the spaces of the ship, and then went to the four containers lashed to the deck.

"Open it," the Soviet officer demanded brusquely, pointing to one of the containers.

Kim motioned to his bosun. The man broke the seals, unlatched the container doors and threw them open. The Russian entered with a flashlight and Kim followed right behind him. The container was redolent with the smell of rough-cut wet lumber. There were scars and fragments, a few pieces of bark, and the other detritus of a heavily used shipping container.

Kim watched the Soviet officer closely. The triumph the man had displayed upon matching the container numbers with a list in his hand turned into disappointment. He stepped out of the container.

"Open these three," he instructed, a little less sure of himself.

Kim nodded again to his bosun. The other three containers were opened and searched. They, too, were empty and smelled of lumber.

The officer motioned to a member of his boarding party

and the man unclipped a marine radio from his belt and gave it to the officer. An animated conversation ensued with someone on the other end. Though Kim had no formal training in Russian, he had worked the ports in the area long enough to get the gist of the conversation. It was clear that the *Lady* did not have what they were expecting to find. The officer leading the boarding party handed the transceiver back to the sailor and approached Kim.

"Please accept my apologies, Captain. Evidently we were mistaken. We will leave your ship immediately and you may resume your voyage."

Kim nodded curtly but said nothing, not trusting his voice. When the boarders had finally departed, he called to his third officer.

"Mr. Smith, please get us under way on our former course. You may call the next watch. You have the bridge."

"I have the bridge, aye, Captain."

With that, Kim left the bridge and went to the small head in his private quarters and threw up. That had been too close, much, much too close.

****

The phone rang and rang. A groggy voice finally responded, "This is Chernikov. Yes?"

"General, it is Mikhail."

"Mikhail, I have been relieved of command. You must make your report to Sergei in Vladivostok."

"I heard, sir, and I am so sorry. I'm just calling because I thought you would want to know. The containers on the *Lady of Singapore* were empty. The boarders found the exact containers, the numbers matched and everything, but there was nothing there. I—I guess I was wrong, sir. I don't know what to say."

"Empty? Surely they were aboard the ship, hiding somewhere?"

"*Nyet*, Comrade General. The entire ship was searched. Nothing. That must not be how the Americans extracted, sir. I don't know how they got away but it was not on that ship, General."

"And the American activity around the Kurils?"

"Sir, I do believe it has something to do with the extraction of their assault team and the prisoners, but we have not yet figured out how they did it."

"Mikhail, do you believe that they are still here?"

There was a long pause. Finally Udovin responded sadly, knowing that his boss would be held responsible by the high brass in Moscow, "*Nyet*, Comrade General. I think they have gotten away, free and clear. But we don't know how."

****

A cold wind gusted over the bow of the *Vinson* as the Landing Signal Officer (LSO) carefully guided the container down to the deck with his lighted batons. The deck crewmen swiftly detached the slings. Freed from its cargo, the Super Stallion glided slowly toward the bow, staying well clear of the superstructure. A second LSO brought it down to the deck, while the first one was receiving the next container. Nearly out of fuel, the other choppers hovered off the stern on the starboard side, waiting their turn for landing. The containers remained sealed until all the helicopters were recovered and the containers could be dragged forward of the bridge on the starboard side, freeing the deck for fixed-wing flight operations.

The first container held the now-freed prisoners, wounded SEALS, and those who had attended them. A growing crowd of onlookers, some of whom knew what was going on, clustered on the deck around the base of the carrier's island. When the container's doors were thrown open and the SEALs that had been serving as medics stepped out, a roar of approval went up from the onlookers. Many rushed forward to help, and a steady stream of stretcher-bearers began to ferry the freed prisoners and the seriously wounded SEALs down to sickbay. The next two containers held healthy SEALs, and the walking wounded. They were greeted with loud cheers. As they exited the SEALs formed a somber line in front of the fourth container.

At first the sailors raised another cheer when its doors were thrown open, but they quickly fell silent as SEALs emerged with stretchers bearing the body bags of their fallen buddies. Instinctively the *Vinson's* sailors formed a line opposite the SEALs, and both lines snapped to attention and held their salutes as the dead on their litters were carried between them and taken below to the ship's morgue.

Last out of the container were Commanders Clausen and Rainer and Major Jacob Kelly. Admiral Bridger, who had been observing the procession in the background, came up and threw his arms around his weary men. "Well done, Marcus. Well done, Tom. Welcome home. Just in time for Christmas." He turned and held his hand out to Jake. "Falcon, you can sail with my SEALs any day. Great job, son. Welcome home."

Chapter 39

Galina sat on her bed wrapping the Christmas gifts she'd purchased for the Bates and for her Chinese host family. Though Christmas in Siberia was celebrated on a different day and with somewhat different traditions, Galina was enjoying being part of a family—the Bates family—and wanted to celebrate their way.

Sitting on her pillow was a special gift—one she didn't expect to ever deliver. The year prior she'd handsewn a shirt for Jake, and he'd taken it with him when he fled the logging compound above Sidima, in Siberia. She'd kept his measurements and ever since she'd come to America she'd been making him another one. After putting the finishing touches on it early this morning, she wrapped it in gaily colored paper as the tears spilled from her eyes. Jake had been missing since the middle of November, and she was convinced he was gone forever. She looked again at the beautifully wrapped package on her pillow, and felt empty inside. Finally she dried her eyes, determined not to cast a pall over the family festivities. She smiled as she looked about her room. Her losses were great— but so were her blessings. She found herself humming a carol as she put a decorative bow on a gift for Susan.

The house was brightly decorated, and fragrant with the bayberry candles Susan had lit. The boys were excited, Roger and Susan were excited, and there was an air of expectancy about the home. Galya heard the phone downstairs ring, and the happy clatter from the kitchen quieted. In a moment she heard Susan climbing the stairs, followed by a knock at her door. Glancing quickly around her room to make sure nothing was showing that would spoil a Christmas morning surprise, she answered, "Come in."

Susan opened the door and stood in the doorway with a huge smile on her face and tears running down her cheeks. "Galya, dear, we just got a phone call. Jake's alive! He'll be here tomorrow!" Galina burst into tears of joy and relief. Hugging each other, the two women danced around the room, unable to contain their joy.

****

At 0700 hours on Christmas morning, Jake descended the stairs of the C-9B Skytrain. He'd hopped a ride on a scheduled military flight from Coronado to NAS Alameda. Waiting for him at the bottom of the steps were Roger and Susan Bates, and Galina Toporova. He dropped his bags and she raced into his arms. They embraced for what seemed like an eternity, eyes squeezing back tears of joy. Neither were able to speak. It was a blessed Christmas day.

Jake Kelly was never able to tell Galina about the real reason behind his disappearance, since Operation *Thunderbird* remained classified, as it does to this day.

****

America and the western world enjoyed its Christmas of 1987. News was good. The American economy was roaring back. The future looked terrific.

For ten American families it was a Christmas wracked with grief and questions—but no answers. The widow of a SEAL simply had to accept that her husband was killed in the line of duty. It was rare that she was given an explanation of how he'd died or why the mission was worth her husband's life. She wasn't given the opportunity to weigh the enormous cost to her loved one, herself, and her children, against the benefit— the good achieved by her husband's death. It was an entirely one-sided equation. It was a hard, bitter pill to swallow.

There were likewise forty-nine Soviet families bearing the

same kind of loss. Their sons, husbands, and fathers served and fought with honor, too. They bore no responsibility for the corruption of their political masters or the criminal machinations that drove them. They, too, had to deal with the unanswered questions surrounding the death of their loved ones. Was the cause worth it? They would never know.

And so, though separated by continents, governments, and ideologies there was a shared grief among the special operations community in the Christmas of 1987, experienced by SEALs and *Spetsnaz* alike. It was an unavoidable heartache brought on by the clash of nations, politics, and the ambitions of fallen men. Unfortunately the brave men and women of the uniformed services were the sacrificial lambs.

The joy of what was lost being found was felt in nine homes that Christmas. Loved ones who had disappeared without warning suddenly reappeared. The former prisoners were sworn to secrecy, but there were official visits to reassure families that their loved one had not simply snapped and wandered off for a year. The explanations always fell short and weren't entirely satisfying, but they answered enough questions to placate the suspicions and concerns of mystified family members. The joy of reunion stilled the doubt.

It was determined by the respective western governments that nothing would be said—the secret of Project *Krasnyy Voskhod* would be held close to the vest. This was not a decision provoked by kindness, or some sort of live-and-let-live philosophy. It was political blackmail. If and when the Union of Soviet Socialist Republics stepped over the line in the opinion of NATO, *Krasnyy Voskhod* would be revealed before the world in all its criminality and ugliness. But why, the western governments reasoned, play your ace before you need it?

All in all, the year concluded on a good note, albeit with some unfinished business. It would not remain unfinished for long.

****

Roger Bates and Jim Franks howled at the TV set as Bill

Jensen and Jake Kelly high-fived with joy. The clock ticked down to zero, and the game was in the books. The Denver Broncos had defeated the San Diego Chargers 27-0 in the final game of the regular season, securing the AFC West divisional championship.

Bates turned the set off with disgust and grabbed another handful of popcorn. Franks sat on the couch shaking his head. "Terrible game," he said. "Fouts didn't have any protection. How do they expect him to win when he's spending more time on his back than he is on his feet? Disgusting!"

"Elway's my man," Jake Kelly crowed. "He did it again!"

"He had a little help from, oh, maybe twenty-one other guys, like Sammy Winder and Vance Johnson," Bates observed. "Fouts didn't have a whole lot of help from anyone."

"You win some, you lose some," replied Jenkins, chuckling.

"Easy to say, Bill, when your team just won," Franks said sourly. He took a long pull from his Pepsi and changed the subject, looking at Jake. "When are you going to ask that girl to marry you? She was crying her eyes out up until three days ago! She'd thought she lost you in Ivan-land, then you came back, then you disappeared again and broke her heart. Now you're back, but you still haven't popped the question. What is your problem, boy? Why don't you get off your butt, march upstairs, and ask her right now? If I thought it'd do any good, I'd order you to!"

Jake stood up and walked to the window. He looked out for a moment, then turned and faced Franks. "General, there's one more shoe to drop. There's something I've got to do before I can ask Galina to commit her life to me."

All three men knew what he was talking about.

"Don't do it, Jake," pleaded Bill Jensen. "There's no need. We've brought this matter to conclusion. You went in there and destroyed the camp. The prisoners are free, the Sovs have deep-sixed the program. There's no need, Jake, why put yourself at risk?"

"There *is* a need, sir! As long as Chernikov is alive, I and those I love will be at risk."

"Jake, he's finished! He's going to be reduced to making ice cubes in Siberia, for crying out loud," asserted General Franks.

"General, I don't believe that. This has become personal for him. I've ruined his career, I've made him look bad. He's not going to forget that. He's a snake and he can still strike."

"Is it personal for Chernikov, Jake, or has it become personal for you?" asked Jensen. "This isn't life insurance, this is just old-fashioned revenge and you know it, son."

Jake didn't respond.

****

Falcon finished packing his duffel bag and briefcase. One of his forged passports was hidden beneath the false bottom of his briefcase along with his silenced semi-automatic pistol and spare magazines of ammunition. The other fake passport was in his pocket. He smiled mirthlessly. He would enter the USSR as Jacob Sokolov, an American from Atlanta, Georgia. He would leave it as John Meeker of Denver, Colorado. The irony was delicious.

The documents were perfect. After a few discreet phone calls to some of the friends he'd made in the special operations community, he'd located a man who could not only forge the passports, but the entry and exit stamps as well. By pulling a few strings here, calling in a favor there from his contacts in the intelligence community, Jake was able to obtain the addresses of most of Chernikov's haunts in the Soviet Union. He finally had everything he needed. If he played his cards right he'd be back in the States in time to watch Denver play in the AFC Championship game on the 17th.

He looked at his watch. If he didn't hurry he'd miss his plane. He grabbed his bags. On his way to the waiting cab he checked the mailbox. It contained only a small white envelope —something from Bill Jensen. He stuffed it in his pocket, intending to open it later.

****

Chernikov drove a kilometer past his *dacha*. Nothing looked out of place. He saw no cars parked in the woods, no tracks in the snow. It looked safe. He turned the car around and pulled back into his driveway.

He'd been ordered back to Moscow by Patrikeyev. After a brief meeting with the general, he'd been stripped of his driver and bodyguard, Sergeant Yuri Slavin, and all his aides. He'd been ordered to go to his *dacha* and await further instructions. That had been seven days ago. Three days ago he'd seen the news on television: a high-ranking officer had been killed by a car-bomb believed to have been planted by Afghan terrorists. The victim was Lieutenant General Valeriy Ivanovich Patrikeyev. *This has the stink of KGB written all over it*, Chernikov thought when he saw the broadcast. *So, the purge has begun. And I am probably next. Funny—whether there is a tsar or a Politburo, there are always secret police. Some things never change.*

He exited the car and retrieved the groceries from the trunk. Trudging through the snow, he let himself in the front door. He set the bags down and hung up his overcoat, then paused. *What's that smell? It smells like . . . hot solder.* For the briefest instant cold fear constricted his throat and his hands went involuntarily to his neck. Then he steeled himself. He was no coward and he wouldn't die like one.

"Hello, General."

Chernikov turned around slowly. Facing him was Major Jacob Kelly, gun in hand.

"*Dobryy dyen'*, Major Kelly. I appear to have made a mistake."

"Really, General? What would that be?"

"I've been trying to stay one step ahead of the KGB. Now it appears I should have been concerned about staying one step ahead of you."

"Didn't you get my message?"

"I did. But I didn't believe it."

"Have you decided?" Kelly asked.

"Decided what, Major?"

"Which shoulder I should burn *I love Uncle Sam* onto?"

"Seriously, Major, is all this necessary? Please, just— pull the trigger. Let's get it over with."

"No, sir. You will go to your grave with the love of Uncle Sam written on your body. Kitchen's that way, General. That's where I'm all set up. After you. Keep your hands where I can see 'em."

As they walked past the front window it shattered and Chernikov collapsed. Jake dove to the floor. He got on his hands and knees, below the level of the window, and checked on the general. No pulse. He'd been shot through the head. *Sniper*, Jake thought. He heard a car coming along the road and stopping in front of the house. There was the sound of a car door opening and shutting, and then the vehicle drove away. Jake fled through the back door.

The soldering pencil smoldered on the kitchen table. After thirty minutes or so, it became hot enough that the insulation on the wires melted, causing a short. The pencil burst into flames and shortly after the table itself began to burn. Within minutes tongues of flames were licking the wood roof of Chernikov's *dacha*. Soon the entire structure was ablaze. The heat was so intense Chernikov's nearby auto caught fire. An hour later all that remained was a blackened, smoking mound and the burnt-out shell of an automobile. Other than the teeth, the corpse within had been reduced to ashes by the fiery blaze.

****

Jacob Kelly stood in line at the airport in Moscow, waiting to board the airplane. Two plainclothes policemen approached him and asked in English, "Mr. John Meeker? Could you please come with us, sir?"

His heart sank. Jake looked around and realized he had nowhere to run. Steeling himself for the worst, he followed them through a door off to the side of the passenger area. Two more guards fell in behind him. They walked him down a long hall, then ushered him into a small room. The door shut and locked behind them.

An old man sat on the other side of a small desk, an unlit

cigar clenched between his teeth. Removing the cigar, he smiled coldly when he saw Jacob Kelly.

"Ah, Major Kelly, we meet at last. *Dobroye utro.* I am Anatoly Geredin, director of the KGB."

As Jacob Kelly started to protest, opening his passport, Geredin held up his hands and shook his head. "Oh, I know your passport does not say Kelly, but let there be no secrets between us. I know fully well who you are." Jake acknowledged the Soviet's words with a nod of his head.

"You came back to finish off Comrade Chernikov?"

Jacob Kelly studied the old man and decided, *Oh, what the heck? In for a penny, in for a pound.* "Yes, Mr. Geredin, I did. I was afraid I'd be running for the rest of my life if he remained alive. But someone else got him before I did."

"*Da*, we did."

"You did?" Jake was surprised.

"*Da.* Our agent observed you entering the house through the back door. The *dacha* was bugged so we heard the conversation and we realized why you were there. If you'd killed Major General Chernikov it would have made things . . . messy. Our sniper was already set up so we took him out before you did.

"Now listen to me, Major Kelly. Take a message to your government, straight from the Politburo. Tell them, *we take care of our own problems.* There will be no retaliation for your SEAL raid. Chernikov needed to be killed a long time ago and his recklessness finally caught up with him. His project should never have been allowed to exist. It was a mistake.

"And you, Major, you need not fear our assassins any longer. All of Chernikov's orders have been countermanded. You will be allowed to live in peace in your own country.

"Now, Major, we have one final matter to discuss, then I must get back to my office." He looked at the guards and said, "Leave us." After the room had cleared he pulled out a small electronic device and set it on the table. "The room is bugged," he said with a wry smile. "This will interfere with them so we can have a moment of privacy—a rare thing in the Soviet Union, eh? Now, Major, when is your wedding to

Miss Galina Toporova? Have you set a date?"

"How can you possibly know anything about that?" Jake asked, surprised and not a little worried.

The old man chuckled, a gravelly sound rising from his chest, "I'm the head of the KGB, Major. I know about everything. I've known Galina for years, though she does not know me."

Jake thought, *Every stereotype about the Soviet Union finds a home in this guy, from his clothing to the form of his face to his ideology to his brusque manner. He's probably the most dangerous man in the country. And yet . . . I'm intrigued by him.* "You know Galina?"

"Yes, of course. Who do you think got her out of Siberia into China without so much as a bruise?"

"That was *you?*" Jake queried. He'd heard the story from Galina.

"*Da.* Me. You haven't answered my question. When is the wedding?"

"Oh . . . well, we haven't set a date. I haven't asked her to marry me yet. I plan to do that this weekend."

"She will say yes. She'd be a fool not to, and Galina is no fool. I have a wedding gift for her." He reached into the pocket of his greatcoat, pulled out a small box, and placed it in Falcon's hand.

Jake opened the box. It contained a beautiful engagement ring, a small wedding band with faint Cyrillic characters inscribed inside the band, and a much larger, matching wedding band, also with an inscription.

"These," said Geredin, "were her parents' wedding bands and her mother's engagement ring. Many years ago Galina's father was the *rezident* in the Damascus Embassy. I was one of his field officers. He was the finest man I ever knew, and my best friend.

"An operation went bad and we got tangled in a firefight with a Mossad unit. He sacrificed his life to enable me to get away. As he was dying he gave me his ring to deliver to his beloved wife, and he made me promise to take care of her and their two children, Boris and Galina. When his wife died some years later, I was given the rings with instructions to pass them to Galina when she wed. So I now give them to you. She is the last living member of her family. I place her care into your hands. You will take good care of her?"

"I will, I promise. *Bol'shoye spasibo*, Mr. Geredin."

"*Pozhaluysta*, Sokolov," he responded with a twinkle in his eye.

Jacob studied the old face, and then connected the dots. "Last winter Galina told me that all her life she felt like someone in high places was looking out for her. She said the permits, the equipment, the arrangements with the local Party—it all came too easily. It was you all along, wasn't it?"

"*Da*. It was a rare pleasure for me to use my position to do good for someone, rather than to terrorize them, which is what I usually do. Though she never knew me, I felt that she was my own daughter, and I enjoyed her success from afar and did what I could to contribute to it. But make no mistake about it, Major—had I known *you* were at Sidima, I would have arrested you immediately and you would be dead today."

Geredin struggled as he stood. "And now she is your responsibility. I have fulfilled my promise. I sincerely wish you and Miss Toporova every happiness." Geredin held out his hand in western fashion and Jacob Kelly shook it. "Enjoy your flight, Major."

Geredin opened the door and called one of his guards. "Escort him straight to his aircraft, and don't make him wait in that stupid line. But make sure he leaves the country. Oh, wait! I almost forgot. Major, your passports please."

Kelly handed over his John Meeker passport.

"The other one, too, please."

"I'll need it to get back in my country, sir!"

"Give it to me," Geredin insisted.

Kelly opened his briefcase, and then opened the false bottom. His weapon was in plain sight. He handed over the other passport. "I suppose you want the gun, too?"

"*Nyet*. You have certainly demonstrated that you know what to do with a weapon. I believe I can leave that safely in your hands, Major," answered Geredin dryly. "Here, take this." He put a passport in Kelly's hands. It was a perfect duplicate of Kelly's own, real passport, including entrance and exit stamps.

Kelly looked up, confused. "But how—"

"I told you. I am the head of the KGB—do you really think something like that is hard for us to produce?"

Kelly watched the old man as he hobbled to the door. Geredin turned back, the warmth on his face erased, his expression now hard and cold. "Khrushchev was right. We *will* bury you Americans one day. But we will overcome you from within your own political system, not without. *Do svidaniya,* Major."

****

Thirty minutes later the aircraft was in the air, headed for London and then on to LaGuardia, where he would pick up a connecting flight to San Francisco. Jake settled back in his seat and then remembered he had something in his pocket. It was the envelope he'd received from Bill Jensen the day he left his quarters to fly to Moscow. Curious, he opened it. It contained only an index card. Inscribed on the card in Jensen's handwriting was a quotation:

> *"For it would have been better that man should have been born dumb, nay, void of all reason,*
>
> *rather than that he should employ the gifts of Providence to the destruction of his neighbor."*

Quintilian, *De Institutione Oratoria (XII, 1, 1)*

He thought for a moment and realized, *I was kept from murdering Chernikov, even though it was my intention to do so. Coincidence? Or providence? The one person in the Soviet Union looking out for Galina was the one man who could get her out of the country. Coincidence? Or providence? Maybe Galya is right after all. Maybe I should think a little harder about what I believe.*

He shoved the card into his pocket and tilted his seat back. Within minutes he was asleep, dreaming of his wedding day.

A PRAYER OF MOSES

A DEVOTIONAL STUDY OF PSALM 90

C.H. COBB

The Church has rendered God *safe*.

His wrath is a matter relegated to days of antiquity. It seems rare that we connect the brevity and frailty of this existence with His overflowing anger at sin. Unfortunately, having dispensed with His wrath we've also diminished His holiness and His majesty, and made the cross less necessary.

This study invites the reader to take a second look at God and His wrath—and His Christ—through the eyes of Moses. Suitable for individuals or groups.

Chris Cobb's exegesis of Psalm 90 is solid and sobering. In a world that takes sin lightly, Christianity needs to hear the message of this Psalm which Chris Cobb has brought to life.
Dr. Brent Aucoin
President, Faith Bible Seminary, Lafayette, Indiana

Pastor Cobb's exposition of Psalm 90 combines two sets of ingredients that make it a joy to read: on the one hand, exegetical precision together with the sweep of redemptive history; on the other, technical mastery with warm, personal application. There are Scriptural studies in which the author maintains a safe distance from the reader. Pastor Cobb allows us to get to know him along with the text he is expounding. This, in my opinion, is the best way to do pastoral theology.
John L. Marshall, Ph.D.
Christian Studies/History Department, Eastern University

Please help independent authors

Independent authors usually don't have someone managing their books' publicity plan or marketing. We don't have the support of an organization getting our novels in front of retailers who will carry them in their stores. Other than what marketing efforts we can cobble together on our own, we have only one source of publicity that can encourage others to buy our books, and that's you, our readers.

Your word-of-mouth recommendation, your Facebook comment, your tweet, your Amazon or Goodreads review is likely the only way an unknown author will get the word out about his or her books.

Let me hasten to admit that the reader is certainly under no obligation. If you don't like the tale, or if the editing was sloppy, or the cover or packaging amateurish then by all means don't encourage someone else to read it. The last thing the independent publishing movement needs are products that fall short of genuine quality.

Even if you think the product is the best work since Bunyan's *Pilgrim's Progress* or Tolkien's *Lord of the Rings*, you still aren't obligated. Art doesn't create a debt or obligation on the part of the viewer. You're free to enjoy it and walk away. Artists take that risk when we create our work.

But if you find a tale you like and you'd like to read more by that author, give him or her a hand by letting your friends and loved ones know where they can get a good story. Post a review, mention it on Facebook, send a few emails, tell a few friends. Once the word gets out, a good story will sell itself; but getting the word out is the challenge. Thanks for your help!

About the Author

Chris Cobb's resume reads like a patchwork quilt. He's driven a forklift, worked as a technician doing component-level repair on digital circuitry, been a programmer-analyst, a data-center shift operator, taught high school science and mathematics, and been an Information Technology Director at a graduate school. Most of his career he's been a pastor.

He lives with his wife, Doris, in western Ohio, and is presently the teaching pastor at Bible Fellowship Church in Greenville, OH. They have three adult children, two fine sons-in-law and a wonderful daughter-in-law, all of whom are actively engaged serving Christ in the arts at some level.

Chris received Jesus Christ as his Savior in 1974, and seeks to incorporate a biblically faithful worldview into everything he does, including his writing.

You can find Chris on Facebook, or find additional works by him at chcobb.com.

www.ingramcontent.com/pod-product-compliance
Lightning Source LLC
Chambersburg PA
CBHW070154120726
47909CB00001B/107